W9-BMF-311

THE SWEETEST THING

Alex walked farther into the room, a towel slung over his shoulders, the muscles in his body exquisitely defined by the tank-top T-shirt and running shorts. He was a gorgeous man: long, lean runner's legs; flat, taut abdomen; broad shoulders; defined biceps; strong hands. Alex was perfectly made and as male as they came. Faith found herself captivated by the strands of dark hair that curled so sensuously against his chest.

"See something you like?" Alex asked.

She looked into his eyes and saw amusement and something darker, desire perhaps. His gaze turned bold, traveling down her body, lingering on her breasts so long, she felt them start to tingle . . .

Other Avon Books by
Barbara Freethy

ASK MARIAH
DANIEL'S GIFT
ONE TRUE LOVE
RYAN'S RETURN

Avon Books are available at special quantity discounts for bulk purchases for sales promotions, premiums, fund raising or educational use. Special books, or book excerpts, can also be created to fit specific needs.

For details write or telephone the office of the Director of Special Markets, Avon Books, Inc., Dept. FP, 1350 Avenue of the Americas, New York, New York 10019, 1-800-238-0658.

BARBARA FREETHY

This is a work of fiction. Names, characters, places, and incidents either are the product of the author's imagination or are used fictitiously. Any resemblance to actual events, locales, organizations, or persons, living or dead, is entirely coincidental and beyond the intent of either the author or the publisher.

AVON BOOKS, INC.
1350 Avenue of the Americas
New York, New York 10019

Copyright © 1999 by Barbara Freethy
Excerpt from *The Last True Cowboy* copyright © 1998 by Kathleen Eagle
Excerpt from *The Runaway Princess* copyright © 1999 by Christina Dodd
Excerpt from *The Sweetest Thing* copyright © 1999 by Barbara Freethy
Excerpt from *A Rogue in Texas* copyright © 1999 by Jan Nowasky
Excerpt from *Someone to Watch Over Me* copyright © 1999 by Lisa Kleypas
Inside cover author photo by Dave Dornlas
Published by arrangement with the author
Library of Congress Catalog Card Number: 98-93783
ISBN: 0-380-79481-0
www.avonbooks.com/romance

All rights reserved, which includes the right to reproduce this book or portions thereof in any form whatsoever except as provided by the U.S. Copyright Law. For information address Avon Books, Inc.

First Avon Books Printing: April 1999

AVON TRADEMARK REG. U.S. PAT. OFF. AND IN OTHER COUNTRIES, MARCA REGISTRADA, HECHO EN U.S.A.

Printed in the U.S.A.

WCD 10 9 8 7 6 5 4 3 2 1

If you purchased this book without a cover, you should be aware that this book is stolen property. It was reported as "unsold and destroyed" to the publisher, and neither the author nor the publisher has received any payment for this "stripped book."

To a wonderful editor,
Ann McKay Thoroman,
for her keen eye,
words of encouragement and
unending enthusiasm

Chapter 1

"*What do you think she left you in her will?*"

"Excuse me?" Alex Carrigan turned to the teenage girl sitting on the white leather couch in the reception area. In baggy jean overalls, she looked painfully thin and painfully young to be holding a cigarette between two fingers. Her brown hair was parted in the middle and hung down past her shoulders. Her red cheeks clashed with the orange tint of her lipstick, and her dark eyes blazed with defiance, anger, and something vaguely familiar.

"What do you think she left you?" the girl repeated. "That's why you're here, isn't it? To find out what Melanie Kane left you?"

Alex felt suddenly uneasy. Why was this young girl sitting alone in the San Francisco offices of Monroe and Glass, attorneys-at-law, at three o'clock on a Friday afternoon? Why wasn't she with someone? And more important, why was she looking at him as if she knew a big secret?

"Maybe Melanie left you a million dollars," the girl continued, tilting her head to one side as if considering the odds of that possibility. "Maybe she won the lottery. Melanie always said she was going to win the lottery." Her lips trembled slightly at the notion. "Or she might have left you her pink Porsche. You know, the one she got at the gas station that's as big as a cereal box. Melanie always said someday she'd get one she could drive. Course, nobody believed her. She was always dreaming a dream."

"What's your name?" Alex demanded, as the hairs on the back of his neck began to tingle.

"Don't you know?" The girl stared into his eyes for one long, breathless second. "I'm Jessie."

Alex's stomach turned over. *I'm going to name her Jessica if she's a girl.*

No, it couldn't be. He racked his brain trying to remember when that baby had been born. It had been summer when Melanie had gone into labor. In fact, Sacramento had been in the middle of a heat wave, the temperatures in the valley rising past one hundred degrees, even in the dark of the night.

Their tiny studio apartment over the California Grill had turned into an oven by late afternoon, and they'd taken to sleeping on a thin mattress on the floor in front of a noisy fan. Alex hadn't cared that they were living below the poverty line and about to have a baby. At eighteen, life had seemed like one big adventure.

"Melanie used to talk about you," Jessie continued. "She said you had incredible blue eyes."

Alex blinked against the intensity of her gaze—*her brown eyes, eyes that reminded him of Melanie.* But unlike Melanie, who never looked past the surface, Alex had the feeling Jessie could see right through him, into his past, into his heart.

"What else did Melanie say?" Damn! Why had he asked that?

"She said you had long dark brown hair, and once she made you wear it in a ponytail because she thought it was sexy."

Alex cleared his throat and dug his hands into his pockets. He doubted Melanie would have recognized him today. His hair was shorter, just past his ears, and he no longer lived in torn blue jeans and tank tops, but rather business suits, starchy white shirts, and silk ties—at least when he was working, which was most of the time. His business was his life.

"She also said you were a great kisser," Jessie continued with a speculative smile.

Alex felt even more uncomfortable. "I'm sorry about your mother. Melanie was your mother?"

"Most of the time, except when a guy came around. Then we were sisters." Jessie tapped her unlit cigarette against her leg. "Got a light?"

"Aren't you a little young to be smoking?"

"Aren't you a little late to be playing dad?"

Her words cut to the quick. Alex stiffened and immediately shook his head against the accusation in her eyes. "I'm—I'm not your father. I don't know what Melanie told you, but I am definitely not your father."

"How do you know?"

Alex's mind raced to answer the question. How did he know? Because Melanie had told him the truth the day after Jessie's birth. After he'd invested nine months of his life taking care of Melanie and the baby, after he'd gone to sleep listening to the baby's heartbeat, after he'd fallen in love with the infant he believed was his—Melanie had told him he was not the father. Melanie had also told him she wanted to raise her child with the baby's real father, Eddie Saunders.

Alex had been furiously angry, but he'd never doubted Melanie's sincerity. Why would she lie? He'd been willing to take care of her. Hell, he had been taking care of her, working as a clerk at a local shoe store during the day and taking college classes at night.

During their nine months together, he'd fallen in love with her and her baby, only to have his love shoved back in his face. It was the last time he'd let himself get that close to anyone.

"I just know," he said to Jessie, then shifted his feet restlessly, wishing the receptionist would come back.

He wanted someone to tell him why he'd been ordered

to appear on this day, at this time, for the reading of a will of a woman he'd been married to for nine months, thirteen years earlier. It didn't make sense that Melanie would leave him anything after the way they'd parted. They hadn't spoken since the day she'd taken her baby and left him all alone.

He checked his watch. It was ten minutes past three. He was tired, hungry, and irritated. He'd just finished a grueling ten-day business trip for his company, Top Flight Athletic Shoes, and he'd been hoping to get home early. Not that there wouldn't be problems waiting for him at home. According to his part-time housekeeper, his grandfather had arrived at his apartment the day before with a suitcase and a note from his doctor stating that his grandfather shouldn't live alone anymore.

A sudden gust of wind rattled the windows, and Alex's uneasiness increased as he saw the tree branches blowing restlessly against the panes of the old Victorian house that now served as an office building in the Marina District of San Francisco. Maybe it was the wind—or the Carrigan curse, which had brought him here today. He could still hear his grandfather's deep, booming voice . . .

And the winds will curse your life until you return to where it began . . .

His grandfather had told him about the curse in the dark of the night, the wind howling through the trees like a hungry vampire. Alex had been eight years old at the time and his mother had just left his father—because of the curse, his grandfather told him, because of something terrible his grandfather had done when he was a young man.

Alex had wanted desperately to believe it was black magic that had torn his family apart, but in the morning his father had told him that his mother was in love with another man. So much for the curse.

"Mr. Carrigan?"

Alex turned his head as the receptionist finally returned

to her desk. A smartly dressed woman in her mid-thirties, she welcomed him with a cool smile.

"Mr. Monroe will be a few moments. He's on the phone."

Alex had the sudden urge to flee. Listening to the wind and thinking about the curse had drawn goose bumps down his arms. "Look, I've been on a business trip for the past week, and frankly I have no interest in anything Melanie Kane may have left for me. So if Mr. Monroe will be longer than five minutes, I'm out of here."

The receptionist frowned. "You really do need to wait, Mr. Carrigan. Can I get you some coffee? A soft drink?"

"No."

"Please, sit down."

"Fine." Alex took a seat at the other end of the couch, trying to ignore Jessie's steady gaze. He pulled his cell phone out of his pocket and dialed his office. His secretary picked up, sounding as efficient as always.

"Hey, Theresa, it's me. Any messages?"

"Of course. You're a popular guy these days. Did you see the spread in *Entrepreneur Magazine*? They picked us as one of the top five companies to watch."

"I saw it," Alex replied, still feeling a surge of pleasure that his efforts were finally being rewarded. "What else is up?"

"The ad guys want to know if you've signed Elijah James yet."

"No," Alex said with annoyance. He'd been chasing the young basketball star for three months with absolutely no luck. "I have a meeting with him tomorrow at the Coliseum. I'm determined to bring him into the Top Flight family."

"Well, you usually get your man—or woman as the case may be. There are a few other messages, but they can wait until Monday. Oh, one last thing. Amy said to tell you she just signed that young tennis star from Argentina, Rita Seranno."

"Way to go, Amy."

"And she wanted to know if you mind her taking a few days off in Rio as a bonus."

"What did you tell her?"

"To get her ass back here."

Alex laughed. "You're good, Theresa, very, very good."

"I'll remind you of that come bonus time. Oh, and call home if you're not there already. Your housekeeper left me a hysterical message about your grandfather. I didn't even know you had a grandfather."

"Unfortunately, I do. I'll see you Monday."

Alex hung up and dialed his home number.

"Hello? Hello? Señor Carrigan's residence."

He smiled at the sound of his housekeeper's heavily accented response. Gloria Delgado had arrived from Nicaragua six years earlier, but still didn't feel comfortable with the language. She also tended to get upset easily.

"It's Alex, Gloria."

"Oh, Señor Alex, I am so sorry."

His muscles once again tensed. "What are you sorry about?" He hoped she'd simply broken something or missed a dirty spot on the floor.

"I have lost your grandfather," she said dramatically.

It wasn't the response he was hoping for. "What do you mean, you lost him?"

"You asked me to watch him, but he doesn't like my coffee, so he go."

Alex winced as a torrent of Spanish followed. When Gloria finally paused for air, he said, "It's okay. I'll find him. He can't have gone far. Did he say anything before he left?"

"The wind. He say the wind is bad. There are evil spirits dancing. Me, I think I don't understand so good."

"Oh, you probably understood just fine."

"He also say he want cake. Yesterday he want cake. Today he want cake. Every day he want cake."

"Right. I think I have an idea where he may have gone."

"I can't wait, Señor Alex. My niece is sick, and my friend has no car, and—"

"That's okay. I'll be home shortly. Thanks, Gloria."

The door to one of the offices opened, and Alex slipped his cell phone back in his pocket. An older man stepped through the doorway. His hair was pepper gray, the expression on his long, narrow face as somber as his navy blue pin-striped suit.

"Mr. Carrigan?" He extended his hand. "I'm Harrison Monroe, Melanie Kane's attorney."

Alex stood up and shook the man's hand, feeling tense.

"Please come in," Harrison said.

Alex walked into the inner office, not realizing until he was inside that Jessie had followed him. "This is a private meeting," he told her.

"Actually, Jessica is involved." Mr. Monroe gave his tie a nervous tug. "Won't you both sit down?" He waved his hand toward the leather armchairs in front of his desk.

Jessica didn't move. Alex didn't either. The ground beneath his feet suddenly felt like quicksand. "What do you mean Jessica is involved?"

"It's complicated."

"No it's not," Jessie interrupted, putting her hands on her hips. She looked Alex straight in the eye. "Don't you get it yet? I'm your inheritance."

"That's impossible." He looked to Mr. Monroe for reassurance, but he found none. "I'm not her father."

"Your name is on her birth certificate," Mr. Monroe said evenly.

"It is?" Alex was surprised Melanie hadn't put Eddie's name there. "Even so, I'm not Jessie's father."

"You were married to Ms. Kane at the time of Jessica's birth. Isn't that correct?"

"Yes, but I'm not her father."

"And you were married for a total of . . ." Harrison Monroe walked over to his desk and checked a piece of paper. "Nine months and fourteen days."

"I don't remember exactly how long it was, but that

sounds about right. I'm not her biological father, though. That honor belongs to a guy named Eddie Saunders.''

Harrison opened the file folder on his desk and pulled out a folded piece of paper. ''Did you write this note, Mr. Carrigan?''

Alex had a sinking feeling in the pit of his stomach. The paper was old and faded with crease marks, as if it had been tucked away in someone's jewelry box for thirteen years.

Alex could still remember sitting down at his student desk, staring at the loose-leaf paper in his notebook, wondering how he could possibly be a father when he'd only just finished high school. But he couldn't let Melanie do it alone. He knew what it was like to grow up without two parents. So he'd picked up a pen and written Melanie a note.

''Take it,'' Harrison urged.

Alex took the paper from the lawyer's hand and slowly unfolded it.

Dear Melanie,

I want to marry you. I want to be a father to my baby. Please call me. I can't stand not knowing what you're going to do.

Love, Alex

''That is your writing, is it not?'' Harrison asked.

''It's mine.'' Alex folded the note and handed it back to Harrison. ''At the time, I believed I was Jessie's father. Later Melanie told me the truth. She left me to go back to Jessie's real father, Eddie Saunders. We got a divorce. Eddie should be responsible for Jessie, not me.''

''I'm sorry, but Ms. Kane didn't mention anyone by that name to me.''

''She married him.''

"No." Harrison shook his head. "The only marriage she participated in was the one with you."

"She told me she was going to marry him."

"She didn't. And it was her wish that you take Jessica in the event of her death."

Alex stared at Mr. Monroe in horror, then looked at Jessie's defiant face. He couldn't take this kid. He couldn't parent this smart-ass girl. He wouldn't know what to do—what to say.

"This is not going to happen," Alex said wildly. "I—I refuse."

Jessica walked around the desk and sat down in Mr. Monroe's oversized chair. She leaned back and kicked her feet up on the desk. "I told you he wouldn't take me."

"Yes, well." Mr. Monroe looked from Jessie to Alex. "If you refuse, then I suppose I'll have to call Social Services and have them find her a foster home."

"Great, maybe I can get a smoke there," Jessie said. "I don't need you anyway. You're probably—probably a big—a big jerk." Jessie's mouth trembled, and she sniffed back a sob. "Mom said you were a good guy, but you're just like the rest. I'm glad—really glad you're not my dad."

Alex sucked in a deep breath of air as her words cut him deeply. He'd wanted to be her dad once. But Jessie wasn't his. *She wasn't his.* The words rang through his head like a mantra. Melanie had lied to him about Jessie. Melanie had betrayed him. Why should he bail her out now?

Only it wasn't Melanie who needed a bail-out, it was Jessie. And as he looked at her, he wondered if he could really turn his back on her.

"Mr. Carrigan, may I speak to you alone?" Harrison didn't wait for an answer. He pulled Alex into the hall and shut the door so Jessica couldn't overhear them.

"Mr. Carrigan. Putting aside the fact that you don't believe you're Jessica's father—"

"I'm not."

"As I said, putting that aside for now, I must tell you that Ms. Kane wanted you to take Jessie. She told me you were the only person in the world who could give Jessie the kind of home she deserved. Won't you please reconsider?"

"I can't."

"San Francisco is filled with homeless children. The foster care system is stretched to the limit. Jessica just lost her mother. She's terribly alone right now, and I know she hasn't made the best impression, but underneath all that sass, she's a scared child."

Alex knew that. But she wasn't *his* child. And he wouldn't take care of her—not again.

"Jessica needs you, Mr. Carrigan."

Alex stared at him for a long moment. "You never said—how did Melanie die?"

"She had ovarian cancer. She didn't find out until the very end. She was only in the hospital a week before she died. I met with her at the request of a social worker. Melanie was very concerned for Jessie's future. I did try to find you, but Melanie thought you might be in Sacramento."

"That's where we lived together. I spent my senior year in high school there while my dad did a photo spread of the state legislature in action." Alex didn't know why he was explaining, except that it helped to prolong what he knew was coming.

"Yes, well, it took me a while to find you. By then it was too late for Melanie to ask you herself."

"There was a time when I would have gladly been that child's father. Thirteen years ago to be exact. But now I'm building a business—Top Flight Athletic Shoes. I travel a lot. I have commitments on my time. Jessica should go to someone who can give her a home."

"I'm well aware of your situation, Mr. Carrigan. In fact, I did a background check on you."

"What the hell for?"

"I told Ms. Kane I wouldn't feel comfortable sending

Jessica to a man, even if he was the father, who hadn't bothered to pay child support or maintain contact with Jessica over the years."

"This is unbelievable." Alex shook his head in amazement that the conversation continued despite his innocence. "I didn't pay child support because I wasn't the father. How many times do I have to tell you that?"

"Ms. Kane did say that she hadn't wanted you to support her," Mr. Monroe conceded.

"Thank God for that. So what did you find out about me?"

The attorney sent him a steady look. "Your athletic footwear business is very successful. You employ over three hundred people in San Francisco and throughout the country. You mingle with sports celebrities on a frequent basis. You are considered to be a very eligible bachelor, although you aren't known for long-term romantic relationships. You don't appear to smoke or do drugs, and you run several miles a day, probably to balance the enormous amount of junk food you put into your system."

"Very good. Did you find out what brand of toothpaste I use?"

"I didn't consider it necessary."

"You only considered it necessary to invade my privacy."

"For the child's sake, yes. Let me give you the bottom line, Mr. Carrigan. In the eyes of the law, unless proven otherwise, you are Jessica's father and thereby required to support her. Now, if you wish to put her up for adoption, I must tell you that twelve-year-old girls are not very adoptable. Jessica will more than likely end up in the foster care system until she's eighteen. Then she'll be on her own. Of course, she may run away before then. She's not unfamiliar with life on the street. She and her mother were homeless most of this past year."

Homeless? Melanie with the beautiful brown eyes and the big dreams had ended up living on the streets with her baby? Alex felt a sudden thrust of guilt. But Melanie had made her choice. She'd picked a life without him.

''I'm not her father,'' Alex tried one last time, knowing even as he said the words that it was futile to protest. ''I'll take a DNA test to prove that.''

''DNA tests take time, but that's certainly your prerogative. In the meantime, you may wish to pursue Eddie Saunders. If he is in fact Jessica's father, perhaps he'll want her. In fact, I can recommend an excellent private investigator.''

''I'll bet.''

''Until then Jessica needs a home.''

Alex sucked in a deep breath and let it out, thinking long and hard about his options. Once again, Melanie wanted him to care for her baby until the real father showed up.

How could he do that again?

How could he not?

''Fine. I'll take Jessie, until we find her real father.'' It would be okay. He'd get Gloria to come more often, and his grandfather would be there, too, he thought dismally, suddenly realizing how crowded his simple life had become.

''Good.'' Mr. Monroe opened the door to his office. ''Jessie? Mr. Carrigan has agreed to take care of you.''

Jessie shrugged. ''Whatever.'' She got up from the chair and sauntered over to Alex. ''Can I have five bucks?''

''Why?''

''So, I can buy a lighter.''

Alex plucked the cigarette out of her hand. ''I live in a nonsmoking apartment.''

''Oh, shit.''

''And nonswearing.''

''Where do you live? A fucking church?''

Alex stared at her defiant face in amazement. ''Did your mother let you talk like that?''

''All the time.''

''Okay, well off you go,'' Mr. Monroe said, ushering

them out of his office before Alex could change his mind. "I'll have my investigator call you, Mr. Carrigan."

"You better," Alex grumbled as he walked out of the office with Jessie. The hall was empty. He pushed the elevator button and crossed his arms in front of his chest. Jessie did the same, her expression of disinterest as deliberate as his own.

"You know, if you're not cool, I'll just leave," Jessie said, her gaze fixed on the wall.

"And go where?"

"Wherever. I don't need you. I don't need anybody."

Her words rang through to his heart. They were his words, and he'd said them over and over again, growing up in his own shattered family.

"Why don't we just try to get along, Jessie? It will make it easier on all of us. By the way, where are your things?"

She pointed to her worn backpack, still avoiding his eyes. "Right here."

"Is that it?"

"I travel light."

Alex had liked to travel light, too. Only, now he was acquiring baggage by the minute.

The elevator doors opened, and they stepped inside, riding down to the first floor in silence. They crossed through the lobby, and Alex opened the front door for Jessie. A gust of wind blew her hair up in an arch, and Alex was suddenly blinded by a swirl of dust.

"It sure is windy," Jessie proclaimed.

"It sure is," he muttered.

And the winds will curse your life until you return to where it began . . .

Chapter 2

"*My grandson wants to lock me up in a home* for the crazy." Julian Carrigan rested his elbows on the small round table in front of him, the long, worn sleeves of his coat creeping up over his plump forearms. He stared down at his café mocha as if he were searching for an answer in the dark chocolate.

"Are you sure?" Faith Christopher walked around the bakery counter and slid into the chair across from him. It was almost closing time at Faith's Fancies, a small French bakery/café in downtown San Francisco, and Faith was ready for a break.

"I'm sure," Julian replied, casting a wistful glance around the cafe, which was now devoid of customers. "I'll miss this place."

Faith smiled as he looked around the room. She'd worked hard to make the bakery cozy and inviting with dark wood paneling, warm orange-red curtains and inviting photographs of pastries on the walls. There were bud vases with fresh flowers on each of the four small tables and a complimentary rack of magazines and newspapers in the corner. She invited people to linger, to relax, to enjoy. And this old man had done just that, yesterday afternoon and today. She'd wondered if he was going to be a regular customer, now she wasn't so sure.

The one thing she was sure about is that the elderly

man was in dire need of a friend, not to mention an iron. His suit had obviously once been an expensive purchase, but it was now old and worn, as wrinkled as the faded white shirt he wore underneath.

Julian stared at her through weary blue eyes. His white hair stood up in short, straight tufts on his head. His face was lined, his hands aged, his shoulders slumped. He seemed to be carrying the weight of the world on his back.

"My grandson says he doesn't have room for me, but he lives in one of those fancy apartments up on the hill. It's got three bedrooms." Julian took a sip of his coffee and shook his head. "It's all gone bad, you know. My whole life, one thing after another."

"There must have been some good times in your life," Faith ventured.

"There were some . . . a long time ago. Before the curse."

"The curse?" Faith couldn't help but sit forward in her seat. Although she considered herself firmly grounded in reality, she was intrigued by the idea of magic.

"I was cursed more than fifty years ago to live without love. Not just me but everyone in my family. I didn't believe in the curse at first. But it came true. I wish I could set things right. Sometimes I think it might be worth trying, but I couldn't do it alone."

"What about your grandson?"

The old man snorted. "It would be a cold day in hell before he'd help me."

"Other family?"

"No. My son is a bigger SOB than my grandson. Guess they take after me." He paused. "My friends are all dead. I soon will be, too, I suppose."

"Don't say that." Faith was touched by the deep sadness in his eyes. She understood loneliness. She'd been alone since the beginning, abandoned in a church pew with nothing but a worn blanket and a St. Christopher's medal around her neck. From foster home to foster home, the loneliness had only grown, not because people didn't care about her, but because she didn't belong to anyone, to anyplace. She had no blood ties in the world, at least none that she knew about.

It wasn't until she'd met Gary Porter that she'd finally felt as if she belonged to someone. Her stomach twisted into a knot of sadness. Gary had left her too, not willingly, but he was gone all the same, her friend, her lover, her protector.

"I'm sorry. I didn't mean to upset you." Julian's gaze was concerned as it settled on her face.

Faith forced a smile and pushed the memories of her doomed love affair to the back of her mind where they belonged. "You didn't."

"Then why aren't you smiling anymore?"

"I'm angry with your grandson."

"Alex?" Julian raised an eyebrow. "You don't even know him."

"He sounds like a monster."

"Most women love him. He's very dashing."

"Dashing, huh?"

"Handsome, attractive, a—a hunk as they say nowadays."

Faith laughed. "He must take after his grandfather."

"Perhaps in my day," he said with a touch of arrogance that Faith sensed had once been a bigger part of his personality. "I've been married five times, you know."

"Five? Wow. And where are all your ex-wives?"

"I don't know." He shrugged. "I didn't treat them all that well, I'm afraid. I did so many things wrong, Miss Faith. May I call you that?"

"Of course. We all make mistakes."

"I made more than my share. And now my grandson is paying."

Faith wrinkled her nose in confusion. "I don't understand. I thought you said he was putting you in a home. It sounds like you're the one who's paying."

"I'm the one who brought the curse upon the family. The old Indian warned me about what would happen. He said, *The winds will curse your life until you return to where it began . . .* " Julian looked out the window. "It's windy today."

"It's always windy in late March," Faith said, trying to lighten the dark mood that had settled over his features. "One of my foster moms used to say that the wind was just God's way of doing some spring cleaning."

Julian's somber expression didn't change with her whimsical explanation. "The wind brings with it disaster, change, evil. The monster roars . . . and the monster kills."

Faith shivered in spite of the fact that the bakery was quite warm. Despite her foster mom's reassuring explanation, the wind had always scared her, too. Faith had grown up in Southern California where the Santa Ana winds would blow up unexpectedly, lighting the nearby hillsides on fire. One of her foster homes had been on just such a hillside.

She had vivid memories of the day the fire had come down the hill into the backyard. Her foster father had stood on the roof, hosing down the shingles. Her foster mother had hustled her and the other children into a van just minutes before the fire breached the back fence. They'd lost everything. Faith had moved on to a new home, a new family, but she'd never forgotten the hot smothering smell of the fire on the wind. Evil? Yes, she could believe it came with the wind.

"If only I could make it right." Julian drew her attention back to the conversation at hand. "Then I could die with peace in my heart, knowing that my family would no longer be cursed."

"Maybe I could help," Faith said impulsively. "What would you have to do to get rid of this curse?"

Julian hesitated. He looked around to make sure no one was close enough to overhear them, then he dropped his voice down to a whisper. "Find Suzannah."

"Who is Suzannah?" Faith asked in the same hushed voice.

"The love of my life."

"One of your wives?"

He shook his head. "No."

Faith waited for him to elaborate, but he didn't say another word. Finally she asked, "When did you last see her?"

"Fifty-six years ago."

Faith's jaw dropped open. "That's a long time. She might be . . ."

"Yes, I know. But I can't get rid of the curse unless I find her. She has something that I need. Do you think you could help me?"

Faith hesitated. She saw her assistant and almost mother-in-law, Nancy Porter, watching her from behind the counter. Nancy had a worried expression on her round face, and Faith could tell from the set of her jaw that she didn't particularly like Julian Carrigan. But then, Nancy had become very protective of Faith since Gary's death two years earlier. In many ways, Nancy had taken over Faith's life where Gary had left off.

After her oldest son's death, Nancy had volunteered to help in the bakery that Faith and Gary had started together. Nancy had also insisted that even though Gary had died before their wedding, Faith was still a part of the Porter family, and as a member of their family, she would receive all of their love and all of their attention.

Sometimes too much attention, but Faith would never tell Nancy that. Faith owed everything she had to Gary and his family. She wouldn't have had the bakery or her apartment or the family dinners without the Porters—Nancy and her husband, Chuck, and their younger son, Ben, and their daughter, Kim.

"It's too much to ask," Julian said abruptly, patting her hand. "Please forgive me. You're a young woman with a life of your own, a business to tend. I don't know what I was thinking. It's just that this damn curse has not only destroyed me but also my son, and now, I fear, my grandson as well. It will never end unless I make it right.''

''I want to help you. But some things cannot be changed. I learned that a long time ago.''

''Faith?'' Nancy called to her from behind the counter. ''May I speak to you for a moment? In the back?''

''You go on,'' Julian said. ''I've already taken up too much of your time.''

''I'll be back in a minute.''

Faith got up and went into the kitchen. Since her assistant baker, Leslie, left by noon each day, Faith and Nancy were alone. Nancy leaned against the large, marble-topped table set in the center of the kitchen, her arms crossed in front of her chest. A small woman, barely five foot two, Nancy had blond hair, hazel eyes, and a rosy-cheeked complexion. Her round arms were made for hugging, and she usually had a ready smile, unless, of course, she was worried about one of her kids or Faith—which appeared to be the case at this moment.

''You shouldn't be offering to help that man, Faith. He's a stranger.''

''He's a lonely old man.'' Faith picked up a mixing bowl and carried it over to the sink to be washed. She wasn't sure she liked the fact that Nancy had taken it upon herself to listen to their conversation.

''He could be a con artist. He was here yesterday, too.''

''Because he has no one to talk to. He told me his grandson is putting him in a home. I feel sorry for him.'' Faith took a sponge and wiped down a splash of chocolate on the counter by the sink. She didn't want to snap at Nancy, even though her questions were progressively more irritating. Sometimes Nancy acted as if Faith didn't have a smart thought in her head.

''You're such a soft touch, Faith, and so impulsive.''

Faith silently counted to ten. ''The only thing he's tried to con me out of is a chocolate éclair.'' She rinsed the sponge in water and set it on the edge of the sink.

"So far. He's trying to get your confidence. That's why they call it a con game." Nancy walked over to the sink. "When you least suspect it, he'll steal something from you. I saw a case just like this on one of those talk shows."

Faith smiled and patted Nancy on the shoulder. "Steal what? We don't keep enough cash on site to make anyone happy. And I can always make more pastry."

"He might try to talk you into investing in something."

"I promise you I won't give him any money."

"I hope not. Anyway, I wanted to ask you if you're coming to dinner tonight. Ben will be there. He told me you two went sailing last weekend."

"Yes. We had a lot of fun."

"You and Ben get along so well."

"He's a wonderful guy." Faith's smile tightened somewhat as she remembered their good-bye. After two years of solid friendship, Ben had kissed her good night. For a second she'd thought she was kissing Gary. Maybe that was why she'd responded. But she should have told Ben right then that she wasn't interested in being anything more than friends. Although she had to admit it had been a nice kiss, comforting, caring, warm, and she'd missed being with a man.

"Faith?"

She started, feeling a rush of color warm her face. "What?"

"I don't think Gary would mind."

"Mind what?" Good heavens. Had Ben told his mother about their kiss?

Nancy shook her head. "Nothing. I shouldn't have said anything. You are coming for dinner, right? It's Friday night."

Faith nodded. Friday night dinner and Sunday morning brunch at the Porters' were a tradition, and she knew she couldn't disappoint Nancy by saying no. Besides, Ben had called earlier and asked her to come, and she'd already promised. "I'm looking forward to it."

"Good. I'll go then, as soon as I send that man on his way." Nancy headed back to the front of the bakery.

Faith followed her, determined not to let Nancy hurt the old man's feelings. But Faith didn't have a chance to say a word to Nancy, because when they entered the front room, Julian was arguing with another man.

"What's going on?" Faith asked sharply.

The younger man turned to her with blazing blue eyes. Faith took a step back out of self-defense. His blue eyes were exactly the same as Julian's. His face had the same square shape, the same stubborn jaw, but where Julian's hair was white, this man's hair was dark and thick, his skin tan and unlined, his build strong and intimidating.

Dashing, she thought, remembering Julian's description. Or at least he would be if he were smiling, if his stance weren't filled with aggression, if he didn't look like he wanted to hit someone.

"Who are you?" the man asked.

"Faith Christopher. I own this bakery."

"Faith, do you want me to call the police?" Nancy asked, hovering by the phone on the counter.

"I don't think that will be necessary. Will it?" she asked the man. Faith might have been a soft touch, but she hadn't lived in six different foster homes without learning how to stare down an intimidating glare.

"No. My grandfather and I are leaving."

"So you're the obnoxious grandson."

Julian laughed, then coughed to cover it up.

Alex turned to the old man. "What did you tell her?"

Julian shrugged. "You're not interested in anything I have to say. Why start now?"

"Because obviously you've been telling this woman a pack of lies."

"Judging by your behavior just now, I doubt that," Faith said, supremely irritated by the way Alex treated his grandfather. If she'd had a grandfather, she would have treated him with respect and love and patience for his years.

''We're leaving.'' Alex put his hand on Julian's arm.

''Ow,'' Julian said with a dramatic wince. ''Please, please don't hurt me.''

''Now, you stop that right now, you big bully,'' Faith said, storming forward.

''Oh, dear,'' Nancy muttered.

Faith took Alex's arm and pulled him toward the door, her fingers twisting the material of his suit coat into a knot.

''What the hell are you doing?'' Alex demanded, shaking himself free of her determined grasp.

''Showing you the door. This is my bakery, and your grandfather is welcome to stay here as long as he likes. I certainly will not allow you to abuse this dear old man in front of me. I have half a mind to call the police and have you arrested.''

Alex's jaw dropped open. ''What? I'm not abusing him. I'm taking care of him.''

''Oh, sure, by putting him in a home where he'll be strapped to a bed for hours on end.''

''I'm not doing that.'' He turned to Julian. ''What did you tell her?''

''I told her the truth.''

''You wouldn't know the truth if you fell over it.''

''And you'll never know it either unless you open your eyes and see, and open your ears and hear.'' Julian stood up with dignity and pride. ''It's all right, Miss Faith. I'll go now. I don't want to cause you any trouble. You've been more than kind.''

Alex clapped his hands. ''Very nice performance, Grandfather. Did you also tell Miss Faith that you're an actor? That you've acted on and off Broadway for the past thirty years? Did you tell her that you spend each day of your life playing out another character, and today it happens to be the old, abused, and neglected grandfather? Which, by the way, could use some work.''

"You wound me, Alex. So eager you are to play me for the fool."

"And I should be happy you're blackening my name all over town?"

The door to the bakery opened and a little girl walked through the door, a petulant expression on her heavily made-up face. "What's taking so long, Alex?"

"I told you to wait in the car, Jessie."

"Who is this child?" Julian demanded.

Jessie crossed her arms in front of her chest and sent Julian a defiant look. "I'm his kid, Jessie. What's it to you?"

Faith wasn't sure who looked more surprised by the declaration, Julian or his grandson. But if this child was any example of Alex Carrigan's commitment to his family, he was sadly lacking. The makeup on Jessie's face barely disguised the dirt on her neck and around her ears. And she was far too young to be wearing so many cosmetics.

"She's not my kid," Alex growled, sending Jessie a stern look. "Stop saying that."

"Then what are you doing with her?" Julian asked.

"Watching her temporarily, until her real father is found."

"He's ashamed to admit he's my dad," Jessie said, her attitude suddenly changing as her gaze traveled over to the bakery trays filled with desserts. She gave a heartfelt, dramatic sigh, much like the one Julian had just uttered. "I don't blame him for not wanting me. I haven't had a bath in a long time. I haven't eaten in a long time, either."

"Oh, for heaven's sake. Let me get you something," Faith said.

"I'll do it," Nancy offered, stepping up to take Jessie's order.

"I want one of those, and one of those, and one of those," Jessie said, pointing to several different trays.

"Oh, my, you are hungry," Nancy said, as she bustled to fill the girl's order.

"I just got her twenty minutes ago," Alex said defensively, looking from Nancy to Faith. "I haven't had a chance to feed her or throw her into the bath. Because I've been looking for you," he added, turning to Julian. "You were supposed to stay put."

"The wind." Julian's eyes lit up with understanding. "She came with the wind, didn't she?"

"No, she came with a letter and a lawyer."

"It's the curse."

"It's not the damn curse." Alex threw up his hands. "I wish you'd stop blaming everything on some ridiculous story."

"Then how do you explain this child's sudden appearance in your life?"

"The untimely death of her mother. Now that you've told your sob story and had your cake, can we go?"

"I just got my food," Jessie said, taking the bag from Nancy.

"You can eat in the car." Alex took out a twenty-dollar bill and handed it to Nancy, who gave him change without a word or a smile. "Actually, you can hold it until we get home," Alex said.

"But I'm starving."

"Oh, let the girl eat," Julian said.

"I just got my car washed."

Faith shook her head in disgust. How shallow! The man cared more about his car than his daughter.

Alex caught her accusing look. "Fine, she can eat in the car."

As Jessie skipped out of the bakery, Julian picked up Faith's hand and kissed the back of it. "Good day, my dear. I apologize for bringing my troubles to you. But I thank you for listening to an old man."

"It was no bother." She sent Alex a sharp look, then dropped her voice. "If you need anything at all, please call me. My last name is Christopher. Faith Christopher. I'm in the phone book."

"You are too kind. Thank you." Julian squared his shoulders and tossed his chin in the air. "We can go now, Alex."

Julian walked out of the bakery with his head held high. Alex paused at the door.

"You really are naive," he said to Faith. "You actually believed his act?"

Faith bristled at the all-too-familiar accusation. She wasn't naive. How could anyone with her background be naive? Maybe she just liked to believe in the goodness of people. Was that a crime?

"Your grandfather was right about one thing," she said. "You're a jerk. And if anyone deserves to be cursed, it's you."

Alex laughed. "Oh, the curse. Right. I think I'd rather be a jerk than a sucker."

Faith pushed him out the door, and slammed it on his mocking laughter. "Idiot. Arrogant, obnoxious son of a bitch," she said more loudly, wishing he could hear her, but he was gone.

"Good heavens, Faith. I've never seen you so worked up," Nancy said.

"That man!" Faith shook her head. "I'm sorry. But I pity his grandfather and that little girl, whoever she is. I have half a mind to call Social Services and—"

"Faith, they're not your business. Don't get involved. Besides, you heard that man tell you his grandfather is an actor. You can't believe a word he said."

"Maybe he wasn't acting."

"You always look for the best in people. I admire that, I do. But sometimes it gets you into trouble."

Faith gave up, knowing she wouldn't find an ally in Nancy, not on this subject. She took off her apron and hung it on a hook behind the counter. It was past closing time, and she was more than ready to call it a day.

As she systematically removed the trays from the display counter and set them in the large refrigerator in back, Faith couldn't help but go over the earlier scene. She had to admit that Julian's tale of woe and his ramblings about an evil curse had caught her imagination. She'd always believed that some things in life couldn't be explained with logic.

Then again, if Julian was an actor, he could have been having fun at her expense. That was what his grandson thought, his obnoxious, fantastic-looking grandson, Alex Carrigan. She could still see his piercing blue eyes, hear the sexy timbre of his voice, feel the muscles packed beneath his business suit. Oh, Lord, if that man had gotten to her, she definitely needed to get out more.

"I'm finished," Nancy said, returning to the kitchen, purse in hand. "Do you need anything else, Faith?"

"No. I'll see you later."

"Come about seven. And feel free to change clothes if you like."

Faith looked down at her simple floral sundress. "Change? I didn't realize we were going formal tonight."

Nancy laughed somewhat nervously. "I just thought you might want to get out of your work clothes. Why don't you wear that pretty blue knit dress that Gary gave you? I know Ben loves it. You know, speaking of Ben, he told me the other day he wants to settle down and have a family."

"Were you telling him how much you want grandchildren at the time?"

"Maybe. You still want children, don't you, Faith?"

"More than just about anything," Faith replied, feeling the familiar ache in her gut that always accompanied the thought of a baby. If Gary had lived, they would have had a child by now, and she would have finally had someone tied to her by blood. But he hadn't lived, and her womb was empty, so empty. She put a hand to her abdomen and rubbed it.

Nancy's gaze followed her motion and Faith instinctively pulled her hand away.

"You don't have to pretend with me, Faith. I know how much you wanted a baby. Gary told me that you were going to start trying right away."

Faith blinked back an unexpected tear. She thought she'd finished crying ages ago, but sometimes her loss overwhelmed her.

"I know Gary wouldn't have wanted you to live alone the rest of your life."

"Is that a nice way of telling me it's time to move on?"

"I want you to be happy, Faith. I want all of my kids to be happy. If only they would cooperate."

Faith gave Nancy an impulsive hug. "You're the best."

"I try." Nancy walked toward the door, then paused. "Faith, I want you to know that—well, I approve."

"Approve of what?" Faith asked, but Nancy was gone.

Benjamin Porter hadn't known engagement rings came in so many sizes and shapes. He'd foolishly believed they were all the same, a simple diamond on a band of gold. The tray in front of him held diamond clusters, sharp blue sapphires, fiery rubies, and colorful opals. They sparkled as the late afternoon sunshine drifted through the window of the jewelry store, reminding him that it was time to make a decision.

"This is the one you wanted to see, isn't it?" the clerk asked, as she selected a ring from the tray and held it out for his inspection.

"Yes." Ben took the ring from her hand and gazed at the diamond solitaire. The square diamond was perfectly cut, a beautiful gem, one a woman could wear proudly for years to come and perhaps hand down to her daughter or granddaughter or great-granddaughter. That was what life was all about, family, children. Nothing else mattered—at least to his parents.

Since his brother, Gary, had died, the family name was left to him to carry on. His younger sister, Kim, could have all the children she wanted, but none would bear the Porter name, and that meant more to his father than anything.

"Do you like it?" the clerk asked. She was a pretty young girl with dreamy eyes, and the name tag on her chest read "Mandy."

"It's nice." He knew the word was inadequate to describe the ring in his hand, but he felt uncomfortable, awkward. He'd never bought a ring for a woman before, especially not a ring with as much meaning as this one.

"I think it's gorgeous. If my boyfriend surprised me with a ring like that, I'd make him very, very happy."

Ben smiled at the seductive purr in her voice. He had a feeling Mandy made her boyfriend very, very happy quite often. "I'm just wondering if I shouldn't let her pick out her own ring."

"I don't know. It's incredibly romantic for a man to buy an engagement ring for the woman. It's like he's picked out something special just for her. Call me old-fashioned, but I think it's a nice tradition."

Tradition. It was a word Ben had grown up with. *You've got to play baseball, son, it's a tradition. All the Porter men cut the turkey at Thanksgiving, it's tradition. All the Porter men surprise their wives with an engagement ring, it's tradition.*

Gary had known instinctively how to stay in line with the Porter family traditions. He'd never screwed up the way Ben had. No, Gary had played varsity baseball and won a scholarship to Stanford. He'd majored in business and founded his own investment firm just as his father had wanted. And Gary had gotten engaged to a beautiful, loving woman just as his father had wanted. The only thing Gary had done wrong was die.

God, Ben missed his big brother. He hadn't realized how much he'd depended on Gary to run interference with the family until he was no longer there to do it. Now it was just him against them. Although they would gasp in horror if they knew he felt that way.

Since Gary's death, his parents had gone from bragging about Gary to bragging about Ben. Whereas before Ben was the second son, the middle child, now he was the only son. And all their dreams, all their desires, were focused on him. They no longer deplored his job at the art gallery as low paying and on the road to nowhere. He was suddenly their brilliant son working with priceless paintings. And his studio apartment in the Haight district was no longer a former hippy slum, but a cozy artist's loft.

Gary's death had certainly raised Ben's worth. He had to admit, he liked being their favorite son. It felt good to see pride in their eyes, to feel their love. It made him feel high, and he'd fast become an addict for their praise.

"If you want to make a deposit, we could hold the ring for you while you think about it," Mandy said, obviously sensing he wasn't convinced to buy.

Ben hesitated, seeing an out. He could make a deposit. He could think about it. He could change his mind. He could forget this crazy idea. No, he was being a coward at far too many things in his life. It was time for him to take this step. His position in the family would be solidified forever with this move. He would marry and have children. It was tradition.

"I'll take it."

"I'm sure she'll like it," Mandy replied. "Shall I wrap it up for you?"

"That would be great."

Mandy took the ring from his hand. "You must love her a lot."

Ben smiled as he remembered their kiss. He could do this. He could make her happy—make everyone happy.

"Do you think she'll be surprised?" Mandy asked.

Ben offered her a wry smile. "I think she'll be shocked. I just hope she says yes." The rest of his life depended on her answer. Without this marriage, without the children they would have together, he would be nothing.

"This ring ought to convince her that you're the man," Mandy said cheerfully.

"That's what I'm counting on."

Chapter 3

Faith. The name should have described someone saintly looking, not a gorgeous redhead with flashing green eyes, long legs, and great breasts. Alex had to admit Faith Christopher had caught his eye. Of course, she had a temper to match her hair and an idealistic streak to match her name, which meant she was definitely not his kind of woman. In fact, he didn't know why he was thinking about her. He certainly had plenty of other people to worry about, such as his Grandfather and Jessie.

With a sigh, Alex pulled off his tie, tossed it over the kitchen chair, and set to work opening the cartons from Mei Ling's Chinese Restaurant.

Jessie wandered into the kitchen. "Can I have a drink?"

"Sure, help yourself." Alex tipped his head toward the refrigerator. "I hope you like Chinese food. I got a little of everything so you can have your pick."

"Whatever."

Jessie grabbed a can out of the refrigerator and sat down at the kitchen table. It wasn't until she'd taken a few sips and burped in appreciation that Alex noticed she was not drinking a soft drink but instead had a beer in her hand.

"Hey, give me that." He grabbed the can out of her hand. "What do you think you're doing?"

"Having a drink."

"You're twelve, Jessie. Way under the limit."

"I'll be thirteen in three weeks."

"Great. Then you'll be legal to be a teenager. Drinking beer is still a few years off."

"You're no fun." Jessie settled back in her chair with a scowl.

"Yeah, well, you're not exactly a barrel of laughs yourself. By the way, you're in my chair."

"I don't see your name engraved on it. Why can't you sit over there?"

"Because this seat has the best view of the television."

"Cool," Jessie said, reaching for the remote control.

"Oh, no, you don't. I always watch ESPN." Alex grabbed the remote out of her hand, feeling like his life was spinning out of control.

"I hate sports."

Alex silently counted to ten. "Fine. We won't watch anything." He walked over to the cupboard and pulled out three plates and set them on the table. Then he opened the silverware drawer, grabbed some forks and knives, and handed them to Jessie. "Why don't you set the table?"

Jessie sent him a blank look. "What do you mean?"

"Put the forks and knives out."

"Oh, you mean like in a restaurant."

"Yeah."

Jessie bit down on her lip as she studied the silverware, and it suddenly occured to Alex that she had no idea where to put them but was too proud to ask.

"You know, on second thought, why don't we just leave everything stacked, like a buffet?"

"Whatever." She sat back in her seat with a sigh of relief.

"I say, is supper ready?" Julian asked, as he paused in the doorway. "I'm famished, and it's been simply ages since I had a proper supper."

"Why is he talking like that?" Jessica asked.

"My grandfather is now playing a British royal."

"You mean he's pretending?"

"You catch on quick, kid." Alex handed his grandfather a plate. "The servants have all been thrown into the dungeon. You'll have to help yourself."

Julian frowned. "You were never much fun as a child either."

Alex sighed. Jessie had proclaimed him a bore, and now his grandfather had seconded the opinion. It was easy for them to be foolish. They didn't have responsibilities, people depending on them.

Julian sat down at the table next to Jessica and helped himself to some rice and stir-fry beef. Alex took the chair across from them, hoping they could have some semblance of peace for at least a few moments.

"About the curse," Julian began.

"What curse?" Jessie asked, waving her fork in the air as she stared wide-eyed at Julian.

"I don't think we should talk about that right now." Alex sent his grandfather a stern look. Julian, as usual, ignored him.

"It began a long time ago, my dear, in the holy grounds of the ancient ones, the Anasazi."

"The ana— Who?"

"Grandfather, please not now. We're eating."

"The Anasazi are believed by some to be the first human beings to walk the earth. They lived in the Southwest in a place called the Four Corners where Utah, Arizona, Colorado, and New Mexico meet. I spent a summer in northern Arizona, traveling through the desert, visiting the various ruins, the national monuments to a time gone by."

His voice faltered for a moment, then he continued. "We explored many canyons that summer, all the famous ruins, but one day I ventured off the main trails and found myself in a place that seemed untouched by man. The air was so quiet that afternoon." He paused for a long moment, letting the tension build. "I wandered for hours until I saw this incredible rock formation. It appeared as if two butterflies were dancing. I stopped and stared, completely captivated. I had to get closer, to figure out how the sandstone rocks could have taken on such an unusual shape. I had to climb up the side of a canyon wall to get to the butterflies, and I was almost there when I saw an opening under a ledge, a small cave that couldn't be seen from the ground. I stopped, wondering . . . I decided to peer inside, almost afraid of what I would find. But the cave seemed empty. I walked in a little further and there it was."

"What?" Jessie breathed.

"A beautiful, perfect pot, black on white, standing where it must have stood for centuries. I couldn't quite believe it. Even fifty years ago, most of the ruins had been discovered, picked over, and yet I'd found something remarkable. And I took it."

Alex cleared his throat, not liking his own intense reaction to the story that never failed to draw goose bumps down his spine. "Grandfather, do you really need to tell this story again?"

"Yes. If Jessie is your daughter, then it is imperative she know about the curse upon our family."

"Jessie's not my daughter, and there is no curse on our family. We just have bad luck, that's it."

"I said the same thing for many years. I told myself it was only bad fortune that caused me to lose jobs, to marry so many women, to wander aimlessly around this earth."

"You just have a short attention span, that's all." The food in Alex's stomach twisted into a knot.

"No, I brought the curse of the gods down upon my family. I must set it right before I die." Julian looked from Jessie to Alex. "I don't wish to scare the child, but I may not have long to live."

Alex took in a deep breath. The words hurt, more than they should have. His grandfather had never spent much time with him. Julian had been a wanderer all his life. In fact, Julian had only spent time with Alex when he needed an audience. Which was probably why he'd come to visit now.

Still, Alex had to admit Julian's skin looked pale, almost translucent, and his hands shook slightly as he raised the fork to his lips. He knew the old man had already had two heart attacks, both supposedly mild, but Julian was seventy-four years old, he might not have that much time left.

"What did the doctor say?" Alex asked.

"He said I should make my peace now before it's too late."

"Did you talk to my father?"

"Your father is in Africa, shooting bathing-suit models in the wild kingdom."

That sounded like Brett Carrigan. Another wanderer, just like Julian.

Was Alex the same? Destined to travel from one location to the next, one woman to the next, never setting down roots, never feeling connected to anyone? Was that truly the curse of the Carrigans or just a weak family gene? He certainly hadn't had much success finding true love. After his disastrous marriage to Melanie, Alex had shied away from anything serious, devoting himself to his business. It had seemed enough—until today. Until Jessie had reminded him of the child he had once longed to have.

Not that this smart-ass girl was his vision of the perfect child. Not by a long shot. Although he had to admit Jessie had Julian's flare for the dramatic. Was it possible she really was a Carrigan? Where had the lies begun and ended? It all seemed so blurry now.

"What did you do with the pot?" Jessie asked, impatient to hear the rest of the story.

Julian's mouth tightened in a grim line. "I took it back to show Suzannah."

"Suzannah?"

"More rice?" Alex interrupted, disliking the intensity

in his grandfather's eyes. The old man looked like he'd forgotten they were even there.

Jessie frowned at him. "Shush. I want to hear the rest of the story. Go on," she urged Julian.

"What? Oh." Julian took a deep breath. "When I took the pot to Suzannah, she touched it and became angry, hysterical, almost panicked. She said it was wrong to take it, that it might have come from a burial site. She begged me to return it. I told her it was a long trip, and I wasn't sure I could even find the cave again. She insisted that I leave at once, that afternoon." Julian paused. "I became angry. I couldn't believe she wanted me to take the pot back. I told her she could take it back if she wished. That's when Suzannah reached for the pot and . . ."

"And what?" Jessie demanded.

"It broke. It split into two perfectly symmetrical pieces."

"Oh, no."

"Oh, yes."

When his grandfather didn't elaborate, Alex leaned forward in his seat. He'd forgotten the power of the story until now. "Tell her what happened next," he said, impatient to hear the end.

"The wind came down through the canyons, howling and screaming in pain. We were standing in a trailer, and it shook as if there were an earthquake. For a moment, I thought an angry God had decided to pick us up and heave us across the land. I remember everything falling off the shelves, and Suzannah hanging on to the counter with one hand, the other clutching her half of the pot. She screamed at me that . . ."

"That what?" Jessie asked.

Julian shook his head. "I can't remember what she said. I just knew that I had to get help. I took my half of the pot and went into the town to talk to one of the Indian guides we had met earlier that summer. He was an older man, and he'd seen many a burial site. When he saw the pot, his eyes lit up with a fury almost as spectacular as the wind. He told me that I had unleashed a powerful curse. I begged him to tell me how I could fix what I had done. And he told me that—''

''The winds will curse your life until you return to where it began . . .'' Alex finished.

Julian met his gaze. ''Exactly.''

''So why didn't you take it back then?'' Alex demanded, even though he'd asked the question a dozen times before.

''Because I needed the other half. You know that. When I returned to the trailer, Suzannah was gone. I looked all over for her, but she had vanished. The next day I called her home in California. Her great-aunt had no idea where Suzannah was.'' Julian's eyes darkened. ''It was then I realized Suzannah had run away to meet me in Arizona.

''Her aunt told me that Suzannah was a bad girl and as far as she was concerned, Suzannah was dead. Three months later I finally got up the courage to go to her aunt's house. I thought that surely Suzannah would have returned by then. As far as I knew, she had little money. A man answered the door. He said he'd just moved into the house a week earlier and had no idea what had happened to the former owners. I didn't know what else to do. I didn't believe in the curse at first, but as the days turned to weeks, then months, then years, I realized I had lost the love of my life, and I would never know true love again and neither would anyone in my family.''

''Wow,'' Jessie breathed.

''I must find her,'' Julian declared. He rose to his feet. ''I must find Suzannah before I die. I must obtain the other half of the pot. For this curse shall not be broken until the pottery is returned to the land, until the gods are appeased. With my last breath I will fight to protect my family from the evil that I created. I shall no longer ask what they can do for me but what I can do for my family. I have a dream . . .''

"Who is he now?" Jessie asked Alex as Julian launched into a speech.

Alex sighed. "Martin Luther King and maybe a little John F. Kennedy."

"Who?"

"Never mind." Alex clapped his hands. "Take a bow, Grandfather. Act One is over. Now, does anyone want dessert?"

"Would you like some dessert, Faith?" Nancy asked as she cleared away the dinner plates.

"No, thanks, I'm full." Faith sat back in her chair and smiled at the Porters gathered around the dining room table. Kim, Gary's younger sister, was a twenty-five-year-old law student. A slender brunette, she had an easy laugh, a stubborn nature, and an independent spirit. She loved to argue, thrived on conflict, and reminded Faith a bit of Gary in the way she went after what she wanted.

Ben, on the other hand, was more reflective, more introverted, than his siblings. Ben loved books and music and art. He loved to sail and paint. His spirit was free, although sometimes a bit lonely, Faith thought. Before Gary's death, she'd noticed that Ben was often on the outside of the circle, as much a spectator at the family gatherings as Faith.

Even tonight he seemed out of it. "Are you all right, Ben?" Faith whispered as Nancy and Kim cleared the table, and Chuck stood up to pour another glass of wine from the bottle on the credenza.

Ben leaned forward, looking into her eyes. "We're good together, don't you think?"

She stared at him uncertainly, not sure what he was asking. "What do you mean?"

"I mean, we get along. We never fight. We like the same movies. We both want kids. We even like the same food—most of the time, except you like it a bit spicier than I do. And, uh . . ."

"Ben, what are you talking about?" Faith asked, cutting him off in midramble. Her stomach began to turn, the muscles in her neck tensing with his every word.

"I'm talking about you and me. About . . ."

Faith didn't hear the rest of the sentence, because Gary's voice rang through her head.

"I'm talking about you and me," Gary said with a laugh. "We should get married, don't you think?"

"Just like that—you want to marry me?"

"I love you. You love me."

"But I don't have a family. I don't even have a name," Faith protested.

"I'll give you mine. You'll be a Porter, and you'll never be alone again."

Faith took in a deep breath and let it out.

"Faith, did you hear me?" Ben asked.

She didn't know if she'd heard him or not. Was there a question she was supposed to answer? Ben seemed to be waiting for something.

"So, Faith, Nancy tells me you had quite a scene at the bakery today," Chuck Porter interrupted, as he sat down at the table, a glass of red wine in his hand.

Faith looked over at Gary's father, relieved to have him back in the conversation. She didn't like the way Ben was looking at her. It reminded her of Gary. She picked up her water glass and took a long sip, trying to calm the butterflies in her stomach.

"Tell me what happened," Chuck ordered, and Faith didn't dare refuse. Chuck was a large man, well over six feet, with a girth to match his advancing years. He was a good man, very protective of his family, although rather stern at times. But he'd always treated Faith like a daughter, which seemed to give him the right to criticize and to give orders.

"It was nothing, really," Faith began. "We just got in the middle of a family dispute."

"Maybe I should come down to the bakery tomorrow afternoon in case that man comes back and gives you any trouble."

''He's an elderly man. He's not dangerous.''

''His grandson could be,'' Nancy said, scooting back into the conversation as she and Kim returned to the table. ''He had a nasty temper.''

''I didn't know the bakery business was so exciting,'' Kim interjected. ''And apparently overflowing with men. Maybe I should stop by more often.''

''Julian Carrigan is in his mid-seventies, Kim, and his grandson is, I don't know, early thirties, I'd guess.'' Faith couldn't help the sudden catch in her voice when she thought of Alex. In fact, she'd been thinking of him all evening. He had gotten under her skin, and she didn't know why. He was too good-looking to be anything but trouble.

''Maybe Ben could stop by,'' Nancy suggested. ''He could handle that young man for you.''

Actually, Faith didn't think Ben's light, wiry frame would match up all that well with Alex's athletic build.

''No one has to handle Alex,'' Faith muttered. If she didn't put a stop to this now, Nancy would have Ben and Chuck standing guard in her bakery every afternoon.

Nancy raised an eyebrow. ''Alex? You remember his name?''

Actually, Faith remembered everything, the curve of his lips, the breadth of his shoulders, the slight indentation in his chin . . . She took in a breath. ''His grandfather called him Alex.''

''Was this Alex guy cute?'' Kim asked.

''Honestly, Kim, you have a one-track mind,'' Nancy replied before Faith could answer. ''As if Faith would be interested enough to notice.''

''You didn't notice?'' Kim asked.

Faith shrugged. ''He was nice-looking.''

''Ben, I think you should definitely come down to the bakery tomorrow,'' Nancy said. ''Just in case that man returns and tries to make trouble for Faith.''

''He's not going to do that,'' Faith said. ''Good heavens. You're all making a big deal out of nothing.''

Nancy sat back in her seat, looking somewhat hurt. "We care about you, Faith. That's all."

Oh, damn. Now she'd done it—insulted the only family who'd ever really wanted her to be a part of them.

"I'm sorry. I'm not used to people worrying about me."

"We love you," Nancy said. "We have from the first minute Gary brought you home."

"She's right, Faith. You're like a daughter to us," Chuck added.

"And a sister," Kim said with a cheerful smile.

"Ben, don't you have anything to say?" Nancy asked. "About how much Faith means to you, to all of us."

Ben cleared his throat. He looked from his mother to Faith. "Actually, I do. I . . . um. I have an announcement. Well, it's not really an announcement, but more of a question—a question for Faith."

"About what?" Faith asked, noting the red flush creeping up from his neck.

"Uh, well." He cleared his throat again, then reached into his pocket and pulled out a small box. "This is for you."

Faith stared at the beautifully wrapped package, no bigger than a ring box. Oh, Lord!

"It's not my birthday," she said warily.

"I know. Please, open it."

Faith took the box from his hand. She slowly loosened the silver ribbon and lifted the lid to reveal a velvet ring box. Her heart began to race. Her breath came short and fast as she remembered the last time a man had given her a ring box. Gary had asked her to marry him at a family picnic. She had hated being the center of attention then and she hated it now.

And what—what was Ben thinking? She looked into his face and saw her friend, her supporter, but not—not her lover. Never her lover. Although that kiss . . . Oh, man, that kiss. He must have thought . . .

Ben reached across the table and opened the velvet box. The diamond sparkled accusingly.

''Oh, Ben,'' she whispered.

''Will you marry me, Faith? Say yes.''

Chapter 4

Say yes? Faith couldn't say anything. She could only stare in bewilderment at the emerald-cut diamond ring nestled in a bed of white velvet. She'd played this scene before, two years earlier, but the ring was different, the man was different. Everything else was the same.

Faith turned her head to see Nancy smiling encouragement, her round, rosy cheeks expressing her pleasure. Kim hovered behind her mother, her youthful eyes shining with romantic enthusiasm. Chuck sat at the other end of the table, sipping a glass of red wine with a satisfied smile, as if her answer were a foregone conclusion.

Faith's gaze drifted to the empty seat beside her. Ben sat across from her, not next to her—never next to her. That had been Gary's seat. How could she marry Ben when he'd never sat beside her at the dining room table?

It was a silly question, but she couldn't answer it. Hysteria rose through her like bubbles of champagne, making her feel dizzy and giddy. She couldn't catch her breath. She couldn't speak. Instead, a wave of irrepressible laughter swept through her, and it was all Faith could do to hold it back. Finally a chuckle escaped, then a laugh, then another. She covered her mouth with her hand.

''Faith?'' Ben questioned, his eyebrow quirking in an endearingly familiar arc.

Although they had always been close friends, there were moments when Faith knew her behavior completely baffled Ben.

"Do you think this is a joke?" Ben asked.

Faith shook her head, trying desperately to stop laughing, but the giggles continued to spill out of her and her eyes began to stream with tears.

"Because it's not," Ben said forcefully. "I love you and I want to marry you."

"You've just taken her by surprise, Ben," Nancy said, her eyes concerned. "Isn't that right, Faith? Oh, dear, you're not crying now, are you?"

Faith shook her head again, but she couldn't deny the tears that streaked down her face.

"I always laugh and cry at the same time," Kim added, trying to lighten the tense atmosphere.

"Your mother cries when she's happy," Chuck said, patting Ben on the shoulder with a reassuring hand, but he, too, looked a bit alarmed.

"Are you crying because you're happy?" Ben asked.

"I'm—I'm surprised," Faith finally got out. She took several deep, calming breaths. "I didn't expect this tonight."

"I would have asked you in private, but it's always been a Porter tradition to ask for a woman's hand in marriage in front of the family."

"I know," she whispered, thinking of the last time.

"I would never try to take Gary's place. You know that, don't you?"

"No one could take Gary's place," Nancy said. "But we love you, Faith, and Ben loves you, and, well, I don't think Gary would want you to spend the rest of your life alone."

"No, he wouldn't want that." Faith wiped her eyes with the edge of her napkin. Gary would have been the first one to encourage her to go on with life. God, she missed him.

"This will be perfect," Kim said earnestly. "We'd really be sisters. I've wanted a sister forever.''

Faith had wanted a sister, too, and a family like the Porters to call her own. Her favorite daydreams had been about falling in love and getting married and having children. She'd made up dozens of imaginary families over the years, but none had come close to the Porters.

And she cared about Ben. They shared a lot of interests, and they'd always enjoyed each other's company. In fact, they were frighteningly compatible. They'd never had an argument or even a difference of opinion in all the time they'd known each other.

But marry him?

''Maybe we should let the kids talk,'' Chuck said.

Nancy seemed reluctant to leave the table without a firm commitment from Faith, but her husband's sharp glance made her get to her feet. ''I'll start the dishes.''

''I'll help you, Mom,'' Kim said.

The room fell silent with the exit of the Porters, broken only by the ticking of the grandfather clock in the hallway, counting off the seconds of her life, Faith thought. She glanced down at the beautifully cut diamond ring. It was a gorgeous ring, and suited to her taste, but that didn't surprise her. She and Ben had always shared the same taste in jewelry. Was that enough to base a marriage on?

Of course not, she told herself. Then again, she'd lost the love of her life. Maybe it was time to settle for a comfortable love, to find joy in being part of this family, to have the babies she yearned for. Ben would make a good father. What was she thinking? They'd never even slept together.

''Did I blow it?'' Ben asked quietly.

''You surprised me.''

''I was hoping that would work in my favor,'' he said with a guilty smile.

''I don't know what to say.''

''Don't say no.''

''How can I say yes, Ben? I—''

He cut her off with a shake of his head and a pleading smile. "Don't say no, Faith. I know you still love Gary, but consider this. My parents love you. My sister loves you. And I love you. We could make you happy if you'd let us. We want you to be a part of our family."

Ben was bringing out the big guns, hitting her where she was the most vulnerable, the most needy. And Faith caved in like a marshmallow on a hot fire. "Okay, I'll think about it."

A smile spread across Ben's face. He turned his head toward the kitchen door and called, "You can bring out the champagne now, Mother."

"Ben, I said I'd think about it."

"Close enough."

"Oh, I'm so happy," Nancy said, bursting into the room. She flung her arms around Faith and gave her a tight hug. "This is just the best news."

"I said I'd think about it," Faith said again.

Nancy stopped abruptly, looking from Ben to Faith. "What's to think about?"

"She needs a little time," Ben cut in. "But I'll take a maybe right now, because I'm convinced that she will say yes."

"Of course she'll say yes," Chuck boomed out as he popped the cork on the bottle of champagne. "She knows a good man when she sees one."

"I'd love to be a bridesmaid," Kim said. "But only if you want me. If you'd rather have a friend, I'll understand. I'm just so happy that you and Ben are in love."

You and Ben are in love.

Faith wasn't in love with Ben. She was in love with Gary. Faith tried desperately to conjure up Gary's handsome face, but the image in her mind was dull and vague, and his features kept blending into someone else, maybe Ben, she thought at first; maybe this was the way it was meant to be. Gary fading into the shadows so Ben could take his place.

Faith squeezed her eyes shut, trying to concentrate, trying to see the answer. When it came, her eyes flew open in astonishment, because the face her mind had conjured up was not Ben, but Alex Carrigan, or maybe it was the devil—a devil with sharp blue eyes and a dazzling smile.

Alex took a deep breath and raised the weights over his head one more time, feeling his biceps strain with the last repetition. Slowly he brought the weights down and took another deep breath of satisfaction. He exercised every day, determined to make his body as lean and mean as any athlete he worked with.

Alex sat up and reached for the white terry cloth towel he had set next to the treadmill. He wiped the sweat from his face and stood up. Four miles on the treadmill, a series of weights, and he still felt tense, not the usual euphoria that accompanied a good hard workout but rather a feeling of anxiety about a life that was spinning out of control.

The sound of canned laughter playing on his television in the living room and the sound of baroque music coming from his guest bedroom reminded him that his small weight room/laundry room was his only oasis of privacy in what had once been his castle. He was now relegated to the dungeon, so to speak.

Alex walked over to the window, picked up his water bottle on the way, and took long, deep gulps while he stared out at the city of San Francisco. The lights of the Golden Gate Bridge sparkled through the fingers of fog creeping across the city. He loved this town, the crowded, narrow, crooked streets, the bicycle messengers and Rollerbladers dashing between the cars, the honking horns, the delicious smells coming from every neighborhood: garlic and oregano from the Italian restaurants in North Beach, the mysterious Far Eastern scents emanating from the Chinese restaurants in Chinatown, and the raw, fresh smell of the sea coming from Fisherman's Wharf.

This was his town. He had arrived as an awkard youth escaping from a past and a childhood that had been more embarrassing than joyous. In San Francisco he had become a new person—a man. He had built a business in the industrial area in the southern part of the city. He now had offices, employees, a warehouse, inventory, and a name, a name he was proud of, a name he wanted to make into a household word—Top Flight Athletic Shoes.

He wanted every kid to lust after a pair, every parent to run frantically through malls trying to find the shoes on the night before Christmas. He wanted professional athletes to mention his shoes every time they came before the camera. He wanted advertisements that people would remember. He wanted the public to feel as if the shoes freed their souls—as they had freed his soul.

Alex smiled as the familiar fantasy grew in his mind. As a child, he'd spent fourteen years in orthopedic shoes because his feet turned inward. His parents had been oblivious to his embarrassment and shame and simply told him he'd have to wear the shoes until his feet changed. They didn't care about the taunts he'd suffered at school and on the playground. They'd never realized how hard he had had to fight to play the games he wanted to play, to wear the shoes he wanted to wear.

Nobody had ever understood him. Nobody had ever tried, he thought cynically. Certainly not his mother or his father, nor his grandfather for that matter. After his parents split up, Alex had truly done everything alone, and he'd grown accustomed to the solitude of thoughts and plans and dreams. Now his grandfather wanted a piece of his life. And Jessie wanted another. But neither one of them would last.

He'd suffered through more entrances and exits than his grandfather, who'd been in the theater all of his life. For Alex, the departures had always come from people who promised to stay, who promised to care about him. Well, no more.

He didn't believe in long-term relationships. He knew his grandfather would be gone with the first new show opening on Broadway, and Jessie—well, eventually her real father would show up to claim her, the way he had before. And Alex would once again be left alone. It would be easier if they'd just leave now before he started to care about them.

With a sigh, Alex checked his watch and realized it was almost ten. It was time Jessie got to bed. Maybe he could talk his grandfather into retiring for the night, so he could have a few minutes of peace.

Alex swung the towel around his shoulders and walked out of the laundry room and through the kitchen. Off to his right, a hallway led to two smaller bedrooms. Off to his left was the dining room, living room, and master bedroom at the far end of the apartment. It was a spacious apartment and one he had worked long and hard to afford. Only, now it didn't seem as big as it used to be. Jessie was sleeping on a futon in the den, and his grandfather had taken over the guest bedroom.

Alex decided to go after Jessie first, and he knew exactly where he'd find her, in front of the television set. As he walked down the stairs into his sunken, usually starkly neat black and white living room, he found Jessie had tossed the pillows from the couch onto the floor and was lying on top of them. A bag of corn chips on the oak coffee table was ripped open and spilling onto his baseball-card book, and two cans of Coke had left wet rings on the wood.

He'd never considered himself a neatnik, but Jessie was making him feel like Felix Unger.

"Time to clean up, Jess."

Jessie didn't even acknowledge his presence.

"Jessie. I'm talking to you."

He leaned over and snapped his fingers in front of her face.

"What?" she asked with annoyance.

"It's time to clean up, hit the shower, and go to bed."

"It's early, and I'm not tired. Besides, I took a shower a couple of days ago."

"It's almost ten."

"So? I stay up until midnight."

"Not here you don't. Come on, let's go." He walked over to the television and turned it off.

"Hey, that was the best part."

"If you know that, you must have already seen it."

Jessie made a face and slowly got to her feet. She took a moment to stretch, and with her arms raised over her head, she looked very thin, her collarbone and ribs standing out in sharp relief against her thin knit T-shirt. Catching him staring, she lowered her arms and crossed them self-consciously in front of her waist.

"How about that shower?" Alex asked.

"If you think I'm going to take my clothes off in front of you—"

"No! No, of course not. I assume you can handle that yourself."

"I can handle everything myself."

He certainly hoped she could handle a lot, because what the hell did he know about twelve-year-old girls? "I'll leave you to it then."

"Fine. I'll take a shower, but only because I want to, not because you told me to."

Julian applauded from the doorway. "Very nice exit line, my dear," he said with a twinkle in his eye as Jessie headed for the hall. "But you might want to tilt your head up just a bit more. There's nothing quite so beautiful and proud as a boldly upturned chin."

"You're nuts," Jessie proclaimed as she walked down the hall.

"At last, something the kid and I agree on," Alex said.

"Excellent comeback." Julian walked slowly into the room with the aid of his cane and gradually settled himself into the black leather reclining chair that was Alex's favorite.

Alex didn't know if Julian was playing the part of a crotchety old man or if he truly had become one. That was the problem with his grandfather. Julian was a very good actor.

Julian let out a sigh and rested his head against the back of the chair. ''That's better.''

''Are you all right?'' Alex sat down on the couch. He knew the words sounded grudging, but he was afraid that Julian would suddenly laugh and yell ''Gotcha,'' the way he'd done so many times when Alex was a boy.

''I'm old,'' Julian said in a somber tone.

Alex didn't know what to say. He could talk up a streak at work. He could sell just about anything. But with his grandfather, silence stretched between them like a high wire, and Alex was afraid one misstep would lead to a terrible fall.

He shook his head at the wimpy thought, because it reminded him of how often he'd felt like a coward where family was concerned, and how many risks and challenges he had deliberately taken to prove to himself and everyone else that he was as brave as they come, only to find himself, in moments like this, terrified of a simple conversation.

''What are you going to do with her?'' Julian asked.

It took Alex a moment to switch gears. ''I don't know.''

''Is she yours?''

''No. Her mother told me I wasn't the father. She had no reason to lie.''

Julian smiled cynically. ''There's always a reason to lie.''

''Let's talk about you. We need to discuss our long-term plans. If you can't live alone anymore, then we'll have to find you somewhere to live where you'll be comfortable.'' Alex frowned, remembering his grandfather's earlier lies. ''And you won't be strapped to a bed or tortured.''

''I want you to help me find Suzannah,'' Julian said abruptly.

''What? No.'' Alex shook his head. ''I will help you find a condo. I well help you move your things down from Seattle. I will even let you live here for a while, but that's it."

Julian leaned forward, his weary eyes suddenly sharp and piercing. "I must do this, Alex. I don't have much time, and I need your help."

"She's probably dead, Grandfather. It's been years."

"We won't know until we try to find her."

"You've had decades to find her. Why now?"

"Because I'm dying."

Alex swallowed hard, the simple statement taking the breath out of his chest. "You're exaggerating."

"And if I'm not?"

"It's pointless." Alex stood up and paced around the living room, which had once seemed large and carefree but now seemed cramped and filled with responsibilities. "I don't have time to look for some woman you spent a summer with fifty years ago. I have a company to run. I am this close to signing Elijah James," he said, putting his thumb and index finger an inch apart.

"Elijah who?"

"A basketball player, Grandfather, a giant in terms of height, ability, and celebrity recognition. If I can get him to endorse Top Flight Shoes, we'll be on our way to the top."

"The top of what?"

"The top of everything, the athletic shoe business, the money, the—well, everything."

"Your total happiness and success in life depends on having this giant wear your shoes?"

Why did his grandfather always make his dreams sound foolish? "Elijah is a good part of my future success, yes. I've spent the past ten years building this company. It may not seem important to you. I'm not opening on Broadway or anything, but it's important to me."

"I can see that. More important than me."

"Since when was I first on your list?"

Julian ignored that comment as he always did. He

could dodge insults better than anyone. "If you won't help me, I will ask Miss Faith."

"Who? No, absolutely not. You will not involve her in this fantasy of yours."

"I'm doing it for you," Julian said as he got to his feet. "For your own good."

"She's going to think you're a crazy old man, if she doesn't already."

Julian smiled knowingly, his blue eyes twinkling. "You liked her."

"Don't be ridiculous."

"She's not for you."

"Who said I wanted her?"

"You will."

"And why is that?" Alex couldn't help asking, nor could he help remembering the fire in Faith's eyes, the softness of her lips, the curves of her body.

"Simply because you can't have her. You always want what you can't have. Just like the shoes you always coveted. You've built an entire career about getting the right kind of shoes."

Alex didn't want to touch that piece of pop psychology, preferring to stay with Faith. "Who says I can't have her?" If there was one thing Carrigan males did well, it was attract women.

"Oh, Alex," Julian said with a laugh. "You may know more about business than I'll ever know or ever care to know. But you'll never know more about women."

"And you have such a great track record? Five ex-wives, and no one who gives a damn about you now." Julian paled at Alex's harsh words, and Alex once again felt guilty. "I'm sorry. I didn't mean that."

"Of course you did. But you're right, I'm alone, and no one gives a damn about me, because we're cursed." He paused, his eyes darkening. "*And the winds will curse my life until I return to where it began.*"

"I will not allow you to involve that woman," Alex said.

"You can't stop me."

Alex opened his mouth to retort, when it suddenly occurred to him that the air had grown hazy, and his apartment smelled distinctly like smoke. Smoke!

Alex and Julian raced down the hall and into the bathroom. Jessie, with stringy wet hair and a freshly scrubbed face, sat Indian style on the floor in Alex's navy blue bathrobe, smoking a cigarette.

"Hey, I'm taking a shower," she complained. "Don't you knock?"

"I told you, no smoking," Alex yanked the cigarette out of her hand and tossed it into the toilet. "Now, where is the rest of the pack?"

"That was the last one."

"Are you lying?"

"No."

Alex shook his head. Her eyes were still defiant but a bit uncertain; unfortunately he couldn't read her any better than his grandfather. "I won't allow you to smoke, Jessie. Get that through your head."

"You can't stop me," she said, echoing his grandfather's earlier words.

"I can stop you and I will. Do you understand?"

"Yes," she said sullenly.

"Good." Alex slammed out of the bathroom, furious at the chaos in his life.

Jessie looked up at Julian with an uncertain smile. "He's mad."

"He certainly is. Thank heavens. It's been a long time since I heard any real emotion in his voice."

"I don't think that's a good thing," Jessie said, getting to her feet.

"It all depends on your perspective, my dear." Julian stroked his chin. "That's the best damn exit line I've heard the boy give. There might just be hope for him yet."

Chapter 5

Faith's Fancies was quiet on Saturday morning. Instead of the usual frenzied businessmen and women on their way to work in downtown San Francisco, the patrons were more relaxed, less stressed, content to sip their coffee and nibble on a pastry while perusing the newspaper. While Faith needed the hectic pace of the work week to meet her bills, she couldn't help enjoying the leisurely pace of Saturdays.

The only drawback to today's slow influx of customers was that she had too much time to think—about Ben and the Porters. Thankfully, Nancy didn't work on Saturdays, so Faith didn't have to put on a happy face—or her engagement ring. Faith still couldn't believe Ben had asked her to marry him. She also couldn't believe she'd said maybe.

She wasn't in love with Ben. Then again, maybe she'd never be in love again. That depressing thought brought a sigh to her lips and a heaviness to her heart. Still, she supposed she was lucky that another man wanted to marry her, another good, honorable man. Just because Ben didn't make her heart race, or her palms sweat, or send a flutter of butterflies into her stomach, didn't make him a bad choice for a husband.

The bell over the door jangled, and Faith looked up with a cheerful smile, eager to take her mind off her thoughts. A genuine sense of pleasure filled her when she saw the old man's face, his halting gait, sharp blue eyes, and windblown hair. In the morning light she could see a trace of his grandson in Julian Carrigan, and she had a sense that he must have been quite a ladies' man in his day. After all, he'd snagged five wives. She couldn't imagine even wanting to get married that many times.

"Mr. Carrigan, good morning."

Julian walked slowly to the counter, leaning heavily on his cane at times. He had exchanged his suit coat for a long brown overcoat that was just as worn, just as wrinkled. She wondered if Alex had ever considered buying his grandfather a decent coat.

"Good morning to you, Miss Faith. You're looking lovely."

"And you are quite the charmer. What can I get for you?"

"I'd like one of those cinnamon rolls and a latte, please."

"Coming right up."

"I wanted to apologize—for my grandson's boorish behavior yesterday. He doesn't do well in the wind."

So they were back to the wind. Faith didn't want to pursue that line of conversation, not after a sleepless night listening to the windows rattle. She'd kept hearing Julian's deep voice telling her that evil came with the wind. She'd finally pulled the blanket over her head.

"Anyway, Alex had no right to speak to you the way he did," Julian continued. "I'm afraid I irritate him. He wasn't angry with you but with me."

"Please don't give it another thought. I haven't."

"You're very kind."

She was also a liar. Even with the covers pulled up over her head, she'd thought about the Carrigan men, especially Alex. Every time she'd tried to concentrate on Ben's earnest face, Alex's rough features had filled her mind. She was apparently a sucker for a five-o'clock shadow, a great body, and blue, blue eyes.

When Faith handed Julian his latte, his own blue eyes sparkled as if he knew a secret—or he'd read her mind. Faith cleared her throat and smoothed her apron over her hips. "That will be three dollars and twenty-seven cents."

"A bargain at any price." Julian handed her a five, and she made change for him while he found a seat at one of the small tables. Instead of making him come back for his change, she walked around the counter and over to his table. "Here you go."

"Thank you. Do you have a moment, Miss Faith?" Julian looked at the two other people sitting in the bakery. One was reading the newspaper and the other was engaged in a book.

"Sure. What's up?"

Julian urged her to sit down. "I wanted to show you something." He dug into the pocket of his overcoat and pulled out a photo. He stared at it with a yearning smile that filled his eyes with sadness. After a moment, he handed it to her as if he were turning over a cherished treasure.

Faith took the photo with a sense of reluctance. She had the feeling that she was being sucked into quicksand, and no one would be able to pull her out.

"Please look at it."

Come into my parlor, said the spider to the fly.

Faith took a deep breath and looked at the picture. It was a black-and-white photo of a young girl with long hair that hung past her breasts. Her light-colored eyes were wide and filled with beautiful innocence. A small smile touched her lips, a hint of a dimple appeared at her chin, as if she wanted to really smile, but was holding back. She wore a simple light-colored clinging knit T-shirt with a V neck. Around her neck hung an old-fashioned cameo locket.

"She's very beautiful," Faith said, turning her gaze to Julian. "One of your wives?"

"No." He paused, his lips suddenly trembling. "The

one I should have married. The only one.'' He put a shaky hand to his mouth and struggled for composure.

Faith couldn't help reaching out to him. She put a hand on his shoulder and touched him with the reassurance of an old friend. ''Are you all right?''

After a moment, he nodded. ''That picture was taken the day before Suzannah left. She told me she loved me.''

Julian took the photo from Faith's hand and stared at it. ''This was the last time I saw her look so innocent, so untouched by sadness. I hurt her.''

''You were young, foolish.''

''Selfish,'' he corrected. ''I took something that wasn't mine. What happened next was retribution.''

''We all make mistakes, Mr. Carrigan.''

''I must fix this mistake, Miss Faith.'' His eyes filled with determination. He threw back his shoulders and lifted his chin. ''I must do this for my family.''

''I think it's admirable that you want to fix things for your family, but do you think you can?''

''With your help.''

''Oh, no.'' She shook her head. ''I couldn't. I wouldn't know how. You need a private investigator or someone like that.''

''I need a friend.'' He captured her gaze with his lonely blue eyes. ''For a friend may well be reckoned the masterpiece of nature.''

His simple statement touched her heart. ''That's lovely.''

''Ralph Waldo Emerson said the words, but the sentiment is mine.''

Faith knew that she could not resist his plea. The man was all alone, or at least alone with an unfeeling grandson. She knew what it felt like to be lost in a sea of people who really didn't give a damn. ''I'll help you,'' she said.

Julian smiled with relief. ''You won't be sorry.''

''I also may not be much help.'' Faith stood up and walked over to the counter. She pulled a piece of paper off her notepad and grabbed a pencil. ''Why don't we start with Suzannah's full name and what you know about her. Then maybe we can think of a plan of attack."

"Good idea."

Faith set the paper and pencil down on the table, then looked up as the door blew open and another windblown Carrigan walked into the bakery.

"You should have brought me with you," Jessie declared, tucking her wild hair behind her ear. "Alex wanted me to eat oatmeal and a grapefruit."

"That sounds like a healthy breakfast," Faith offered.

Jessie made a face. "It's disgusting. Can I have a chocolate éclair?"

"Do you think your—your father would mind?" Faith still wasn't quite sure of their relationship.

"No." Jessie tipped her head toward Julian. "You can put it on his tab."

Julian laughed. "I'm not running a tab."

"Well, you'll pay, won't you?"

"Why should I?"

"You're my great-grandpa." Jessie suddenly smiled, and the movement transformed her defiant face into a much prettier picture. "And you know how much better this food is than what Alex has at home. Besides, since my mom died, I haven't had anyone to really cook for me, and, well, this place kind of smells like home, you know." Jessie turned to Faith. "You even remind me of my mom. She had red hair just like you do, and the softest eyes and—"

Julian's big booming laugh startled not only Faith and Jessie, but also the other customers, who quickly gathered up their things and left.

"After that speech, you must be my great-grandchild," Julian declared.

Faith looked from Jessie to Julian, slowly catching on that she was being conned. "I don't look like her mother, do I?"

"I have no idea, but I find it doubtful. And I happen to know she's been living on the streets off and on for the past six months, so I doubt this bakery smells much like home."

"Thanks for blowing my cover." Jessie dropped into the chair next to Julian and crossed her arms in front of her chest. "I thought you were cool."

"You overplayed the scene, my dear. The smells of home, yes, but the reference to your mother, too much."

Faith didn't follow much of their conversation, but one part lingered in her head. Jessie had been living on the streets. Why? Where was her mother?

"Jessie? That's your name, right?" Faith asked.

Jessie nodded.

"I'll give you an apple-cinnamon pastry for some straight answers."

"Like what?"

"Where is your mother?"

Jessie licked her lips, her face once again taking on a haunted, waifish look. "She died two weeks ago."

Faith stared at her in dismay. Was she being conned yet again? Or was that real pain in the child's eyes? Of course, it would explain why she'd suddenly come to live with Alex. "I'm sorry."

"Can I have my pastry now?"

"Sure. How about some milk to go with it?"

"Okay."

Before Faith could get the pastry, the door opened once again. She hadn't had this much traffic on a Saturday morning in weeks. Of course, it was yet another Carrigan. She was beginning to wonder how many of them there were. Alex didn't look any happier this morning than he had the night before, although he was dressed more casually in a pair of beige slacks and a rugby shirt that made those damn butterflies flutter in her stomach.

She hastily turned away and busied herself behind the counter.

"So here you both are," Alex said with annoyance. "I made breakfast at home, you know."

"You call that breakfast?" Jessie asked.

"Yes, I do. I made you a very nutritious meal."

"Boring," Jessie proclaimed. "This is much better," she added as Faith set the promised pastry down in front of her.

"I hope this is all right," Faith said.

"I appear to be outvoted."

Faith walked past him to clear some empty dishes from a nearby table, and he caught a whiff of her perfume, which smelled exactly like sugar and spice and everything nice, he thought whimsically. The sleeves of her knit dress were pushed up over her forearms and the dress clung to her breasts beneath the white apron. There was a smudge of flour on her face, but the rest of her skin was pure peaches and cream. He'd never met a woman who reminded him so much of food. But not just any food, comfort foods, warm, lush, spicy, sweet, heavenly . . . Damn, she was attractive, soft and womanly and curved in all the right places.

He cleared his throat and looked over at the display of pastries. Maybe he was just hungry. That had to explain the yawning ache in his gut. He'd gotten up early and run two miles before showering. He just needed something more substantial than a grapefruit to take his mind off—off of Faith.

"Do you want something, Mr. Carrigan?" Faith asked as she returned to her post behind the counter.

Did he want something? He had a feeling her beautiful green eyes would glaze over with shock if he told her exactly what he wanted. He returned his gaze to the pastry trays. "Let's see. I'll have one of those," he said, pointing to pastry filled with cinnamon-covered apples. "And a cup of coffee, black, no cream."

"Are you sure you wouldn't like a little sugar?" she asked with a glint in her eye.

"Why? Do you think I need to sweeten up?"

"Just asking."

"Black is fine."

"I imagine it is."

''What is that supposed to mean?''

''You just seem like a man for which everything is black or white, no messy shades of gray, not even in your coffee.''

''Now, why do I get the feeling I'm being insulted?''

Faith shrugged, her smile a mix of innocence and mischief, but then everything about her seemed to be a contradiction, from her sharp words to her soft body. She had a wickedly sexy body and an angel face. Alex had a feeling he was in big trouble.

''It was just an observation,'' Faith said.

''Do you usually analyze people who buy pastry from you?''

''Only the interesting ones.''

''So I'm interesting now?''

''In a traffic-accident sort of way.''

Alex couldn't help a small grin at that reply. She was certainly direct. ''Thanks, I think.''

Faith set his order on a tray, and he handed her a twenty-dollar bill.

''Are you paying for your daughter as well?'' Faith asked.

Alex sighed. ''Are you going to believe me if I tell you she's not my daughter?''

Faith sent him a steady look. ''Why wouldn't I?''

''Because I'm sure you've heard a different story from them.'' He tipped his head toward Julian and Jessie, who were suddenly concentrating on their food.

''I've heard a lot of different stories from the three of you. I have to admit, you're certainly a colorful family.''

''That's one word for it. I suppose you come from your basic middle-class, white bread, two parents, two kids, and a white picket fence family. No liars, no theater players, no long-lost children appearing on the doorstep—'' Alex stopped abruptly as her face paled and her eyes lost their shine. ''What did I say?''

''Nothing.'' Faith squared her shoulders. ''You're absolutely right about me. In fact, you're a very astute man, perceptive beyond belief. If you'll excuse me, I have to take something out of the oven."

As Faith hurried into the back room, Alex turned to his grandfather. "What did I say?"

Julian shrugged. "You're always so smug."

Alex set his food down on the table and sat in the chair across from his grandfather. He drummed his fingers on the tabletop, wishing Faith would come back. He no longer felt hungry but guilty, as if he'd kicked a small kitten. Damn. What the hell was the matter with him these days? He usually got along great with people.

Alex stood up. "I'll be right back," he said decisively. He ignored the Employees Only sign and walked around the counter and into the kitchen.

Faith wasn't taking anything out of the oven. She was leaning against a large marble table in the middle of the room, her arms hugging her waist, her head bowed. He wished he could see her face, but her hair hid her expression from his eyes.

He hesitated, wondering if it wouldn't be better just to leave her alone. But he couldn't seem to turn around, to walk away, to forget the haunted expression in her eyes. "Faith?"

Her head jerked up. Streaks of tears ran down her cheeks, which she rushed to wipe away.

"What? Do you need something? I'll get it right away. I just burned myself on the stove, and I needed a minute to pull myself together."

Faith moved to get past him, but Alex grabbed her by the hand. The touch of her fingers sent an electrical shock through him. If they'd been standing on carpet instead of a cement floor, he would have discounted the sudden connection as nothing more than a carpet spark. But this was different. This was—too much. He dropped her hand, but the energy still crackled and sizzled in the empty space between them.

"I—"

"I—"

They both started and stopped at the same time. "I'm sorry," Alex said. "I know I said something to upset you, although I'm not sure what."

"It was nothing."

"It must have been something."

Faith's eyes glittered with unshed tears that once again contradicted the smile on her lips. "Just me being overly sensitive. Please forget it. I should get back to work."

"Not before you tell me you accept my apology."

"You don't owe me one, Mr. Carrigan."

"I said something about your family—"

"I don't have a family."

Her words were stark and filled with an emptiness that went beyond anything he'd ever felt.

"I'm sorry again." The words sounded inadequate in the face of such bleakness.

Faith threw her head back and he could see the fight return to her eyes. "Why are you sorry? You didn't leave me."

"But someone did."

"Everyone did."

He didn't know what to say. He barely knew her, yet they'd suddenly become intimate. She'd shared something personal, and he'd never encouraged that type of sharing with a woman, especially one he'd never had in bed.

"Please, don't say you're sorry again. I don't even know why I told you that." Faith shook her head, as if she also felt bewildered by the sudden confidence.

He felt better, safer now, sure she wouldn't reveal anything else that would make him want to hold her, comfort her, do something to take the sadness out of her eyes. He suddenly realized his fingers were clenched into fists. He'd been wanting to touch her since he'd walked into the room. Thank God he'd resisted.

Faith tucked her hair behind her ear. "I think we better check on your grandfather."

Alex hesitated. "I feel like we got off on the wrong

foot. I'm not usually so . . ." He tried to think of the right words to describe his behavior.

"Obnoxious, arrogant, judgmental," Faith offered helpfully.

"We did get off on the wrong foot." He offered her an apologetic smile. "I'm really not that bad. It's just that my grandfather came out of nowhere along with Jessie, and, well, my life is a little stressed right now. I don't usually yell at strangers."

"Just at your family."

"They tend to bring out that side of me."

"Look, Mr. Carrigan, you don't owe me any explanations, and I should really get back to work. Excuse me."

Alex stared after her, noting the proud posture. One moment she'd seemed vulnerable, the next invincible. He wondered which was her usual attitude, not that it mattered. The last thing he needed was another complication in his already complicated life. And a woman, especially this woman, would be a definite complicaton.

Julian sent Alex a quizzical look when he returned to the front of the bakery.

"Everything all right?" he asked.

"Fine," Alex replied, noting that Faith was already busy with a customer. He finished his pastry in a couple of quick bites and wiped the back of his mouth with a napkin. "I have to go to the office."

Julian raised an eyebrow. "On Saturday?"

"That's right, Grandfather. Most athletes work Saturdays and Sundays."

"But you're not an athlete, you're a shoe salesman," Julian pointed out, somehow making it sound as if Alex worked at the local mall for four dollars an hour.

"Elijah James has promised me fifteen minutes before practice today at the Coliseum. With any luck, this will be my chance to sign him to a long-term contract. With his endorsement, Top Flight will be on its way."

"Can I come?" Jessie asked.

"No, I'll be working."

"But Elijah James is cool. Please let me come."

"Sorry, Jessie, but I don't have time for distractions today."

Jessie sat back in her chair, her shoulders slumping with rejection. "You can't leave me alone on our first day together. You're supposed to be taking care of me."

Alex frowned at the wistful note in her voice. "You can stay with Grandfather. I'll only be gone an hour or two."

Julian immediately shook his head. "She can't stay with me. Miss Faith and I are—" He stopped, glancing at Faith, who was handing a bag to a customer.

"Are what?" Alex demanded, looking from Julian's guilty face to Faith's guilty face.

"Nothing," Julian said. "Nothing at all."

"You don't really believe in curses and black magic, do you?" he asked Faith.

"I don't think I said I did." She walked around the counter to collect their dishes from the table.

Alex put a hand on her arm. "Then why are you encouraging him?"

"Is that what I'm doing?" She pulled her arm free.

"Yes, that's what you're doing. He's a sick man. He doesn't need the stress."

"Oh, Alex, leave her out of it," Julian protested.

"I told you not to involve her." Alex glanced over his shoulder at Julian.

"And I told you that I was going to find Suzannah with or without your help." Julian rose to his feet. "I have some things to show you, Miss Faith. I would bring them here, but perhaps it is best if you come up to the apartment. We live just down the street. It's the tall gray building, the Centrillion. We're on the twenty-first floor, number 2107."

"I have a clerk coming in at noon. I could probably come up then," Faith replied.

"Perfect. I will see you later."

As Julian left the bakery, Alex turned his attention back to Faith. She backed up a few steps, until her palms came to rest against the front of the display case.

There were no longer any tears on her cheeks or sadness in her eyes, just a simple steadfast determination that surprised him. Somehow, Julian had drawn not only her sympathy but also her loyalty. But Faith was in for a wild-goose chase, not to mention a long hard fall when she realized she was being conned. Alex could almost feel sorry for her, if she weren't so stubborn and headstrong and determined to make him the bad guy.

"Are you sure you want to do this?" Alex asked.

"I just said I'd help him make a few inquiries."

"You'll never find this woman. It's a waste of time. He hasn't seen her in fifty years. She might be dead."

"It's my time."

"He probably made the whole thing up. My grandfather is the ultimate liar. He's never met a story he didn't want to act out. This is just another one. Can't you see that?"

"What I see is a very lonely old man who wants to make peace. What's wrong with that?"

"Things are never what they appear to be with my grandfather. You don't know him. You can't believe him."

"I don't know you either. Why should I believe you?"

"I give up." He looked down as Jessie slid her arms around his waist. Her attitude had gone from willful defiance to puppy-dog loneliness, and he wasn't sure which was harder to take.

"Please, let me come with you today," Jessie said wistfully. "I won't be any trouble. It will be good for the two of us to get to know each other, don't you think?"

Alex sighed. He couldn't handle yet another argument. It was easier to give in. "Fine. You can come."

Jessie gave him a quick hug that accompanied a squeal of delight. At least he'd made someone happy today.

"But no smoking, no swearing, and no autographs."

"Whatever. I'll wait for you out front."

Jessie headed to the door and Alex moved closer to Faith, deliberating invading her space, standing close enough to see the pale bridge of freckles that dashed across her nose and smell the cinnamon clinging to her skin. She was beautiful, sexy, and he wanted her.

The realization struck him like a lightning bolt. He'd moved in to intimidate her, but now that he was here, all he could think about was touching her, kissing her. His gaze fell to her mouth and her lips slowly parted, letting out a slight breath of air. She was so close, so very close.

"You're in my way, Alex," she whispered.

Alex raised his head and looked into her beautiful green eyes. "And you're in mine."

"All you have to do is take a step back."

"That's all you have to do."

"I can't move."

"You know what I mean." He paused. "I hope you won't regret getting involved with us, Faith."

"I'm not involved with you, only with your grandfather."

Alex slowly smiled. "If you're smart, you won't go near my apartment today."

"As long as you won't be there, I'm sure I'll be safe."

"I wouldn't count on it. Where my grandfather goes, trouble usually follows."

Chapter 6

"I should warn you," Julian said somberly as he held a cardboard box in his hands. "By looking at this pot, by touching it, you may very well bring the curse upon yourself."

Faith swallowed hard, unnerved by the serious glint in his eyes. She didn't believe in magic or curses, not really. Julian was just acting, she reminded herself, spooking her as he probably had done dozens of times in countless plays. But she couldn't help the shiver that ran down her spine as he set the box on the coffee table in Alex's living room and slowly opened it.

For a moment, Faith thought of stopping him, of running from the room, of admitting that this was all a terrible idea. But she couldn't move. She couldn't speak. She could only watch as Julian unwrapped what seemed like layers and layers of tissue paper.

Finally he got down to the last piece. Faith caught her breath as he pulled out a piece of pottery that had once been a stunningly crafted black and white vase.

As Julian had said, the pot had broken in half, but in perfect symmetry. There were no jagged edges, only a clean line of separation. She could almost believe it had been made in two pieces, then put together, so clearly defined was his portion of the pottery. It had been painted black, with jagged white lines running around the neck and the bottom portion of the vase. It was a beautiful piece of art, one she could hardly believe was centuries old.

"Would you like to touch it?" Julian asked.

She met his gaze, saw the perceptive glint in his eye. He knew she didn't believe him.

"You can check to see if it's made in China or some such place," he added.

"I'm sure you wouldn't be showing it to me if it said that."

Julian smiled. "You're right. It's the real thing, Miss Faith. I found it under a precipice in a cave buried deep in a wild canyon protected for centuries from the weather and man . . ." His voice drifted away. "Until, of course, I came along. I thought it was just a pretty piece. But I should have known by the markings on the wall."

"Known what?" Faith whispered, taken back in time by the magic in his voice.

"Nothing, never mind."

"But—"

"Just take it. You don't need to know anything more." His gruff voice allowed her no argument.

After a moment, Faith picked up the pot from the table. It was smooth and cool to the touch. She closed her eyes and slid her fingers up and down the sides. Whispers of voices rang through her head. She couldn't understand what they were saying, but there was joy and anger and sadness and love all mixed together, then fear. It swept through her like a flame catching fire.

They were chasing her, the voices grew into a thundering roar, and the wind, the wind sent shivers down her spine. The vase suddenly became warm in her hands—or was it simply that by holding it, she'd made it warm? In a rush of confusion, Faith opened her eyes and saw Julian staring at her in horror.

"It got you. Oh, my God, it got you."

"What do you mean?"

"I saw it on your face. You heard them."

Faith set the pottery back in the box, suddenly desperate to get it out of her hands. "I didn't hear anything. Nothing."

"I didn't think it would hurt you," Julian muttered. "I touched it and I didn't hear anything."

"Neither did I." Faith refused to remember the feeling of stark terror that had come over her.

"What have I done? What have I done?" Julian got to his feet and paced around the room.

"Mr. Carrigan. Please, you're making me nervous."

Julian stopped abruptly. "Suzannah heard them, too, the ghosts of the past. That's why she dropped the pot. That's why she ran away. I didn't tell you . . ."

"Tell me what?"

"In the picture you couldn't see . . ."

"See what?" Faith demanded in frustration as he refused to complete a sentence.

Julian stared at her for a long, tense minute. "Suzannah had red hair and green eyes—like you."

"Lots of people have red hair and green eyes. It doesn't mean anything."

"There was a story." He shook his head. "No, I can't remember how it went."

He was lying. This time she could see clearly that he was not telling the truth. Whatever the story was, he remembered it clearly. Faith opened her mouth to question him further, then wondered if she really wanted to hear it. Her stomach was twisting with uneasiness and she had a sudden pounding headache behind her eyes.

"I have to go," she said, getting to her feet.

"Suzannah said the same thing," Julian replied. "She was suddenly so afraid. She thought they would . . ."

The silence drew out. Faith couldn't stand it for another second.

"They would what?"

"They would kill her."

"Who?"

"The voices. The gods. The spirits. I don't know. She wouldn't tell me what they said."

"But they didn't kill her," Faith said, trying to be logical.

Julian stared at her for a long moment, and the truth came to her with blinding clarity.

"That's what you want to find out, isn't it? Why did you wait fifty years?"

"I didn't. I tried before, but I couldn't find her. She simply vanished."

"Then why do you think you can find her now?"

"Because now I have you. I knew it the first moment I saw you."

Oh, God! He was crazy and scaring the hell out of her. Faith tried to tell herself he was a harmless old man, but there was a sharpness to his expression, a clarity to his gaze, that told her he knew exactly what she was thinking.

"I don't want to hurt you, Miss Faith. I just want your help."

"I can't help you." She put up a hand to stop him from interrupting. "I can't. This is too weird."

"I'm afraid it's too late for you to say no."

"Of course I can say no."

Julian shook his head. "I would be happy to let you go, but they won't. That's what the old Indian said."

"I don't care what some old Indian said." Faith practically ran to the door. "I'm leaving, and I'm not coming back."

The pictures on the wall shook as Faith slammed the door. Julian sank down on the sofa and pulled out his photograph of Suzannah. "I've done it again," he whispered. "Forgive me."

But there were no words of forgiveness, only silence. He set down the photo and picked up the vase. "Speak to me." But again, he heard only silence. "Why won't you talk to me?" He asked the question, but deep down he knew the answer. The old man had told him, he just hadn't wanted to believe.

Melanie had always told Jessie she could be anybody. All she had to do was close her eyes and believe. So Jessie closed her eyes and propped her feet up on the bench in front of her. Right now she wanted to be a superstar basketball player, the adored celebrity of millions of fans.

As her fantasy grew, she could hear the lights being switched on and off as the Oakland Coliseum was prepared for the evening game, the static sounds of the microphone being tested for loudness, the distant voices of Alex and his partner, and Elijah James and his agent, and finally the slow, soothing bounce of a basketball against the hardwood floor.

Oh, what a sweet life—to be rich and famous and tall. Jessie smiled to herself and blew a huge bubble out of her mouth, popping it with a reassuring bang. She could imagine herself riding in limousines, signing autographs, wearing long silvery dresses that glittered in the spotlight. And off to the side would be her father, smiling proudly, beaming with delight, saying, "That's my daughter."

Her smile faded and tears crowded her closed eyes. She wouldn't let them out. She wouldn't. So she sniffed instead and tried to get the fantasy back, but it wouldn't come. When she opened her eyes, she was just a little kid sitting in the grandstands, waiting for a man who couldn't stand her to finish his business.

Alex was a nice-looking man, tall, strong, great hair, beautiful eyes. Melanie had always picked studs to sleep with. Too bad none of 'em ever wanted to hang around, Jessie thought, hardening her heart against the charming smile that swept across Alex's face as he tried to talk Elijah into something. Alex was just another one who'd left.

Course, Melanie had never really wanted any guys to stay. "We've got places to go, sweet pea," Melanie used to say when they'd pack up and head out for somewhere new. "You and me—we're going to be rich someday and living the good life. You'll see. All you have to do is believe." And so they'd gone to New York so Melanie could play on Broadway, only she'd ended up waiting tables in a backstreet deli. Then they'd gone to Nashville, so Melanie could break into the country music scene, only she'd ended up dancing in a cage, showing off her boobs.

Jessie wasn't supposed to see her mom dancing that way. She'd never been supposed to see anything her mom did. But she had, because it got lonely waiting, and Melanie always needed help. And when her mom needed help, she always said, "I love you, sweet pea," and Jessie liked hearing her say that.

Course, Melanie wouldn't be saying it anymore. She'd known she was gonna die for a lot longer than she'd told that lawyer guy. They'd looked for Alex all over Sacramento. She still remembered Melanie's words—that last night. "The lawyer will find Alex for you, Jessie. It's time you met your dad."

And Melanie had died—gone and left her with some guy she'd screwed a hundred years ago. Only Alex didn't think he was her dad. And shit, he was probably right.

Jessie sighed. She'd tried so hard to believe, but the last few months, living in the back of a car or some seedy motel, hadn't given her much to believe in. And lately she'd begun to think that believing was worse than not. It hurt—just like finding nothing in her stocking when Melanie had assured her that Santa Claus would find the red sock hung out on the car's antenna. Course, there wasn't no Santa. And there wasn't no dad. Alex didn't want her. There was no sense in believing that he did.

The only person Alex wanted was Elijah James. He'd been talking to him for almost twenty minutes, trying to convince him to wear some stupid shoes. As far as Alex was concerned, she was invisible. Melanie had always told her that besides believing, sometimes you have to go get what you want, instead of waiting for it to come to you. Jessie tipped her head to one side. There must be something she could do to get Alex's attention. But what? She rested her chin on the back of her hand and watched as Alex picked up a basketball and tossed it at Elijah.

"I'll shoot you for the contract, Elijah. Whoever misses, loses." Alex heard his desperate challenge echo through the cavernous arena, bouncing off the sponsor signs, the slick hardwood basketball floor, the press box, and the scoreboard descending from the ceiling like a spaceship about to land.

In a few hours the arena would be packed with fans come to watch the Warriors' new twenty-year-old, seven-foot rebounding sensation, Elijah James. But right now it was just the two of them. Actually, it was the four of them. Elijah's agent, Matthew Denning, and Alex's more conservative business partner, Charlie Hayes, were hovering on the sidelines, looking as shocked as Elijah at Alex's suggestion.

He knew it sounded crazy, but he'd run out of words to convince Elijah, and Alex had learned long ago that he'd never get anything unless he fought for it.

"You want to shoot me?" Elijah asked in a disbelieving southern drawl, as he crossed his muscled arms in front of his massive chest. "You sell shoes, man."

"What's the matter, don't think you can beat me?"

Elijah laughed. "I could beat you with one hand tied behind my back."

"That won't be necessary. I'll let you use two."

"Uh, Alex. You want to think about this?" Charlie asked, sweat beading along his forehead. "Elijah is a professional athlete."

Alex shrugged, refusing to back down. If Top Flight was going to compete with the big boys at Nike, they needed the big athletes to endorse their shoes. Elijah had already admitted he liked their shoe, loved it, in fact. They'd even come to terms on the money and the cut on future profits. Elijah just wasn't sure he wanted to sign with an upstart company like Top Flight over an established league sponsor.

"It's a simple bet," Alex reiterated, watching Elijah battle with his pride. Having spent the last ten years studying athletes and creating shoes that would make them better and faster, he knew the way they thought, and he knew which buttons to push.

Elijah could no more resist taking a dare than Alex could resist making one. In some ways they were two of a kind; he'd just chosen to play his game in a different venue.

"I'll need to confer with my client," Matthew said, drawing Elijah away from them.

Alex turned to Charlie. "We've got him."

"You're crazy."

"We're at an impasse. Elijah wants to sign with us, but he's afraid we're not good enough. We have to prove to him that we are."

"By shooting free throws?"

"It's the only language he understands. Elijah wants to go with a company he respects. All we have to do is get him to respect us, by showing him that we're confident, we're bold, we take risks."

"I don't take risks. You take risks, usually against my advice."

"True." Alex took a practice jump, feeling the bounce from his Top Flight Airborne Shoes. "But I can do anything in these babies." He felt a renewed sense of energy and confidence. Shoes made the man. And today he was the man.

"So what's the deal?" Elijah asked, his eyes skeptical as he peered down at Alex like some powerful god.

"I win, you sign. You win, I pay you ten grand just for your trouble."

"Oh, shit," Charlie said.

"Relax, I know what I'm doing," Alex said.

"Last time you said that, you lost ten grand in the stock market."

"That was different. I didn't know anything about software, but I do know my hoops." Despite his bravado, Alex knew the bet was risky. But dammit all, he had struggled like hell the last ten years to build a company that would attract the top athletes. He couldn't let Elijah slip through his fingers, not when he was so close to getting the success he'd dreamed about.

"Fifteen grand," Matthew Denning said, stepping forward, his eyes lighting up at the prospect of easy money. "If you're that confident."

"Eleven," Alex countered.

"Twelve."

"Deal." Alex turned to Elijah. "I'll even go first."

"I think I'm going to be sick," Charlie murmured, taking a seat in the first row. "Do you know how much twelve thousand dollars is going to set us back?"

"I'm not going to lose." Alex grabbed a ball and walked onto the court with Elijah. That was when he realized just how short he was compared to the towering giant. Okay, six foot wasn't particularly short, but next to Elijah, he felt like a midget.

Height had nothing to do with free-throw accuracy, Alex reminded himself. After having faced the doubts of a dozen basketball coaches, he had learned how to prove himself with at least one shot, the free throw. He'd done it by practicing about three thousand times a day, dunking balls, clothes, toys, sticks, and anything else he could get his hands on through every receptacle he could find, from real hoops to wastepaper baskets and even through the branches of the trees in his backyard.

Of course, he'd had plenty of time to practice, growing up alone all those years. He shook off the negative thought and concentrated instead on the line underneath his feet and the basket in front of him. It suddenly seemed a million miles away.

Alex bounced the basketball, one, two, three times, taking a deep calming breath with each one. He could do this. He could. He just had to concentrate. No fear, he told himself.

"You gonna shoot or what?" Elijah demanded.

Alex replied by sending the ball through the basket with a clean swish. He felt a surge of relief and his confidence returned. He could do this.

Elijah grabbed the ball and walked to the line. He bounced twice and sank the ball through the basket. Alex grabbed the rebound and headed back to the line.

He bounced the ball three times again and shot. Good.

Back to Elijah. Another basket.

Alex stepped up again. As he raised his arms, he heard a moan. Distracted, he turned his head. Jessie was standing on the sidelines, holding her stomach.

"I feel sick, Daddy," she said pitifully.

Alex hesitated.

"Hey, if you gotta take care of the kid . . ." Elijah said with a shrug.

"Hang on a second, Jessie. Just sit down, okay?"

Holding her stomach, Jessie stumbled into one of the seats in the front row. Alex turned back toward the basket. Concentrate, he told himself. It's just you and the basket. He shot the ball. It went in. Alex let out a sigh of relief.

"I think I'm going to throw up," Jessie announced.

"Charlie, take care of her."

"Take care of her? Who is she?" Charlie asked in bewilderment.

"She's—she's a kid I'm watching for a few days."

"What do you want me to do? I don't have any kids."

"Rub her back or something."

"I'm not a cat," Jessie protested, sending them both a dark look.

"I'll be done in a few minutes, Jess, please."

Elijah bounced the ball. "Are we shooting hoops or what?"

"We're shooting hoops. And you're up."

Elijah sunk the basket. Alex stepped up and shot before Jessie could say another word. Back to Elijah, then Alex.

Jessie screamed. "It hurts, Daddy."

Charlie tried to pat Jessie's back, but she pushed his hand away and ran out to the court, throwing her arms around Alex's waist. She sobbed into his stomach, rough, garbled words that Alex couldn't understand.

"All right, Jess, I'm done," Alex said in resignation.

He watched his dreams walk away with Elijah. He'd been so close, so very, very close to having exactly what he'd always wanted. And he'd lost it. Jessie's arms tightened around his waist and she looked up at him with tears in her eyes.

"I'm sorry, Daddy."

Daddy. He felt a rush of unexpected tenderness at the word. Even though a part of him wanted to correct her, he couldn't do it. She looked so little and lost. "It's okay, Jess. You want to go to the bathroom?"

Jessie nodded.

Alex looked over at Charlie. "Sorry, partner."

"No problem. We only lost Elijah and twelve grand. Not bad for a Saturday morning's work."

"You're always an optimist. That's what I like about you." Alex punched him on the arm as he led Jessie toward the bathrooms.

"And by the way, since when do you have a daughter?" Charlie asked after him.

Alex paused. "Since yesterday."

"That was fast."

"Tell me about it. Look, can you hang around for a while? See if you can set up another meeting with Elijah."

Charlie sent him a doubtful look. "I'll try, but I think you gave it your best shot. Too bad the kid got sick."

"Yeah, too bad." Alex glanced down at Jessie, who no longer seemed to be in pain. "Feeling better?" he asked suspiciously.

"I burped," she said with an angelic smile. "I guess it was just a bubble."

Alex looked over at Charlie. "Just a bubble. Who knew?"

"Can we go home now, Daddy?" Jessie asked, tugging on his arm.

Alex had a feeling if he said no, the mysterious stomachache would reappear. "You messed that up on purpose, didn't you, Jess?"

Her eyes widened and she shook her head. "I didn't mean to mess anything up. I just felt sick and then I got scared. I'm only twelve, you know."

"Give her a break, Alex, she's just a kid," Charlie said. "So where's her mother?"

"Dead."

Charlie raised an eyebrow. "And you're the long-lost father?"

"No, I'm the long-lost stand-in."

"What does that mean?"

"It means I need a private investigator."

"Pete Sloan is doing PI work now," Charlie replied, naming a mutual friend who had spent several years in the San Francisco Police Department. "He might be able to help you."

"Good idea. I'll call him when I get home."

"Alex . . ." Charlie stopped him one more time. "We've got a lot to do in the next few months with the upcoming trade show and the quarterly sales meeting. Not to mention we need a new warehouse location and possibly an entire new ad campaign. If you can't find her real father, maybe you better find a baby-sitter or . . ."

"Or what?"

"A wife."

Jessie tugged on his arm. "Daddy, I feel sick again."

Alex smiled grimly. "So do I."

Chapter 7

Fifteen ten-year-old girls filled the lobby of the art gallery on Geary Street. After thirty minutes of being lectured to by Ben and his assistant, Isabelle Scalini, they were ready for the second half of their tour, a chance to actually paint. Ben enjoyed the school groups. He'd always felt comfortable with kids. They were so accepting of themselves, open to new ideas, to exploring life rather than just accepting it. Sometimes he wished he could go back to those trouble-free days.

He clapped his hands to get their attention, and after a moment of giggles and chatter, they quieted down.

"Is everyone ready to paint?" he asked.

"I am. I am," they cried, raising their hands, their faces filled with enthusiasm.

"Good. First thing we do is ask you to put on the smocks that you'll find on the table over there. Then we're going to assign each of you to an easel. We're working with watercolors today and you'll have your choice between painting from our props"—he waved his hand toward a bowl of fruit and also a table laid out with a lady's fan, a pair of opera glasses, and a vase with a long-stem red rose—"or you can paint whatever you want. Use your imagination. Just try to remember some of the art that you've seen. Use contrasting colors. Don't be afraid to be bold. When you're done, we have juice and cookies."

He smiled at the accompanying cheer. "So get your smocks and have fun. We'll break in about thirty minutes."

Ben stepped aside as the two adult leaders helped the girls on with their smocks. After he gave a few more instructions, the girls got under way, and he returned to the front of the gallery to help Isabelle lock up for the evening.

"Mrs. Constantine called and said she wants to buy this seascape," Isabelle said as she took one of the paintings off the wall and set it on the counter. "She didn't even flinch at the price. And I actually raised it five hundred dollars because she seemed so eager."

Ben smiled. Isabelle knew far more about making the gallery profitable than he did. In fact, opening the gallery to children's groups had been her idea and had met with resounding success. Unfortunately, she knew far less about the actual art on display. So while she increased sales, he concentrated on developing artists to display. They made a good team, so good, the owner of the gallery had moved to Paris and left them with free rein over the day-to-day operations.

"How are the girls doing?" Isabelle asked. "They're a lively bunch today."

"No kidding."

Her dark eyes twinkled with amusement. "I saw a couple of them giving you the look. One even asked if you were married."

Ben's muscles tightened involuntarily. Isabelle thought she was joking. Little did she know . . . He glanced over his shoulder toward the back room where the girls were involved with their paintings. "I meant to tell you," he began.

"Tell me what?"

"I asked Faith to marry me."

Isabelle's jaw dropped. "You did? Why?"

"Aren't you going to say congratulations?" He picked up the invoice Isabelle had set on the counter and added it into the computer, so he wouldn't have to look at her face.

"Congratulations," Isabelle said slowly.

"Thank you." He hoped that would be it.

"But, Ben, why?"

Finally he looked at her, seeing the confusion in her eyes. "Faith is a wonderful woman."

"You don't love her."

There it was—simple, direct, honest. What else could he have expected from Isabelle? She always said exactly what she thought.

"I like her."

"You like her. So what? I like my butcher, Mr. Hurlihy, but I wouldn't marry him."

"Because he's got a gut the size of the Transamerica Building."

Isabelle made a face. "You know what I mean. Liking someone doesn't make them a viable life partner. Does Faith love you? I know she was crazy for Gary, but she's always treated you like a friend, a brother."

"I kissed her the other day. It was nice." Ben drummed his fingers on the counter, thinking about Faith's response. It had been a pleasant surprise, assuring him that he could do this.

"Well, that's certainly the way most men talk about their future brides."

"Look, she wants kids, so do I. Maybe it's not the greatest love affair in the world, but we're well suited. Faith is smart and kind and beautiful. I could do a lot worse."

"I've got nothing against Faith. You know that. I think she's great. But, Ben—she's not for you."

"I'm getting older. It's time to move on, to get with the program."

"You have plenty of time to move on."

"Do I? Gary thought he had lots of time, but he's

dead.'' Ben felt a sharp spike of pain at the memory of his brother. He wished he could talk to Gary. Gary would have understood that Porter men needed to marry and have children and raise families with pride and dignity. Of course, if Gary were still alive, Ben would hardly be contemplating marriage with Faith.

''Gary caught a bad break, but that's no reason to rush into marriage with Faith,'' Isabelle replied. ''Does she even want to marry you?''

''She's thinking about it.''

''Have you told—''

''No.'' Ben cut her off with a shake of his head.

Isabelle's eyes filled with understanding. ''It won't be easy. You can't be happy being someone you're not.''

''I can't be happy being who I am,'' Ben replied, knowing it was the truest statement he'd spoken all day. ''My family loves Faith. This is the right thing to do.''

Isabelle didn't say anything for a long moment. The only sounds came from the gallery where the girls were expressing their individuality—something Ben had never been able to do.

''Maybe Faith will say no,'' Isabelle said finally. ''I'm sorry, but I almost hope she does. One of you has to think rationally about this.''

''There's nothing rational about love.''

Isabelle sent him a pointed look. ''We're not talking about love.''

''Well, Faith won't say no.'' Despite the lack of a passionate love affair between them, Ben knew what Faith wanted more than anything—a family. And that was one thing he could give her. It would be enough—for both of them.

Ben had sent her flowers, not red roses, but lilacs in a small pot. He knew her so well, Faith thought, as she put the plant on her kitchen sill. He knew all her favorites, flowers, food, movies, books. But he didn't know her—not really.

Ben knew she collected antiques but not why—that by filling her apartment with old, old things, she would find some connection to her past. Faith glanced over at the kitchen counter, at the old-fashioned bread box that must have once been a home for fresh bread sweated over by some mother who baked for her family every morning. And then there was the waffle iron, hopelessly outdated and awkward, but a favorite because it had come in a box with a picture of a family sitting around a Formica-topped table eating waffles with blueberries on top. No—Ben didn't know about the waffle iron or the bread box.

Faith left the kitchen and wandered into her small living room. Her apartment was on the third floor of an old building in Noe Valley, the southern section of San Francisco. In the late afternoon the sunlight streamed through her windows and cast shadows on the photographs on the mantel.

Ben knew she liked picture frames, but he didn't know why—that by filling her house with framed pictures of people, she felt a part of something. He didn't know that she barely knew the people in the photographs, that she could only imagine what their lives were like. No—Ben didn't really know about the picture frames.

Faith sat down on the couch and rested her head against the back of it. She smiled to herself at the colorful array of pillows piled on each end of the couch and the blanket draped over the back.

Ben knew she liked pillows and blankets and warm woolen coats and handmade quilts, but he didn't know why—that they kept her warm, that they took away the cold emptiness of her surroundings, that they made her feel like she was enveloped in someone's warm embrace. No—Ben didn't really know about the pillows.

But if she married him, if she became Mrs. Benjamin Porter, she could put pictures of Ben and their children in the frames. Nancy would make a quilt for their first baby. Kim would bring in books and toys and more things to make her apartment look like a home. And Faith would have someone to share waffles and homemade bread.

It could be perfect. Everything she wanted. And Ben.

A good man. A caring man. A kind man.

She would say yes, Faith decided impulsively. Say yes, and forget everything else.

The relief of making a decision overwhelmed her, and Faith closed her eyes, suddenly weary. It had been a long day, up early at the bakery, then visiting with Julian . . . Her mind drifted to the broken pot, and her fingers began to tingle. She took a deep breath and smelled smoke, the heavy scent of pine and something else, something darker. Her thoughts began to wander. She tried to stop them. She didn't want to remember—didn't want to hear those voices, the thundering roar of the wind.

Suddenly images began to float through her head.

Faith could see the dancing flames of a fire, hear the pounding of drums and the muttered, then passionate chanting of dozens of unseen voices. She wanted to move closer but couldn't, suddenly drawn to the shadows behind her.

Out of the darkness he came, a strong, handsome warrior, wearing nothing but a strip of cloth that hung loosely around his hips. His muscles were dark and sleek and powerful. His face was proud, his jaw strong, his light-colored eyes intense. He held out his hand to her.

She felt torn between him and the people by the fire, between the darkness and the light, between what was right and what was wrong. He reached out his hand, and a desire so overwhelmingly powerful convinced her to take it. His touch burned her fingers. The wind began to roar. She'd done something wrong, something terribly wrong. But she didn't understand. There were suddenly voices and faces and fear.

"No," she screamed, feeling the angry spirits surround her.

They wouldn't listen. They were coming for her. And she suddenly knew why. Betrayal.

Faith blinked her eyes open and sat up, her heart pounding, her hands sweaty, her chest heaving with the nightmarish daydream. She reached for the pillows on the couch and pulled them to her. Even though the evening was warm, she grabbed a blanket and wrapped it around her. She was cold. She was scared. And she was alone.

What was happening to her? She'd always had an imagination. In fact, it had kept her going through the long, lonely nights of her childhood. But now her mind was traveling a different path, and she seemed to have no will to stop it. Since she'd touched the pottery, she'd felt electricity running through her, as if she were a conduit to some secret past.

But she didn't want to know their secrets. Didn't want to feel their pain. Someone had been hurt. A man and a woman. Julian and Suzannah? Somehow she didn't think so. The pain seemed deeper, darker, older.

The doorbell rang, and she started in alarm, suddenly filled with the panicked thought that the spirits had come for her. Silly. There were no spirits, no ghosts. She took a deep breath and walked over to the door. "Who is it?" she asked.

"Ben."

She opened the door with relief, pleased to see his warm brown eyes, his friendly face. "Oh, Ben." She hugged him, and he squeezed her back.

"Does this mean your answer is yes?"

"May I come in?" Alex asked, standing at the doorway to his grandfather's bedroom.

"Yes." Julian waved him into the room, without looking up, his eyes focused on the letter in his hand.

Alex waited for a moment, taking the time to look around his guest room. He had furnished it sparsely with a double bed covered by a forest green comforter that matched the green rug and the green curtains at the window. There was an oak chest of drawers in one corner and a small writing desk against the wall. A window seat brightened by the late afternoon light looked so inviting he walked over and sat down.

He rarely came into this room. And he rarely had guests. He'd always preferred his privacy. Sometimes he wondered why he'd even bought this luxury condo with its three bedrooms and large living room/dining room. It wasn't as if he needed the space. He'd just needed the look of being successful.

His gaze turned to his grandfather, whose white hair was in complete disarray. A pair of reading glasses slid halfway down his nose and his hand shook slightly as he slowly lowered the letter to the bed.

"What's all that?" Alex asked, pointing to the packet of letters.

"My letters from Suzannah."

Alex raised an eyebrow. He'd never known there were letters. Never once while telling the story of the curse had Julian shared that piece of information. "She wrote to you?"

"I thought I'd told you about the letters."

"No, you didn't." Alex cleared his throat. "Look, Grandfather, we need to talk." And the last thing he wanted to talk about was the infamous Suzannah.

Julian removed his glasses. He rubbed his eyes, then returned the glasses to his face. "I suppose we do, but first, I want you to listen." Julian picked up the letter, took a deep breath, and began to read.

" 'We must meet in Arizona this summer, Julian. I have been learning about the historic sites of the ancient Anasazi, and I am eager to see where they really lived. I know there must be a wonderful world out there, and I long to see it.

" 'Did I tell you that my great-grandmother was born in Arizona? Before she died she told me so much about the desert, the deep canyons, the blue sky, the vast silence, the mystical sense of a past filled with people who danced with the spirits.

" 'I think I must be like the spirits, Julian. No one

understands me here. Since my parents died, I am all alone. My great-aunt is so stern. She goes to church every day to pray for my soul and makes me pray for forgiveness every night before I go to bed. She doesn't like my clothes. She doesn't like the way I talk, and she hates it when I dance.

" 'Perhaps I am truly wicked, Julian, for I can't stop dreaming about you. I long for you in ways that I know must be wrong. I have your picture hidden beneath my pillow and your letters are locked in a box in my closet. I know if my aunt found them, she would make me stop writing you. But I can't do that. You mean so much to me.

" 'Please say you will meet me this summer. I must see you in the flesh. I must know if our love is as real as it feels to me.' "

Julian's voice trembled on the last word and he once again removed his glasses and wiped his eyes. "How wrong she was to invite me."

Alex didn't know what to say or do. He felt uncomfortable with such a display of emotion, and deep down, a bit jealous that his grandfather had experienced a love that still moved him. Then he reminded himself that his grandfather had gone on to find equal happiness with five other women. So much for everlasting love. It didn't exist. And this search for Suzannah was born of sentiment and a yearning to recapture a youth forever lost.

"You don't understand." Julian watched Alex with a perceptive gaze that was now free of tears. "How could I expect you to—with the curse of the Carrigans marked on your brow?"

"Last time I looked, my forehead was free of any marks, Grandfather."

"You're so literal, Alex. Do you never look beyond the surface?"

"What's the point? If people don't say what they mean, why should I dig deeper? And frankly, this sudden yearning for a lost love seems rather ridiculous. You had plenty of time to find this woman—if you really wanted to.''

Julian's gaze turned troubled. ''You're right. I suppose a part of me was afraid of finding her again. I wanted to know what happened to her, and at the same time I didn't. I was terrified that my actions had brought the curse into her life. It was easier not to know. It was easier to live with the ignorance than with the truth.''

''She probably married someone else and lived happily ever after.'' Alex refused to let his grandfather's passionate words touch him again. ''And if you were afraid to find her before, why now—when it's far too late to change what happened? Why add more stress to your life when you should be relaxing, taking things easy, planning for a comfortable future? We should be looking for condos.''

''Because you want me out of your way,'' Julian said flatly, his voice no longer filled with emotion.

Alex felt more comfortable with this response. This was the grandfather he knew, the one who was too busy to let a little boy mess around with his costumes or his paints, the one who got married every other year and spent more time with other people's families than with his own. This was the man who had never remembered Alex's birthday but couldn't seem to forget a woman he'd known for a few short months more than fifty years ago.

''I don't blame you really,'' Julian said. ''I suppose it's what I deserve. Your grandmother always said we reap what we sow.''

His grandmother, Bess. Alex hadn't thought of her in years. She'd been Julian's first wife, and they'd divorced when Alex's father, Brett, was five years old. Apparently Bess had found Julian in the arms of another woman. Like father, like son, Alex thought, remembering his own father's infidelities. The only difference in the two generations was that Bess had kept her son with him. His own mother had chosen to leave him with a father who cared more about getting screwed than raising a son.

Alex shook his head, disgusted with the turn of his thoughts. He'd wasted too much time already feeling sorry for himself. He didn't do that anymore. There was no point. He had a good life now, a business that gave him a great sense of accomplishment. He didn't need a family or a wife to mess up the happiness he had found in his work.

"Neither one of us would be happy living together," Alex said. "You know that as well as I do. I suggest that tomorrow we spend some time looking for a suitable place for you to live. We can still see each other, but you'll have your space, and I'll have mine. As for this quest of yours—I don't think it's healthy for you."

Julian arched one eyebrow. "And you're so concerned? Now who's acting?"

"I'm not acting. I don't want to see you get your hopes up and find out this woman died years ago or that she can't be found, or that she married someone else, had ten children, and lived a happy life. Either one of those scenarios is going to hurt you." Despite his resentment toward his grandfather, Alex didn't want to see the old man get hurt, because one thing had become apparent in the last twenty-four hours: Julian was old. He was tired and his body was winding down. Maybe it was an act, but Alex didn't think he was that good.

"There is one other scenario," Julian said. "We find Suzannah alone and still suffering from the consequences of my thievery. She still has the piece of pottery. We glue it back together, return it to the holy grounds, and restore peace to our families."

"Oh, for God's sake . . . What are the chances, Grandfather? Where would you even start?"

"I would start with Miss Faith."

Faith. Alex's stomach turned over. The name immediately drummed up the image of red hair sparked with gold, flashing green eyes, soft, full lips, a hint of a smile, a speck of a tear. Damn. Why couldn't he forget the details?

''Faith will help me,'' Julian said. ''She won't be allowed to do otherwise.''

''Allowed? What are you talking about?''

Julian seemed to hesitate, his eyes darting from a brown box on the desk to the letters on the bed. Finally he looked at Alex. ''She agreed to help, that's all.''

''That's not what you said.''

''Let it alone, Alex. None of this need concern you. I'm sure you'll be busy selling your shoes next week. No doubt we'll rarely see you.''

Everything his grandfather said was true. So why didn't he let it alone? What did he care if his grandfather spent his days on a dusty search through old phone books? He wasn't going to find Suzannah. And in time Faith would come to realize that and go away.

''Fine.'' Alex stood up. ''Just do it during the day when I'm not here, okay? By the way, I met with a private investigator this afternoon.''

''A private investigator?'' Julian's eyes lit up. ''To help me find Suzannah?''

''No. To help me find Jessie's real father.''

Julian looked both disappointed and irritated. ''I see. And what will finding this man accomplish, Alex? Perhaps he's married with three other children and doesn't want another. Or what if you find him, and he's a terrible person, a drunk? Will either of those scenarios make you happy?''

Alex could hardly admit that those two possibilities scared the hell out of him. ''There is another scenario. He could be a great guy desperate to have a relationship with his long-lost daughter.''

''So you do have an imagination on occasion. That's encouraging.''

''Why do I try to talk to you?''

''Because you can't stand it when someone doesn't agree with you. We're more alike than you think.''

''That is the scariest thing you've said all day.'' Alex walked to the door.

"Alex?"

Alex paused in the doorway. "What?"

"I would have wanted her, too."

"Who? Faith?" Alex's eyes narrowed. "I don't want her. If there were a photograph in the dictionary next to the word *homebody,* it would be of Faith."

"That's what you need, Alex, someone to make you a home."

Alex shook his head. "I don't need anyone, and I certainly don't need a woman named Faith."

"Faith?" Ben asked, eagerness lighting up his eyes as she brought him a bottle of Beck's beer. "You still haven't answered my question. Have you decided to say yes?"

Faith realized her enthusiastic greeting a few minutes earlier had probably given Ben the wrong impression, but she'd been so glad to see him, to be distracted from . . . No, she wouldn't go down that road. She needed to concentrate on the here and now, not on some crazy daydream about people who had lived centuries ago.

"Here's your beer." She handed him the bottle. "I hope it's cold enough. I picked it up at the store earlier, but I forgot to put it in the refrigerator until a while ago."

"My beer is fine, and you're stalling."

She sat down on the couch and waited for him to do the same. "I'm still not sure, Ben. We're friends, good friends, maybe best friends. But we've never—you know."

Ben looked down at his beer bottle, then back at her. "In the beginning it seemed too soon."

"It has been two years, Ben. Last weekend was the first time you kissed me."

"And you kissed me back."

This time she looked away. How could she explain that he'd reminded her of Gary? It would sound insulting and hurtful, and the last thing she wanted to do was hurt Ben. He'd stood by her since the day they'd told her Gary was dead. He'd dragged her out of her apartment and out of her depression. He'd helped her to go on, to go back to work, to make the bakery that she and Gary had dreamed about a success.

"Faith. I think we'd be good together. I know I'm not the love of your life. I wouldn't try to take Gary's place in your heart if that's what you're worried about."

"It's not that."

"Then what?"

How could she explain? It wasn't just Gary she missed, it was the feeling of excitement, anticipation, the butterflies in her stomach, the racing pulse at the end of a kiss, the heat, the passion, the sense of falling, loving, being. Could she have that with Ben?

She studied his pleasantly handsome face. It wasn't as if he weren't attractive, as if other women hadn't wanted to go out with him. He'd always had plenty of dates, just no one serious that she could remember. And she liked so much about him. She wanted to be attracted to him. She wanted to love him.

"Kiss me," she said suddenly.

Ben started. "What?"

"Kiss me." Before he could move, she leaned forward and pressed her lips against his.

He quickly responded, sliding his hands around her back. Faith closed her eyes and enjoyed the sensation of being in a man's arms, feeling a man's mouth on hers, inhaling the scent of musk aftershave. It was the smell that did it, that brought back all the memories. It was the same aftershave Gary had used. For a moment, she remembered the way he'd kissed her, and she instinctively reached for the same feeling, taking the initiative with Ben, pushing him to deepen the kiss, hoping, praying, wanting to feel what she'd felt before.

And she heard bells—maybe there was magic after all. But then Ben broke the kiss and the ringing continued. It was the telephone. She looked at it in dismay, irritated at the intrusion when she was trying so hard to get lost in Ben's arms.

"Do you want to get that?" Ben asked.

No, she wanted to go back to the kiss, to the elusive feeling for which her heart still hungered. When she didn't move, Ben picked up the phone, which was on the table next to him.

"Hello," he said. He looked over at Faith. "Yes, she's here. Hold on." He held out the receiver to her. "For you. It's a man."

Faith's heart skipped a beat. A man? The only men who called her at home these days were Ben and his father. "Hello?"

"Miss Faith?"

"Mr. Carrigan." Her body tensed at the sound of Julian's voice. She was reminded of her earlier dream, of the strange images and feelings she had experienced.

"I'm sorry that I frightened you earlier."

Faith twisted the telephone cord between her fingers. "You didn't frighten me. I just let my imagination run wild for a minute there."

"I must admit to feeling a bit shocked by your reaction. The expression on your face—well, you looked just like Suzannah. I had the strangest sense of déjà vu." He paused. "I had no idea, Miss Faith. I'm sorry for pulling you into this, for exposing you to the curse."

Faith didn't know what to say to Julian or to the questioning look in Ben's eyes. She knew she couldn't talk about it now, not with Ben sitting right next to her. "Can I call you back? I have company at the moment."

"Of course. I'm sorry to disturb you. I just wanted to apologize and tell you that I understand your reluctance to help me pursue my quest. You're a lovely young woman with your whole life ahead of you. Why would you want to waste a second of it on a foolish dream? Please, accept my apology. I won't bother you again."

A rush of guilt swept through her. Julian's words reminded her that he was an old man with one last hope of finding peace, and she was being selfish. Or was she just succumbing to the wiles of a con man? She knew Alex didn't believe in his grandfather's story. Then again, she didn't get the feeling Alex believed in much of anything.

"Good night, Miss Faith."

"Wait," she said impulsively. "Don't be sorry. What you want to do is very noble. I hope you find Suzannah."

"I hope so, too."

"I wish I could help, but . . ." Her voice drifted away. What reason could she give him? She was too busy? She was too smart to play sucker? Or she was too afraid of the emotions, the images, the voices, the drums, the wind, and the sense that she was being drawn back into a dream, a nightmare, a life that was not hers?

"I understand," Julian said.

"Thank you. Good night."

"Who was that?" Ben asked curiously as he hung up the phone for her.

"Julian Carrigan, the elderly man who came to the bakery yesterday."

"The one Mother thinks is a con artist."

"Yes, but she's wrong."

"Why is he calling you, Faith? What does he want you to do for him? And why do you look so pale?"

Faith ran a hand through her hair and tried to smile. "Because I'm tired. It's been a long day, Ben. And Mr. Carrigan isn't after my money, believe me. He's just lonely."

"So let him find his own girl," Ben said with a smile, leaning over to kiss her.

Although he let his lips linger, Faith no longer had the energy to pursue the passion, and after a moment she pulled away. Ben looked disappointed.

"Next time I'll let your machine pick up the phone," he said.

She smiled. "Next time."

Ben stood up. "Tomorrow—brunch at Mom and Dad's?"

"Of course." She got to her feet and walked him to the door.

"Do you want me to pick you up?"

"No, I'll meet you there. I have some errands to run in the morning."

"Okay." Ben paused. "Tomorrow would be a good time to sit down with Mother and pick a date."

"I haven't said yes yet. You don't want to rush me into a quick decision, do you?"

"As a matter of fact . . ."

"Ben."

"You're right. You need time. But just think about this. Mom and Dad will be celebrating their fortieth wedding anniversary this coming June. We could have a double wedding ceremony. They could renew their vows, and we could pledge ours. It would be incredible, the binding of one generation to another. We could have that, Faith. Who else has that?"

Faith felt a rush of emotion at his beautiful and romantic plan. She, who had never felt tied to anyone, could be connected to generations of Porters, to family traditions, to timeless love. All she had to do was say yes. Before she could utter the word, Ben was gone, giving her the space she'd asked for but no longer wanted.

She thought about calling out for him, then decided against it. She closed the door and leaned against it. Tonight she would dream about the future. And tomorrow—tomorrow she would say yes.

Chapter 8

Faith didn't dream about the future. She dreamt about the past—the distant past.

Dawn rose over the canyon, illuminating the dark lines of "desert varnish" that streaked the walls. She felt so small here, closed in by the cliffs surrounding her. A lone eagle soared far overhead, and she knew instinctively it was a sign of something. But the knowledge of what it meant lay just beyond her grasp or her memory.

Thunderheads dotted the morning sky, but the air was too dry for it to rain. It hadn't rained in days. The gods were angry. With her, she thought suddenly.

A sense of being watched came over her, and she turned her head, wondering who she would see this time. An old woman stepped through the open doorway of a home tucked into the belly of the cliff. Her face was weather-beaten, having spent a lifetime in the hot desert sun where the wind carved lines in the people's faces as deep as the canyons.

The woman gestured for her to come. She didn't want to leave. The pot wasn't ready yet. She looked down, caught by the realization that she was holding the pot. She traced one of the markings and felt a powerful desire, an elemental sense of lust.

Shocked, Faith looked up and around. There was a man watching her now. It was not the warrior. This man was short and squat. His hair was thick but lifeless, his eyebrows bushy, his mouth set in a fine line. His shadow reached to her bare feet, to the pot, and she held it closer to her breast, feeling a desperate need to protect it.

His expression grew angry. Faith turned as the woman came up behind her. She spoke, but Faith couldn't understand her words. Then the woman grabbed the pot from Faith's hands and shoved her toward the man. His hands encircled her waist as tightly as a snake. She struggled against the constricting bonds as the coil wove around her.

She panicked as his face faded away and his arms became the slithering body of a snake, a boa constrictor winding its way around her waist, her bare breasts, her neck, until she could no longer breathe.

Faith gasped and sat up in bed, breathing in and out until she could refill her lungs. She could still feel the cool slick skin of the serpent wrapping itself around her body. God! What was happening to her?

Who were these people she was dreaming about? And why were they haunting her? What did they want from her? Faith suddenly remembered Julian's words. *'You won't be allowed to walk away.'*

Faith scrambled out of bed. She ran to the bathroom and poured water on her face. She rubbed her skin dry with the rough edges of a terry cloth towel until her face stung from her efforts. Then she returned to the bedroom.

The normalcy of her surroundings, the hand-sewn quilt she'd picked up at the county fair, the colorful rug hanging on the wall, her shoes on the floor, the mystery novel opened on the night table, reminded her that she was living in the twentieth century, not some distant past. She was a pastry chef, not a potter, and she'd never lived anywhere near the desert.

Her clock read 8:00 A.M. and she decided it was time to get up. Besides that, she didn't think she could take another dream like the last one.

She'd hoped to sleep in this morning. The bakery was

closed on Sundays, her one day of rest. Faith pulled up the covers on her bed. She usually slept so peacefully, in a small cocoon on one side of her double bed. But this morning it looked like she'd had a party the night before, and her head ached with the memories of her restless dreams.

Faith pressed her hands to her temples, debating her options. She could go into the bakery and get a head start on tomorrow's baking. With Easter only a week away, she had dozens of orders to fill for pastries and cakes, some of which needed to be delivered midweek.

Work would be good for her—if she weren't so tired, if she weren't so filled with a desperate need to find out more about that damn pot.

Julian had been right. It was too late for her to forget about it. She had to know more. She had to know what the markings on the pot meant—if Julian knew of its history, if he had any idea why she was suddenly convinced she knew the original owner of that pot.

That sounded ridiculous even to herself. But the nagging thought wouldn't go away, not even after a hot shower and a quick cup of coffee. Finally, giving in to the urge, Faith pulled on a pair of jeans and a knit T-shirt and drew a brush through her hair. It was too early to go visiting; the Carrigans were probably still asleep. She smiled grimly at that thought. Then again, they'd robbed her of a peaceful night's sleep. She owed them.

Ninety-seven, ninety-eight, ninety-nine, one hundred. Alex lay back on the floor, letting his abdominal muscles breathe before he put them through another hundred sit-ups. He'd been working out since seven, thirty minutes on the StairMaster and another thirty minutes on weights. He almost felt strong enough to face the day.

He knew that most people looked at him and saw strength in his well-defined muscles. But inside he was still the thin, weak, sickly kid with the awkward feet. No matter how much he changed the outside, he couldn't seem to change the inside. That was probably what he kept striving for—some inner sense that he was as successful as he appeared to be to others.

And he was successful, he reminded himself. Okay, losing Elijah was a momentary setback. He still had hopes Elijah would sign with them. He just had to think of a new strategy, one that wouldn't set them back another twelve thousand dollars. He winced at the memory. He'd been so close—until Jessie.

She was something else, a piece of work, just like his grandfather. He was convinced now that her sudden illness had just been a play for attention. After all, she'd been fine the rest of the day, her usual smart-ass self.

Alex rolled his neck, trying to ease the sudden tension in his muscles. On one hand, he hoped the private investigator would come up with Jessie's father as quickly as possible. On the other hand, he couldn't quite face letting her go so soon. Alex shook his head. Of course, she had to go. There was no other option. Alex wished he'd given Pete Sloan more to go on other than a name and where he thought the guy had gone to school.

School. It suddenly occurred to him that Jessie should probably be in school. She was twelve years old. What was that? Seventh grade? Eighth? He didn't even know the name of the closest school, much less its location. Maybe they were out for Easter break. Did they get the week before Easter off or the week after? Maybe his secretary would know. Theresa knew everything.

Alex mentally added that to his list of things to do, right after checking the real estate section of the newspaper for condos. It was a good day to take his grandfather out and get him used to the idea of relocating into a smaller place of his own. Then they'd have to talk about selling his grandfather's small house in Seattle, which he'd bought at the time of his last marriage ten years earlier. According to Julian, he'd never liked the house and would be glad to get rid of it. So that just left moving the rest of his things to San Francisco. Alex mentally added two more items to his list.

Alex still couldn't figure out how Julian had ended up alone after five trips to the altar. Surely that should have netted him at least one ex-wife willing to care for him in his old age. But apparently not. The concept of family certainly wasn't what it was cracked up to be.

"Daddy?"

The childish voice reminded him that *his* family had become a lot more complicated in the past two days. Alex took a deep breath and let it out, then glanced at the doorway where Jess stood in a pair of old cotton boxer shorts and an oversized T-shirt. Her brown hair was a tangled mess, her eyes still sleepy, her cheeks flushed. She looked far more angelic than he remembered, more innocent, more needy.

He wouldn't let that thought take root. He was only a temporary baby-sitter, nothing more. In a few days her real father would come and collect her, and that would be that.

"Daddy?" Jessie drew her hand over her eyes as she yawned.

He didn't like what the word did to his gut, twisting and turning it with utter simplicity. Daddy. He could still remember rushing Melanie to the hospital all those years ago when he'd believed he really was Jessie's father. He could still smell the antiseptic in the delivery room. He could still see Jessie's tiny red face, hear her squeal of protest at being pushed into the cold cruel world. Most of all he remembered the feeling of utter wonder and completeness that he had a child, someone to love, someone to love him.

"Alex," she said this time. "Doorbell. She's in the living room."

"Who's in the living room?" Alex sat up and grabbed a towel off the bench.

"You know—her."

Jessie stumbled out of the room before he could get a

more definitive explanation of exactly who "her" was. But Alex had an uneasy feeling he knew exactly who was waiting in the living room, and she was definitely not on his list of things to do.

Alex walked through the kitchen and dining room and paused in the archway that led into the living room. Faith stood by the window, framed by the early morning sunlight streaming through it. She reminded him of an angel, her reddish blond hair billowing in a cloud around her shoulders, her womanly figure molded softly by the light blue knit T-shirt that clung to her breasts and the faded, well-washed blue jeans that curved with her hips.

He didn't think he'd ever seen a woman who struck him as so utterly feminine, even in a pair of jeans. There was no way she should be single. She should be someone's wife, someone's mother. Then she wouldn't be haunting his thoughts. She'd be out of reach. And he suddenly wanted her out of reach.

He wondered why she wasn't married. He knew that *home* and *family* were important words to her, especially since she'd grown up alone. Even now, she stared at the photos on his mantel—photos he had never wanted to display, but his housekeeper, Gloria, had found them in the bottom drawer in his desk, framed them, and set them out.

A home should have pictures of family, Gloria had told him. He hadn't wanted to tell her that those family pictures were nothing more than a camera trick. His father had been an expert photographer, almost making Alex believe that the photos were truly a reflection of life, that the look of love in his mother's eyes was real. Alex hardened his heart against that painful memory.

Faith reached out and picked up a photo—the one of his mother holding him the day after he was born. Why had he let Gloria put the pictures out? They didn't mean anything. They only gave the wrong impression—that he cared, and he didn't care. Not one little bit.

But Faith seemed to care. She looked at the photograph

with an expression of such wistful longing, Alex had the sudden irrepressible desire to race across the room, pull her into his arms, and kiss her until the lost look disappeared from her eyes.

His urge vanished as Faith started and caught him staring. She hastily set the photo down on the mantel. "Hello."

"Good morning."

"Is that you?" She waved her hand toward the photo.

"Yes."

"Your mother was beautiful. She probably still is. I didn't mean to make it sound like she's dead, or maybe—maybe she is." Faith's ramble stopped abruptly as embarrassment filled her eyes. "I'm sorry."

"She's not dead and she may still be beautiful—I wouldn't know. I haven't seen her in fifteen years."

"Fifteen years? Good heavens! Why not? I mean, she is your mother."

"A title that never suited her and one she never really wanted. She divorced my father when I was eight years old. I didn't realize at first that she intended to divorce me as well." His jaw tightened. "I used to sit on the steps every evening, imagining that she'd come home just as the sun went down and the moon came up, because she'd always told me that was her favorite time of the day. But she never did come home." He shrugged. "Eventually someone would find me sitting on the step and make me go to bed."

"Someone?" Faith questioned softly, her heart caught by the image of a forlorn little boy, waiting every night for his mother to come home. Maybe there was more to Alex Carrigan than met the eye. "Not your dad?"

"My father? Never." Alex drew himself up, as if he were sorry for having revealed such a personal memory. "What do you want from me anyway?"

"Nothing—from you. I didn't come here to see you."

"Then why are you here?"

Alex walked farther into the room, a towel slung over

his shoulders, the muscles in his body exquisitely defined by the tank-top T-shirt and running shorts. He was a gorgeous man, long, lean runner's legs, flat, taut abdomen, broad shoulders, defined biceps, strong hands. Alex was perfectly made and as male as they came. Faith found herself captivated by the strands of dark hair that curled so sensuously against his chest.

"See something you like?" Alex asked.

She looked into his eyes and saw amusement and something darker, desire perhaps. His gaze turned bold, traveling down her body, lingering on her breasts so long, she felt them start to tingle.

"Uh, what are you doing?" she asked.

"Looking at you."

"You're staring, actually."

"*Actually,* you are, too."

She couldn't deny that, so decided it was safer to change the subject and cross her arms in front of her breasts. "I came to see your grandfather. Is he here?"

"Don't know."

"Could you find out?"

"I could." Alex didn't move a muscle. Instead, he continued to look at her as if she were a puzzle he couldn't quite figure out.

"Well?"

"Why do you want my grandfather? I know he thinks he's a stud. But surely you can get someone your own age."

Faith stiffened at his sharp words. So much for thinking he was nicer than he'd first appeared. "You know why I'm here and it has nothing to do with—well, you know."

"With sex."

Faith licked her lips and played with the St. Christopher medal that hung around her neck. Just the mention of the word *sex* had actually drawn her gaze down to a part of him she had no business wondering about. And he knew. She could see the amusement in his eyes, and it irritated the heck out of her. She felt like a blushing schoolgirl, and she was nothing of the kind.

"Maybe I should come back later."

"Maybe you shouldn't have come at all. In fact, why did you come?" Alex planted his hands on his hips in a stance that was purely aggressive. "Did you come to help an old man search out his lost love? Because I don't get it. Why would you take the time to bother? You're a busy woman. You have your own business. Your own life. Why do this? Unless . . ."

"Unless what?"

"You're looking for an inheritance. If so, I hate to break it to you, but the old man hasn't got much more than that broken pot and a million stories to sell."

"How dare you! I have no interest in your grandfather's money."

"Then maybe it's me you're after. *San Francisco Magazine* called me one of the ten most eligible bachelors in the Bay Area."

"Bully for you. I didn't see the article, and if I had, I'd probably question their taste."

"Ooh, that hurts." Alex put a hand to his heart.

"I hope it does."

Faith tried to walk past him, but he caught her by the arm.

"Wait."

"Why? So you can insult me again?"

Alex let out a breath and shook his head. "You were in my dreams last night. I didn't like it."

His words startled her. When she looked into his eyes, she no longer saw dislike but fear. The emotion humbled him, made him far less arrogant, far more likable.

"I can't stop thinking about you," he muttered. "What is it about you? You're not my type. Not at all."

"And you're not mine. That's why I haven't been thinking about you at all . . ." Her voice drifted away as she realized that wasn't true. She had seen his image the day before—in her dream. The warrior. It all came back.

He'd stood in the shadows, but his build, his stance, the set of his jaw . . . She clapped a hand to her mouth. "My God, it was you!"

"Who was me?"

"In my dream. At least I think it was you. No, it couldn't have been. You were wearing a loincloth and you were carrying a spear."

"That was some dream. Did I pound on my chest and call you Jane?"

"No." She shook her head, unable to laugh it off as he was trying to do. "We were caught in something, something terrible, and the pot—the pot was there. Your grandfather's pot. I could see it. And it wasn't broken. It was whole. And there were pictures on it. And . . ." She looked into his eyes. "I felt like I knew what they were, what they meant. As if I were the one who had put them there."

Alex didn't say anything for a long moment. Finally he ran a hand through his hair and shrugged. "Oh, hell. He got to you, didn't he?"

"You don't believe me."

"I believe you have a very good imagination."

"I thought the same thing, Alex. I told myself it was like putting a seashell to my ear and imagining that I could hear the ocean. But then yesterday afternoon I took a nap, and I dreamt about the pot, and last night the dream came again, only different, like someone was showing me the pieces of a puzzle one at a time." She wished she could make him understand. "I feel like I'm being haunted by ghosts, and you look remarkably like one of them."

"We're attracted to each other, Faith. If you want to add in a Tarzan-and-Jane fantasy, that's fine."

"It's not fine, and it's not it. The dreams have to do with the pot, with the symbols painted on the side."

"Then why am I in your dreams?"

Alex touched her face, drawing his finger down the side of her cheek in a simple but intimate gesture. Faith couldn't stop the shiver of anticipation that ran down her spine. He was too male, too close, and he moved closer still.

"You're not going to kiss me, are you?" She hated the breathless note that carried in her words, but she couldn't quite seem to catch her breath.

He paused to smile at her. "Yes, I think I am."

"No, you can't."

He raised an eyebrow. "No?"

"I just came by to see your grandfather. Why can't you get that through your head? Or are you such a—such a stud that you think every woman wants you? Because I happen to prefer my men a little . . ." She searched wildly for a reason why she should not kiss him. "A little less—sweaty."

His smile broadened. "Is that a fact? I think a little sweat between us could be a good thing."

"Well, here's another fact, Mr. Carrigan. I'm almost—almost engaged." There, she'd done it, pulled out the big gun and fired away. She'd never considered Ben a lifeline before, but today he was right there where she needed him.

"Is that like being almost pregnant?" Alex reached for her hand. "Where's the ring?"

She yanked her empty hand away from his sharp gaze. "I, uh, it's being fitted."

"You're serious? There really is someone in your life?"

"Yes."

"That's good," he said slowly.

"It is? I thought you were interested in me." Now that she'd made him back away, she found herself filled with regret. What would have been the harm in one little kiss? She should have kissed him. She could have used it for comparison if nothing else.

"I shouldn't be interested. You're the kind of woman who should be married, and I don't intend to ever get married."

"Why not?"

"I've seen too many marriages end in divorce."

"Your grandfather."

His eyes narrowed. "And my father and mother, who have each been married twice. For a while they were considering naming the divorce court Carrigan Court."

Faith tried to smile, but she felt more sad than amused. "Hasn't anyone in your family stayed married?"

"None, not since my grandfather brought the infamous curse down upon our heads."

"You don't believe in the curse."

"I don't believe in much of anything."

"That's too bad."

"If you don't believe, you don't get hurt."

And Alex was a man who'd built so many walls to protect himself, he was trapped inside a fortress of his own making. No one could get in, but Faith also had the feeling he couldn't get out.

"You should have longer hair," she said.

His jaw dropped. "Excuse me?"

"Then you could let it down like Rapunzel, and I could climb up and rescue you." She sent him a whimsical smile.

"I don't need rescuing."

"Don't you?"

"Don't be ridiculous." He laughed, as if she'd made a joke, when they both knew she hadn't.

"Am I interrupting something?" Julian's voice broke the intimacy between them.

"No," they replied at the same time, stepping away from each other in perfect unison.

Julian looked from one to the other, a perceptive gleam in his crafty blue eyes. "I see."

"You don't see," Faith said immediately. "I came to speak to you, not Alex. I'd like to see the pot again."

"I thought you weren't interested in pursuing this."

"I wasn't." Faith glanced at Alex, wishing he'd leave, but he seemed intent on listening to their conversation.

"But I keep seeing the pot in my dreams."

Julian paled slightly. "In your dreams?"

"Yes. It's not like a normal dream where I'm still myself. It's like I'm someone else, then I'm not. I'm watching it, and I'm living it at the same time. I know it sounds crazy. I feel crazy."

"You're not crazy. You're caught, a conduit to the past. The old Indian said it could happen. He was talking about Suzannah at the time, but perhaps he also meant you."

"I wasn't even born when you took the pot."

"I don't think that matters. It's your spirit, a friendly spirit that they would want."

"That who wants?"

"Oh, come on. Friendly spirits? The two of you sound ridiculous," Alex interjected. "You've gone overboard, Grandfather, even for you."

Julian ignored him. So did Faith. She was more interested in his grandfather's tale.

"What exactly do you mean, Mr. Carrigan?"

"The spirits want your help. That's why they speak to you. That's why they spoke to Suzannah. They need someone to undo the harm I did."

"Then why don't they speak to you?" Faith asked.

Julian hesitated. "I haven't told you everything. I'm not sure I should. I never meant to endanger you, to bring the curse down upon your head. You must believe me."

"What haven't you told me?"

"That pots such as these were sometimes buried with the dead, holding their spirits together for all of eternity." He lowered his voice dramatically. "When I took the pot, I disturbed the spirits. I broke the sacred bond between two lovers. And that is why I will never know true love, nor will anyone in my family—not until I take the pot back, until I reunite the lovers, who are lost in eternity."

"Oh, my God," Faith whispered. She knew the tale was true. She'd seen it in her dreams.

"They want your help," Julian said. "The question is—will you give it?"

Chapter 9

"The question is—will you believe this bullshit?"

Alex put a hand on Faith's shoulder and spun her around to face him. "My grandfather tells a great story. Applaud if you must, but please, please think twice about believing him. I can't tell you how many times I've bought in to his story, only to have him yell 'gotcha' at the end."

Faith looked into Alex's worried blue eyes, wondering if he was truly concerned about her or something else.

"I'm not yelling 'gotcha.' " Julian drew her attention back to him. "Not this time."

"Not this time? You couldn't tell the truth if your life depended on it," Alex replied.

"This is the truth, Alex, and my life does depend on it. More importantly, so does yours. And perhaps Miss Faith's as well." Julian gazed into Faith's eyes with simple sincerity. "I hope you will believe me. I am telling the truth. Perhaps I led you on a bit in regards to Alex putting me in an old folks' home. But this is the truth."

"See, I told you." Alex pounced on Julian's words. "He was lying then, and he's lying now."

"Everything I've told you about Suzannah is true."

Faith sighed, not sure whom to believe. She was saved from a reply when Jessie walked into the room.

"Is there someone in the bathroom?" Jessie asked,

looking sleepy and bemused. "The door is closed and I need to take a piss."

Her pragmatically crude statement cut through the lingering mist of ancient legends and curses. For a moment there was silence, then Alex started to laugh. "This is the real world, Faith—crotchety old grandfathers who want to relive their youth and irritating children who should have their mouths washed out with soap."

"What did I say?" Jessie demanded. "Shit. I just want to go to the head."

"Where have you been living?" Alex asked. "And more importantly, who have you been living with? I know Melanie didn't talk that way."

Melanie? Faith wondered if Melanie was Jessie's mother, which was immediately followed by the question of what had happened between Melanie and Alex that had left him with custody of a child he didn't seem to think was his.

"Melanie talked whatever way she was supposed to. She could do southern," Jessie said with a perfect drawl, "or New York," she added with nasal intonation. "But she was really good at sweet talk. That's what got so many dudes using our head, you know?"

It was clear that Alex didn't know, that he was as baffled by Jessie as he appeared to be baffled by Julian. In fact, Alex seemed completely out of step with everyone in his family. His expression reminded Faith of that little boy on the steps he'd described earlier. He wasn't a boy now, but he still looked lost.

"There's no one in the bathroom," Alex said finally. "You can use it. But clean up your act while you're here, Jess."

"Fine," she grumbled.

As Jessie ambled off, Alex said, "I need coffee." He glanced at Faith. "I suppose you'll still be here when it's ready?"

"I would like to see the pot again."

"I can't convince you, can I?"

Faith slowly shook her head. "I'm not choosing to believe your grandfather over you. I'm simply keeping an open mind."

"Right."

Faith let out a breath as Alex left the room. "He doesn't like me."

Julian's gaze followed Alex down the hall. "I'm afraid he likes you too much. He doesn't want to see you get hurt—by me."

"I don't think you could hurt me."

"I hurt Alex, more times than I realized. It's no wonder he doesn't believe in anything. I put the doubts there."

Faith knew she shouldn't pry, but she wanted to know more about Alex, why he seemed such a contradiction, so strong and yet so vulnerable. "He said his mom ran out on him when he was a boy."

Julian looked surprised. "He told you that?"

"I don't think he meant to. I was looking at a photograph, the one on the mantel."

"Alex's mother loved him, but she suffered the curse of the Carrigans as we all did. Or perhaps I should say her husband, my son Brett, suffered the curse, and in turn she was touched by it as well. Brett couldn't be satisfied with one woman."

"But to leave her child behind . . ." The concept had always been unacceptable to Faith, perhaps because she, too, had been left behind.

"The man she wanted didn't want Alex. She made a choice."

"That's terrible."

"I don't think she truly realized how badly she hurt Alex until much later. She thought that by leaving him with Brett, she was giving him the male influence that he needed. But Brett never paid Alex much attention. He was too busy making a name for himself as a photographer. And I was too busy getting married and divorced to notice,'' Julian added with a shameful smile. ''We're a self-centered bunch, we Carrigans. I wouldn't advise getting involved with Alex.''

Faith squared her shoulders. ''I have no intention of getting involved with Alex.'' She forced herself not to think about their almost kiss. It hadn't happened. It wouldn't happen. He'd told her she wasn't his type, and he certainly wasn't hers. She wanted a family and a family man, someone who'd be around forever. Someone like Ben. ''Just show me the pot and I'll be on my way.''

A half hour later Faith sat cross-legged on the end of Julian's bed. She'd meant to leave after seeing the pot, after convincing herself it was nothing like the one in her dream. Unfortunately, seeing the pot had only made the images reappear in her head along with the strong smell of woodsmoke. She'd asked Julian if he smelled it, too, but he'd only smiled and said no, all the while watching her as if he thought she might go into a trance.

She'd also questioned him about the markings. He pointed to one and said it meant marriage or love; he wasn't quite sure if there was a distinction. Faith had a feeling there was a definite distinction.

Then Julian had switched the conversation to Suzannah, which was why she was now being handed a packet of letters, faded yellow with age.

''What are you doing?'' Jessie asked, walking into the room with a bowl of cereal in her hand. She took a slurping bite, then sat down on the window seat across from Faith.

''I'm showing Faith my letters from Suzannah,'' Julian replied. He took a seat in the straight-back chair in front of the desk. ''We began as pen pals, you know. It was a class project between two schools. I was living in Connecticut at the time, and Suzannah lived in Burbank, California. We started out with the usual small talk about our favorite ice cream—strawberry—what we liked to do—

watch old movies—then moved on to more personal things as we came to know each other."

"Cool," Jessie said.

"Perhaps Miss Faith will read one aloud for you. My eyesight isn't what it used to be."

Then why did his eyes look so sharp and so clear? Faith wondered, as she undid the ivory-colored ribbon that held the letters together.

"I can't believe you kept the letters," Faith mused. "I didn't think men were all that sentimental."

"We can be on occasion." He reached for a letter written on pink stationery. "Read this one."

Faith opened the envelope and slid the letter out. The paper still carried a lingering scent of a woman's perfume.

Dear Julian:

I sprayed the stationery with my favorite scent. I love gardenias. In fact, I'm wearing one in my hair right now. Whenever you smell gardenias I want you to think of me.

If my aunt saw me now, she'd make me take the flower out of my hair. She thinks everything I do is wicked. Last Saturday she found me dancing around the house in my shorts. She said dancing like that was a sin, so I had to say a lot of extra prayers.

Did I tell you my aunt has this crazy idea that I should marry her best friend's son? He's old, almost twenty-five, and he's studying to be a minister. I want to attend college or go to New York and dance in a show. My aunt thinks I should get married. She said girls don't need college, they need husbands.

I wish you were here, Julian. I wish I could see you and you could see me. I feel like you're the only one in the world who understands me.

Write back soon, Julian. Your letters fill my heart with such joy.

Love,
Suzannah

Faith smiled at the romantic ramblings of a young girl on the brink of womanhood. "She sounds lovely and young."

Julian smiled back. "She was seventeen, a senior in high school. We were both a little bit lonely, a little bit different. Suzannah liked to dance. I liked to act. Neither one of us fit in at our high schools. Maybe that's why we were so drawn to each other."

"I've never met anyone who fell in love by mail. It's nice. You liked her before you knew what she looked like. Nowadays there's so much importance placed on physical attraction." An image of Alex immediately floated through her head, but Faith pushed it away. "Your attraction to Suzannah must have been mental and emotional, at least in the beginning."

"And in the end. I loved her very much. She is my biggest regret."

"Did you screw her?" Jessie asked.

"Jessie!" Faith looked at the girl in astonishment.

"That is a personal question," Julian said, with an edge to his voice. "And one I don't intend to answer, young lady."

"Melanie said everyone screws before they're seventeen. She was fourteen. And I'm almost thirteen, so I figure I'll be doing it soon," Jessie said matter-of-factly.

"You won't do anything of the kind," Faith said firmly, disregarding the fact that this girl was none of her business.

"What's it to you? You're not my mother."

"Maybe not, but I'm a woman, and I can tell you for a fact that doing 'it' before you're ready, which is not at fourteen, is a huge mistake."

"Why? Sex is no big deal."

"Oh, Jessie, it's a very big deal."

Jessie made a face and lifted the cereal bowl to her lips, drinking the last bit of milk. When she finished she had a milk mustache and an even younger appearance.

"You should talk to Alex," Faith said.

"Alex doesn't care what I do."

"I'm sure that's not true."

"What do you know?" Jessie got up from the window seat and left the room.

Faith sighed. "I guess she told me."

"Jessie is a frightened little girl. Despite her rather colorful language and boasting statements, I don't think she's nearly as confident or secure as she appears to be."

"No," Faith agreed, thinking of the children she'd grown up with at various homes. While she'd often retreated into a make-believe world of books and movies, some of the other kids had reacted like Jessie, attacking the world before it attacked them.

Faith stood up and set the letters on the bed. "I'll have to read the rest later. I'm supposed to be somewhere in a few minutes." She paused. "If you'll write down what you know about Suzannah, her first name, last name, middle name, birthdate, place of birth, anything you can remember, I'll stop by the library and look it up on the Internet."

"Oh, yes, of course. I was thinking of going to the library and hunting through the white pages, but I'd forgotten that people get around so much faster these days."

"Well, it will be a start, Mr. Carrigan. We may not find anything."

"But you'll help me?"

"I don't seem to have any other choice. Alex was right."

"I was right about what?" Alex entered the room with two mugs of steaming coffee. He handed one to his grandfather and the other to Faith. "I added a little cream and sugar to yours. You seem the type."

Faith accepted the mug and took a small sip. ''Perfect. That's frightening.''

''Almost as frightening as believing I was actually right about something,'' he said with a grin. ''So enlighten me.''

''You won't like it.''

''That doesn't surprise me.''

''Well, you were right about me being caught by your grandfather's story. I'm going to help him find Suzannah.'' Faith sent Alex a challenging look. There was more between them than a simple disagreement over a legend. Alex didn't want her in his life. He was controlled, organized, methodical, and logical. She could see it in the orderly appearance of his apartment, the starkness of the furniture, the clipped tones of his voice. He didn't want to be attracted to her because she was the opposite of him, emotional and sentimental.

She should be grateful that he didn't want her. He wasn't the right man for her either. She wanted a man who would commit, marry, have children, and be her best friend as well as her lover. She'd only known Alex for two days, but instinctively she knew he was not that man.

But he was awfully attractive, she thought with a sigh, and he had a way of looking at a woman that made her feel like she was the only one in the room.

''So what's the next step?'' Alex asked, his expression now carefully guarded.

''The Internet.''

''A little computer investigation, huh?''

''I think it's a good place to start. Maybe Suzannah is in a phone book somewhere.''

''That would make it easy.'' Alex turned to the door. ''I'm going to clean up, then take off to the office, Grandfather. Can you keep an eye on Jessie? I'll be gone for a couple of hours.''

''I suppose.'' Julian leaned over the desk where he was writing something down on a pad of paper. He ripped off the top page and handed it to Faith. "That's the information you'll need to find Suzannah."

"Thanks. I'll call you later if I find anything. Oh, Alex." She ran her St. Christopher medal through her fingers as she faced his questioning glance. "Could I ask a favor of you?"

"What's that?"

She tipped her head toward the fractured pot lying in a box on Julian's desk. "Would you pick up the pot?"

"Why?"

"Because I asked you to. He hasn't touched it, has he?" Faith asked Julian.

The old man shook his head. "No, but it won't matter, Miss Faith."

"You don't know that."

Alex looked from Julian to her. "Is it booby-trapped?"

How could she answer that question in view of her recent nightmares? "I don't know. Touch it and tell me if you hear anything or if you smell anything."

Alex shrugged and walked over to the desk. He picked up the pot and held it in both hands, then up to one ear. "I might be able to get the Giants game if I tilt it."

"You don't hear anything." Faith felt incredibly disappointed. If he was the warrior in her dream, why didn't he hear the voices, feel the heat of the fire, the brush of the wind? Why didn't he smell the damn smoke that was even now creeping over her senses? "Never mind."

"Here, you hold it," Alex said, handing her the pot.

She reached out to push it away, but even the small contact sent a jolt of electricity through her.

"No, take it away."

When Alex didn't immediately comply, she repeated her command. "Now. Do it now." She suddenly felt like she couldn't breathe. The snake was back, wrapping itself around her neck. She pulled at the neckline of her shirt, trying to breathe.

"What's wrong with you?" Alex demanded, still holding the pot between his hands.

Faith couldn't answer. She felt hot, light-headed, dizzy. She couldn't breathe. She closed her eyes and couldn't open them. Her feet wouldn't move, and she felt herself sink to the floor.

"Faith?" Alex's voice called to her. Or was it the warrior?

Chapter 10

*Ben parked behind his mother's dark green mini-*van and walked up the driveway to his parents' house. His parents had bought this house in the Westlake District of South San Francisco just after their first wedding anniversary, and they'd never lived anywhere else. The trees they'd planted all those years ago had grown and flourished just as their children had grown and flourished, nourished by a loving family.

Nancy was a strong believer in putting down roots, in making things last. Their lives were steeped in long-standing traditions—the same rosebushes bloomed year after year, the house was always repainted off-white, and as sure as the sun came up, his father would seek the morning paper with a cup of coffee in his hand. There were never any surprises in the Porter household. At least there hadn't been until Gary had died, upsetting everything.

Hadn't Gary known Porter men were supposed to live into their eighties? It was tradition.

Ben's gut twisted at the reminder of his loss. Gary was gone. He couldn't take over the Porter family as intended. That would be left to the second son. To Ben. He was afraid he'd blow it. And if he blew it, there'd be nothing left of the family. In fact, he knew that he could single-handedly destroy the peace and contentment his parents had taken forty years to build.

"Ben!" Nancy threw open the front door and hurried down the walk to give him a hug. He towered over her now, but she could still give a mean squeeze, and Ben relished every second of it. He remembered all the times he and Gary had walked home from school together and Gary had been greeted with the big hug, while Ben had received a casual touch on the shoulder.

"Well, did she say yes?" Nancy asked.

Ben laughed and extricated himself from his mother's arms. "Not yet. It's only been two days."

"I know. But she has to say yes. I do so want her in the family. It was meant to be."

"I think so, too."

"Is Faith here?" Kim called from the steps, shading her eyes as she looked out at them.

"She should be here any time," Ben replied. "She had a few errands to run this morning."

Nancy chattered away as they walked up to the house, talking about wedding invitations, a church that overlooked the ocean, and a banquet hall that was incredibly cheap, as well as a million other details that went in and out of Ben's head.

When he reached the house, Kim started up where Nancy had left off, telling him about the best place to get bridesmaids' dresses, asking him how many ushers they would have and if she could invite her boyfriend. Ben didn't know what to say except yes. He just hoped Faith would come up with the same answer. He hadn't felt this much a part of the family in years.

"Come into the living room," Kim said. "Mom picked up some invitation books from the stationery store. We can only keep them until tomorrow."

"You don't have to pick one today," Nancy said, as she pushed him down on the sofa and placed an enormous book on his lap. "But you should at least narrow down some choices."

The book was enormous and stuffed with sample invitations. Ben had no idea what he was supposed to be looking at. "Maybe we should wait for Faith."

"Now, now, Ben. The groom should have just as much say as the bride." Nancy sat down next to him and flipped the pages. "I want to show you the one I picked out for when your father and I renew our vows. Here it is. What do you think?"

"It's nice," he said, trying to infuse some enthusiasm into his voice, but he was beginning to feel like he had unleashed a tornado with his spontaneous wedding proposal.

"It's perfect, old-fashioned maybe, but it's almost the same one we had before, and you do know how your father likes tradition." Nancy smiled up at him, happiness radiating from her eyes like a rainbow after a long winter. "Last night I had the most incredible idea. We could get married together. Wouldn't it be lovely? You and Faith standing right next to your father and me?"

"It would be great, Mom."

"I can't think of anything that would make me happier." She gave him a kiss on the cheek, her eyes tearing up at the prospect of a double wedding. "Of course, if you want your own day, I'll understand."

"Let's just wait and see what Faith wants."

She nodded, then turned to Kim, who was sitting on the opposite couch looking through one of the other invitation books. "Can you get your brother a soda, Kimmie?"

Kim made a face. "You always did wait on the boys, Mother."

"Because we deserved it," Ben said.

"Yeah, right."

"Please, Kim."

"Okay," she said, giving a long-suffering sigh as she left the room.

When they were alone, Nancy dropped her voice to a hushed note. "Ben, before your sister comes back, well,

I just wanted to tell you how proud I am of you. You've grown up to be a wonderful, courageous man."

Ben felt his insides begin to shrivel. He wasn't courageous. He was as big a coward as they came. If his mother knew him, really knew him . . . No, he wouldn't go there.

"Marrying Faith, starting a family, it's so right. Everything I wanted for you. I love you, Ben, so much."

She didn't love him, she loved the son her mind had created. Part of him wanted to stand up and shout, *Look at me. See me, not Gary, not the son of your daydream, but me, your real, flesh-and-blood, and incredibly flawed son.* But Ben didn't say anything. He wouldn't and couldn't take that smile off of her face.

"Ben. I've been waiting for you," Chuck boomed from the doorway, his voice echoing through the house. "Come with me, son."

"Oh, you. Say whatever you have to say right here," Nancy said. "We're picking out wedding invitations."

"That's woman's work. You save that for Faith. Ben, I need to see you in the den."

"You better go," Nancy said, taking the invitations off of his lap. "We'll look at these when Faith gets here."

"Right."

Ben felt a bit wary as he made his way to the back of the house. He hadn't been in his father's den in quite some time. It wasn't Ben's favorite room of the house, mainly because it wasn't just a den but a trophy room, and most of the trophies belonged to Gary. The others belonged to his father, who had been quite an athlete in his day. Even Kim and his mother had brought home trophies. Only Ben had neglected to contribute to the trophy shelf, although it wasn't for lack of trying.

The gold still glistened, Ben thought, as he walked into the room and over to the glass case. He wondered if that was what his father did in here every night—polish trophies. Chuck always said he liked to get away and read his sports magazines, but the trophies never had a lick of dust on them.

"Sit down, son." Chuck motioned to the well-worn couch along one wall. "I've got something for you." He reached into the top drawer of his desk and pulled out a small box. Then he sat down next to Ben on the couch. "This is something I was going to give your brother." Chuck cleared his throat, suddenly overcome with emotion.

Gary. Always Gary. Ben wished he'd asked Kim to get him a beer. It would have taken the edge off this conversation. But there was nothing to do but sit and wait for his father to finish.

"This has been passed down from generation to generation, to the firstborn son," Chuck continued, his attention solely focused on the box.

His father had been the first son as well, Ben realized. Maybe that was why he'd always valued first but never second.

"Gary's gone now," Chuck said, his voice gruff with sadness. "He'd want you to carry on, as I do." Chuck slowly opened the lid of the box and took out a watch, a solid gold pocket watch.

Ben had seen the watch in the family movies. His great-grandfather had been given the watch for dedicating fifty years of his life to the same engineering firm that had designed and built some of the biggest bridges in the world. His great-grandfather had been a strong and courageous man. In fact, all the Porter men had dreamed big dreams and accomplished most of them.

"Take it, son." Chuck held the watch in his hand.

Ben hesitated. His hand seemed small compared to his father's hand. And that didn't begin to describe how he felt on the inside. He wasn't Gary. He couldn't begin to step into his big brother's shoes.

"Go on now, Benjamin. It won't bite."

Ben finally wrapped his fingers around the smooth roundness of the watch.

"There's an inscription inside. Open it."

Ben did as he was told, knowing already what it would say. "The best of the best, William Alan Porter," he muttered.

"The best of the best. That's who we are, Benjamin. That's who you are." Chuck slapped him on the back. "I'm proud of you, son. You've changed in the last two years, become the man I always knew you would be."

He'd become Gary, that was who he'd become. He was a paler version, but close enough for parents who desperately wanted their son back not to see the differences between them.

"You and Faith make a fine couple. She'll do you proud, stand by your side. She's a loyal one, that girl. And she's got backbone."

It was a good thing one of them did, Ben thought dismally.

"What's the matter, son? You look down in the dumps for a man who should be celebrating."

"She hasn't said yes yet."

"Oh, she will. Soon as she thinks two seconds about it. You'll see. You keep that watch for your son, Ben. And promise me you'll tell him about all the other Porter men. Make him proud to be one."

"I'll do that, Dad." Ben looked at the watch in his hand, feeling the weight of its responsibility down to the tips of his toes.

Chuck stood up. "I hope Faith is here. I'm hungry. Coming, son?"

"I'll be there in a minute."

"Don't want to keep a woman like Faith waiting. In fact, I'll let you in on the secrets to a successful marriage. Don't drink too much. Don't swear too much. Don't ever forget her birthday and never tell her she looks fat. You follow those rules and you'll die a happily married man."

She was to be married when the moon turned full. It would be soon. Her heart cried out its sorrow. For she would not give herself to the man she loved but to another, the one she had been promised to on the day of her birth.

Faith struggled to free herself from the dream, but it would not let go. She could smell the woodsmoke, feel the cold of deep night approaching, and she knew he would come soon.

Tonight she would give him the pot she had made for him, telling him what she could not say with words. She looked down at the pot, and a tear fell from her eye, washing away the last bit of dust, streaking the final edge of color.

Faith started as she heard a sound behind her. It came from the opening to her room. A tall shadow cut off the moonlight, enshrouding her in darkness. When the shadow moved, he was there, entering as silently as the wind. His presence warmed her like the sun. Her warrior.

He called to her with his eyes and she ran to him. She had one last night. She would take it and her soul be damned.

His lips touched hers and the heat drew the fire through her soul. She wanted more. She opened her mouth and felt his breath wash over her like a warm evening breeze. She melted into his kiss, into his body, into his soul.

He called her name. She didn't want to speak of the future or the past. But he called her name again, and said . . . "Faith! Faith! Come on now, breathe."

She felt his lips touch hers again, but this time it was different. Faith opened her eyes, disoriented by the dream, by the fact that she appeared to be lying on the floor, and Alex was leaning over her. "What? What happened?"

"You passed out," he said, worry running through his eyes.

"Oh, my God." She put a hand to her lips in bewilderment. "Did you kiss me?"

"I had to. I didn't think you were breathing."

"He was going to give you mouth-to-mouth," Julian said, entering Faith's vision from behind Alex's broad shoulders. "Fortunately, that wasn't necessary."

Fortunately? Faith could still taste Alex's mouth on hers, feel the heat of his breath.

"Do you pass out often?" Alex asked.

"Never. It was—it was the pot." She darted a quick look around to see where it was. "Where did it go?"

"I put it away," Julian replied. "It disturbs you so much."

"Didn't you smell the smoke?" Faith asked. "I couldn't catch my breath. I thought I was suffocating."

Alex's hands tightened on her arms. He searched her eyes with a grim look on his face. "Did you eat anything this morning?"

She looked at him in a daze, unable to comprehend the simple words. Finally they sank in. "No. I didn't eat."

"That's it then. You're hungry. Probably low blood sugar. That's why you fainted. Let's get you some food."

Faith knew she hadn't fainted because of lack of food. It had something to do with the pot, the damned pot. And the dream. "She was going to marry someone else."

Alex stared at her, his blue eyes shadowed with concern. "Who? You?"

"Not me. Well, maybe me. The woman in my dream. She's supposed to get married, but she loves someone else, someone she can't have."

"Yeah, okay. Whatever you say."

"You didn't hear anything when you touched the pot?"

"Sorry."

Faith sighed and struggled to get up. She still felt a bit dizzy, but the smell of smoke was gone. "I should go. I'm probably late. What time is it?"

"Almost eleven."

"Oh, no. I was supposed to go to brunch at ten-thirty."

"I don't think you should go anywhere, Miss Faith," Julian said. "Let Alex get you something to eat first. You still look pale. I must say, you scared us.''

Faith looked at Alex and saw the tension set in his jaw and face. ''Did I scare you?''

''Let's just say, it's not every day women fall at my feet.''

''Really? I would have thought that a common occurrence for one of San Francisco's most eligible bachelors.''

A small smile crept across his face. ''Touché. Do you like pancakes?''

''I'm supposed to be somewhere.''

''I don't want to be responsible for you passing out in your car halfway across town. Come on, have some breakfast with us.''

Faith hesitated. She never missed Sunday brunch at the Porters'; it was tradition. Nancy would have strawberry crepes and egg frittata and bacon and sausage, even though Chuck wasn't supposed to eat any of those things. If she didn't go today, it would be the first time she hadn't gone since . . .

''I should go,'' she murmured again, feeling torn between Alex and Ben, the Carrigans and the Porters.

''Here's another idea.'' Alex took a deep breath. ''I can't believe I'm saying this, but it seems we have to get to the bottom of something, although I'm not sure what. Anyway, I'm going in to my office today. I have a computer with Internet access. You're welcome to come with me and use it.''

''You're willing to help me?'' she asked with surprise.

''I'm willing to let you use my computer. That's as far as I go.''

It was a tempting offer. The library computers were often jammed with users, especially on a Sunday. Of course, if she went with Alex, she'd definitely have to skip brunch. Still, she did want to learn more about the pot, if for no other reason than to figure out why she'd fainted for the first time in her life.

''All right,'' she said impulsively. ''Thank you. I still

can't believe you're even offering this much."

"As I said, it's not every day a woman falls at my feet."

"It's not every day a man gives me mouth-to-mouth."

Alex smiled in a way that was pure male, pure sex. "Next time I kiss you, you'll be awake."

"Next time? You're pretty confident."

"Actually, I'm beginning to realize that some things are inevitable. I have a feeling a kiss between you and me is one of them."

"I'm the one who's helping your grandfather with the Carrigan curse, remember? The crazy idealist who is not only having strange dreams but even stranger fainting attacks? I'm sure you could find a less complicated woman."

"I'm sure I could. But I'm not sure it would be quite as much fun."

Faith decided it was past time to change the subject. "May I use your phone?"

"There's one in the hall. I'll show you." Alex led her down the hall toward the kitchen, stopping in front of a small desk set in an alcove. "Help yourself."

"Thanks. And thanks again for trying to revive me."

"You're welcome. Make your call. I'll warm up the griddle."

Faith smiled to herself as he walked away. She had a feeling Alex didn't give himself nearly enough credit. Not many men would have taken in a child and an eccentric grandfather in the same week, not to mention a pastry chef who was hallucinating on a daily basis.

Faith dialed the number for the Porters, knowing that excusing herself at this late hour would not go over well. But she had to admit to feeling relieved that she wouldn't have to sit through brunch and answer questions about the engagement. Last night she'd decided to say yes. This morning she just didn't know.

"Hello?" Nancy's cheerful voice cut into her thoughts.

"Hi, it's me, Faith."

"Faith, honey. We were getting worried about you. Are you all right?"

Was she all right? She felt shaky, light-headed. Maybe she was hungry. Maybe she was crazy. She didn't know anymore.

"Faith?"

"I'm sorry, Nancy. I can't come today."

"But, Faith, Ben's here. We're all expecting you. I made that egg frittata that you love so much. And, well, between you and me, we have some champagne on ice just waiting for a celebration."

Faith put a hand to her head as the beginning of a headache began to take hold. "Could I talk to Ben, please?"

"Faith, I know I promised not to press you, but Ben is my son, and I love him very much. I hate to see him so unsettled."

Whose fault is that? Faith wanted to ask. The wedding had been Ben's idea in the first place. Most men would have at least asked their potential mate in advance before bringing the entire family in on the decision.

"I'm sorry, Nancy, but I really do need to talk to Ben."

"All right. Just a minute."

Nancy came back on the line a second later. "Ben has gone to the store with Chuck to pick up some soda. I know he'll be so disappointed if you don't come."

"I'm not feeling well," Faith said, her lie quickly becoming the truth. "I need to rest."

"Oh dear. Maybe we should come over there and bring you some food."

"No. No, thank you." She tried to ease the sharpness out of her voice. "I need some time alone. You understand, don't you? I've been working so hard, and with Easter next weekend I have a zillion things to do this week. I just need a few minutes to catch my breath."

"I'm sorry. I'd forgotten what a busy time this is for

you. I'll come in extra early tomorrow and give you a hand."

"I'd appreciate that. Tell Ben I'm sorry and I'll call him later. And give my apologies to everyone else." Faith hung up the phone before Nancy could utter more protests. When she looked up, she caught Alex watching her from the kitchen doorway.

"Who's Ben?" he asked, holding a spatula in his hand. He looked so annoyed she almost thought he was jealous.

"Ben is the man I'm going to marry."

"The one you don't love," he said, quoting the words from her dream.

"That dream wasn't about me."

"Wasn't it? When you fainted, you had this incredible smile on your face, like you'd just seen the love of your life. You don't have that look anymore."

"That was a dream. This is reality."

"So you do know the difference. I was beginning to wonder."

Chapter 11

Faith found four Suzannah Brocks on the Internet, one living in San Diego, another in New Jersey, one in Dallas, and the last in New Orleans. It was something, but not enough. Faith flexed her fingers, trying to think of what to do next. She had no idea if Suzannah Brock had married, but it seemed likely since fifty years had passed. She probably wasn't listed under Brock at all. Still, it was something. Faith printed out the page and considered the possibilities.

A search through the Web finally took her to a site that checked vital statistics, births, deaths, and marriages in various counties throughout the country. For the first time, Faith felt a thrill of excitement. She typed in "Suzannah Brock" and the birth date Julian had given her. Next, she filled in "Los Angeles County" and waited for the computer to process the information. While the computer light blinked on and off, Faith leaned back in the leather chair and stretched her arms over her head.

She had to admit that using Alex's computer was a lot more comfortable than trying to get on one of the computers at the main library. Here she had a nice chair, a small refrigerator full of sodas, and plenty of privacy, the latter for which she was extremely grateful. Alex had assured her he could work just as well in the conference room, and he'd vanished there soon after they'd arrived.

With the computer still asking her to wait, Faith decided to stand up and stretch, maybe even explore a bit. She couldn't help but be curious about Alex. The photos on the far wall immediately drew her attention, and she walked over to take a closer look.

Alex appeared in almost every photo with athletes from a variety of sports. He certainly seemed to get around, from football stadiums to outdoor tracks, to soccer fields and basketball arenas. Everywhere she looked, there was Alex and his shoes. She smiled to herself, wondering how he'd ever decided to go into the athletic shoe business.

The rest of the office looked as neat as his apartment. With the exception of a stack of shoe boxes in one corner, there was little clutter. There were no overflowing files on his desk, no cute knickknacks, just a no-nonsense phone, a blotter, and a green potted plant. She had a feeling that little touch had come from someone else.

Across from the desk were two chairs. Against the far wall was a comfortable leather couch, much like the one in Alex's living room, and a glass coffee table. There were windows along one side of the office, but they offered nothing more than a view of the warehouse district.

Judging by the size of the warehouse next door with the Top Flight logo and the number of offices in this building, Alex's company was very successful, and he was the man at the top.

She had a feeling that being in control was very important to Alex. That was why he couldn't believe in a curse. He wouldn't be able to control a stormy wind, a haunting spell. She smiled at the thought of him trying to wrestle the wind. She could almost see him, with his dark hair blowing, his blue eyes sparkling with energy and passion.

He was truly a warrior. She wished she could share the dream with him, make him see it as she did. Maybe then he would understand why she was captivated by the tale. It was no longer as important for her to find Suzannah for Julian, but to find the other half of the pot. She didn't think the dreams would go away until she did.

"Find anything?" Alex asked, as he opened the door to his office and stepped inside.

Startled, she turned abruptly, catching her foot on the carpet. She stumbled, and Alex moved swiftly to catch her. His strong hands on her waist kept her from falling, but they didn't keep her from feeling. His touch brought immediate awareness, something he must have felt, because whatever he was going to say stilled on his lips. He simply stared at her. She knew what was coming. They'd been moving toward this moment from the first day they'd met.

Alex pulled her toward him.

"Not a good idea," she muttered.

"You are awake this time?"

"Alex, don't."

"One kiss, then we'll both know."

She wanted to ask him what they'd both know, but she didn't get a chance. His mouth covered hers in a demanding manner that was far too intimate for a first kiss, far too warm and deep and inviting.

It was a kiss that touched her soul, fed her hunger, quenched her thirst. It was a kiss that made her want another and another and another. Alex obliged, his mouth moving over hers again and again and again.

She molded her body into his, feeling the hard angles of his hips and pelvis, the broad expanse of his chest, every long, hard inch of him. And it wasn't enough. She wanted more, much more.

"Damn." Alex's eyes glittered, his breath coming rough and ragged. "You're good."

"I—I am?"

"I wasn't expecting so much—passion. I guess the red hair should have clued me in." He touched her hair with a tender hand. "You have great hair, a great smile." His gaze traveled across her face. "Soft, soft lips and beautiful, beautiful breasts."

Her breasts tingled at his words, at his look. She

wanted his hands there, and his mouth. Lord, what was she thinking? She couldn't do that with him. He was a stranger. She didn't even know him.

"I should finish up," she said hastily.

"You can finish me up. Right here. Right now. We're all alone."

She flushed, not as quick with the sexual repartee as he was. "I don't think so. That would be a mistake."

"Probably. But I could live with it."

Faith moved away from his amused grin. She needed space, a chance to think without him touching her. "I'll just get back to work."

"That easily?"

"I didn't say it would be easy. But it's the right thing to do. You said yourself I'm not your type. And you're not mine." The words came out in a rush before her conscience could call her a liar.

"I also said that kissing you would tell us what we both needed to know."

"Which is what?"

"We need each other in a very basic way."

Faith swallowed hard at the word "basic," feeling a sense of lust for him that did in fact feel as essential as breathing. She didn't, however, intend to act on that feeling, because the power of it frightened her. She'd loved Gary. She'd made love to Gary a dozen times or more. But she'd never felt so addicted to a kiss, so desirous of another.

The traitorous thought kicked her in the gut. How could she have forgotten Gary? A man she had intended to love for all time? It had only been two years.

She shook her head, still feeling an enormous sense of guilt. "I'm sorry," she whispered.

"For what?"

She'd been talking to Gary, to his memory, not to Alex, but Alex didn't know that. "I was supposed to marry someone else."

"Like in the dream. This guy Ben."

Ben? Oh, Lord, she'd forgotten about Ben, too. She was a terrible, terrible person.

"As far as I'm concerned, if you're not married, you're still free to kiss someone else, especially if you're still only 'almost' engaged," Alex said.

"You don't understand." She walked over to the chair behind his desk and sat down.

"Then tell me."

Alex perched on one corner of the desk, his gaze still fixed on her face. He was certainly one of the most attentive men she'd known.

"I wasn't talking about Ben, but Gary."

He raised an eyebrow. "Gary? Good grief, Faith. How many men do you have waiting in line to marry you?"

Faith sighed, knowing she would have to explain, at least part of it. "Two years ago, I was engaged to be married to Gary Porter. We were really, really happy." She took a deep breath, preparing for the pain that she knew would accompany the rest of her explanation. "Three weeks before the wedding, Gary was killed in an automobile accident. A drunk driver ran a red light. Gary died instantly. He was on his way to see me."

"I'm sorry. That must have been very rough."

"Things happen." She stood up, feeling restless. She didn't like the tenderness on Alex's face, the compassion in his eyes. It made it more difficult to be strong, to stand straight and tall and alone—when what she really wanted was a hug.

Alex came up behind her and slid his arms around her waist, drawing her back against his chest. He nuzzled her neck with his lips. "It's okay to remember."

She turned in his arms and buried her face in the curve of his neck. She hadn't been held in a very long time.

Alex didn't move. Nor did he speak. He just let one hand drift through her hair, while the other held her tight against his body, as if he could give her some of his strength. She never would have guessed he had such a core of patience in him. He always seemed to be in a hurry. He drove a fast car, led a fast lifestyle, but for now he seemed content to let the seconds pass without a word or a glance at the clock on the wall.

"Thanks," she said finally, offering him a weak smile. She stepped out of his embrace. "I seem to be thanking you a lot today."

"So who's Ben?"

"Ben is Gary's brother."

Alex looked surprised. "His brother?"

"It's not like that. It only happened recently. We've been friends since Gary died, but it was just lately that we started thinking about being something more."

"That explains the unofficial engagement. What are you waiting for, Faith? Are you still in love with Gary? Because I've got to say, you didn't kiss me like you were in love with someone else."

"I forgot for a second. Is that a crime?"

"No."

"It feels like one. I really want to be married. That's why Ben's proposal is so appealing."

Alex nodded as if that came as no great surprise. "You were made for marriage, for kids."

"I want children, more than anything. And Ben wants kids, too."

"But you don't love him."

His accusation drew a silence between them. "I care about him."

"That's it? You care? I was feeling sorry for you, but now I'm beginning to feel sorry for Ben."

"You don't have to feel sorry for either one of us. My life is not your business." She took a deep breath. "Don't kiss me again."

He seemed to view her words as a challenge. "Why shouldn't I? You liked it."

"Too much. I just told you I want to be married. That should scare you off."

"It should, if I had any sense. I'll agree to one thing, though. Next time we kiss, it will be your call."

"I will never make that call."

"Never say never. That's my motto. By the way, I usually get what I want."

"You don't want me, remember?"

"I'm trying to, Faith. I'm trying very hard to remember that fact."

An hour later Faith picked up the phone to call Julian. Thankfully, Alex had his home number on autodial.

"Mr. Carrigan. It's Faith. I found something, actually two things."

"Oh, dear God in heaven. I can't believe it. Tell me, please."

"Well, first of all, Suzannah's aunt Bernice died about three weeks after Suzannah returned from your trip to Arizona."

There was silence on the other end of the phone. Finally, Julian spoke. "That would explain why the house was sold a few months later. So Suzannah was left all alone in the world. I don't understand why she didn't come looking for me."

"You said she was religious. Perhaps she couldn't get over the fact that you'd stolen something holy and that together you'd broken it."

"That must be it. Otherwise, I'd have to consider that she never really loved me, that it was all a lie."

"Let's not think that yet. Actually, I believe there's another reason why she didn't contact you. Are you sitting down?"

"She's not dead. Please, tell me she's not dead."

"She got married, Mr. Carrigan, just a few months after her aunt's death."

"No. I can't believe that. So soon?"

"She was all alone in the world," Faith reminded him.

"But—go on. Who did she marry?"

"Someone named Harry Conrad. At the time of the marriage he apparently lived in Pasadena, California. That's where they got married."

"Harry Conrad." Julian repeated the name as if it were a clue to a puzzle. "I think that was the man Suzannah was supposed to marry. In her letter she said her aunt wanted her to marry a young man from their church who was studying to be a minister, but she couldn't imagine living with such a stern man. Why would she have said yes? She wanted to go to college. She wanted to dance."

"Women had fewer options in those days, Mr. Carrigan Maybe she didn't have money for college. With her aunt gone, she might have felt she had no other choice but to marry."

"She was so filled with light and joy, my Suzannah. I can't bear the thought that she lived with someone cold and unforgiving. Unless . . ."

"Unless what?"

"She was doing penance for both of us, for the sin I committed."

"You don't know that. Maybe Harry Conrad wasn't a bad guy. We don't have enough information."

"What do we do now?"

"Look for Suzannah and Harry Conrad, starting with the Pasadena phone book, then checking all the others. Who knows? We may get lucky. I'll call you back."

As Faith hung up the phone, Alex walked into the office. She offered him a brilliant smile.

"You found something," he said.

"I did. Suzannah Brock married one Harry Conrad." She handed him the paper she'd printed out.

"It could be the same person."

"It has to be, Alex."

"Even if this is her, it doesn't mean she's still alive or that she lives anywhere near Pasadena. Good grief, she married this guy just a few months after her trip to Arizona."

"That's right. But even though it was a long time ago, I still think we have a chance of finding her. Don't be such a pessimist. This is a real lead. I can't quite believe it. Aren't computers wonderful?"

"I'll say one thing for you, Faith. You choose to see the best in things." He tipped his head toward the window. "Did you happen to notice it's getting dark outside? You've been at this for hours. It's almost six o'clock."

"I didn't realize. You should have made me stop earlier."

"I got some work done. I came by a while ago, but you were so involved, I decided not to disturb you. Now I'm hungry."

"Me, too."

"Come on, we'll pick up a pizza on the way home, and you and Grandfather can plan out your next step."

"I almost hate to quit now."

"It's been fifty years, Faith. Another day won't matter."

"That's true."

He waited while she turned off the computer and gathered her notes. Then they walked out of the office together.

"You've built yourself quite a company, haven't you?" Faith commented as they reached the lobby area.

"I've tried. We're not at the top yet. We still have a way to go." Alex hated the sense of failure that followed his words.

Faith looked surprised at his reaction. "You don't feel like a success, even with all this?" She waved her hand toward the array of offices that tomorrow morning would be filled with his employees, dedicated to designing, manufacturing, and selling his shoes.

"It doesn't feel like enough." He pushed the button for the elevator. "I'm not the best yet."

"How will you know when you're the best? When every person on the earth is wearing your shoes?"

"Maybe."

Faith put a hand on his arm. She was an affectionate person, someone who used her touch as much as her words to communicate, and she didn't even realize it. Her gaze was focused on his face, and her eyes seemed determined to convince him of something.

"Don't you think you've set your expectations a bit high?"

Hell, his expectations had always been too high, especially where people were concerned. But he wouldn't tell her that. He tapped the elevator button again. "Where is the damn elevator?"

Faith laughed.

"What's so funny?"

"You're always in a hurry."

"I have places to go."

"Maybe if you'd slow down, you'd enjoy where you are right now."

His muscles tightened as her words once again created an atmosphere of intimacy between them. "Is that an invitation?"

"No. It was a general statement about life."

"Too bad." He liked the way she reacted to him, how sensitive she was to his moods, how passionately she responded to his touch. But he'd promised her he wouldn't kiss her again. Damn.

The elevator doors opened, and they stepped inside, remaining quiet for the short trip down to the first floor.

"This is all pretty impressive, you know," Faith said, as they continued out to the parking lot. "You're not that old."

"Sometimes I feel really old."

Alex unlocked the car door and opened it for her. She hesitated before getting in. "What about Jessie, Alex? Are you going to keep her?"

Jessie? He'd been wondering that same thing most of the day. And he'd felt guilty for leaving her alone all day with his grandfather. He'd done it partly for his own self-preservation. The less time he spent with her, the less chance he had of coming to care about her.

"I don't know," he said finally. "I'm hoping we can

find her father. I hired a private investigator, although I probably could have just let you loose on the Internet."

"One missing person is enough for me."

"Hopefully this detective will come up with her father fast. I still haven't figured out if she's supposed to be in school tomorrow. I don't suppose you know."

"Sorry. I'm not up on school schedules."

"Neither am I. In fact, I'm not up on twelve-year-old girls at all, especially ones who talk like truck drivers. Actually, I've never been able to figure out women, no matter what age they are."

"We're not all that difficult to understand. We're just people."

"Yeah, right."

"Well, whether or not you understand women is beside the point. We're talking about a young girl with her whole life ahead of her. Maybe you should think about keeping Jessie. She needs a home, and she needs a family."

"You're right. Jessie does need a home and a family. But all I have to offer is a roof over her head."

"That's not true. You have a lot more to give." She paused, looking into his eyes with absolute and honest sincerity. "You know, Alex, with your grandfather and Jessie, you have the makings of an incredible family—if you want it."

A family? Hadn't he longed for a family most of his life, only to be disappointed over and over again? "I don't think so. I have a tendency to drive people away. No one stays for long."

"I'd stay somewhere forever if I found the right man."

He smiled, wishing for a foolish instant that he were that right man. "I believe you would, Faith. I believe you would." He watched while she slid into the passenger seat. "So is this Ben the right man? The one you care about but don't love?"

He shut the door before she could reply, because he didn't really want to know her answer.

Chapter 12

Ben strode into Faith's Fancies just after twelve noon on Monday. He'd tried phoning Faith several times on Sunday, but her machine had answered him every time. He'd told himself she was probably sleeping, but when she hadn't returned his calls this morning, he'd begun to worry. He'd even driven by her apartment, but she wasn't home. That meant she was at least well enough to go to work and well enough to speak to him.

Nancy greeted him with her usual loving smile. "In the back, honey. She's baking up a storm. We're really busy today."

Ben could see that. The bakery was packed, and there were two other clerks waiting on customers. He slipped around the counter and headed into the kitchen. He found Faith up to her elbows in dough. Her apron was soiled. Her hair spilled out of her hairnet, and her face was flushed from the heat of the ovens.

She started when she saw him. "Ben. What are you doing here?"

"I was worried about you. Didn't you get my messages?"

Yes, she'd gotten all five of them. But by the time she'd left the Carrigans, it had been after ten, and she hadn't wanted to call or explain where she'd been all day.

"I figured you let the machine pick up your calls so you could rest."

Faith didn't want to contradict him, so she concentrated on the pastry dough between her fingers. "I'm really busy today, Ben. Leslie had to leave early, so I'm the sole baker. Was there something you wanted?"

"Yes, as a matter of fact."

His exasperated tone drew her gaze to his face. "What?"

"The wedding, Faith. An answer, if you don't mind."

"You promised not to push."

"I don't think I am pushing."

"Ben, you asked me to marry you completely out of the blue four days ago. Don't you think I could at least have a week to think about it?"

Ben began to pace around the kitchen, looking like a caged tiger. She'd never seen him so worked up. Usually he was the picture of calm. But today his tie was askew and his shirt was coming untucked from his slacks.

"Okay, what's really wrong?" she asked.

He stopped his pacing and stared at her. "I'm afraid the longer you wait, the more chance there is that you'll say no. And you can't say no, Faith. I want to persuade you. I want to wine you and dine you and show you how good it can be between us. But you were sick yesterday, and today you're busy, and who knows what tomorrow will bring. I feel like you're avoiding me."

She looked away, knowing that his words held more than a little truth. But she hadn't figured out her feelings yet. And she didn't want to push him away when a part of her still longed for everything he had promised—kids, a family, a home. "I'm just busy, Ben. Can we do this later?"

"How about tonight?"

Actually, tonight she'd promised Julian she would continue her search for Harry Conrad. In fact, Alex had promised her access to his computer again anytime after five. "I can't. How about tomorrow night? We can have dinner at the Clam House. Say seven o'clock?''

Ben frowned at being put off for yet another day, but eventually nodded. ''All right. I guess if that's the best you can do. Just promise me you'll really think about us, while you're punching and pummeling that dough. Actually, maybe that's not such a good idea if you start thinking I look like that piece of dough.''

Faith laughed. This was the teasing friend she remembered. Ben smiled back at her. ''By the way, my father gave me the watch.''

Faith knew exactly what watch he was talking about. Gary had often talked about his great-grandfather's watch and how he would one day inherit it. Poor Gary.

''At least you'll have it, too, when we get married,'' Ben said. ''So in a way Gary will share in it. Because he brought you into the family.'' He shifted his feet somewhat awkwardly. ''I never expected to get it. It was always meant for Gary, the first son.''

''You deserve it, Ben. Just because Gary was born first didn't make him any more a Porter than you.''

''He always seemed so much more a Porter than me. My father gave it to me because of you, Faith.''

''Don't be silly.''

''It's true. He wants me to pass it down to our son. I'm the only one who can ensure the name goes on, the last Porter.'' He laughed, but his smile didn't reach his eyes. Instead he looked worried. ''I never thought it would feel like such a responsibility.''

''I'm sure you're up to the task. Even if you and I didn't—''

''Don't say it.''

''You would find someone else. You're a great guy.''

''I want you, Faith. It has to be you.'' He walked over and kissed her, taking advantage of her trapped hands to linger over her mouth.

It was a nice kiss, and she tried to give him back what he wanted, but she couldn't help comparing the kiss to the one she'd shared with Alex. It came up sadly wanting.

There wasn't any chemistry between them. Friendship, yes. Caring, yes. But passion, no—at least not yet.

Ben seemed somewhat desperate to ring her bells, and looked disappointed at the end of the kiss. She felt much the same way, wanting to feel something with him, her best friend, the nicest guy in the world, the right man to marry.

"I'll see you tomorrow night, Faith. We'll talk."

"Tomorrow," she promised cheerfully. But when he left the kitchen, she let out a small sigh. Why, oh why, couldn't she be attracted to him? And could she really contemplate a marriage without that essential ingredient?

"Faith, I need you out here," Nancy called from the doorway, looking perturbed about something.

Faith wiped off her hands and went out front. Her clerk, Pam, had her hand around the wrist of a scruffy-looking girl wearing jeans with big holes at the knees and an incredibly small midriff sweater that clung to her flat chest. Faith smiled at the defiant look in her rebellious brown eyes. "Hello, Jessie."

"I told you I knew her," Jessie said to Pam. "And I didn't do anything."

"She stole three madeleines when I was helping another customer," Pam said. "See, the crumbs are still on her mouth."

Jessie quickly wiped her mouth with her free hand, looking as guilty as sin.

"I saw her, too," Nancy said. "I told you that family was nothing but trouble."

Faith took one look at the long line of customers and knew they had to end the scene now before she lost any more business. "Jessie, come with me."

"I think she'll just run if I let her go," Pam said. "Don't you think you should at least call her parents?"

Faith sent Jessie a stern look. "Even if you run, you know I'll find you. I know where you live."

"You do?" Nancy asked in surprise. "How do you know that?"

''Uh—can we talk about this later? We have customers waiting.''

Nancy frowned but obediently tended to the next customer in line. Faith knew she would face lots of questions later.

''Jessie.'' Faith motioned for Jessie to come around the counter and into the kitchen. ''Why did you do it?'' she asked when they were alone.

''I was hungry,'' Jessie said, directing her gaze toward the floor. ''Alex went to work and didn't leave me any food. I don't know where Julian is.''

''We had half a pizza left over from last night, Jess. You could have had that.''

Jessie shrugged. She walked over to the ovens and peered inside. ''These are huge. What are you making?''

''Framboisine—otherwise known as raspberry almond tart.'' Faith walked over to the oven and pushed on the light switch to check the tart. ''When the pastry and macaroons on top turn gold, it will be ready. Then I'll dust the top with toasted almonds and sugar.''

''It smells so good.'' Jessie inhaled a deep breath and let it out with a sigh of satisfaction.

Faith laughed. ''After you've been in here awhile, you'll barely notice the smell.''

''Is the same thing in the other oven?''

''No, that's noisette.''

''How come everything sounds so weird?''

''*Noisette* is a French word. I'm what's known as a French pastry chef; I make desserts and pastries that are French specialties. Of course, I also make American desserts as well.''

''So what is a noisette? It doesn't sound very good.''

''Oh, but it is. It's a meringue layer cake with hazelnut buttercream.''

''Ooh, yum.'' Jessie offered Faith a rare smile. ''Do you think I could taste it?''

''It won't be ready for a few minutes. Say, aren't you supposed to be at school?''

"Alex called around. They said it was spring break."

Well, at least he'd done that much. Although he had a thing or two to learn about keeping a twelve-year-old girl out of trouble while he was at work.

Jessie opened the refrigerator and her eyes widened at the sight of every sugary ingredient known to man. "This is so cool. I would love to work in a bakery."

Faith couldn't help a smile at Jessie's wide-eyed wonder. She remembered the first time she'd seen the kitchen in a bakery. She'd known right away that this was exactly what she wanted to do.

"Can I help you make something?" Jessie asked.

Faith hesitated. She'd gone home the night before determined not to get any further involved with the Carrigans, and here she was again, about to get even closer. But if she didn't let Jessie help, she'd probably wander the streets, and that wouldn't be good for her.

"All right, you can help. But we work here, Jess. No fooling around. I give the orders, and you follow them."

"Does that mean I have to wash dishes?"

Faith laughed. "Eventually, after we've done some baking. With Easter coming up, I have dozens of orders to get ready for the weekend, so an extra pair of hands would be great."

"I don't actually know how to cook."

"Then I'll teach you."

"Really?"

"Yes. First thing you do is wash your hands and put on a hairnet."

"I have to wear a hairnet?"

"Health regulations."

Faith finished the dough she was working on while Jessie washed her hands and slipped on a hairnet. Then she handed the girl an apron and helped her tie it on. A few minutes later they were mixing flour and salt and rolling out dough.

Jessie was all thumbs in the beginning, uncertain about every new move. She knocked herself in the head with a rolling pin and sifted flour all over her jeans. Faith heard more swear words in twenty minutes than she'd heard in the last five years, but she let Jessie work out the kinks without commenting.

Nancy came into the kitchen several times during the next few hours, trying to catch a quiet word with Faith, but aside from stating that Jessie was working off her theft, Faith didn't explain that she felt sorry for the girl and closer to Jessie than Nancy could ever imagine. It wasn't that long ago that Faith had been twelve and all alone.

Finally, at three o'clock, Nancy went home in a huff, after one last pointed comment about getting too involved with *those* Carrigans.

"How come she doesn't like us?" Jessie asked.

"She thinks Julian is a con man."

"If he's a con man, he's not very good. He doesn't have any money, you know. And his clothes . . ." Jessie wrinkled her nose in disgust.

Faith smiled. "Nancy is very protective of the people she cares about. That's all."

"Can we make éclairs now?" Jessie asked, showing an enthusiasm for baking that had taken Faith by surprise. She'd figured Jessie would be bored after an hour, but it had quickly become clear that Jessie was lonely and longed for something to do, someone to talk to, someone to care.

"No, we're going to make a snowflake next—meringue layer cake with white chocolate mousse. We'll start with the mousse. Can you get the heavy cream out of the refrigerator? It should be on the second shelf."

Jessie walked over to the refrigerator and stared at the contents, finally locating the cream. She took it out and set it down on the table. "What else?"

"White chocolate. I'll get that. It's too high for you to reach."

"Can I have a soda, Faith? I saw some in the fridge."

"Sure, help yourself."

While Faith got out the white chocolate, Jessie retrieved two Diet Cokes from the refrigerator and handed one to Faith.

"Thanks, honey."

Jessie blushed at the endearment, as if she wasn't used to hearing kind words. But then, from the little Faith knew about Jessie's background, perhaps kindness was a rarity in Jessie's world.

Jessie took a sip of her Coke. "Did your mom teach you how to cook?"

"I didn't have a mom, Jess." Faith took a drink, letting the cool liquid soothe away the hurt that always accompanied those words. How many times had she said them in her life—to how many teachers, how many neighbors, how many curious kids? She couldn't remember. It shouldn't still hurt, not after all these years, but somchow it did. And Jessie knew. Faith could see the understanding in her eyes, and a bond was born between them.

"What happened to your mom? Did she die?"

Faith leaned against the counter. "I don't know. She gave me up when I was a baby. I never knew who she was or why she left me. The only thing I have of hers is my St. Christopher's medal." Faith pulled her necklace out from under her apron to show Jessie. "I've worn it since I was a kid."

"Weren't you mad at her for leaving you?"

"Of course I was—I mean, yes, sometimes." Faith ran the necklace through her fingers, remembering the time she'd taken off the necklace and flung it into the garbage, angry at her mother for leaving her alone with people who didn't care about her. But later that night, she'd gone out to the trash and retrieved it. Did that make her incredibly weak, stupid, or just sentimental?

"What about your dad?" Jessie asked. "What happened to him?"

"I know nothing about him."

"I don't know anything about my dad either. I mean, Alex thinks it's this guy named Saunders, but Melanie never said he was my dad. The way she talked about Alex—well, I always thought he was my dad. But he says he's not. He doesn't want a kid anyway, so it's cool."

Faith smiled sadly at Jessie's rambling bravado. She knew what it meant to live with uncertainty, to wonder if anyone would ever really love her. Jessie had had her mother for twelve years, but now she was alone, and Faith couldn't stop herself from giving Jessie a hug.

Jessie broke away as soon as possible, her face a study in embarrassment and insecurity. "Why did you do that?"

"Because I miss my mom, and I think maybe you miss yours, too."

"Maybe—a little." Jessie played with the pull top on her Coke can. "Why did she have to die?"

Jessie looked up, pain shimmering in her eyes like raindrops about to fall.

"I don't know. I guess it was her time."

"Yeah, I guess." Jessie didn't say anything for a moment. "Melanie wasn't a very good mom. I mean, she didn't know how to cook or anything. And sometimes I kind of had to take care of her."

So much weight had been placed on such very thin shoulders, Faith thought sadly. "I'm sure your mother loved you very much, Jessie."

"She said she did." Jessie looked at Faith again, her eyes desperately seeking reassurance. "But she lied a lot."

"Mothers don't lie about that. She kept you with her, Jess, all these years. She loved you. Don't ever doubt that."

"It doesn't matter anymore. She's gone."

"It will always matter, even when you're a little old lady with grandkids and great-grandkids."

Jessie made a face. "I'm never getting married."

"Someday I think you'll change your mind."

"How come you're not married?"

"It just hasn't happened yet."

"Do you like Alex?"

Faith had a feeling that was a loaded question. "Yes," she said warily.

"He's not married."

"No, he's not."

"Melanie said he was a good husband. I think she was sorry they got divorced." Jessie paused. "Do you think there's any chance that you and Alex—"

"We should get back to work," Faith said abruptly.

"Okay." Jessie bit down on her bottom lip. "But—do you think Alex will keep me, Faith? I mean, if I'm really good?"

Faith's heart almost broke with the question. "I hope so, Jess. I really do."

"I don't have time, Pete. I need answers, and I need them now." Alex leaned back in his chair, holding the phone to his ear. "There must be some record of Eddie Saunders. He couldn't have vanished into thin air. Hang on a second." Alex put a hand over the phone and leaned over to sign the paper his secretary put in front of him. "Did I just sign my life away?"

"No, but you gave me a big raise," Theresa said.

"Seriously?"

"Hotel contract for the trade-show reception."

"Thank you." Alex adjusted the phone. "Sorry, Pete. Where were we?"

"Nowhere," Pete replied in his rough, gravelly voice. He seemed to end each sentence with a punctuating cough. He was either a smoker or had a hell of a cold.

"I'm not paying you the big bucks to get nowhere."

"It's only been a few days. Can you tell me anything else about this guy?"

"I told you everything I know."

"Do you remember what he looked like?"

Alex started to say no, then stopped, suddenly remembering that brief painful moment in the hospital room all those years ago. He'd decided to give Melanie one more chance. He'd brought roses and was going to make her an offer she couldn't refuse. But he'd found her in Eddie's arms. They'd been kissing but must have sensed his presence, for they'd turned, and he'd seen the face of the man who was stealing his future right out from under him.

"Beady eyes," he said. "Long face, pale skin, blond hair, no muscle. I don't know what she saw in him."

"Apparently she didn't see enough in him to stick around."

Which was another odd thing. Melanie had told him she was in love with Eddie, and that Eddie wanted to marry her. What had happened to stop them? It didn't make sense.

"I'll keep looking," Pete said. "I haven't been stumped yet. If this guy exists, you'll have him."

"When?"

"Now, that's a tougher call."

"I want you working on this twenty-four hours a day. Whatever it takes. Whatever it costs." Alex took a deep breath. "I want Jessie gone by the end of the week."

"Not much of a family man, huh?"

The words cut deep. "No, I'm not. Just find Eddie Saunders, and when you do, don't let him slip away. It's about time Eddie finally became a father."

Alex hung up the phone and stretched. He felt lousy, like a son of a bitch, wanting Jessie gone. But dammit, he was starting to care. He'd felt it last night when Jessie had asked him to say good night, and he'd found himself tucking the covers under her chin and impulsively kissing her on the forehead as a father would do. A father! But he wasn't her father. He wasn't responsible; Eddie was.

Hell, Eddie was probably married by now with a good wife who baked cookies for when the kids came home after school. In fact, he probably had other kids, and Jessie would have brothers and sisters to play with, a mom to tell her all the "girl stuff," and a dad to lay down the rules and get her to clean up her mouth. Jessie would be better off with Eddie. She needed a loving family, a good home. And Alex couldn't give her that.

You have the makings of a great family, Alex, if you'd let yourself care.

Faith's words rang through his head, but he forced them aside. He didn't want a kid or a wife or even a grandfather. Top Flight was all the family he needed.

A brief knock on his door made him turn around. Charlie stuck his head into the office. "Alex, what are you doing? We're waiting for you in the conference room."

"Sorry, I was just finishing up a call." Alex grabbed his memo pad and met Charlie at the door.

"By the way, I have some good news for you," Charlie said.

"I could use some."

"Elijah James has agreed to another meeting."

"Great! When?"

"Tomorrow evening in Chicago."

Alex paused. Tomorrow evening? How could he go to Chicago with Jessie hanging around, and his grandfather and Faith involved in a crazy quest? Who would keep them out of trouble?

Charlie sent him a curious look. "What's wrong? I thought you'd be jumping for joy."

"It's not a good week for me to leave town. I got the kid and my grandfather . . ."

"So your grandfather can baby-sit. This is Elijah James, Alex. I've never seen you put family before business."

That was because he'd never had a family before. The thought shocked him. He didn't have a family now, he reminded himself, just a few people spending a few days with him. They'd be gone with the next good wind, if past experience was anything to go by. And he'd be left with nothing. No, make that Top Flight. He'd be left with Top Flight. "You're right. What was I thinking?"

"I have no idea," Charlie said, a speculative glint still lingering in his eye.

Alex walked out of his office and stopped by Theresa's desk. "I need tickets to Chicago tomorrow morning as early as you can get 'em."

"Already done, boss. You're out of here on the seven A.M. flight."

"Thanks."

"Do you want to get some dinner tonight after the meeting?" Charlie asked, as they walked down the hall to the conference room. "We should go over your new strategy for signing Elijah. I'm assuming you have one."

"Of course I have one." Actually, he didn't, but he'd think of one before tomorrow.

"Good."

"But I'm busy tonight."

Charlie quirked an eyebrow. "A date? I thought you'd sworn off women since you caught Sherry poking a hole in her diaphragm."

Alex's lips tightened at the memory. "It's not a date."

"Then what is it? A business meeting I don't know about?"

"No."

Charlie stopped in the middle of the hallway, forcing Alex to pause. He regarded Alex as if he were a column of figures that was not adding up. "Now I know you must be talking about a woman. You're not usually this evasive. So if not Sherry, who?"

"Faith," Alex said shortly.

"Faith who?"

"Faith—the pastry chef."

Charlie burst out laughing. "A pastry chef? Now, that's a first."

"She's helping my grandfather. I told her she could use the computer here at the office to get on the Internet. Okay? Satisfied?"

"Are you sleeping with her?"

"No." The word exploded from Alex's lips. He would not sleep with Faith. Never ever. Although he had to admit he'd come damn close to making love to her on the couch in his office last night.

"Why not?"

"She's a . . ."

"A what?"

"A damn pastry chef."

"And that makes her bad because . . ."

"Because sweets are very, very bad for you." Alex shook a finger at Charlie. "If you lose control where sweets are concerned, you'll end up in serious trouble."

"But very, very happy," Charlie said. "You know, I've always wanted to date a great cook. Maybe you should give me her number."

"I don't think so." He ignored the smile in Charlie's eyes.

Okay, so he liked Faith. Admitting it did not mean he had to do anything about it. Forewarned was forearmed. And when Faith came to see him later that night, he would make it clear to her that he was only interested in her as a friend of Julian's.

Chapter 13

Faith brought a chaperone; actually she brought two chaperones. Alex should have been relieved. But he couldn't quite shake the disappointment that accompanied Jessie and Julian.

"Good evening, Alex," Julian said, as he walked into the office, leaning a bit more heavily on his cane than usual.

His grandfather wore the same old gray suit he'd had on a few days earlier, the wrinkles in his coat mirroring the wrinkles in his face. Alex couldn't understand why his grandfather continued to wear the same clothes despite the fact that he had brought other items in his suitcase. Alex made a mental note to take Julian shopping as soon as possible. He didn't want Julian's act of the poor, neglected elderly man to gain credence with the state of his clothes.

"Hello, Alex," Faith said, her smile somewhat nervous. "I hope you don't mind that I brought along Julian and Jessie."

"Faith thought I might enjoy seeing the computer in action," Julian explained.

"It doesn't sing songs or tap-dance, Grandfather."

"Is that a fact? Now I am disappointed."

"Couldn't you at least wear some of your other

clothes?" Alex complained. "I'm sure half of my office staff now thinks I'm starving you."

"Ah, Alex. 'It is a melancholy truth that even great men have their poor relations.' "

Alex sighed and caught a look of amusement on Faith's face. "See what I go through."

"Who said that?" Faith asked.

"Charles Dickens, my dear." Julian took a seat on the couch.

"We brought dinner," Jessie said, setting a large brown bag on Alex's desk.

That explained the incredible smell that accompanied them. Usually he associated Faith with cinnamon and sugar, but tonight she smelled like peppers and hot sauce. In fact, she looked hot. While she was distracted with unloading the food, Alex had a chance to take a good look at her—another mistake. She wore a short black knit dress as plain and simple as it was sexy. It showed off her breasts and her legs—her long, long legs. Alex swallowed hard.

"Alex, do you want a burrito or a hot tamale?" Jessie asked impatiently.

"What?" Alex asked, suddenly realizing he was still staring at Faith.

"A burrito—"

"That's fine." Alex took the wrapper from her hand. He hesitated. "Unless you want it," he said to Faith.

"I like tamales."

"Faith likes everything hot," Jessie added. "She insisted on getting that sauce with the jalapeños in it."

Alex smiled at Faith as Jessie chattered on about something.

God, Faith was gorgeous. He couldn't take his eyes off of her. She moved so gracefully, leaning over the desk to set up the picnic dinner, gently scolding Jessie for swearing. Her glorious red hair brushed the tops of her breasts, swinging in such a tantalizing way, he wanted to reach out and catch a strand between his fingers and brush it against . . .

Faith cleared her throat and he wondered if she could read his thoughts—if that explained the warm flush of red that colored her cheeks. "Alex, would you like a soft drink?"

"Sure, thanks." He took the can of Coke out of her hand and popped the top. Maybe a drink would cool him off.

Theresa knocked on the half-open door, then walked into the room with her purse in hand. "Looks like a party." She sent Alex a curious look. "And no one invited me."

"It was a surprise party," Alex replied.

"I'll bet. Aren't you going to introduce me?"

Alex didn't appear to have a choice. "My grandfather, Julian Carrigan."

"Charmed." Julian stood up and took Theresa's hand in his. He brought it to his lips. " 'She walks in beauty like the night, of cloudless climes and starry skies; And all that's best of dark and bright meet in her aspect and her eyes.' "

"Oh, wow," Theresa said as Julian kissed her hand. "That is incredibly beautiful."

"He stole it from Lord Byron," Alex said, taking a bite of his burrito.

"I don't care. No one ever said such a thing to me." She frowned at Alex. "How come you don't talk to me like that?"

Alex rolled his eyes. He waved his hand toward Jessie. "Theresa, meet Jessie. She's, uh—staying with me for a while."

"Lucky her," Theresa said, sending Jessie a broad smile, which quickly became more curious as she turned to Faith.

Alex could almost read his secretary's mind. He never brought women to the office, never took them to company socials, never let them host a cocktail party in his apartment, never mind a taco party in his office. His private life had always been kept separate from his business life, until tonight.

"Faith Christopher," he said at Theresa's pointed look.

"Nice to meet you," Faith said, shaking Theresa's hand.

"Likewise," Theresa said. "Have you known Alex long?"

"Not really, no."

"Faith owns a bakery down the street from me."

"That sounds like a fun job."

Faith smiled. "It has its moments."

"I'd probably turn into a big lump of dough if I worked in a bakery. I have quite the sweet tooth. So does Alex, but he's so much more controlled about it than I am." Theresa sent Alex a sly look. "At least he used to be."

"I still am," Alex said.

"Actually, after about the first week of gorging myself in cooking class, I learned to enjoy the smell of cooking as much as the taste," Faith explained. "It's the only thing that saves me. Would you like something to eat, Theresa? We have plenty." She waved her hand toward the spread on Alex's desk.

"No, thanks. With any luck, my husband has dinner waiting for me at home. Have fun, but not too much fun. Don't forget you have an early flight, boss." Theresa waved and left the office.

Silence followed her exit. Alex took another bite of his burrito, wishing he'd had the chance to break the news. He hadn't thought of how his trip would affect Jessie or Julian.

"You're leaving?" Faith asked, a look of surprise on her face.

Did she care? He couldn't help the shimmer of pleasure that ran down his spine. "I have to go to Chicago tomorrow."

"Oh."

"Business. It can't be avoided." He glanced at Jessie, who dropped her gaze to her taco. Then he looked over at Julian, who stared back at him with displeasure etched in his blue eyes.

"Of course," Julian said. "You must attend to your business. What could be more important than that?"

Alex stiffened at the implied criticism. "It's an important meeting, Grandfather." He tossed his burrito down on the desk. He'd suddenly lost his appetite.

"I'm sure it is. What about Jessie? Who's going to watch her? Who's going to make sure she gets something to eat and doesn't wander the streets? Or have you arranged for a baby-sitter?"

"I haven't had a chance." Alex looked at Faith, hoping to find an ally, but she appeared to be as annoyed as his grandfather. "I just found out about the meeting a few hours ago. Elijah James is going to give me one last chance to sell him on my shoes. I can't say no."

"You have other responsibilities," Julian said, "like your daughter."

"She's not my daughter. She's . . ." Alex's voice trailed off as Jessie jumped to her feet, so abruptly she knocked her taco off the desk.

"Oh, shit," she said, then ran out of the room without bothering to pick up the mess.

"Why do you have to hurt her like that?" Faith demanded, her green eyes flashing. "She's just a little girl. It's not her fault you don't want her. She hasn't done anything to deserve your attitude."

"My attitude? You don't know anything about my attitude." Alex stood up and planted his hands on his hips, as annoyed with her as she was with him.

"It doesn't take a rocket scientist to figure out you're scared to death of loving someone."

"I am not scared of love. But she's not mine."

"Then why did you take her at all? Why not just let her go to foster care if you don't give a damn about her?"

"I don't know. Maybe that's what I should have done.

But I didn't. Now I have to work, and I need a little help."

"You need more than a little help," Faith muttered, as she cleaned up Jessie's mess.

"What does that mean?"

"It means you're as selfish as they come, thinking only about yourself. Every time you deny that you're her father, you break a little bit more of her heart."

"But I'm not her father. And it's pointless to pretend that I am. Because any day now Eddie Saunders, her real father, is going to come back and claim her. It's better if she doesn't get attached to me."

"Better for who? For you or for Jessie?"

Faith threw the remains of Jessie's food into the trash and walked out of the room.

"Oh, hell." Alex sat down in his chair with a weary sigh. It had been a long day, and it was getting longer by the minute.

Julian walked over and patted him somewhat awkwardly on the shoulder. The Carrigans had never been affectionate, and it had been a long time since Alex had felt a fatherly hand on his back.

"It's all right, Alex."

"I screwed up." He hadn't needed Faith or his grandfather to tell him that. He'd seen the damage on Jessie's sweet face.

"Screwing up appears to be a family trait. I'll watch Jessie for you tomorrow. I shouldn't have said anything—I know your business is important to you."

"Thank you for acknowledging that fact."

Julian smiled somewhat sadly. "Faith was right about one thing. You are scared of love."

"Everyone I love has left. What's the point? Love is a waste of time. I prefer to invest in reality, in business."

"Does your business keep you warm at night?"

Alex avoided Julian's pressing gaze. "It keeps me sane at night. When I want to go a little crazy, I find a nice woman who wants to have some fun—for a night."

"Just one night? I suppose you leave before the sunrise, too."

"No one brings up the word *commitment* in the dark, but in the daylight, it's surprising how fast it springs to mind."

"You're far more cynical than I imagined, Alex."

"Am I?" Alex asked, meeting his grandfather's eye. "I bet you've run a few times in your life."

"Not like you." Julian paused. "Have you never cared about anyone enough to want to spend the night? Have you never loved to the depth and breadth and height your soul can reach?"

"No," Alex said shortly. "I don't think that kind of love exists. I've never seen it. You never showed it to me, not even with grandmother. You left her for the first short skirt that walked by. And my father goes through women as fast as he changes channels. A little sex, a few laughs. That's all I want from a relationship."

"And all you give."

"That's right."

"I feel sorry for you."

"And I feel sorry for you," Alex said strongly, as he stood up. "You're chasing after a dream that doesn't exist. You want to remember this woman, Suzannah, as being the great love of your life. But you didn't work very hard at finding her or at keeping her in the first place. Now, with the rose-colored glasses you've trained on the past, you'd like to believe she's pining away for you somewhere, that she remembers you with the same passion. The truth is, she probably married someone else and lived happily ever after without you."

Julian sent him a steady look. "That may be, but I have faith." He smiled. "I don't mean Faith Christopher. I mean faith in love and hope and dreams."

"Fine, live in a dreamworld. It's no business of mine. Just don't expect me to live there with you. Now, if you'll excuse me, I'm going to the conference room, where I can work in peace and quiet." Alex picked up a stack of contracts he wanted to review and walked to the door.

"You'll never have peace," Julian called after him. "Not until we break this curse."

"Then break the damn curse so I can get on with my life."

Alex closed the door behind him and leaned against it. Jessie and Faith were nowhere in sight, which was a relief. He needed a moment to get his head together. He closed his eyes and took a few deep breaths, wondering why his life was suddenly in such turmoil. No one had ever wanted to have him in their lives. Now everywhere he turned, someone wanted a piece of him. He'd shut off emotion a long time ago. He didn't know how to turn it back on.

Maybe Faith was right. Maybe he was scared of love. Because he knew he couldn't do it. He didn't know how to do it. One woman for all time? He smiled to himself. All time? Who was he kidding? No one stuck around that long.

Although . . . he could almost believe it of Faith. Maybe because she still wanted what he'd given up on—a home, a family, children. She'd never had it, none of it. But he had had it and seen it ripped away. Why go down that road again? He had a nice home, a successful business, enough money, a few friends . . . What more could he ask for?

A wife? A daughter? He tried to quiet the tiny voice inside his head that told him he was lying. He did want a family. He wanted it so bad it hurt.

"Alex?"

He opened his eyes. The uncertain voice belonged to Jessie. She stood next to a desk, her hair falling out of its clip, her eyes red. There were no smart words coming from her mouth, no defiant muttering. She just looked lonely and sad. And he felt like he should be shot, whipped, knocked against a wall. No punishment would be too great for what he'd done to a little kid. He should have known better. Hadn't he suffered just such cruel, uncaring words from people who had no time for him?

"I can go," Jessie said.

The knife went deeper, and he took a deep breath. "Go where?"

"Wherever. I'm not your kid. You shouldn't have to keep me."

"Oh, Jess." Alex ran a hand through his hair and shook his head. "I'm sorry. It's not your fault. None of this is your fault."

Jessie looked surprised at his change in attitude. "You're sorry?"

"Yes." He paused, debating just how much he wanted to tell her, but she had a right to know the truth. "I was angry when your mom told me I wasn't your dad. She'd lied to me for almost a year. It wasn't just that I'd taken care of her, it's that I'd come to think of you as being mine, and when she told me you weren't, when your real dad showed up at the hospital, it hurt."

Jessie stared back at him, wide-eyed. "You wanted to be my dad then?"

"More than anything."

Silence fell between them. Jessie ran her finger along the edge of the desk. Finally, she looked at him. "Melanie talked about you all the time. She told me about your first date at the drive-in."

"She told you that, huh?"

"And how you went to the prom together. She said you were someone she could always depend on. She needed somebody like that."

Alex saw a wealth of wisdom in Jessie's young eyes. She probably knew more about life now than Melanie ever had.

"Melanie wasn't very good at—at a lot of things," Jessie added. "I used to have to remind her to buy milk and stuff. She was always losing things, her money, her keys."

"I remember. I gave her a key chain once—it had a

license plate with her name on it—so big I didn't think she could lose it.''

Jessie offered him a tentative smile. ''She probably did.''

''Yeah, probably.''

''Melanie said you were good at rescuing people. I think that's why she told the lawyer about you.''

''Rescuing people? I wonder why she said that.''

''Because you married her when she was having me. She got pregnant two years ago, but she had to have an abortion because the guy didn't want it. Maybe she would have done the same thing if you hadn't married her. Maybe that would have been better. I was just a mistake.''

Alex's fists tightened in a sudden, unexplainable fury. ''Don't ever say that, Jessie. You are a beautiful person, not somebody's mistake. When Melanie found out she was pregnant, she was scared, but she wanted you more than anything. And so did I.''

''Really?'' Her voice blossomed with hope.

''Really. Want to know a secret?''

''Yes.''

''I used to talk to you when you were in Melanie's stomach. She'd be snoring away,'' he said, drawing a grin from Jessie. ''But I'd lean over and whisper all sorts of things to you. I used to tell you the important stuff, like the baseball stats.''

''I like baseball,'' Jessie said with a shy smile.

''So do I. We should go to a game sometime.''

Her smile faded, and Jessie looked uncertain. ''There aren't any games for a few more weeks. I won't be here then.''

''Maybe you can come back for a visit, after we find your father.'' For some reason the thought didn't please him as much as it had earlier. ''Until then, you're not going anywhere. I said I'd take care of you, and I will.''

''You don't have to.''

"I want to, Jess. I do. If you can put up with me and my grandfather."

"I guess," she said, back to her usual unconcerned shrug that covered up so much.

"But I have to go to Chicago tomorrow. You won't run away while I'm gone, will you? Promise me?"

"I promise."

He tipped his head toward his office. "You better get some dinner, before it's all gone."

"I'm not really hungry. I ate a lot at Faith's today."

His eyes narrowed. "What did you say?"

"I ate a lot at Faith's."

"What were you doing there?"

Jessie's eyes filled with guilt. "Uh, baking."

"Faith invited you?"

"Uh, sure."

"She did? Jessie?"

Jessie ducked into the office before he could question her further. Deciding to let well enough alone with his grandfather and with Jessie, he headed toward the reception area and caught sight of Faith trying on a pair of Top Flight Athletic Shoes for women. He smiled as he walked over to her.

"How do they feel?"

"Oh," She looked up, startled. "Fine. Sorry. I heard you and Jess talking, and I didn't want to interrupt."

"I apologized to Jess. I didn't mean to hurt her, Faith."

"I know."

Alex dropped down to his knees in front of her. "You have to lace them up to get the proper fit. May I?"

"You don't have to do that."

He wrapped a hand around her warm ankle. "I want to."

Faith licked her lips as the heat of his hand raced up her leg and sent tingles throughout her body. She tried to pull her dress down over her thighs, but it seemed to be stuck.

"Don't worry, Faith. I can't see—much."

His blue eyes were positively wicked, and his fingers seemed to be far busier caressing her ankle than tying laces.

"Alex—the shoe," she reminded him.

"Oh, sorry." He laced up her shoe and leaned back. "Stand up and try them out."

Faith felt a little foolish wearing tennis shoes with her short black dress, but she had to admit they felt incredibly comfortable. "Wow, these are nice," she said, enjoying the thick padding under her feet. "I should wear them at work."

"You should," Alex agreed, as he stood up. "In fact, before you leave, we can pick out a few more pairs for you. Those are cross-trainers, designed for pretty much anything, but we also have running shoes, basketball shoes, soccer shoes. Whatever you like to play, we've got a shoe for it."

"Whatever I like to play?" Faith challenged, unable to resist teasing him. "Are you sure you have a shoe for that?"

He answered her with a grin. "Oh, definitely. In fact, I'd be happy to help you try them out."

"Do you always give your customers such personal service?"

He took a step closer. "Only the special ones."

"Am I special?"

His eyes darkened. "Unfortunately, yes."

"Why, Alex?" She wasn't teasing anymore. She really wanted to know.

He put his hands on her shoulders and lowered his head. She thought he was going to kiss her, but his lips touched the corner of her ear, and he whispered, "You were right about me, Faith. I'm afraid to love someone like you."

Love? She hadn't been talking about him loving her. Although she had to admit, right now the idea had some merit.

Alex's lips touched her neck, his hair brushed her

cheek. She closed her eyes and breathed in the warm male scent of him. She could lose her mind right here, in his arms, and not even care. His mouth teased her collarbone, a glancing, tantalizing caress that left her wanting so much more.

Finally Alex lifted his head, taking the warmth with him. Faith blinked her eyes open to find him watching her, his expression no longer mischievous but serious, somber, questioning.

"Faith? It's your call."

She stared at him, remembering his promise not to kiss her again, and her vow not to ask him.

"Oh, hell," she said, catching his face in her hands. She pulled him to her and planted her mouth on his, teasing, tasting, taking until there was no doubt she had completely lost her mind—and just possibly her heart.

Chapter 14

Alex pulled away a few minutes later. He looked deep into her eyes. "Faith?"

"What?"

"I don't think you should kiss me again."

"Why not?"

"Because I want to take you to bed."

Her breath caught in her chest. "You—you do?"

"Now."

"Jessie. Your grandfather . . ."

"I don't think they should go with us." He smiled, then kissed her on the cheek, trailing his lips across her face to the corner of her ear.

"Alex, stop."

"Why?"

"I'm supposed to be searching the computer tonight."

"I'd rather you were searching me."

She took a step away from him, smoothing out her hair. "I'm going to go back to your office before anyone comes out here and gets the wrong idea."

"And what idea would that be? That you like me? That I like you? That we want each other?"

"It's not as simple as all that."

"Sex is pretty simple."

"Not to a woman."

"You're right. Sex would never be simple with a

woman like you.'' Alex ran a finger down the side of her cheek. ''You are so soft. So incredibly soft.''

Goose bumps ran down her arms, but she tried to ignore them and focus on what was important, what needed to be said. ''I don't just sleep with someone for the heck of it.''

Alex slowly smiled. ''No kidding.''

''Okay, you think you know me pretty well, but you don't. For a second there, I was tempted.''

''More than a second, Faith, and I think if we're being honest, you're still tempted. So am I.'' His eyes met hers. ''Because it hasn't felt this good in a long time—maybe it's never felt this good. Maybe we should explore just how good it's going to get.''

''And maybe we should let our imaginations fill in the rest. It might be safer.''

''But not as much fun.''

She ducked away from him as he attempted to kiss her again. ''Time to work, Alex. I need to help Julian find Suzannah, and you have to prepare for your trip. We can't forget our priorities.''

''I think my priorities may have changed.''

''Faith?'' Jessie's voice rang through the empty offices. ''Where are you? We can't make the Internet work.''

Faith glanced over her shoulder, thankful that Jessie hadn't stumbled on to them a few moments earlier. The child was confused enough as it was. ''I'm coming,'' she called. ''I better go,'' she said to Alex.

''So go.'' He held up his hands. ''Am I stopping you?''

Not physically, but emotionally . . . Faith didn't want to leave him. She wanted time, lots and lots of time, to explore his body, his mind, his feelings. She smiled at that thought—as if the very guarded Alex would ever share his feelings with her. He probably didn't even admit to himself that he had feelings.

''What's so funny?'' Alex asked warily.

"Nothing." She sat down on the chair and slipped off the tennis shoes.

"You can keep them, Faith. A token of my affection."

She put her heels on and stood up. "And your grandfather doesn't think you're romantic. He doesn't know you at all."

"He doesn't know me, and neither do you," Alex said, as she walked away from him. "One kiss doesn't make you an expert."

"You'd be surprised, Alex." Faith couldn't help the small surge of pleasure that ran through her as she walked away. Her kiss had never scared a man before. It was a good feeling. Never mind that Alex's kiss had absolutely terrified her. She'd worry about that later; right now she'd just enjoy her brief, sweet moment of power.

An hour later, Faith's attention was focused solely on the machine in front of her. Since discovering that a marriage took place between Harry Conrad and Suzannah Brock some fifty years ago, Faith had become confident that they would find more leads on the two people, and they had, seventeen listings for a Harry Conrad in several different states, and fourteen listings for an S. Conrad or Suzannah Conrad or Susan Conrad in several other states. It would take forever to call each number.

"There has to be some other way," Faith said restlessly, while Jessie stood up and stretched, bored by the relentless whirring of the computer. Even Julian had lost some of his eagerness.

"Perhaps this is impossible," Julian said. "I don't know what else we should do."

"Give it up," Jessie advised. "Melanie always said if a person don't want to be found, she can't be found."

Faith wondered just why Melanie had chosen to impart that piece of advice to her daughter. Had they been on the run, evading bill collectors or some lunatic boyfriend? She could only imagine what Jessie must have seen living on the streets.

"Why wouldn't Suzannah want to be found?" Julian asked wearily. "Why hide from me? Especially if she married someone else, someone who was a good man, a minister?"

"A minister, of course," Faith said, snapping her fingers. "I am so stupid. You said Suzannah was a Baptist, which means Harry Conrad must have worked at the Baptist church in Pasadena, because it would make sense that they would get married in his church."

Julian nodded, a light of hope coming into his eyes. "Yes, of course."

Faith put her fingers to work on the computer and within a few minutes had the listings for three Baptist churches in Pasadena. "What do you think? Shall we make some calls?"

Julian smiled. "We shall. You are truly magnificent, my dear."

Faith laughed. "Don't thank me yet." She checked her watch. "It's seven-thirty. I'm not sure we'll be able to reach anyone."

"Let's try," Julian said impatiently. "I don't think ministers hold regular office hours, do they?"

Faith printed out the page of phone numbers. "Do you want to do the honors?"

Julian immediately shook his head. "I can't. No. I need time. What if Suzannah were to answer? What would I say?"

"Okay, I'll do it." Faith picked up the sheet and dialed the first number. She reached a recording with the suggestion that unless this was an emergency, she should call back in the morning. The same thing happened with the second number. But the third time, they struck gold.

"I'm trying to find a man named Harry Conrad, who might have been the minister of your church a long time ago," Faith said after exchanging a brief hello with the woman who had answered the phone.

"Harry Conrad," the woman mused. "The name sounds familiar. But my husband is out, and we've only been here for three years. I don't know all the names of the previous ministers. I'm sorry."

"Wait. Would you mind if I called back and spoke to your husband?"

"Why do you want to find this man?"

"It's a long story, but I have a friend, an elderly gentleman . . ." Julian frowned at her description, but she ignored him. "He's trying to find Harry because—because he was a good friend of Harry's wife, Suzannah. I know it's been something like fifty years, but it's very important that he locate Mr. Conrad."

"It's such a long time, dear. But hold on a second."

Faith put her hand over the phone. "She's checking something."

"I am not elderly," Julian said grumpily.

"It makes a better story. You should be able to relate to that."

Finally the woman came back on the line. "I have this book," she said. "It's about the history of our church, and yes, I did find the name of Harry Conrad. He was the minister here from 1945 to 1963."

"That's wonderful. Can you tell me any more about him? Maybe where he went after 1963?"

"It says that Reverend Conrad transferred to the First Baptist Church in Monterey, California. I'm sorry, that's all it says."

"Thank you. That's really a help. Would you mind taking my number? If your husband knows anything more about Harry Conrad or his wife, Suzannah, I'd really appreciate a call."

"I don't think my husband will know any more, but I'll certainly call you if he does."

Faith repeated her number and hung up the phone. "We're one step closer. Now we just have to call the church in Monterey. Jessie, would you type in 'First Baptist Church in Monterey, California,' and see if we can find a phone number?"

While Jessie got to work, Faith stood up and stretched. She felt tired but exuberant.

"Monterey is very close, isn't it?" Julian asked.

"About an hour and a half south. But it was 1963, Julian. That's still a long time ago, and he would be your age, probably retired."

"We'll find him, and we'll find Suzannah," Julian said confidently. "I was destined to come here by something stronger than just my wish to see Alex. Meeting you . . . now this. I feel as if we are mere players in a game."

"I just hope we win this game."

"I got it," Jessie said, hitting the print button.

"Got what?" Alex asked as he returned to the office. He set his files on the desk and sent Faith an expectant look.

"Another lead," Faith replied.

He arched an eyebrow. "No kidding. That's great. What did you find out?"

"We found the church that Harry Conrad may have worked at in 1963."

"That's it?"

"This is good, Alex."

"If you say so. It sounds like a long shot. Nineteen sixty-three? That's as close as you've come?"

"It's better than 1948. We've moved seventeen years in one night. I consider that a success."

Alex's smile spread slowly across his face. "I'm beginning to think you were named Faith for a very good reason."

"Are you going to call the church now?" Jessie asked.

"Sure. Why not?" Faith reached for the phone, feeling invincible. Her bubble of pleasure was popped by the sound of a recording, asking that she call back during business hours. "We'll have to try tomorrow."

"Tomorrow?" Both Jessie and Julian echoed the word at the same time, disappointment etched in their faces.

"Sorry, but tomorrow isn't that far away. With any luck, we'll find Harry still working in Monterey."

"I almost wish I was going to be here," Alex said slowly. "Not that you'd need me for anything." He busied himself with some papers on his desk, but Faith had the distinct feeling he was waiting for someone to contradict him, only no one did.

"Alex—" She started, then stopped, not sure what to say. He'd made it clear he thought they were on a wild-goose chase. Maybe she was reading him wrong, thinking he cared, when he didn't.

"What?"

She wished he weren't quite so good at hiding his feelings. His expression was completely unreadable. She didn't know if he was interested, annoyed, or bored. "Do you want to help us?" she asked.

"What would I do?"

"I don't know. I'm sure your ideas are as good as mine."

"I doubt it. But thanks for the offer."

"I'm going to work at Faith's bakery tomorrow," Jessie said. "She's going to teach me how to make chocolate truffles."

"Is that all right with you?" Alex asked. "I don't want Jessie to bother you while you're working."

"It's fine. With Easter coming, I could use an extra pair of hands."

"Easter. I'd forgotten about that."

"Well, it's not too late to color your eggs."

"Nobody does that anymore."

Faith looked at him in surprise. "Everybody does that, Alex. You mean you don't?"

"No. And I can't believe you do." He looked at her as if she'd just said she was an alien.

"It's a tradition, Alex." As soon as she said the word, she realized it was a Porter tradition—not a Carrigan tradition. It was a tradition she should share with Nancy, Chuck, Ben, and Kim, not Alex, Julian, or Jessie. They weren't her family. And Easter was a family affair. Everyone knew that.

"I'd like to color eggs," Jessie said. "Can we, Alex?"

"I don't know how," he admitted somewhat sheepishly. "What do you do?"

"Faith can show us, can't you, Faith?"

Faith swallowed hard, suddenly torn. What was she doing spending so much time with the Carrigans when she should be with the Porters? She had a marriage proposal to consider, among other things. Still, the look on Jessie's face was difficult to resist.

The Porters would have their Easter traditions, even without her, but the Carrigans—they needed someone to lead the way. It was the least she could do for a lonely girl, a sad old man, and a cynical guy who needed a little holiday spirit.

"I could show you," she agreed. "Maybe when Alex gets back from his trip. Because everyone should color an egg at least once in their life. Now, let's clean up, Jessie, so we can go home. I have to be up early tomorrow."

Alex stepped up to Faith and whispered in her ear. "I can think of one other thing everyone should experience at least once in their life. Will you let me show you?"

"No. I'm practically engaged."

He stepped back with a disbelieving smile. "I'd forgotten."

"Yeah, me, too," Faith whispered as he turned away. "Me, too."

Faith didn't have much time to think about either Alex or Ben on Tuesday. Her day began at five o'clock in the morning and it was almost ten before she took five minutes for a cup of coffee. Jessie showed up at eleven, and Faith put her to work making Easter Bunny cookies. Lunchtime came and went with Jessie running down the street to the deli and bringing back two enormous poor boy sandwiches. By three o'clock Jessie declared herself off duty and bailed out in the middle of an ornery bread dough.

Faith waved good-bye, pleased that Jessie had lasted as long as she had. A little hard work was good for a girl. And if the truth be told, Faith had really enjoyed Jessie's company. She had a way of looking at life without all the bullshit. Not that Jessie couldn't fling it on occasion. Faith knew she would have to teach Jessie some manners before she let her wait on the customers. Otherwise, she'd probably flip someone off if they asked for the wrong type of croissant.

Faith smiled and wrestled the dough into a bread pan, then slid it in the oven. She washed her hands in the large sink, sent the pile of dirty pans an evil eye, and decided she needed a break from cooking and the hot kitchen.

When she went out to the front, she found a few people sitting at tables. Pam was helping a customer and Nancy was wrapping up a special order to be picked up later that day.

"How's it going?" Faith asked, stopping by Nancy.

"Better now," Nancy said. "What a day. If I never see a bunny cookie again, it will be too soon."

Faith laughed. "Holidays are good for business. Did Mrs. Sullivan pick up her cake yet? She wanted me to add in a dozen cinnamon rolls. Apparently her son returned from college with a girlfriend and a nose ring. She's not sure which she's more upset about."

"That would be a difficult choice. I never had to worry about my boys doing anything crazy like piercing their nose. Gary and Ben were always so stable, so reliable. Good boys. Of course, Ben isn't married—yet." Nancy sent Faith a pointed look.

Faith sighed. "Was that supposed to be subtle?"

"No." Nancy's brows tightened with worry. "I'm worried, Faith. Ben stopped by last night, and he seems so unsettled, so unsure of himself. I think you need to give him an answer."

"I haven't had time to think, Nancy."

"You've had time to baby-sit that Carrigan girl."

"Jessie was helping me. I feel sorry for her. She's all

alone. Her mother died a few weeks ago, and this is her first holiday on her own."

"She has other family—that man and his grandfather."

Faith sent Nancy a curious look, not sure where the intense irritation was coming from. "Why do you dislike them so much?"

Nancy patted a hand to her hair, looking uncomfortable by Faith's direct question. "I don't dislike them. I don't know them. But I think they're trouble. The girl's mouth ought to be washed out with soap. And her grandfather looks like he sleeps in his clothes. That other man, well, he was awfully rude to you the day he was in, and they seem to be taking up so much of your time. There, now, I've said it. You know I don't like to speak ill of people, especially when they're not around, but honestly, you seem to have taken these people under your wing, like they're a bunch of lost puppies, while poor Ben is left hanging. I don't think it's fair."

Faith didn't know what to say. Nancy had never criticized her behavior so openly, and it stung. "I'm sorry," she said, not sure exactly what she was apologizing for, but obviously she needed to say something. "I don't mean to hurt Ben or to leave him hanging, but you know he took me by surprise."

Nancy threw up her hands in bewilderment. "For heaven's sake, Faith. You've known Ben for more than two years. It's plain to everyone he adores you. He probably had a crush on you when Gary was alive, but was afraid to say something. That's why he hasn't dated much these past few years. He was pining for you."

Pining for her? Surely Ben would have said something in the past two years if he'd truly loved her for that long. He'd always seemed content with friendship. No, it didn't make sense. "I don't think so, Nancy."

"Well, you wouldn't know. You were so wrapped up in grief when Gary died."

"That's true, but a lot of time has passed since then."

"Exactly, which is why I can't understand your attitude. Ben has been so attentive to you, so patient, so caring. Have you just been stringing him along?"

"I've been his friend, and he's been mine. I honestly never thought of him in any other way, until he proposed the other night."

"He said you kissed him. Of course he would think you were interested if you kissed him."

Faith flushed at the accusation. Nancy's reading of their first kiss made her feel like the biggest tease in the world. "I think Ben understands how I feel. It's complicated."

Nancy's lips softened and her eyes filled with compassion, although she still seemed somewhat desperate. "I understand, too, Faith. I know you loved Gary more than life. We all did. But he would want you to be happy with Ben. And we've been waiting so long for you to be part of our family. This was meant to be." Nancy took one of Faith's hands and squeezed it tightly. "We love you so much, dear."

"You know how much that means to me. Thank you."

"You've been good for us, too. If we hadn't had you when Gary died, I don't know what we would have done."

Faith smiled, feeling tears gather in the corners of her eyes. "And if I hadn't had you, I would have been lost."

"I want you to be my daughter, Faith. If I'm pressuring you, I'm sorry, I just want it so much that it's driving me a little crazy." She let out a breath. "And I'm probably driving you crazy. So I'll stop. I won't say anything else. Ben would be furious if he knew I'd said this much." She glanced at the clock. "It's slowed down, so I think I'll go. I want to pick up a few things for Easter brunch. Did I tell you that Chuck is considering wearing an Easter Bunny suit for the kids as long as I put enough champagne in his mimosas?"

"Now, that's a sight I can't wait to see."

"Well, I'll see you tomorrow. Don't work too hard.

You know, you're welcome to come to dinner tonight if you like. I'm sure you don't feel like cooking after baking all day."

"I can't. I'm meeting Ben."

Nancy smiled broadly. "I'm so glad. I'll see you later then. Good-bye, Pam." She waved her hand in Pam's direction and hurried out of the store.

Pam sauntered over to Faith. A slender brunette with three little kids and a no-good ex-husband, Pam was a single mother and the bakery's resident cynic. She was also the bakery's biggest talker. In fact, she sometimes acted more like a bartender than a bakery clerk, listening to her customers' problems and offering advice to the lovelorn whether it was requested or not.

"Mrs. P. sure doesn't like Jessie," Pam said, referring to Nancy. "She was muttering up a blue streak all day about you getting involved with people better left alone. What did that girl do to her anyway?"

"Nothing," Faith replied, as she pulled out an empty tray and set it on the counter. "Nancy is completely overreacting."

"She said some guy was in here giving you a hard time last Friday. I miss all the good stuff."

Faith rolled her eyes. "It was no big deal, a little family fight." Faith grabbed a sponge and wiped off the counter. She didn't particularly want to discuss the Carrigans with Pam.

"So is Mrs. P. getting on your nerves yet about this wedding? And by the way, why didn't you tell me Ben Porter asked you to marry him?"

"I haven't had a chance. And no, Nancy is not getting on my nerves. She's just worried about her son. I can't fault her for that."

Pam frowned as she leaned back against the counter and crossed her arms in front of her chest. "Don't you think it's a little odd, her wanting you to marry Ben after you were with Gary? I mean, it's kind of weird."

"Ben and Gary are totally different people."

"They were brothers. It seems to me that if they're that different, you wouldn't be loving both of them the same. Besides that, I've had a mother-in-law, and you haven't, so I've got experience, and let me tell you, if you think Mrs. P. is in your life now, just wait until you marry Ben."

"I like Nancy—a lot," Faith said defensively. "She's always been wonderful to me, treated me like a daughter."

"I know all that. But let's talk turkey for a second. It seems to me Mrs. P. is afraid to let you go. She's told me a few times that you're her last link to Gary. That sometimes she can almost see Gary in your eyes, because he loved you so much."

Pam waited for a reply, but Faith was too moved by her words to answer. Why hadn't she seen it before? Nancy was trying desperately to hang on to her because of Gary. That was why Nancy was so insistent on Faith marrying Ben and so worried that it might not happen. It probably also explained why she didn't like the Carrigans invading Faith's life.

"She feels threatened," Faith murmured aloud, catching Pam's eye. "You're right. I'm just like the rest of Gary's belongings. She won't change anything in his room. She won't throw away his clothes or get rid of his books or his trophies, because she wants to hang on to Gary's memory. Why didn't I see it before?"

"You were busy making bunny cookies."

Faith made a face. "And Ben—she probably pressured him to marry me. He must think it's his duty or something. What a mess."

"Well, Ben might be in love with you. I don't know that he's not." Pam paused, sending Faith a steady look. "But I don't think you're in love with him. Are you?"

Faith shook her head. "No, but—"

"There are no *buts* where marriage is concerned, Faith. You can't marry him if you don't love him. Marriage is hard enough when the two people actually love each other. You start out with anything less, and it's going to be an uphill battle."

Faith knew Pam was right, that she was only saying out loud what Faith had been unable to voice. Except for one thing. Faith glanced over her shoulder. There was no one left in the bakery, so she felt free to confide in Pam. "I want to have babies, Pam. I could do that with Ben. He'd make a great father. He loves kids. You should see him with the groups that come through the gallery. He's so patient and kind, so attuned to their needs."

"And what will you tell your kids when they ask you why you don't love their daddy?"

"But I do love him—maybe not in a hot and sweaty, passionate sort of way, but I care about him. I would like being part of the Porter family. I've never—well, you know—had a family. I could do worse."

Pam's gaze didn't waver. "Maybe you can have that hot and sweaty thing with some other guy who also loves kids and has a great family. You're not that old, Faith. Why settle now? Why be rushed into making a decision?"

"I'm not being rushed."

"Oh, of course you are. If Nancy had her way, you'd be getting married this Saturday."

"Well, she's not getting her way. If I marry Ben, I'll do it right. I'll have the wedding I want."

Pam let out a sigh. "Well, at least you said *if*. I was beginning to wonder if you were completely crazy. Now tell me something else. Why are you really hanging around with Jessie?"

"I like her. She's a good kid and she's all alone."

"And her father—the one who caused such a scene, and who seems to add a lovely shade of red to your face every time his name comes up?"

"I like him, too," Faith admitted. "But Alex Carrigan is not the marrying kind, Pam. He's a jet-setting bachelor who's not interested in settling down."

Pam nodded knowingly. "No wonder you're still

hanging on to Ben. You're using him like a shield to keep this other guy away."

"I am not."

"I'm always right, Faith, you know that."

"Go home, Pam. I'm sure your children could benefit from some of your wisdom."

"They don't listen to me either," Pam said with a laugh. "So you're meeting Ben tonight?"

"That's right."

Pam paused at the end of the counter. "I saw a look in your eyes today that I haven't seen in a very long time, and I don't think Ben put it there. Maybe you should go see the man who did."

Chapter 15

Alex paced restlessly around his hotel room. It was a nicely decorated room with a huge king-size bed and a view of Lake Michigan. But it felt empty. He felt empty. Damn, it wasn't supposed to be this way.

He'd signed Elijah James to a very sweet deal a couple of hours earlier, then watched the Warriors beat the pants off the Bulls. He should be celebrating tonight, not sitting alone in a hotel room with Nick at Night on television. Impatiently he picked up the remote and soared through twenty-seven channels before hitting the Sports Network. Satisfied that he'd found something to occupy his attention, he leaned back on the bed and loosened his tie.

This was enough, he told himself. He was exactly where he wanted to be. He'd signed the athlete he needed and had already called the ad guys to start working on a campaign to launch Elijah as their new spokesperson. Everything was going exactly as he'd planned.

With a sigh, Alex looked over at the phone, wondering if he should call home. Jessie could be a handful for anyone, especially an elderly man. They could have gotten into all kinds of trouble. And with Faith aiding and abetting at every turn, who knew what they were up to? They might have turned his kitchen into an Easter egg factory. He smiled at the thought, more amused than displeased.

Following an urge he'd been fighting all night, he reached for the phone and dialed his home number. He wondered if Faith would be there. The threesome had certainly become fast friends the past few days.

The phone rang three times before Julian picked it up. "Carrigan residence."

"Grandfather, it's me."

"Alex. Did you sell your shoes?"

"I signed Elijah, if that's what you mean."

"Ah, then you'll sell more shoes."

"Eventually. How are things going? Are you managing all right?"

"Well . . ." Julian paused. "Jessie dyed her hair three different shades of purple, and she brought home two boys this afternoon. One had a ring in his tongue."

"What?" Alex jerked up in the bed. "I thought you were watching her."

"They smoked marijuana in front of the television, and I'm afraid Jessie spilled beer all over your couch."

"And what exactly were you doing?"

"Me? Well, I was thinking up a story to tell you, of course."

"What?"

"Gotcha."

Alex held the phone away from his ear. Damn him. Damn him. And Faith wondered why he didn't believe the old man.

"Let me talk to Jessie," Alex said finally.

"I'm sorry, Alex. I couldn't resist. You act like I've never taken care of a child before."

"Well, have you?"

"I've raised several children for various times in their lives, including you."

"And you did a fine job," Alex mocked. "Playing part-time dad to your wives' offspring for as long as you were married hardly qualifies you for father of the year."

"Running off to Chicago and leaving Jessie with me hardly qualifies you either."

"I can't talk to you."

"You don't even try."

"I do try," Alex said. "What happened with the search today?"

"Nothing. Faith called the church in Monterey, but the pastor was unavailable, and no one else had any information. He's supposed to call back tomorrow or the next day."

"I'm sorry. I know you must be disappointed."

"I am, but I haven't given up. Faith won't let me lose hope. She's an incredible young woman, taking on my quest as if it were her own. Hold on a second, Alex. Here's Jessie."

"Hey, Alex. I made five hundred bunny cookies today."

"No kidding. How many did you eat?"

"Only three. Faith says if we eat all our work, it'll take that much longer."

"She's a smart lady. Is she there?" Alex tried to sound casual.

"Nope."

His anticipation dimmed. He'd thought, hoped . . .

"When are you coming home, Alex?"

"Tomorrow morning," Alex said, feeling strangely dejected. "I'll be back by lunchtime."

"Okay. Can I go now?"

"Yeah, sure. 'Bye, Jess." He muttered the words to the dial tone in his ear. So much for being missed. Not that he cared. In a few weeks, both Jessie and Julian would be gone. There'd be no one to call at home, no one to tell him a bundle of lies and yell "gotcha," no one to share their excitement over making five hundred bunny cookies.

You have the makings of a great family, Alex, if only you'd let yourself care.

How, Faith? How do I let myself care? And what if no one cares back? What then?

He couldn't take that chance.

* * *

Faith took the chance that Ben was still waiting for her, even though she was an hour late. She'd had to stop for gas, then realized her wallet was at home on the kitchen table. One trip back to her apartment, another to the gas station, then an unexpected traffic jam on Third Street had brought her to the Clam House at eight o'clock, a good hour past their designated meeting time.

The Clam House was a popular seafood restaurant and bar in the Richmond District neighborhood. Its clientele was on the young side. The atmosphere tended to be noisy, but the fish was fresh and the drinks were good, so it was always busy.

Faith paused in the doorway, taking a moment to let her eyes adjust to the lighting. The bar to the right was overflowing with customers, even on this Tuesday night. And there were several couples waiting in the lobby to be seated for dinner.

Faith walked over to the maître d'. "Excuse me, I'm looking for someone. His name is Ben Porter. We were supposed to meet for dinner, but I'm late, really, really late."

The girl checked her reservation list. "Mr. Porter did check in. I think he's in the bar. I told him to tell us when you got here."

"Thanks." Faith strolled into the bar, hoping she would find Ben nursing a beer and not too angry with her. She should have left the bakery earlier, but she had to admit she'd been stalling. She knew she had to tell Ben something tonight. It wasn't fair to leave him hanging. She just didn't know what to say. Her head kept saying no, but her heart kept saying maybe, especially when she thought about the babies they would have. She did so much want to have children. Of course, she still had time, but not as much time as she'd had two years ago or five years ago. How long could she put it off? And if not Ben, then who . . . ?

No. She shook her head at the foolish thought. Alex

had already said he was not the marrying kind. She'd be a fool not to believe him.

Faith went up one aisle and down the next. It was crowded, and the lighting was so bad she could hardly see some of the tables.

"Where are you, Ben?" she muttered. "Where are you?"

Ben came out of the rest room and stopped by the pay phone in the back hall. His head spun as he stared at the numbers. Shit! He was drunk. He hadn't meant to get drunk, but sitting alone in the bar all night, thinking about what he would do if Faith said no, or what he would do if Faith said yes, had led him into ordering more and more drinks, so many he'd lost count. He should probably just get the hell out of here. Go home. Call Faith. Hope she wasn't in an accident.

"Ben? Is that you?"

Ben turned his head sharply, too sharply. He had to brace his hand against the wall to keep his balance. The features of the man in front of him swam before his eyes. Oh, God, not him.

"Hello, Ben." Tony Benedetti, one of the artists on display at Ben's gallery, stared at him through somber brown eyes, disappointed eyes, disapproving eyes.

Why did he always seem to bring out those emotions in people? Ben wondered.

"I thought I'd hear from you," Tony said. "The last time we were—"

"I've been busy." The words came out in a slur, and Ben cleared his throat. "I might have a buyer for one of your paintings, the Mendocino seascape. I'll let you know. I better go. I'm meeting someone."

Tony put a hand on his shoulder. "You're wasted, man."

"I've had a few beers. I'm fine."

"You're not driving, are you?"

"I'm fine," Ben repeated.

"You can't drive in this condition. Give me your keys."

"I'm meeting someone." Had he already said that? Ben couldn't remember. He just wanted Tony to go, before he said or did something that he shouldn't do. "I'm getting married." The words came out before he could stop them.

Tony stared at him for the longest time. "Congratulations."

"Thanks." Ben pushed off the wall. "Gotta go. I'll see ya."

Tony grabbed his arm. "Once you start running, you can never stop."

"Ben, there you are," Faith said, waving at him from the end of the hall.

He shrugged Tony's hand off of his arm. Thank God, Faith had come. He'd be all right now. Faith walked down the hall and gave him a hug. She wrinkled her nose when she looked at him.

"Good heavens, Ben. You smell like a brewery." She looked over at Tony. "Hello. Are you a friend of Ben's?"

Tony nodded. "A good friend."

"Really? I'm Faith Christopher."

"Tony Benedetti."

Faith extended her hand. "It's nice to meet you. Are you here alone? Maybe you'd like to join Ben and me for a drink, or . . . ?"

"No," Ben burst out. "He has to go. Don't you have to go, Tony?"

"I do." Tony turned to Faith. "Don't let him drive home."

"I—uh, okay." Faith gave Ben a closer look. "Ben, are you drunk?"

"I had a few beers while I was waiting for you. You're late."

"I'm sorry. I've never seen you look so . . ." She couldn't think of words that wouldn't sound insulting or surprised. But Ben did not look like Ben. His shirt was coming out of his pants. His tie was askew. His face was flushed and his eyes glittered with an emotion she didn't recognize. Was he angry with her? Or just drunk?

"What do I look like, Faith? Like a man who has run out of patience, maybe?"

"Ben, you're shouting."

Faith looked over her shoulder, relieved to see they were alone in the corridor, at least for the moment.

"So that's why you won't marry me? I'm too loud. Funny, I always thought Gary was the loud one, the strong one, the best one." His anger deflated like an empty balloon. "Oh, hell, what's the use? I can't be Gary."

"No one wants you to be Gary."

He smiled bitterly. "Everyone wants me to be Gary."

"I don't."

"Yes, you do. Because if I were more like Gary, you would have already agreed to marry me. Instead, you're wondering if you can settle for second best, for the second son. I always come in second."

"Ben, I think you should go home."

"Yeah, why not?" He reached into his pocket for his keys.

Faith grabbed them out of his hand before he could react. "I'll drive you."

"I'm not that drunk."

"Yes you are. And no matter what you think, Ben, I am your friend."

His eyes met hers. "I want you to be more than my friend. I want you to be my wife."

"We'll talk about it later, okay?"

"I'll be a good husband, Faith. You won't be sorry."

Faith slipped her hand under his arm. "Let's go home."

He didn't move. His face took on a bleak look. "Home? Where the hell is that?"

"I know where you live."

"I'm not talking about where I live. I'm talking about who I am."

"Okay, well, let's start with your apartment building. We'll figure out the rest later."

Ben didn't say much in the car. Instead, he seemed dazed. Faith helped him up the stairs to his apartment and unlocked his door. She followed him inside, turning on the lights as he stumbled toward the bathroom with a sudden groan. A few seconds later, she heard the distinct sounds of someone who'd had far too much to drink.

She stood restlessly in the hall for a few moments, not sure what to do. She could hardly leave him like this. What if he was truly sick? What if he needed help getting into bed? Finally she took off her sweater and set down her purse. She waited for Ben to come out of the bathroom, then helped him into his bedroom.

He fell spread-eagle on the bed, passing out before his body hit the mattress. She took off his shoes and his tie, then loosened his belt and pulled the comforter over his body.

"Faith," he muttered, blinking open one eye. "Don't you love me?"

She smiled. "Of course I love you, Ben. You're my best friend."

"Hate that word. Friend. Want a lover."

"Shh, go to sleep."

Ben closed his eyes and she walked to the door. She paused there for a moment, knowing that in the morning they would have to talk, really talk. She didn't want to hurt Ben, but obviously the stress of her indecision had put him over the edge. She had to give him an answer. In the morning, she promised, then turned off the light and headed to the living room. She'd sleep on the couch, just in case he needed her. It was the least she could do.

Faith fought the dream that took her back in time, to the dark caves and the stunning canyons, the blue sky, the lone cry of an eagle, the vast emptiness of the desert.

She saw the butterflies dancing, the rocks at the top of the cliff that called to her each day. She wondered what lay on the other side of the walls that surrounded her.

But she couldn't escape from this canyon, nor the paint being applied to her face. There were women everywhere, with dark eyes and rough, thick hair. No one smiled as they helped her dress, as they smeared colors on her face and braided her hair. And suddenly she knew what they were doing. They were preparing her for the wedding.

She wanted to cry out that her name was Faith, that she didn't live with them, that she wanted no part of the marriage they had planned, but she couldn't speak. It was like watching herself in the mirror, but she was unable to touch her own reflection.

The young women suddenly disappeared as silently as they'd come. Faith turned around and saw the old woman, her shoulders stooped, her hair white, her eyes angry. She grabbed Faith by the hand and pulled her out of the cave. She saw someone waiting for her. It was not the warrior, but the other man, the one she would marry.

The old woman placed Faith's hand in his. Faith felt her skin crawl and terror take over her soul. No. No. No. The anguished cries filled her heart.

He took her toward the circle of fire and drums.

Then in the darkness, in the shadows, she saw the warrior. He held out his hand to her. She looked from the man beside her, to the old woman waiting in front of her, to the circle of dancers who had always protected her—then back to the warrior.

His eyes commanded her to choose—the light or the darkness—her duty or her destiny.

Then he held up the pot, and she knew what she had to do . . .

Faith awoke in a sweat, her heart pounding, her pulse racing, bells ringing, the sun shining in her eyes, confusion clogging her brain at the unfamiliar surroundings. Finally she caught her breath and looked around. She knew this place. It was Ben's place, and the stiffness in her neck and shoulders reminded her that she'd spent the night on Ben's couch.

Just a dream, she told herself, just a silly dream.

She sat up and straightened her clothes, suddenly aware that the ringing continued. It was the doorbell. Since Ben seemed to be asleep, Faith got up to open the door, expecting to see a friend of Ben's, maybe Isabelle from the art gallery or Ben's neighbor, John, who always seemed to drop in unexpectedly. But when she opened the door, she found herself staring at Nancy.

"Ben—" Nancy's mouth fell open in surprise. "Faith?"

Chuck's face appeared behind his wife. "Faith?"

"Uh, good morning." Faith suddenly saw herself through their eyes, a woman standing in their son's apartment with wrinkled clothes, mussed hair, and a guilty expression on her face.

Nancy flung her arms around Faith. "Oh, I'm so happy. You said yes. I knew it."

"Welcome to the family, daughter," Chuck said gruffly.

"Uh, uh . . ." Faith stuttered, trying to say something, but what? "It's not what you think."

"Oh, Faith, we're not that old-fashioned. We expected you and Ben to be sleeping together," Nancy said, as she walked past Faith into the apartment.

"We're not sleeping together."

"Now, don't get all embarrassed." Chuck set a crate of oranges on Ben's kitchen table. "We were young once, weren't we, honey?" He put his arm around Nancy and smiled down at her.

Oh, Lord. What now?

"Mom? Dad?" Ben stumbled into the room in his boxers and a T-shirt. Somehow in the night, he'd obviously awoken long enough to take off his pants.

"Congratulations, son." Chuck slapped Ben on the back.

Ben stared at Faith in bewilderment, as if he wasn't

sure what she was doing there. She waited for him to explain what had happened, but Ben suddenly smiled, and said, "I thought I dreamed about you last night, but you're still here. It was real. You've made me so happy."

Oh, no, he didn't remember what had happened. "Ben—"

"You won't be sorry, Faith. I'll make you the happiest woman alive." He grabbed her by the shoulders and planted a long kiss on her lips.

"Oh, this is too much for me," Nancy said, tears welling up in her eyes. "I may have lost a son, but I've gained a beautiful daughter. You will call me Mom, won't you, Faith?"

"And call me Dad," Chuck said.

"You can call me anything you want," Ben said with a grin. "As long as I can call you wife."

"Ben."

"What?"

She had to say no. She had to tell them it was all a mistake, a terrible mistake. She hadn't just made love to their son—even if it looked like it. And she wasn't just teasing him along—even though it looked like it. And she wasn't the most ungrateful woman on the face of the earth—even though it looked like it.

Three pairs of eyes focused on her face, demanding loyalty, love, commitment. They were waiting. She had to say something.

"Ben?"

"Yes, darling?"

"I think you better put on your pants."

Chapter 16

While Ben put on his pants, Faith put on a pot of coffee. While it was perking she called the bakery. To her relief, her assistant, Leslie, was hard at work and would handle things until Faith could get there.

When Faith got off the phone, Nancy told her that unfortunately she and Chuck could not stay for coffee. Chuck had a doctor's appointment and Nancy wanted to go with him to make sure he understood the dietary restrictions they were putting him under to lower his cholesterol. Faith didn't much care where they were going as long as they went soon. She needed to talk to Ben alone, before the situation got even more out of hand.

When Ben reappeared, his hair wet from a recent shower, she handed him a cup of coffee and watched him take a grateful drink. Judging by his pale face, she doubted he was feeling particularly fine this morning, not after all he'd had to drink.

"Thanks. I guess I had too much beer last night."

"A bit. Don't you remember what happened?"

"Only the part where you agreed to be my wife."

"Ben, that didn't happen," she told him, trying to be as gentle as she could be.

"You're denying it—after everything you said last night? Are you deliberately trying to hurt me?"

"Ben, I didn't say anything last night. You were drunk. I brought you home."

Ben stared at her accusingly. "You undressed me."

"I loosened your belt."

"You took off my shirt."

"I undid the top two buttons."

"You slept with me."

"I slept on your couch."

Ben set his coffee cup down on the counter and reached for a bottle of aspirin. He washed the two tablets down with a swig of coffee. "You just told my parents we were getting married," he said, his eyes pained. "They're very happy."

"They jumped to conclusions, Ben. You know they did."

Ben stared at her for a long moment. "You always told me how much you wanted a family, how you longed for children to hold in your arms, how you worried that you'd never find that kind of happiness. I'm offering you exactly what you want. Why won't you take it? What am I doing wrong?"

"Nothing." She shook her head, wishing she could make him understand. "Actually, you're doing everything wrong."

"Well, that narrows it down."

"You're my friend. I can't seem to get past that to something else. I'm sorry." She put a hand on his arm. "I wish I could feel what I want to feel."

"Which is what, exactly?"

She shrugged, feeling self-conscious as she tried to explain. "I want to feel my stomach take that tumble when I see you. I want to feel a tingle every time I hear your voice. I want to be swept away."

"And you don't feel those things with me?"

"Do you feel them with me, Ben?"

"Yes. Absolutely."

"Then I'm sorry, because I don't mean to hurt you."

Ben slid his arms around her waist so gently she

couldn't pull away without insulting him, so she stayed. "Love can grow, Faith. It's like a garden. You plant the seeds in the dirt and for a while it looks like nothing, but after a few storms and a few good sunny days, you find a blossoming plant, thriving where there once was nothing."

"That's beautiful, Ben." And it was beautiful. Why oh why couldn't she feel passion for this romantic, caring, sensitive guy?

He kissed her softly on the lips. "Why not see if we can get something to grow between us?"

"I'm sorry, Ben. But as one of my foster moms used to say, sometimes you can't grow corn in a wheat field."

Ben's arms fell to his sides and his expression turned bleak. "I can't change your mind?"

She shook her head, wondering why there was so much desperation in his voice. "I'm sorry. But I think we're better off friends."

"Friends, right. Great. Wonderful. That should make everyone happy."

"I better go. I should have been at work two hours ago." Faith picked up her purse and sweater and headed for the door.

"Faith, don't tell my mother yet."

"Ben, she wants to plan the wedding."

"I need time to figure out what to tell them. They're going to be disappointed."

"I know. All right. But we can't let this go on too much longer. It will only make it worse."

"Just promise me, Faith. You won't say anything to my mother."

"I promise."

A couple of hours later, Faith wished she had never made that promise. Nancy arrived at the bakery shortly after one o'clock with her arms full of wedding magazines, lace samples, and a calendar. Pleading busy, Faith managed to avoid any lengthy discussion, but only because she agreed to look through the magazines later that night.

Satisfied with that, Nancy tended customers, and Faith pummeled dough in the kitchen, taking out her frustration on another five hundred bunny cookies, not to mention several bunny cakes and a giant torte in the shape of an Easter egg.

Just after four o'clock, Nancy stepped into the kitchen, her good mood apparently gone. "There's someone on the phone for you, Faith. Alex Carrigan."

Nancy said his name as if there were dirt stuck between her teeth.

"Thank you." Faith reached for the phone on the wall.

Nancy frowned and disappeared through the door.

"Hello," Faith said. "I've got it, Nancy." She waited for the click, ensuring their privacy. "Alex?"

"Hello, Faith. Did you miss me?"

Faith's stomach tumbled as shivers ran down her spine. She closed her eyes and leaned against the wall. He was the wrong man at the wrong time. But she wanted him so much, she could hardly stand it.

"I'll take that as a yes," Alex said, when Faith didn't answer. "You are still there, aren't you?"

"Yes." She had to pull herself together. She had to stop losing her breath every time she heard his voice, saw his smile. "I was just getting something out of the oven," she added belatedly. "What did you say?"

"It wasn't important. I'm calling because Grandfather has some news."

"He does? That's wonderful. What is it?"

"He wants to tell you himself. Tonight."

"Tonight?"

"Can you come over for dinner?"

"Well . . . uh. Sure, I guess so."

"That's what I like, an enthusiastic yes. Why do I feel like I'm twisting your arm behind your back?"

"You're not. I'm just busy this week. But dinner sounds nice. Shall I bring something?"

"Just yourself. I'll pick you up around six."

"I can drive myself."

"I know you can, but I'd like to talk to you alone for a few minutes."

Her stomach tumbled once more. "All right. It's out of the way, though. I live in Noe Valley."

"That's fine."

"I'm at 3312 Domingo Street, Apartment 5B. I'm on the third floor, and the elevator is broken."

"I'll wear my stair-climbing shoes."

Faith smiled. "I'm sure you have some, too. How did it go, Alex? Your trip?"

"It went great. Elijah James signed on the dotted line. You know what impressed him?"

"You mean besides the shoes?"

"Yes."

"Your charm, your wit . . ."

"You think I'm charming and witty?"

"I think you're digging for compliments, but if you don't want to tell me what Elijah liked about you, you don't have to."

"He thinks I'm a great dad." Alex sighed. "I really snowed him, didn't I?"

He was so hard on himself, so afraid to admit he might actually like being a father, not to mention the fact that he might even be good at it if he gave it a try.

"You didn't snow anyone, Alex, except maybe yourself. Jessie told me what happened at the Coliseum. You were pretty cool."

"I didn't have much choice."

"Sure you did. You made the right choice, and I'm glad to hear Elijah did the same. Congratulations."

"Thanks. It—it's nice to share it with someone—someone whose paycheck doesn't depend on being nice to me."

"Hey, I'm just hoping for a good dinner."

Alex laughed. "I'll see you at six, Faith."

"See ya."

Faith hung up the phone with a smile. It faded at the sight of Nancy standing in the doorway, looking extremely put out.

"I don't understand. You're going out with another man when you're engaged to Ben? What's going on, Faith?"

Oh, dear. This was getting more complicated by the moment. Faith wanted to tell Nancy the truth, but she'd promised Ben.

"It's not what you think," she said. "I'm helping Alex's grandfather locate his long-lost love. That's it."

"I don't understand you, Faith. Why are you spending so much time with these people?"

"Because they need my help." Faith knew her excuse was weak. But what else could she say?

"Maybe Ben would like to help, too. Why don't you call him and see?"

It was a dare, plain and simple.

"Ben is busy tonight," Faith said, hoping it wasn't a total lie. Ben better be busy—busy thinking up a way to get them both out of this mess without hurting Nancy or Chuck or Kim any more than they had to. "And speaking of busy, we should get back to work."

"If you're smart, you'll call Mr. Carrigan back and say no," Nancy said on her way out the door. "Those Carrigans are nothing but trouble."

Alex Carrigan was not only trouble, he was also late. Faith paced restlessly around her living room, knowing she should not be this impatient to see the man. He was all wrong for her. Yet in many ways he seemed so right. He was charming, handsome, sexy. But that was just the surface, the guy everyone saw. She had had glimpses of another man, one with a core of kindness and compassion, one who'd obviously fought his own demons of loneliness, and one who needed family as much as she did—even though he wouldn't admit it. Or maybe she just wouldn't accept that anyone could turn their back on love that was there for the taking.

Faith pulled her necklace out of the collar of her soft knit sweater. The St. Christopher's medal calmed her the way it always did, but it also reminded her that she had played it safe for a very long time. She hadn't taken many chances in the past two years. Instead, she'd stayed wrapped in the warm cocoon of Porter love, protected, sheltered, in hiding from the outside world.

It had taken Alex Carrigan and his grandfather and Jessie to shake her up, to make her realize she'd fallen into a rut. She could see now that it would have been a terrible mistake to marry Ben—and to think she'd actually considered that option. Thankfully, she'd realized in time that she didn't want to settle for pleasant and caring. She wanted love and passion. She wanted to feel the butterflies in her stomach, the shivers of anticipation. She wanted to have it all, not just a friendship, but the sensual pleasures of love between a man and a woman.

Faith walked over to the mantel and picked up the photograph of Gary. She'd taken the shot on a sailing trip, and she smiled as she realized how happy and carefree Gary looked with the wind sweeping through his hair. The photograph was only three years old, but it seemed a lifetime ago. She would have been happy with Gary. But it wasn't meant to be. So she'd gone on alone. The story of her life.

Marrying Ben would have meant the end to being alone. But she would have still been missing something, something important, love—deep, soul-searching, body-aching, heartbreaking love. That was what she wanted.

She knew she wouldn't find that love if she stayed tucked away in her cocoon. She had to let the Porters go the same way she'd let Gary go. It was time to leave the nest, to try to fly on her own.

''You can't steal second with your foot still on first,'' one of her foster dads used to say. And he was right. It was time she took her foot off the base. It was time she took a risk.

The doorbell rang, and she jumped. So much for being ready. Faith wasn't sure she could open the door, much less give in to her other desires. The doorbell rang again. Patience was not Alex's middle name.

She moved to the door and opened it. "Hello, Alex."

"Hello, Faith." He smiled at her, that slow, dangerously sexy smile that lit up his eyes and face and made her heart melt. How did he do it? One look and she could barely remember her own name.

"Come in," she murmured. "Unless you think we should get going?"

"Not yet. I want to talk to you alone." He stepped into her apartment and looked around with a curious smile. "Nice."

"Thank you. I just got home, so it's kind of messy."

"Everyone always says that."

"I bet you don't. It would take an earthquake to mess up your apartment, not that you have much to fall or break."

He made a face. "Are you implying my apartment is empty?"

"*Sterile* would be a better word. You could perform surgery in your living room."

"And what would we do here in your apartment—hold a flea market perhaps?"

Faith couldn't help but grin. She was a pack rat and proud of it. "At least my place looks lived in."

"No kidding." Alex paused by the mantel to pick up a wood carving of a ship. "Where did you get this?"

"Africa."

"Really? Were you on safari?"

"No, my—a friend brought it back." Her smile faded away as she remembered the pride in Gary's eyes when he'd shown it to her. He'd always loved ships, and this one was special. He hadn't really given it to her. He'd simply left it at her apartment. A few weeks later, he was dead, and she became the owner of one of his dreams.

"Your fiancé?" Alex questioned gently, his gaze probing hers with quiet speculation.

"Yes. Gary loved to sail. His big dream was to buy a sailboat, but he never did."

"Too bad."

"Do you think we should go?"

"In a minute." Alex moved on to the photographs, and Faith tensed. He didn't look at them casually the way most people had, the way Gary had, the way Ben had. "Who are all these people, Faith?"

"Friends," she lied.

"You sure have a lot of friends." He picked up a photo and studied it carefully, then set it down. *He knew.* She could see it in his eyes.

"Okay, that picture came with the frame," she confessed. "A lot of them did. I just like the way they look. And, well, you know I don't have many of my own to put up."

"Except this one. Gary?" He tipped his head toward the photo she'd so recently studied.

"Yes."

"Good-looking guy."

"Alex, what did you want to talk about?"

He shrugged and moved over to the credenza where she had a display of miniature teacups. Then his gaze moved to the round lamp tables, the potpourri holders, the set of ceramic owls, the ancient radio, the dried flower arrangements decorating the walls. He didn't miss a thing.

"You sure have a lot of stuff, Faith."

"Do you mean junk?"

"I wasn't criticizing."

"Weren't you?" She crossed her arms in front of her waist. She didn't care what he thought. This was her home, her haven, her nest. Maybe she wasn't quite ready to leave it after all.

"I like it," Alex said. "It's you. This room is filled

with color, emotion, and life, all the things you wanted to have growing up, I'll bet.''

It was a lucky guess. He couldn't be that perceptive. ''I didn't have much as a child. I was always moving and usually had to share a bedroom with someone. My foster moms used to tell me that I couldn't take things with me, because they'd need it for the next kid. When I finally grew up, I vowed that someday I would have a home filled to the brim with everything.'' Faith paused, a bit unsettled by his intense gaze. He was far too interested in her for a man who just wanted a one-night stand. So what did he want? And why? ''Would you like a drink?'' she asked, instead of the questions she really wanted to pursue.

''It's not a sin to be an orphan, you know.''

''It's not a blessing either.''

Alex walked over and took her hand. He pulled her to the couch and sat down next to her. ''What happened to your parents, Faith?''

Faith stared at him for a long moment. ''Are you sure you want to know that much about me?''

''I find myself wanting to know everything about you.''

''And that surprises you?''

''Scares the hell out of me.''

She let out a breath. ''Me, too.''

''So tell me about yourself.''

''It's a pretty short story. When I was six days old, I was left on a church pew, wrapped in a blanket, with a St. Christopher's medal around my neck. A nun found me. She's the one who gave me my name. The police tried to locate my parents, but no one ever stepped forward, and I became a ward of the state.''

''I'm sorry.''

''It wasn't so bad. You can't miss what you've never had, right?'' She leaned back against the couch. ''Actually, that's not true. I did miss it, or at least what I imagined family life would be, the world I saw on television.

I used to watch 'The Brady Bunch' and imagine that I was one of the girls. Or sometimes I'd pretend that the Cleavers had a daughter, a sister for Beaver." She smiled. "I used to sit in my bedroom or wherever I could find a quiet spot, and I'd write down names on pieces of paper of all my imaginary brothers and sisters. I always made up big families, with parents who spent all their time playing with their kids. It's silly. I know that now. And believe it or not, I try not to wallow in self-pity, at least most of the time."

She offered him a wary smile, not sure how he was taking her confession, since his gaze remained so guarded. After a moment, Alex reached out and took the St. Christopher's medal in his hand. "So this is all you have?"

"No. I have all this." She waved her hand around her crowded apartment.

"Now I understand the decorating scheme."

And she had a feeling he really did understand. "Sorry you asked?"

He shook his head, a small smile playing at the corner of his lips. "No."

"Really?"

"I wasn't an orphan, Faith, but I spent a lot of time alone, especially after my parents divorced. I used to wish for a brother."

"You? The man who wants no family?"

"I didn't always feel that way. I grew up on sitcom television, too, you know. It reminded me of what I didn't have."

"Because your parents divorced."

"Because they didn't give a damn about me."

"I'm sorry, Alex."

"Like you said, it wasn't so bad. I wasn't abused, just ignored. Hardly a crime by anyone's standards."

"Except a small boy wanting a loving family."

"The only real loving families are the sitcom families.

They're good for a half hour. If they had to go any longer, they'd end up like the rest of us."

"The Porters are a pretty wonderful family, supportive of each other, caring, loving."

Alex stared at her for a long moment, and she suddenly wished she hadn't brought up the Porters, because she knew what the next question would be.

"So, any update on the engagement?"

"It's over," she confessed, not sure it wouldn't have been better to lie when she saw the pleased look in his eyes.

"That's the best news I've heard all day."

"Is it?" She turned sideways on the couch, wanting him to see that she was serious in what she was about to tell him. "I believe in marriage, Alex. I want a husband, babies, grandchildren. It's all I've ever wanted."

"You're a little young for grandchildren."

"You know what I mean."

"I do," Alex agreed. He played with her fingers, studying the empty spot on her left third finger. "You want a ring."

"I want a commitment."

His eyes met hers. "Then why didn't you say yes?"

She took a deep breath, feeling like she was about to step out on the high wire. But for better or worse, she was ready to make that move. "He wasn't the right man."

"Don't say it," Alex warned, reading so easily between the lines.

"He doesn't make me feel the way you do. It's the truth. Why should I lie?"

"I want to be honest with you, Faith. The husband, kids, grandkids routine isn't for me."

"I know."

"I shouldn't have come here tonight."

"Probably not. Why did you?"

He gave a rueful shake of his head. "Because I couldn't stop thinking about you, about the way you felt in my arms." His voice grew thicker. "I wanted to know if it was as good as I remembered."

"It couldn't have been that good," she said with a sigh.

"Shall we find out?"

It would have been safer to say no. But she was tired of playing it safe.

When he leaned forward, she met him halfway, as eager as he was to know the truth. Was he as good as she remembered?

His mouth pressed against hers, gently at first, then more forcefully as the warmth between them exploded into a hot, hot fire. She moved her mouth under his, restlessly, impatiently, wanting him to open up, so she could slide her tongue inside, so she could really taste him.

Finally he complied with a groan, and she found herself taking the initiative, cupping his face with her hands, holding him to her as if he were a lifeline and she were drowning. And she was drowning, hopelessly, madly, foolishly . . .

He broke the kiss, his breathing ragged, his blue eyes glittering with passion, with need. "Damn, Faith. You sure as hell can kiss." He tangled her hair in his fingers as he placed his mouth against hers once more, sliding his tongue along her lips, teasing, tantalizing.

"It's not enough," she murmured, pulling back slightly.

"What do you want from me?"

"Everything." It was the truth, the simple basic truth. She didn't just want his kiss; she wanted his touch, his taste, his body, his soul. She'd never wanted so much from a man and never dared to ask for it.

"I can't. You know I can't."

"You won't."

"It's the same thing."

"It's not. You have a choice."

Alex stared at her. "Did you break up with your boyfriend because of me?"

Faith shook her head, wanting there to be no misunderstanding. "I broke up with him because of me, because I couldn't love him the way I should, the way I could love—"

"Don't say it, Faith. You'll regret it."

"Will I? Or will you?"

"I can't change who I am. I can't be who you want me to be." His gaze met hers with brutal honesty. "I would very much like to make love to you right now, but I won't marry you, and I won't pretend otherwise."

His words cut deeply, reminding her that she wasn't good enough to be loved, to be wanted, to be married. Alex suddenly seemed like all the people in her life who'd looked at her and said, "She's pretty, but we can't keep her forever, you know. She's not right for us."

Faith pulled away from him and jumped to her feet.

Alex followed suit. "I didn't mean to hurt you." He reached for her, but she stepped away.

"You didn't hurt me. You told me the truth. I appreciate that."

"It's not because of you. It's me. We both know it's me."

Faith smiled, her heart filled with sadness and the self-pity she'd so recently denied feeling. "Oh, Alex, we both know it's me. I'm the little orphan girl who nobody wanted. Why should you be any different?"

"You are so wrong, Faith."

"Am I? Do you know how many times I hoped someone would adopt me? Do you know how many times I listened at the keyhole, desperately wanting to hear someone say, 'We love Faith, we have to have her. She would be perfect for our family'?"

"Faith—"

"About twenty times," she answered for him. "And every time I'd think, this is the one who will love me. And every damn time I was wrong. You'd think I would have learned by now."

"You should have learned by now. As I have. I can't believe you're willing to take a chance on loving anyone after everything you've been through."

"Because I still want love. And I still have hope that one day I'll find the right man, who will love me back."

He stared into her eyes for the longest time. "Do you know the definition of faith? It's an illogical belief in the impossible—like you or me believing we could fall in love and marry and live happily ever after. It can't happen."

Faith felt some of the tension and anger dissipate at the hopeless note in his voice. Suddenly it became clear how hard he was fighting to stay away from her, and it was that knowledge that made her soften.

"You are so scared to let me in, and I can't seem to keep you out. I know you're wrong for me, but that doesn't seem to stop my stomach from taking a dive every time I see you."

"And you think I don't feel the same way? I want you so much it hurts. Why the hell do you think I came here tonight?" His eyes blazed. "I'll tell you why. Because I can't stop thinking about you. Because you've gotten under my skin and turned everything upside down and sideways. Because you made me start thinking that maybe there could be a happy ending. Dammit, Faith. I don't want to believe in you. I don't want to buy in to this love story, only to hear you say 'gotcha' at the end. I've been a sucker too many times."

"That wouldn't happen."

"It happens to me more than you think."

"I'm not your grandfather."

"Thank God for that."

A tiny seed of hope blossomed within her. "You really can't stop thinking about me?"

"I can't. And I'm not just saying that because I want to go to bed with you." He smiled. "Although I do very much want to go to bed with you. The way you kiss. Hell, Faith, you have a very wicked mouth."

Her stomach took another tumble. A shiver shot down her spine. She couldn't have him for a lifetime, but she could have him now. Why not?

Because he'll hurt you. Because you'll fall in love with him. Because one night won't be enough.

She couldn't argue with her conscience. She also couldn't argue with her desire.

Faith very slowly and very deliberately raised her hands to his chest. She slipped open the first button of his shirt, then the second. She heard him catch his breath, felt his hands tighten on her waist. She moved on to the next button and the next, letting her fingers graze for just a moment against the warm skin of his chest, his stomach, his abdomen.

"Faith, you better stop."

"I don't want to." She pressed her lips against his chest, and he groaned.

"I can't make any promises," he said.

"I'm not asking for any."

"You said—"

"I know what I said," she sighed. "Don't remind me."

"I don't want you to have regrets."

"Regrets are probably inevitable, but I'll deal with those tomorrow. Right now I just want you."

"Are you sure?" He gave her one last chance to run.

Chapter 17

"*I'm sure.*" *She moved her hands to his belt buck-*le. "Can we get rid of this?"

"Be my guest." He leaned into her, nuzzling her neck with his lips, drawing a line of fire from the lobe of her ear to the sensitive pulse in her throat. His mouth was so hot, so enticing, she could barely get her fingers to work.

"You're taking too long," he muttered, slipping his hands under the hem of her sweater, spreading his fingers across her rib cage until he reached the swell of her breasts.

She took in a deep breath, wanting him to fill his hands with her. He must have read her mind, because he did exactly that, rubbing the rough edges of his thumbs across her nipples, sending ripples of desire and need throughout her body. He sought her mouth, plunging his tongue inside, demanding, taking, seducing her in ways far more wicked than any she could ever imagine.

"You're killing me," she muttered.

"Likewise, sweetheart."

She pulled his belt free of his pants with a triumphant smile.

He grinned down at her. "Next?"

"Your shirt."

"And yours."

She helped him out of his white dress shirt, and he

returned the favor by pulling her sweater over her head. Faith felt a moment of shyness. She didn't exactly make a habit of baring her breasts, but under his approving gaze, she couldn't help but feel a surge of pride. And when his fingers worked the clasp of her ivory-colored lace bra, she made no move to resist him. She wanted to get closer, lips to lips, breast to breast, hips to hips.

A moment later she was back in his arms, kissing him, touching him, rubbing her breasts against his chest, feeling his hard thighs slip between her legs. He reached for the zipper on the back of her short skirt, and it slipped down with barely a whisper. Her skirt fell to the floor and she stepped out of it, leaving her with only a pair of ivory-colored panties.

Alex rubbed his hands over her buttocks, impatiently, urgently, bringing her into the curve of his pelvis, leaving no question as to how much he wanted her. "We gotta slow down," he muttered.

"Not slow. Fast." She tugged at the snap on his pants and undid the zipper, then pushed them down his legs. "I want to live the way you live, Alex. Take me with you. Show me the fast lane."

He groaned as her hands delved beneath the band of his Jockey shorts. "That's not all I'm going to show you."

She smiled against his mouth as he kissed her again. "I want to see it all."

"And you will. Do you have a bed somewhere around here?"

Before she could answer, his mouth was on her breast, tasting, sucking, nipping, until she could barely think. "Too far away. There's a very nice couch—"

Alex pushed her down on the cushions before she could finish the sentence, his body covering hers, warming her in a way no blanket could. She ran her toes down the side of his leg, nestling into the warm cotton of his socks. "Alex, you're still wearing your socks. Don't you want to take them off?"

He kissed her on the lips. "I'm more concerned about other parts of my body right about now." And he pressed his pelvis into hers, creating a friction of desire that made her head spin.

"Oh." She ran her hands over his buttocks, feeling the strength and power in his body. What would it feel like to have all that power within her? Suddenly she couldn't wait to find out. "Alex, please."

"Protection," he said abruptly, lifting his head.

"Do you?" she asked in a panic, because she certainly hadn't prepared properly for this moment.

"In my pants."

They both reached for his pants at the same time and landed in a tangle on the floor. Alex managed to pull a couple of foil packets out of his pocket. Faith raised an eyebrow at the number.

"Confident, weren't you?"

"Hopeful," he corrected, looking into her eyes with an expression so deep, so loving, so tender, it took her breath away.

She pulled his head down to hers. "Love me, Alex."

And he did—with his mouth and his fingers and his body, filling the empty spaces in her heart, pushing away all the doubts, the fears, the loneliness.

It wasn't fast. It was deep, wet kisses, and long, slow strokes, passion and tenderness that took her so close to the edge, she couldn't help but fall. And when she did, Alex caught her, just as she'd known he would.

"I'm hungry," Faith announced a while later, as she rested her head on Alex's bare chest. They had moved from the floor to the couch, and Alex had pulled the blanket down to keep them warm, although she needed nothing more than his arms around her.

"Hungry, huh? I thought I might need a few more minutes. But if you're hungry . . ."

She lifted her head and smiled. "I was talking about food."

"Oh, that."

"You know—that dinner you promised me."

"Right. Wouldn't you rather just have sex again?"

"You don't have any plans for dinner, do you?"

"We could make plans."

"And your grandfather isn't expecting me?"

"Not until tomorrow," Alex admitted. "I told him you had to work tonight."

"So you could have your way with me."

He grinned as he pulled her down to kiss him. "I think it was the other way around, sweetheart. I distinctly remember you making the first move."

"Me? I'm the shy one, remember."

"You are never what I expect you to be." Alex's voice turned serious. "You are one of a kind, Faith." He stroked the side of her head with gentle fingers, bringing several strands of hair to his mouth. "Soft, silky, sexy—and a genuine redhead."

"You noticed."

"I noticed everything. Although I could use a second look. And a third, maybe a fourth."

"I like a man who thinks big," she said, placing a kiss on his lips.

"Honey, I don't have to think big, I am—"

She put a hand over his mouth and smiled. "I'll be the judge of that." And she let her other hand trail down his chest to his hips. "Mmmm, you might be right after all."

"Faith?"

"What?"

"I'm getting hungrier by the second."

"We don't have any food here."

"Are you sure about that?" He took her mouth with a sureness and a sweetness that was fast becoming an addiction.

She moved on top of him, straddling his hips, suddenly impatient for him.

"Foreplay?" he asked.

"We'll do it later," she said, as he slipped inside of her. "Much, much later."

Julian wandered into the living room and found Jessie flipping through channels on the television set. She paused for a moment at MTV.

"I'm thinking about getting a nose ring," she said.

Julian sat down on the couch and studied the dancers on the television set, each wearing a nose ring. "I suppose it goes with some costumes. Are you planning to be in a music video?"

She wrinkled her nose. "Yeah, Michael Jackson wants me to dance with him."

Julian smiled at her. "Sounds like fun."

"You don't take me seriously," she grumbled.

"That's because you aren't being serious. I've been around the block a few times, Jessie, and I know bullshit when I see it."

Jessie flung him a quick look. "I'm going to tell Alex you said 'shit' in front of me."

"I've said worse in front of him. Now, what do you really want to be when you grow up?"

"I don't know."

"Well, what are you good at?"

"I can pick a lock."

"What else?"

"I can steal candy without anyone noticing."

"Well, those talents will get you a nice jail cell, but how about shooting for something a bit more comfortable?"

Jessie went through another round of channels before replying. "My mother—you know—she did it for money sometimes."

Julian listened to the stumbling explanation with a sad heart. Jessie was too young to know so many hard truths. "Was your mother happy?"

Jessie thought about his question, then shook her head. "No. She said it didn't matter, but once—once I saw her crying in the shower. She didn't think I heard her, but I did."

Julian put his arm around Jessie's shoulders. She stiffened but didn't move away. "Did you know Melanie's parents?"

Jessie looked surprised by the question. "No. Melanie said they kicked her out when she got pregnant with me."

"Then you've never had a grandfather or a great-grandfather?"

"No."

"Would you like one?"

"You mean you?" She gazed up at him with a skeptical expression in her eyes.

"Yes, me."

"Alex said you were a lousy grandfather."

Julian sighed. "Ah, but love can teach even asses to dance."

"What?"

"It's a French proverb. It means that people can change with love."

"Melanie said you can't change a man no matter how hard you try."

"Good advice, no doubt. But maybe we can bring out the best in each other. Why don't we try? I'll be your great-grandfather and try to be wise and kind and not too astonished by your language, and you can be my great-granddaughter and try to be patient and kind and not too astonished by my stories."

A smile spread across her face. "You tell awesome stories."

"Well, thank you. I think we're off to a good start in this family business. Now we just need to bring Alex into the circle."

"He's trying to get rid of me."

Julian patted her on the leg. "We Carrigans are pretty hard to get rid of."

"I'm not a Carrigan."

"I believe we just agreed that you're my great-granddaughter, which makes you a Carrigan, for better or worse. Hopefully, not worse. If only we could get rid of the curse." He stood up and walked over to the window. "As long as the wind stays calm, we should be all right."

A gust of wind blew into his face as Alex stepped out of Faith's apartment building. It was dark, almost midnight. The day had been calm, but a night wind had come out of nowhere. He couldn't help the shiver of uneasiness that ran down his spine.

And the winds will curse your life until you return to where it began . . .

Alex shook his head and strode briskly to his car, eager to escape from the wind and his guilty conscience. Faith had pretended to be asleep when he left. And he'd pretended to believe her. They'd both known the truth.

He'd wanted to stay the night, to hold her in his arms, to make love to her with the awakening dawn, but sunrise had always scared him. Things looked different in the morning. The promises women didn't care about in the night seemed suddenly more important in the light of day.

He slipped into his car and drove quickly across town. He just wanted to get home and crawl into his own bed—*where it was safe.*

Safe! His conscience railed against the word. What the hell was he doing—sneaking away like a coward? He should have said good-bye at the very least.

Faith probably didn't understand why he'd had to leave. She'd think—oh, no—she'd think it was her again, that he was leaving her because she wasn't good enough, wasn't special enough. She was confident on the outside, but insecure down deep where it mattered. And he knew that. He'd no doubt hurt her. And that was the last thing he'd wanted to do.

He shouldn't have gone to her house at all, shouldn't have kissed her, shouldn't have made love to her, shouldn't have created a relationship bound to end in disaster. Faith wanted all of a man, and he couldn't give her that much. He didn't have that much to give.

Alex parked his car in the lot beneath his building and took the elevator up to his floor, hoping that both Jessie and Julian were fast asleep.

One out of two wasn't bad. Julian sat on the couch in the living room, holding the piece of pottery in his hands. He stared at the markings as if he could somehow decipher them.

Alex tossed his keys on the table and sat down in the chair across from Julian.

Julian looked up after a moment, his eyes troubled. "We must break the curse, Alex. If we don't, you and Faith—it can never be."

Alex felt a chill sweep over his body. He shook his head. "Faith and I will never be—curse or no curse."

"You love her already."

"I don't—love her." Alex tripped over the words, knowing that he felt something for Faith. But it couldn't be love. Infatuation maybe. Lust definitely. But love—no, he wasn't ready for that. Still, he couldn't quite forget the way she'd felt in his arms, her breath in his ear, her voice calling his name. She'd been a generous, giving lover. He should have expected that. She was one of the givers in life, and he was one of the takers.

"She loves you, too," Julian said.

Alex wanted to deny it, but he'd felt Faith's love. She hadn't said the words, but the way she'd kissed him, the way she'd touched him . . . He knew she didn't make love lightly, that she'd given herself to him for a reason. He just didn't want to know the reason, because then he might have to do something about it.

"She shouldn't love me. We both know why. And it's not because of a curse. It's because of a weakness in our family to love, to commit, to stay anywhere forever. Carrigans live for the moment, not for the future. And Faith—she needs a man who will be there in the morning, every morning."

"You should have stayed with her tonight."

"I couldn't." Alex stood up. "I'm going to bed, Grandfather. I'll talk to you later."

"You can't run away, Alex. It's too late for that." Julian glanced toward the window. "The wind—it's picking up."

"The wind comes and goes, Grandfather."

Julian leaned back against the couch. "I fear we're running out of time." He put a hand to his heart and closed his eyes.

"What's wrong? Do you feel ill?" Alex walked over to the couch, disturbed by the pallor of his grandfather's skin. Was it another act? Or was his grandfather really fading away in front of him? Alex touched Julian on the shoulder, compelled to make sure he was still there, still alive.

Julian opened his eyes. "We must find Suzannah soon, for both our sakes."

"Do you want me to get you something—call the doctor?"

"What I have can't be cured by a doctor."

"There is medicine available for your heart."

"Not for a broken heart."

Alex sighed. "You can't die from a broken heart."

"I wouldn't be so sure of that. What are you going to do about Faith?"

Alex stared into his grandfather's eyes and wished he knew the answer to that question, but he came up short. "Nothing."

"She could give you so much."

"But what could I give her?"

Julian didn't answer. His silence said it all.

"Good night, Grandfather."

"Sleep well, Alex."

Faith shivered as the early morning breeze blew through her hair. She fumbled with the keys to her car, finally managing to unlock the door and slip inside. While she warmed up the engine, she turned on the heater to take off the morning chill.

The heat reminded her of the night before, of Alex, of the love they'd made and the love they'd shared, and the love he'd taken away when he'd slipped out of bed just before midnight and gone home without a word.

She'd pretended to be asleep. He'd pretended to believe her.

Faith sighed and pulled away from the curb. The night was gone. It was morning. Time for a reality check. Alex was a great guy, a wonderful lover—a one-night stand. Not that she couldn't probably have him for a second night or maybe even a third. But she couldn't have him for a lifetime. Who was she kidding? She couldn't even have him for one whole night.

He hadn't lied to her. He hadn't made any promises. She had absolutely nothing to be angry about, but she couldn't help the spurt of annoyance at his hasty departure. She'd heard women complain about men falling asleep right after sex. She'd rather have had that than a man who got out of bed at the speed of light.

She'd told him to go fast. He'd simply taken her at her word, she told herself.

Besides, she had other fish to fry this morning. Ben. She absolutely could not go through another day of lying to Nancy, especially not after having spent at least part of the night with Alex. She couldn't do it. She'd have guilt written all over her face.

A few minutes later, Faith pulled up in front of Ben's apartment building. It was early, barely six, but she wanted to catch Ben before she went to the bakery.

Faith turned off the car and made her way into Ben's building. The buzzer was broken, so she headed straight up the stairs and rang the doorbell. No one answered, so she rang it again. She didn't much care if she was waking Ben up. He'd created this problem with his hasty proposal. It was about time he helped her fix it.

After a moment, she heard footsteps, then a clatter and

a muffled curse. When the door opened, she saw Ben hopping on one foot, dressed only in a pair of boxer shorts.

"What happened?" she asked.

"I stubbed my toe. What are you doing here?"

Ben didn't look happy to see her. In fact, he looked downright angry.

"Can I come in?"

"I—uh, I'd rather you just say what you have to say and go. I have to get dressed for work and, well, I'm in a rush. Can we talk later?"

"No, we can't talk later." She pushed past him in irritation. "I'm not going through another day with your mother planning our wedding."

Ben put a hand on her arm as she headed for the couch. "This isn't a good time, Faith."

"Why not? You don't have to be at work until eight-thirty."

Before Ben could reply, she heard the toilet flush and the faucet go on.

"Oh, my God! You have a woman here." Her jaw dropped open in shock.

"You said no, Faith. What's it to you?"

"I'm surprised, that's all. Yesterday you seemed desperate to marry me, and now you're with someone else." She shook her head in bewilderment. Something wasn't right. "If you have someone else in your life, Ben, why are you holding on to me? Why don't you ask whoever spent the night to marry you?"

"Yeah, why don't you?" a man said.

Faith swiveled around, caught off guard by the deep male voice coming from the hallway. Her eyes widened. It was the man from the restaurant. The one who said he was a friend of Ben's. And he was wearing boxer shorts. And Ben—Ben was wearing boxer shorts. And there was only one bedroom, one bed.

"Oh, my God!" she said.

"It's not what you think," Ben said quickly.

"It's exactly what she thinks," the other man said. "We met before, Faith. Remember? Tony Benedetti."

"Of course I remember. What's going on?"

Ben licked his lips, his gaze darting back and forth between his friend and Faith.

"Tell her, Ben. Tell her what's really going on," Tony said.

"Faith, I—I can't." Ben slumped down on the arm of a chair.

Faith stared at him for a long moment, knowing the truth despite his inability to tell it. "Ben, you should have told me."

He looked at her through reddened, pain-filled eyes. "How could I?"

"I'm your friend." Faith paused and glanced at Tony. "Would you mind if I speak to Ben alone?"

"Go ahead. Maybe you can get him to stop denying who he is and what he wants."

Tony vanished into the bedroom, and Faith took a seat on the couch across from Ben. Finally Ben looked at her and said, "You wouldn't have been my friend if you knew the truth about me."

"How can you say that? I don't judge people. But, Ben, I don't understand why you asked me to marry you when—when you're gay."

"Because I don't want to be gay." Ben jerked to his feet. "I don't want to be different. I want to fit in. I want to be the son my parents want. My father gave me that watch, Faith, to pass on to my son, to tell him about the Porter men." Ben shook his head in utter defeat. "I'm not much of a man."

"You're a very good man. You're smart, personable, articulate, artistic, sensitive, romantic."

He gave her a rueful smile. "If I was all those things, you would have said yes. But thanks for trying to make me feel better."

"You are all those things, but we both knew something was missing between us. Chemistry."

"I know. I thought we could make it happen. I would have been a good husband. I would have been faithful to you."

"And you would have lost yourself along the way." She got to her feet. "You have to tell your parents."

"No! No way. And you can't tell them either. I'll find another woman to marry. It can still work. I'll just have to start over."

"You can't marry someone and pretend to be straight. It wouldn't be right."

"I won't be pretending. I'll be straight. I'll give it up. I can do it."

"Ben, your parents love you. They might be surprised. Okay, they might be shocked, and it might take a few days for them to come to terms with the new you, but I believe they will come around. Because they're your family."

Ben shook his head. "You have such an idealized view of family, Faith. Make no mistake. This would kill them. They already lost one son. I won't make them lose another. I'll carry this secret to my grave."

Faith wanted to argue, but didn't know what to say, how to convince him. Maybe he was right. Maybe she was giving his family more credit than they deserved. But she'd seen firsthand how they protected one another, how they showed their love and affection every day of their lives.

"Did Gary know?" she asked, as the silence drew out between them.

"He suspected. He never asked me outright, but he told me once that he hoped I'd be happy no matter what anyone else thought. I sort of figured he knew."

"He wouldn't have held it against you."

"No, Gary was the perfect son."

There was no rancor in his voice, no anger, just a simple acceptance of a basic fact, at least the way Ben saw it.

"I don't think your parents expect you to be perfect."

''Maybe not. But they certainly don't expect me to be gay.''

''You have to tell them we're not getting married.''

''I will,'' he promised, but he sounded a bit vague.

''When?''

''When the time is right.''

''Today, Ben. Your mother is driving me crazy.''

''They've given you so much, Faith. Can't you give them a few days of happiness before we break their hearts again?''

His sharp words were grossly unfair, but they still hurt. ''You created this situation, Ben.''

''Not entirely. You could have said no outright. But admit it, you were tempted, just as I was, to give my parents the wedding they wanted, and to give yourself the family you wanted. Well, family comes with good and bad, and right now you're going to have to take some of the bad, because I need time to figure things out.''

''You don't need time, you need a kick in the butt.'' Faith stormed over to him. She grabbed his arms and gave him an impatient, frustrated shake. She was so angry, she wanted to hit him. ''Stop feeling sorry for yourself. Stand up. Be who you are.''

''Easy for you to say. You don't have a family to lose.''

His words shot through her like a bullet, and she fell back a step. His words hurt her deeply, because he was right. She'd been pretending the Porters were her family, but they weren't, and they never would be. It was about time she faced that fact. They loved her because of her connection to Gary, not for herself.

''I'm sorry, Faith. I didn't mean to hurt you.''

''You're right. I don't have a family to lose. But you have a family to keep.''

''And I'll keep them by not telling the truth. Since Gary died, for the first time in my life, my parents have been proud of me. And it feels good, damn good. I don't want to lose it. I know—I'm an ass, a needy, pitiful ass.

But God help me, I can't seem to stop wanting their approval.'' His eyes filled with pain. ''As soon as I tell them our wedding is off—not to mention the other—I'll go right down to the bottom of the list once again.''

Faith squared her shoulders and thrust her chin in the air. She instinctively went into survival mode, the way she'd done every time she'd had to leave one family to go to another. She knew that her relationship with the Porters would never be the same after this. She'd have to go on alone, but she would do it.

''Faith, just give me some time.''

''No.'' She was getting tired of all the men in her life calling the shots. ''This is not my problem, Ben. It's yours. I won't continuc to lie to your parents. It will only hurt them more in the long run. Fix this, or I will.''

Chapter 18

Nancy didn't come to work that day. Instead she called in sick with a cold. Faith offered sympathy and hung up before Nancy could quiz her on the wedding. Despite her intention to end the pretense, she didn't want to do it over the phone or while Nancy was ill.

Instead, she took out her anger and frustration and bewilderment on every piece of rough dough she could find. She must have looked angry, because Pam and Leslie kept their distance most of the day. Jessie dropped in before lunch, but after a few minutes, left with a quick "See ya later."

By late afternoon, Faith was simply too tired to fight with herself or anyone else. She'd slept little the night before, reliving every moment with Alex, and she'd spent the entire day thinking about her conversation with Ben.

To hell with the both of them, she decided. In fact, she would have sworn off men entirely if Julian hadn't come into the bakery just before four with one last plea for help. If he hadn't looked so weary, so hopeless, she might have turned on him, too, but she couldn't do it.

Instead she sat down with a cup of coffee and asked him what he'd discovered.

Julian pulled out a piece of paper and handed it to her. There was an address written down, but nothing else.

"What's this?" she asked.

"I spoke with the pastor at the church in Monterey. He called me back late last night. Unfortunately, Harry Conrad left their church in 1982."

"Oh, dear."

"But after Harry left their church, he went to a church in San Jose. I talked to a woman at that church this morning, who confirmed that Harry was the pastor there, but he died two years ago."

"And Suzannah?"

"She knew Suzannah had moved out of the area, but she wasn't sure where. She did, however, have an address for Harry's brother, Russell."

"That's great," Faith said, excitement stirring in her veins. It was unbelievable that they'd traced fifty years in just a few days. "Did you get a phone number?"

"The woman didn't even know if the address was still good. I checked the phone book, and there were lots of Conrads listed in San Jose, but none with the first name of Russell. I can't believe we've come so far only to be blocked now."

Faith patted him on the hand. "Don't despair. This is good news. San Jose is only an hour away."

"Do you really think this is good news?" Julian sent an uneasy look toward the door. "It's getting windier, Miss Faith. I don't like it."

Faith had to admit that the breeze had definitely picked up, but it was spring, and this corridor of downtown San Francisco was always a bit windy. "Let's not worry about the wind for now. I guess the best thing to do is to drive down to San Jose and see if anyone at this address knows Suzannah."

"Do you think it's worth the trip?"

"Definitely. This is our first real lead. I'm just glad Harry's brother lived in San Jose and not halfway across the country."

"Fate," Julian said with a small smile. "I came here for a reason. I knew that here I would find the answers or at least the path to the answers.'' He took the paper out of her hand and returned it to his wallet. ''Then we'll go—as soon as Alex gets here.''

''Alex?'' She couldn't stop the nervous dive of her stomach. ''Why do we need Alex?''

''He said he wanted to go with us.''

''You told him about the address?''

''Of course.''

''Oh, well, the two of you can go without me. I'm kind of busy anyway.''

This time Julian reached out to pat her hand. ''Don't despair, Miss Faith. To every thing there is a season—a time to love, a time to hate.''

His smile eased her tension somewhat. ''I don't think the poet was talking about Alex and me. But you do have a way with words. Not your own words, mind you.''

He grinned back at her. ''Why should I write my own words when there are so many already written? And why shouldn't you love my grandson?''

She started at the direct question. ''Because.''

''Because why?''

She got to her feet and set her coffee cup down on the counter. ''There are a million reasons why I shouldn't love your grandson. The best one being that he doesn't want me to love him.''

''He's afraid of love. You said so yourself. He won't let himself care about Jessie and he won't let himself care about you. If he doesn't care, he won't get hurt.''

''I wouldn't have thought Alex was a coward.''

''My grandson will jump out of airplanes. He'd sail straight into a storm if he had to save someone's life, and he'd walk through fire to sell his damn shoes. But give his heart . . .'' Julian shook his head. ''It's the curse Miss Faith. It must be broken.''

''Do you really think if we find Suzannah and the other half of the pot—if we somehow put it back together and take it back to where you found it—do you really believe that your life, that Alex's life, will change?''

Julian looked straight into her eyes, into her heart. She knew the answer she longed to hear. She wanted to believe in the dream as much as Julian did. "Or are we tilting at windmills, like Don Quixote in his impossible quest?"

"All of our lives will change forever, Miss Faith. I know it. Here in my heart." He placed a hand on his chest. "I have never been more certain of anything in my life."

She wanted to believe him—so much.

They both started when the door opened. Even before the man stepped into the bakery, she knew who it was. She could feel his presence in every tiny nerve ending in her body, every breath she drew.

"Alex," she whispered, putting a hand on the counter next to her. She felt suddenly weak, overwhelmed. She'd made love to this man last night. She'd seen him naked. She'd felt him tremble in her arms. But now, now he seemed like a stranger, so strong and tall and handsome in his charcoal gray suit and red tie. His eyes no longer held the glaze of desire. Instead he looked remote, hard, almost in pain.

"Hello, Faith, Grandfather."

"Alex." Julian looked from one to the other. "I'll wait outside for you. Is Jessie—"

"In the car," Alex said, his gaze fixed on Faith.

She wanted to look away, to walk away, to do something, but she couldn't move.

Alex shut the door and walked toward her, stopping a foot away. "How—how are you?"

"Fine." She swallowed hard and offered him a bright if somewhat nervous smile. It was the best she could do under the circumstances. "And you?"

"Good. A little tired. I didn't sleep much."

Because you were thinking about me? Remembering the way we touched, the way we kissed, the way our bodies fit together . . . ?

"Faith?" He started, then stopped.

"What?" She looked into his blue, blue eyes and saw remorse. "Don't say you're sorry."

"Not for making love to you—for leaving without saying good-bye. I didn't want you to think it was you, that you did anything wrong."

"I knew why you left."

He shifted from one foot to the other. "I don't know what to say."

"Me either."

Another silence fell between them. It had been so easy to talk to him the night before.

"You're angry," he ventured.

She shook her head. "No, I'm not. I had a good time last night. I don't regret what happened."

"Really?" His face took on new life. "I'm glad to hear that. I thought I might have hurt you."

"You were wonderful, Alex. The two of us together are incredible. Only, you'll never admit that."

"Oh, I can admit that, Faith." He moved closer to her, so close she could almost taste him. If he lowered his head. If she raised her head. If they moved just an inch . . .

"I told myself to stay away from you. A foot between us at all times," he murmured.

His mouth was so close to hers, they couldn't have gotten a penny between them.

"I can't resist," he said.

"Don't."

He kissed her, and all the doubts and insecurities fled with the touch of his mouth on hers. She wanted him in spite of everything. And he wanted her, too.

Alex pressed her back against the counter as his tongue danced with hers, a wild, erotic mating that touched off every erogenous zone in her body. She wanted his mouth everywhere, giving, taking, loving . . .

The door opened and a cool wind blew some sense between them.

"Oh, excuse me," a woman said.

Faith hastily extricated herself from Alex's arms. "It's okay. What—what can I get for you?"

The young woman stepped up to the counter as Alex moved briskly over to a table, picking up the *Wall Street Journal* as if he had nothing more on his mind than stock quotes.

"I thought I wanted pastry, but—does he have a brother?" she asked in a hushed voice, tipping her head toward Alex.

Faith smiled. "Sorry."

"Too bad. I guess I'll have to settle for a half dozen croissants."

Faith filled the woman's order, took the money, then followed her to the door. She flipped the sign from Open to Closed but didn't have time to turn around before Alex's arms were around her waist, his lips nuzzling her ear.

"You smell good enough to eat."

"That's because I work in a bakery." She turned in his embrace. "One of the fringe benefits of kissing a pastry chef. You get the sugar without the calories."

"Mm-mm, how can I resist that?"

His kiss was tender but brief. "As much as I'd like to indulge my sweet tooth, my grandfather and Jessie are waiting for us."

"For you."

"For us. I'm not going on this quest without you."

"You don't need me."

"I do need you."

She wanted to believe there was more behind his words than just a simple desire to have her along on the search for Suzannah, but she was afraid to read him that closely. Her heart was still bruised from his hasty departure the night before.

"Come with us," Alex urged. "You always know exactly what to say to my grandfather. If we get bad news about Suzannah, I don't know how he'll take it, and it worries me."

She wanted to ask him if that meant he was actually letting himself care about his grandfather, but decided it was too early to rock that boat. "All right. I'll come. Just let me put a few things away and lock the door."

"The car is out front. I'll be waiting."

"Alex?"

He paused at the door. "Yes?"

"Next time you leave, say good-bye. Don't just disappear. I can take a lot, but I can't take that."

Alex nodded. "Is there going to be a next time?"

"I guess that depends on how dangerously you want to live."

He wanted to live very dangerously, Alex decided, as Faith came out of the bakery wearing a short baby pink knit skirt with a white shell and a matching pink sweater. She looked like a cream puff, and he could eat her up, starting with her toes, working his way up those long, gorgeous legs, to her beautifully rounded . . . He took a deep breath and cleared his throat, suddenly aware that Julian was staring at him.

"She's a fine-looking woman, Miss Faith."

"Yes," Alex said shortly. He didn't want to discuss Faith with his grandfather, especially not with Jessie sitting in the backseat. Instead, he turned the key in the ignition, while Faith opened the door to the backseat and slid in next to Jessie.

"Hi, Jess," she said. "Where did you disappear to earlier?"

"I didn't feel like baking today. I don't think I could stand looking at another bunny cookie."

Faith laughed. "I know what you mean."

While Alex concentrated on maneuvering through the downtown traffic, Faith and Jessie chatted about San Francisco and life in general. In just the few days Jessie had been with him, she'd lost a lot of her toughness. Her language still left a lot to be desired, but she was clearly blossoming. Alex couldn't help wondering what would happen when her real father showed up. He knew Jessie didn't believe that would happen. But the investigator had called him earlier that day, saying he expected to have a definite location for Eddie Saunders very soon.

Alex should have spent the rest of the day celebrating instead of worrying, but he couldn't help wondering what Eddie Saunders would be like. Was he a good guy? Would he love Jessie? Would he take care of her, provide for her? Or would he leave her the way he'd left Melanie?

Alex's muscles tensed at the irony of the situation. Melanie had left him for Eddie, and Eddie had left her for God knew who. They'd all ended up alone. Even Jess. He heard her laugh and glanced into the rearview mirror. She and Faith were looking at a magazine and sharing female advice about clothes.

That was what Jessie really needed—a mother. Maybe Eddie Saunders would be married. Then Jessie would have the family she deserved. Otherwise, Jessie would be stuck with him and his crazy grandfather. What kind of a family would they make?

A good one, Faith would say. But only if she was in it. The thought came to his mind and wouldn't leave. If he married Faith, then they could be mother and father to Jessie. They could be a family.

No!

He didn't want a family. He didn't need a family.

"You're quiet," Julian commented. "Worried we'll find her or worried we won't?"

"Just worried," Alex said with a sigh. "I don't have a good feeling about any of this."

"You have to start looking for the bright side, Alex. You can't live the rest of your life in the dark."

"Who says I can't?"

Julian shook his head. "So stubborn. You can't even see you've been offered a gift, several really. All you have to do is take them."

"No, thank you. Those gifts come with strings attached, long, thick, tangled strings."

"You can build a pretty nice nest with string."

"You can also hang yourself," Alex said darkly.

Faith looked away from the magazine, feeling moisture cloud her eyes. Alex's voice held such sadness, such hopelessness. She'd never met a man who truly didn't believe in love. And it scared her, because he sounded so definite, as if there was no chance he would change his mind.

She wanted him to change his mind, she realized. She wanted it more than anything. Because she was falling in love with him. And despite her bravado in telling herself she could handle a one-night stand, she knew she wanted more, much more.

Faith bit down on her lip, holding her emotion in check. She couldn't let him see how she felt. He'd given her what he had to give, and she'd taken it. It would have to be enough.

"That's it," Julian said excitedly, pointing to a white ranch-style house on the corner.

The neighborhood was modest, with small homes, neat yards, and family cars in the driveways. There was nothing sinister here, nothing to explain the sudden uneasiness that assailed her. For the first time, Faith realized just how much she wanted to find Suzannah. She had the feeling that Suzannah would understand about the dreams. Maybe she'd had them, too.

Alex shut off the car and turned in his seat so he could see Faith. "What now?"

"We go up and knock on the door."

Julian stared at the house. "I'm not sure I can do this. What if Suzannah is there?"

"It's her brother-in-law's house," Faith said. "I don't think she's there."

"She could be. I don't know that I can face her."

"Why the hell are you looking for her if you can't face her?" Alex asked wearily.

"I'll go," Faith said quickly. She sent Alex a sharp

look. ''It would be better for Julian to wait here, don't you think?''

''I guess. You wait with him,'' he told Jessie.

Jessie made a face at being left in the car. ''I want to see Suzannah.''

''If she's there, we'll call you,'' Faith said, slipping out of the car. She met Alex on the sidewalk. ''Ready?''

''As ready as I'll ever be.''

''You don't believe we'll find Suzannah?''

''I'm not sure I even believe there is a Suzannah.''

''Someday, Alex, I'm going to make a believer out of you,'' Faith promised. She strode forward and rang the bell, praying that someone in the house could lead them to Suzannah.

Chapter 19

The door opened after a few moments. A young woman stood in the entryway, wearing jeans and a T-shirt, and holding a toddler on one hip. She looked tired and frazzled. "Yes?"

Faith exchanged a quick look with Alex. He shrugged as if to tell her to go ahead.

"We're looking for Russell Conrad," Faith said. "Does he still live here?"

The woman looked taken aback. "My grandfather? You're looking for my grandfather? You mean you don't know?"

Faith felt her heart sink to her stomach. "Know what?"

"My grandfather died six months ago. Were you friends of his?"

"Not exactly," Alex said when Faith couldn't think of what to say next. He tipped his head toward the car. "My grandfather was looking for him. Actually, he was looking for Russell's sister-in-law, Suzannah Conrad. Is she by any chance still alive?"

The woman shushed the baby as she started to cry. "Suzannah Conrad was married to my great-uncle Harry." The woman sent them a suspicious look. "Why are you asking all these questions?"

Alex offered the woman a charming smile. "I'm sorry.

We should have explained. You see, my grandfather was once very good friends with Suzannah.''

''They were sweethearts,'' Faith added, ''before she met her husband, of course.''

''Oh. Well, I wouldn't know about that.''

''My grandfather, Julian Carrigan, has something that belonged to Suzannah,'' Alex said. ''He's ill now, getting up in years, and, well, he'd like to try to find her so he could return it. If you have any idea where she might be . . .''

The woman shifted the baby to her other hip. ''Suzannah moved away after my great-uncle died. I'm not sure where she went.''

''Is there anybody else in the family who might know?'' Faith asked.

''No.'' The woman thought for a second. ''I suppose my grandmother might know where Suzannah is. She keeps in touch with everyone.''

''Your grandmother?'' Faith echoed, feeling renewed hope in their chances of finding Suzannah.

''Yes, but she's not here. She lives in Denver.''

''Do you have her phone number?'' Faith asked.

The woman hesitated. ''If you give me your number, I'll call her. If she wants to call you, she can.''

''Good enough,'' Alex said. He took out his business card and jotted his home number on the back. ''She can reach me at either of these numbers.''

''All right.'' The woman took the card and started to shut the door, but Faith stopped her.

''Please tell your grandmother how important it is that we find Suzannah. An old man's life might just depend on it.''

''I'll see what I can do.''

The woman shut the door without another word.

''Laying it on a bit thick, weren't you?'' Alex asked.

She shrugged. ''It is important to your grandfather, even if it's not to you.''

"Do you think the grandmother is really going to call?"

She took his hand and squeezed it. "We have to have faith."

He smiled. "I'd like to have Faith—in my bed, on the couch. Did I tell you about the Jacuzzi tub in my bathroom?"

She caught her breath at the invitation in his eyes. "No."

"It's big enough for two."

"You're inviting me over to bathe with you?"

"Among other things."

"If I spent the night at your house, I might not leave. I might stay till the morning. Then what would you do?" she asked, half serious, half joking.

"Mmmm, could be a problem—but it might be worth it."

Jessie opened the car door and motioned for them to come, obviously impatient to hear what they'd learned. Faith slid into the car next to her and smiled at Julian. "She's going to have her grandmother call us. She might know where Suzannah is."

Julian's mouth trembled as he tried to speak. "Suzannah is alive? Well, of course she must be if the young woman's grandmother knows where she is."

"She didn't know for sure, but she thinks so." Faith wished she had better news, but at least it was a start. They had actually made contact with Suzannah's family.

"She must be alive," Julian said more confidently. "So what shall we do now?"

"Wait, I guess."

"Wait? That's it? You don't have another idea?"

"Not at the moment, but I have a feeling we're going to hear from this woman very soon. In the meantime, we'll just have to keep positive thoughts and try to stay busy."

* * *

Alex hadn't thought keeping busy would mean participating in an egg-coloring bonanza in his kitchen, but somehow over dinner at Johnny's Rib House, Jessie had convinced him that they absolutely had to color eggs for Easter, which was how he found himself fingers deep in red and green dye.

"You're leaving it in there too long," Jessie told him.

He frowned at her. "I want it dark green."

"Why?"

"Because I like dark green."

"I like to mix colors, red on the top, yellow on the bottom. She flipped her egg over with a deft movement, managing to keep a fine line between her colors.

"Where did you learn that?" Alex asked in amazement.

"Faith taught me."

Faith, of course, their Easter egg guru. He couldn't help glancing at her. She stood in front of the stove, boiling yet another dozen eggs. Her glorious red hair tumbled around her shoulders in a mess of waves and tangles that had come from the wind and Faith's own restless fingers. She had a habit of running her fingers through her hair while she was thinking, and coloring Easter eggs seemed to generate a lot of thought. There were many decisions to be made about stickers and colors and invisible ink that mysteriously appeared when the eggs dried.

He smiled to himself, silently admitting that he was having a good time. The kitchen was warm and cozy. Julian had bypassed the egg coloring, but was sitting at the table reading the newspaper, glancing up every now and then to comment on their progress. And Faith danced around the kitchen, throwing herself into every project with the same boundless enthusiasm and optimism that seemed to be an inherent part of her personality.

She'd been kicked around as a kid; he knew that. He couldn't imagine the total abandonment that she'd gone through. At least he knew who his obnoxious relatives were. She had no idea. Yet she still hoped, she still dreamed. And she tempted him to dream, too, to believe the promise of her sparkling green eyes, her dazzling smile, her soft, loving heart.

"It's going to turn black if you don't take it out." Jessie nudged him with her elbow.

He pulled his egg out of the bowl with a grimace. Jessie was right. His egg was a dark, dirty green and not particularly appealing.

"That looks like shit," Jessie said.

"Watch your mouth."

"Try some pink. That should lighten it up." Jessie pushed another bowl toward him. "You're not very good at this, Alex."

"I haven't had a lot of practice."

"How's it going?" Faith asked, as she came over to the table. She wrinkled her nose at the sight of Alex's poor egg. "Oh, dear. I'm not sure the Easter Bunny will take that one."

"Very funny. Like there is really an Easter Bunny. Even Jessie doesn't believe that."

"You don't believe in the Easter Bunny, Jess?" Faith shook her head in mock despair. "You don't know what you're missing."

"The Easter Bunny never came to my house," Jess said. "Not even when I was little. Melanie said eggs were bad for you anyway." Jessie stirred her egg, her eyes thoughtful and somewhat sad. "We went to one of those hunts once, but I didn't do it. It seemed silly."

Faith put her arm around Jessie's shoulders and gave her a squeeze. "I know, Jess. The Easter Bunny skipped a few of my houses, too. But that doesn't mean we can't still get in the spirit of the holiday, right?"

"The nuns should have named you Pollyanna," Alex said grumpily. How could she still get giddy about a holiday involving a mythical bunny?

"Just because I don't choose to dwell on the dark side of life doesn't mean I haven't seen it. But what's the point? You can either cry or you can laugh. I got tired of crying a long time ago.''

He met the challenge in her eyes and nodded in appreciation. ''So you pick yourself up, dust yourself off, and start all over again.''

She laughed. ''Now you sound like your grandfather.''

Alex was horrified at the possibility. ''I'm sorry, I'll never quote anything again. I promise.''

''I think you need another egg.''

''That's not all I need,'' he whispered as she leaned forward to pick up an egg.

He heard the small catch in her breath and it set off an immediate response, so strong he felt like he'd been kicked in the stomach. He couldn't believe how much he wanted this woman. It was insane, irrational, impossible. Julian looked at him in surprise.

''Are you all right, Alex?''

''I think the vinegar is getting to me.'' He waved a hand in front of his face to cool his heated skin.

''That's not all that's getting to you,'' Faith muttered, her small smile clearly triumphant.

It was a good thing Julian and Jessie were in the room or he'd have laid her down on the table and showed her just how much she was getting to him. Instead he plopped an egg into a bowl of blue dye and prayed for a distraction.

A few minutes later his prayer was answered. The phone rang, and he jumped to his feet, eager to get out of the cozy kitchen, away from Faith, away from the impracticality of his thoughts.

He reached for the phone in the hall. ''Hello?''

''Hello. I'm looking for Alex Carrigan.'' The woman said the words slowly and somewhat nervously, and Alex felt his stomach clench. He had not expected a call. In fact, he'd hoped against it, because then they could have ended the search without any more complications.

''This is Alex,'' he replied, hoping it was just a salesperson and not who he thought it was.

"My name is Dorothea Conrad."

So much for hope. "Yes?"

"My granddaughter said you're looking for my sister-in-law, Suzannah."

He couldn't believe it. There really was a Suzannah. For some reason, he'd never been quite sure, despite the letters attesting to her existence. But here he was, speaking to someone who actually knew Suzannah, someone other than his grandfather. "Mrs. Conrad, thank you for calling," he said finally, not quite sure what to say now that he had her on the phone. He turned around and saw Faith standing at the end of the hall, her eyes expectant and worried. He motioned for her to come forward, mouthing the words, "Dorothea Conrad."

"My granddaughter said you wanted to find Suzannah for your grandfather?"

"That's right. My grandfather, Julian Carrigan, knew Suzannah a long time ago. In fact, they spent a summer together in Arizona when they were just out of high school. He has something that belongs to her, and, well, he's getting on in years, and decided he'd really like to give it back to her before—before long."

Dorothea didn't say anything for a moment. "Suzannah never mentioned your grandfather's name to me."

"It was a long time ago." Alex held the phone out so Faith could hear what Dorothea was saying.

"Well, I'm getting on in years myself, and I can appreciate your grandfather wanting to tie up any loose ends. I just don't know that Suzannah feels the same way."

"Could you ask her?" Alex held his breath, not quite sure when he'd become so caught up in the search. But now he felt almost as desperate as his grandfather.

"Perhaps. It's funny you should mention Arizona, because Suzannah moved there two years ago, after Harry died."

Alex saw the surprise in Faith's eyes, then the understanding. Suzannah had gone back to where it had begun. It was time for Julian to return as well.

"Ask her where in Arizona," Faith whispered.

Alex started, suddenly realizing he was letting seconds go by without saying a word. "Where in Arizona did she go, Mrs. Conrad?"

"She lives outside of Flagstaff. Oh, dear, I probably shouldn't have said that. Listen, I can't just give out Suzannah's address to a stranger. I'll call her and ask her if she'd like to speak to your grandfather."

"That would be great," Alex said. "Before you go, though, can you tell me if Suzannah remarried?"

"No, she didn't."

"Children?"

"No," Dorothea said regretfully. "They never had children. Sometimes I feel bad that Suzannah is all alone in the desert, but that seems to be the way she wants it. She's a very private person, you know. That's why I wouldn't feel right giving out her phone number."

"I can understand that, but if you wouldn't mind calling her, I know my grandfather would appreciate it."

Alex hung up the phone. "She's going to call Suzannah."

"I heard," Faith said, her green eyes glittering with anticipation. "This is unbelievable. We found her." She put her hand on his arm. "Do you know what this means?"

He smiled down at her. "I think we should wait and see what Suzannah says before we start celebrating. She may not even remember my grandfather."

"I don't think Julian is easy to forget."

"You're probably right about that."

"We're close, Alex. I can feel it in my bones." She gave him an impulsive hug, her arms sliding around his waist, her hair brushing against his cheek.

Alex took in a deep breath, the scent of her hair and body arousing him once again. He pulled her tight against his body, wanting to feel every inch of her, to press himself into her warmth, to taste her lips, to touch her breasts, to feel her legs wrap around him. Kissing her again seemed as important as taking his next breath, and he dove for her lips as if only she could provide him with the oxygen needed to survive.

He took her by surprise, delving into the warm cavern of her mouth before she could protest or resist, and she melted into him like a flower opening up for the sun. She bloomed in his arms, her lips lush, her scent intoxicating. He lost all track of time and place. He would have made love to her there, in the hall, against the wall, without a second thought if she hadn't pulled away, if she hadn't put her hand against his chest.

"We can't," she said.

He groaned. "I'm losing my mind."

She let out a long breath of air. "Sometimes, when you kiss me like that, I feel like I lose myself, like I don't know where I end and you begin."

Her words reminded him of how much he'd like to merge their bodies into one, and he had to fight to hang on to some semblance of control. This was Faith. This was the wrong woman, the wrong time. So why did she feel so right, so perfect in his arms?

Faith took a step back, straightening her clothes, which had become entangled in his hands. "I—we should go back to the kitchen."

"And do what—pretend we're not frustrated, pretend we don't want each other?"

"I didn't say that." Her eyes narrowed. "Why are you angry?"

"Because I want you."

"And that makes you mad?"

"As a matter of fact, it does."

She placed her hands on her hips, her eyes filled with fire. "I'm not going to apologize because you want me."

"Did I ask you to?"

"You're spoiling for a fight. Why? Because if we're arguing, you won't want to kiss me?"

Beautiful and smart. He was in very big trouble. "Maybe."

She sent him a long, steady look. "Is it working?"

"No." He offered her a small, helpless smile.

"Too bad for you."

"I don't suppose you want me, too?"

"What do you think?" she challenged.

"I think we're both crazy."

"Yeah, crazy."

"Alex?" Julian stepped into the hallway, interrupting their conversation. "Who was on the phone?"

Alex turned to his grandfather. "That was Dorothea Conrad, Suzannah's sister-in-law."

Julian braced his hand against the wall. "You found Suzannah?" he asked in a stunned voice.

"We found her sister-in-law." Alex hated the disappointment that filled Julian's eyes. He knew the impossible hope that lived in his grandfather's heart, but he wasn't as certain of Suzannah's reaction upon hearing that Julian was looking for her. After all, she'd had fifty years to find Julian as well, if she'd wanted to do such a thing.

"What did she say?" Julian asked.

"She said Suzannah moved to Flagstaff, Arizona, two years ago, after her husband died."

Julian appeared dazed, emotions flitting through his eyes one after another, ranging from surprise to worry, and finally to pleasure. "She went back."

"To where it began," Faith finished softly.

Alex looked at her, seeing the same joy reflected in her eyes. "Suzannah may not want to see any of us." He hated to be the bearer of bad news, but someone in the family had to stay sane.

"She'll see me," Julian said.

"It is strange that she'd go back there after so many years," Faith said. "It wasn't as if she came from there."

"Maybe she just thought it would be a nice place to retire," Alex suggested.

''Flagstaff is not far from where we were,'' Julian said.

''Speaking of where you were,'' Alex began. ''It's been more than fifty years. The landscape has changed. It's possible, even with the other half of the pot, that you may not be able to find the place where the pot was originally buried.''

''I've thought of that, Alex, but there was a rock formation that drew me to that particular place. It looked like two butterflies dancing, very distinctive. I'm sure it would still be there.''

''But . . .'' Alex stopped as Faith swayed slightly, her face now losing all signs of color, her eyes taking on a bemused look.

''Faith! Faith!'' He snapped his fingers in front of her face. ''What's going on? What's happening to you?''

''The butterfly rocks. I saw them in my dream. How could I have dreamt something that I didn't know about until just this second?''

He didn't like the fear in her eyes. He didn't like the truth in her words. ''Coincidence?''

She turned to Julian. ''The rocks were at the top of a cliff?''

''Yes.''

Alex felt suddenly chilled. He didn't believe in hocus-pocus, in dreams, in magic, or even in curses. But dammit all, how the hell had Faith dreamed about rocks that looked like butterflies? Or was she just letting Julian's musings take over her own mind?

''It's real. The dreams are real. They're about the pot. We have to find Suzannah,'' she said to Alex.

''Faith, you're letting your imagination take over your head.''

''I don't think imagination is taking over my mind. It's something else, something darker.''

Alex cleared his throat. He didn't want to hear any more. He didn't want to believe that Faith was some mysterious conduit to the past. ''Okay, fine. We'll just have to wait until Suzannah calls us back. Now, don't we have eggs to finish coloring?''

''Don't worry, Miss Faith. We'll find Suzannah,'' Julian said as he walked away.

Faith turned to Alex. ''What about the other woman? The one in my dreams? I don't think she's Suzannah.''

''Who do you think she is?''

''The one who made the pot.''

Alex stiffened. The pottery dated back to prehistoric times, to the Anasazi, to a culture who had disappeared off the face of the earth, and no one knew why. ''That's ridiculous, Faith. You're just imagining the people who owned that pot. You probably read a story somewhere and now your mind is filling in the details.''

''I'd like to believe that was true.''

''Then believe it, because it makes more sense than anything else.''

Faith's eyes lost their glazed look, and Alex felt a wave of relief. For a moment he'd felt like he'd lost her. ''You're right.'' She shrugged her shoulders and rolled her neck. ''I'm just making up a story to go with the pot. That has to be it.''

''So it's back to reality—to colored dye and bunny stickers.''

''Somehow, I don't think you envisioned colored eggs and bunny stickers as part of your reality.''

''No, but they don't bother me as much as ancient curses and beautiful, passionate redheads.''

Faith slipped her arm through is. ''Alex, deep down in your heart, where your rational mind doesn't go, do you think we'll find Suzannah?''

''I'm afraid we just might.''

''Why afraid?''

His whole body tightened at her question. ''Because finding Suzannah will not be the end. It will only be the beginning.''

Chapter 20

He called to her from the darkness, and Faith wanted to go to him, but how could she? The man by her side had a hold of her arm, a stern, unyielding grip. The ceremony was about to begin. Her marriage ceremony.

It was her duty to go with this man, to be his wife, to bear his children. She put a hand to her womb, feeling a yearning that had nothing to do with babies, but the warrior in the darkness.

She could not forget the heat of his mouth on her lips, the touch of his hand on her breasts, and her heart cried out at the injustice of it all. How could she marry another when she loved him?

She yanked her arm free in a wild burst of rebellion and made her choice, an irretrievable choice. She ran toward the shadows. She heard them call out to her, heard the strange words and knew in her heart exactly what they meant—betrayal, punishment, death.

She seemed to run forever, the warrior, the pot, always just out of reach. "Come to me," she screamed. But he only got farther away. She had thought he wanted her. Now she was chasing him through the canyon, and suddenly she was alone, all alone. Where had he gone? What had she done?

She suddenly wanted to go back to the safety of the

circle and the fire and her family, but the walls of the cliffs rose up around her, coming closer until she was surrounded, entombed. She would die here—now—without him . . . "No," she screamed. "No."

Faith awoke with a rush. She sat up in bed, screaming no, until she realized that no one was listening. She was no longer in the past but the present. Why had the warrior disappeared when she'd gone to him? It didn't make sense. He'd begged her to come, and when she'd chosen him over the other, he'd vanished. Why?

Her head pounded, her heart raced, and the questions came faster than the answers.

"What happened to you?" she whispered to the woman who had invaded her mind. Because surely there was another woman. She couldn't have lived those days. She didn't believe in reincarnation. Of course, she didn't believe in spirits invading her dreams either, until now.

She lay back on the bed, pulling the covers up to her chin, trying to make sense of it all. But none of it made sense. Why had the man run away? She closed her eyes and wondered if the dream would go on if she fell back asleep, if she would find out what had happened to the warrior and the woman who loved him.

The dream wouldn't come. She tried desperately to recreate the images in her head, but they danced away from her like those elusive butterflies.

"Tell me more, dammit," she said out loud, opening her eyes and staring at the ceiling. "It isn't fair to leave me hanging like this." Great, now she was talking to herself. So much for convincing herself that she was not losing her mind.

After a few more minutes of restless tossing and turning, Faith decided to get up. She had a lot of work to do, and she might as well get started. There would be time enough later to sort out Suzannah and Julian and the two lovers from another time, because she had a feeling they would be back. As Alex had said, finding Suzannah would not be the end but the beginning.

* * *

"I've found Eddie Saunders," Pete told Alex just before noon on Friday.

Alex sat down in his chair, surprised by the news. He'd expected Pete to show up with more excuses about why he couldn't find Jessie's father. He'd been prepared to tell him to get on with it already, to get some results. He'd been prepared to yell and scream and even pay more money. He had not been prepared for this.

Pete sat down in the leather armchair in front of Alex's desk. He was dressed in a faded pair of jeans and a rugby shirt. Pete had the weary, reality-worn face of an ex-cop, a divorced father, and an overworked private investigator. He obviously had no time or patience for social graces as he cut straight to the heart of the matter.

"Eddie Saunders lives in Los Angeles. He's a character actor who worked a few years on a television series. He gets bit parts in movies every other year or so and manages to make his mortgage on a modest home in the San Fernando Valley." Pete consulted the small notebook in his hand. "Eddie has been married twice, the first time to Blair Garvey, a soap actress. The marriage lasted eleven months until Miss Garvey took a lover. Eddie stayed single for the next five years, until he married Lucy Jones, now Lucy Saunders, a lingerie model. They've been married almost two years and have no children." Pete paused for breath, his shrewd gaze hitting Alex head-on. "Do you want to know more?"

Alex didn't want to know this much. He felt like he couldn't catch his breath, like he'd been tackled by a three-hundred-pound lineman from the New York Jets. He opened his mouth and searched for air but came up empty.

Pete looked down at his notebook. "Eddie Saunders is a good-looking guy, known to be a ladies' man. He likes to party. Las Vegas is one of his favorite destinations, and he has a weakness for old Scotch. His friends say he's basically a good guy. Tends to be a bit greedy when playing poker and has been known to bet his last dollar on the turn of a card. But since he married Lucy, he's settled down, taken a recurring role on an afternoon soap opera, and is trying to quit smoking."

The guy sounded like a total loser to Alex's mind. A partier. A gambler. A ladies' man . . . Although he had to admit some of those adjectives might be applied to him as well as to Eddie. But Alex immediately sent the thought away. Eddie and he were nothing alike. They were absolutely and completely different men.

"Have you spoken to Eddie about Jessie?" Alex asked finally.

"Nope. I just find my prey, I don't eat them."

Alex made a face at the gruesome analogy. "He might be happy to learn he has a daughter."

"Yeah, right. This is a guy who works out six hours a day, who stares in the mirror more than my ex-wife, and gets to have sex every night with a woman who models underwear. I'm sure he'll be thrilled to find out he has an adolescent daughter."

"Hey, that's not my problem, it's his." But Alex would have to be the one to tell Jessie her father had been found. His stomach turned over at the thought. She would be hurt, devastated. How could he do that to her?

"I have a phone number." Pete shoved a piece of paper across the desk. "And an address. But I should tell you, he left town for a location shoot in Maui. Won't be back for a few days."

"Oh, that's great. Just great." Alex stood up and walked around his office wondering what the hell he should do.

"You can always call him in Maui."

He could do that. Maybe he should do that. Get it over with.

Pete ripped another sheet of paper out of his notebook. "He's staying at the Sheraton Hotel. Here's the number." Pete stood up. "Anything else I can do for you?"

"Not at the moment."

"Then I'll send you a bill."

"Fine. Thanks," Alex said somewhat belatedly.

"No problem. Tracking down missing fathers is becoming quite a lucrative sideline. Just don't be surprised if this guy wants DNA evidence. The thought of monthly child support, not to mention telling the current wife about the old love, tend to bring that out in a man."

"I don't want Eddie to send money to Jessie. I want him to be her father."

"Well, good luck. I think you'll need it."

Alex watched Pete leave, then returned to his desk. He sat down and stared at the two pieces of paper for well on five minutes. Then he picked up the phone.

Faith wiped her brow with the back of her hand, leaving a trail of flour across her forehead. She could feel the grainy powder but was too tired to worry about removing it. She'd been baking since six o'clock that morning without a break, and it was almost lunchtime. Not that she had time to take lunch. She was far too busy for that.

Nancy had called in just before ten saying she was still sick. Faith had told her to stay home. She'd called in Pam an hour early and welcomed Jessie with open arms a few minutes later, setting the teenager to work after a brief course in customer relations.

So far, it seemed to be working well.

"I'm going home," Jessie announced from the doorway.

So much for going well.

Faith looked at the clock and sighed. She had no right to expect Jessie to spend all day at the bakery, but still . . .

"I'll be back," Jessie said. "I just want to get something to eat."

"Oh, good," Faith said with relief. "I'll pay you, Jess, for all your help today. I really appreciate it."

"You don't have to pay me."

"I want to. You have been an angel."

Jessie smiled self-consciously and shuffled her feet.

"I'll be back in a half hour, okay? Do you want me to bring you something?"

"Just yourself. How's Julian, by the way? I never got a chance to ask you."

"He's waiting by the phone for Suzannah to call."

"Well, I hope he won't be disappointed."

"Do you really think he's going to find her? It's been so long."

"I hope so. I'd kind of like to meet her after all that I've heard about her."

"Yeah, me, too." Jessie paused. "Alex said he'd take us to dinner at Fisherman's Wharf tonight and that we could ride a cable car. Do you want to come?"

"No, thanks. I'm going to be baking all night."

"I think Alex is starting to like me," Jessie said somewhat hesitantly. "I'm trying to be good."

"I know you are, Jess, and you're doing a great job."

"Do you think Alex will keep me if I'm really good?"

Oh, Lord, how many times had Faith asked that same question about how many parents? She couldn't remember. She just knew that some decisions could not be swayed by good intentions. "I hope so," she said finally, knowing that Jessie would believe the half answer more than she'd believe anything else.

"Yeah, me, too."

The phone rang and Faith waved Jessie along. She answered it on the second ring. "Faith's Fancies. Can I help you?"

"You can start by telling me just what Faith fancies." Alex's deep, rich baritone voice sent her stomach into its familiar gut-clenching tumble.

"Right about now I fancy a long, hot bath and a soothing massage."

"I like the sound of that."

"And a really comfortable bed where I could . . ."

"Where you could what?" he prodded. "Play naked in the sheets with the man of your choice?"

"No, where I could sleep. I'm tired."

"And I'm disgusted. Your fancies definitely need work."

Faith leaned against the wall. "Why are you calling, Alex?"

"Maybe I just wanted to talk to you, see how you were? I had a dream last night."

She started. "About cliffs and canyons and a wedding ceremony by the fire?"

"No. I dreamt about eggs, yellow eggs, blue eggs, green eggs, pink eggs. And I think I even saw a bunny in there somewhere."

Faith smiled to herself, disappointed that he hadn't had the same dream she had, but at least he wasn't dreaming about profit-and-loss statements. "Alex, I'm busy. I'd love to analyze your dream, but now is not the time."

"Faith, don't hang up yet." His voice turned serious, and she twisted the phone cord between nervous fingers.

"What's wrong? Did you hear from Suzannah?"

"No." He paused for a long, tense moment. "I heard from my private investigator. He found Jessie's father."

Faith felt her heart sink to the floor. Jessie would be horribly disappointed, and she knew exactly what that pain felt like.

"Faith, are you there?"

Faith cleared her throat. "I guess that's good news for you."

"Yeah."

"So when is he coming?"

"I don't know. He's in Hawaii at the moment. He doesn't know yet—about Jess. I have his number. I guess all I have to do is call him."

"Does he have other children?"

"No. Maybe that's good. He might be dying for a kid to love. This could be great for both him and Jess. He's married, too. Jessie will have a mother and a father."

She heard the bleak tone in his voice and wondered why Alex didn't sound excited, exuberant, on top of the world. This was exactly what he wanted. Now he could send Jessie off in good conscience and go back to his bachelor ways.

"So why haven't you called him?" she asked.

"I'm not sure what to say."

"How about—you have a daughter who needs you?"

"That might give him a heart attack."

"Not all men are afraid to be fathers." *Like you*, she amended silently.

"This is the best thing for Jess, to be with her real father.

"Are you trying to convince me or yourself?"

"You, of course."

"There's one thing I don't get, Alex. Why didn't Melanie just leave Jessie to this guy—to the real father? Why pick you? Something doesn't add up. Did it ever occur to you that maybe you really were the one all those years ago?"

Alex didn't say anything for a long moment. She could only hear his breathing, his ragged, worried breathing. Maybe she shouldn't have voiced that question, but it had been nagging at her since she'd first heard the story of Melanie's betrayal.

"Why would Melanie have lied? I was willing to take care of her and Jessie."

"Maybe Eddie had something she wanted. Jessie said Melanie was always chasing after dreams. Maybe Eddie was a dream, for a while anyway."

"That doesn't make sense. He's the father. He's the one. I can't think about it being any other way."

"You mean you don't want to consider that it could be any other way."

"I'm going to call him, Faith. I'm going to tell him to come home and take care of Jessie."

"Then why are you calling me?"

"I don't know. I guess I wanted to talk to someone who understood the situation."

"Well, I don't understand. Jessie loves you."

He drew in his breath sharply. "I don't want her to

love me. I don't want anyone to love me."

"Yeah, well, sometimes you don't get exactly what you want. Jessie was in here a few minutes ago telling me how much she was looking forward to spending the evening with you, to riding the cable cars and having dinner. If you're going to break her heart, can't you at least wait until tomorrow, or better yet, until after Easter?"

"I don't think waiting will make it any easier, but maybe you're right. Maybe I should just wait until Eddie comes back from Hawaii."

"When will that be?"

"A few days."

A little more time to convince Alex that he should fight for Jessie. "I think you should wait. It's only a few days."

"I guess I could do that." Alex sounded more relieved than annoyed. Maybe that was why he'd called her. He'd known she would try to talk him out of it.

The oven timer went off, reminding her of her other responsibilities. "I have to go, Alex."

"Sure. Thanks, Faith."

"For what?"

"For not calling me a son of a bitch even though you were thinking it."

Faith smiled. Alex had a way of cutting through all the bullshit that was rather endearing.

"I don't think you're as bad as you'd like to be. No matter how much you pretend you don't care, you do."

"It's a character flaw. I'm working on it."

"Good-bye, Alex." Faith gave a little laugh as she hung up the phone. It was impossible to dislike Alex. Every time she had him written off as a coldhearted bastard, he said something so honest she couldn't help but admire him.

Or maybe that was simply her character flaw, seeing good in people where none existed.

* * *

The rest of Friday and most of Saturday passed in a blur for Faith, with lots of customers, lots of pickups, and lots of baking. By ten o'clock Saturday night, Faith was ready for Easter to be over, but she had one last thing to do before she could call it a holiday. So she locked up the bakery and walked down the street to Alex's apartment. He buzzed her in and met her at the door with a curious but welcome smile.

"Are you all right, Faith? It's late."

"I know. I'm sorry. Were you in bed?" As soon as Faith said the words, she wished she could take them back, for they reminded her of the time they'd been in bed—together.

He must have read her train of thought, for his blue eyes took on a familiar shine of desire. "No, I wasn't in bed, but I could be persuaded to go there, especially if someone was going with me." He made a face. "Bad line?"

"Bad line," she agreed, stepping into the apartment.

"You look tired. Jess said you've been baking like a maniac."

Faith tucked her hair behind her ear. "Business was good this year. A little too good."

Alex turned her around so he could massage her neck muscles. "You need to relax."

"Mmmm, that feels nice." She leaned back against him. He felt so warm and solid and comfortable, she could almost fall asleep. Then his lips planted a wet kiss on the side of her neck and she shivered. She didn't think Alex was as interested in sleep as she was. "That's enough." She eased herself away from his soothing hands.

"Are you sure?"

"I didn't come here to neck."

"But you have such a lovely neck."

She rolled her eyes. "You're on a roll tonight, Alex. Where's Jess?"

"Asleep—if you can believe it. I took her for a bike

ride down by the Marina this afternoon. I don't think she's had much exercise in a while."

"That must have been fun."

"We had a good time." He shrugged off her silent question. "No, I didn't say anything."

"I'm glad."

"So what's up with you?"

Faith reached into her oversized purse and pulled out a brown paper bag. "Candy."

Alex raised an eyebrow. "For me?"

"No. For believers in the Easter Bunny."

"The Easter Bunny is coming to my apartment?"

Faith laughed. "He's already here. Start hiding the candy, Alex."

"Hide the candy where?" he asked in bewilderment.

"Everywhere, under the couch, behind the vase, all the little nooks and crannies."

"But why?"

"So Jessie can get up in the morning and find it." She returned to the front door, opened it, and brought in a larger paper bag. "I wanted to make sure she was asleep before I showed you this." She opened the bag and pulled out an Easter basket. "I want you to sneak in and put this at the foot of Jessie's bed."

"Oh, Faith." Alex shook his head, his voice thick with emotion. "I can't believe you."

"What's wrong?"

He looked deep into her eyes. "You are incredible. You did all this for Jess?"

"Not just for Jess. Sometimes we all need an Easter Bunny in our lives. You know?"

"I didn't know—until now."

"Well, let's get busy."

"Faith? Would you like to spend Easter with us?"

She hesitated, wishing she could say yes. But she couldn't. "I'm sorry, but I already said I'd go to the Porters' for brunch."

"Right. Well, why not?" His eyes grew guarded once

again. "I'm sure they really know how to celebrate Easter. You'll have more fun. I'm glad you're going there. It's the right place for you."

"When you're done convincing yourself, do you think you could convince me?" Faith asked. "Because the Porters' house, believe it or not, is the last place I want to be tomorrow."

"What about tonight? Where would you like to be tonight?"

"Right here. But we can't. Jessie and Julian—it wouldn't be right."

Alex took her hand. "I don't want you to go yet, Faith. Stay for a while. Help me hide the candy."

"Well . . ." Faith wavered, but once she looked into his blue, blue eyes, she was sunk. "All right. I'll stay, but just for a few minutes."

Chapter 21

After they scattered candy and colored eggs around the living room and stashed the Easter basket at the foot of Jessie's bed, Alex made Faith some hot chocolate with marshmallows. It wasn't a drink she would have associated with this sophisticated man, but Alex seemed just as eager as she was to watch the marshmallows melt into the dark chocolate.

Faith told herself she would leave as soon as she finished her drink, but half an hour later she found herself cuddled up with Alex on a corner of his couch with music playing softly in the background.

She made a halfhearted attempted to sit up, but Alex pushed her back down. "Don't go."

"It's almost midnight."

He stroked her hair. "I'll follow you home when you leave. I don't want you to drive across town this late by yourself."

"I'm a big girl. I can handle it."

"I know *you* can. But I'd worry."

She sat up so she could look into his eyes. "You'd worry about me? Does that mean you're getting involved?"

The corners of his mouth curved into a small smile. "You know I'm involved," he said with a husky catch in his voice.

"Well, that's a step forward."

"Faith, I—"

"No, don't. Not tonight." She didn't want to argue, didn't want to consider all the reasons why they shouldn't be together. "Let's just talk about something else." Faith settled back down on his chest, reassured by the steady beat of his heart. If she couldn't have him forever, at least she could have him for a little while. And here in his arms, she felt protected, cherished—even if it was only in her mind.

"I don't want to hurt you, Faith." His fingers ran gently through her hair. "You've been hurt too much already."

"So don't say anything else right now. Let's just sit here and be together. Tomorrow will take care of itself."

He propped his feet up on the coffee table and pulled her more firmly into his arms. "Sounds good to me."

After a few minutes of companionable silence, Faith spoke. "Tell me about the shoes, Alex."

"What do you mean?" Alex stiffened at her question, not sure he wanted to pursue this conversation either.

"How did you get into the athletic shoe business?"

When he didn't answer right away, she lifted her head, and in her eyes he found the trust, the security, he'd spent a lifetime seeking.

"It's a long story," he said.

"I'm still listening."

"You'll be sorry you asked."

"Tell me anyway."

She turned her body to face him, not even giving him a chance to tell the story to the top of her head where he would have felt more comfortable. No, she wanted to look right at him, to see into his mind—into his soul.

"Come on, Alex. I didn't think it was that hard of a question."

"Well, the shoe business developed out of my childhood."

"You had a lust for athletic shoes as a child?"

"Yes. You see, I wasn't always this good-looking."

She smiled. "Really? I'm disappointed. I thought you were born with these biceps." She pressed her hand against his upper arm.

"No, I had to work for those. I was ugly as sin, especially my feet." Why had he told her that? Why hadn't he just made up some story about wanting to sell shoes because he thought he could make a lot of money? That was what he told most people. But Faith wasn't most people, and she wouldn't believe him anyway. For some reason, she seemed to see qualities in him that he didn't even know were there.

"Go on," she urged, her eyes a gentle, curious green.

"I was born with feet that turned inward. Pigeon toes, they used to call them." He deliberately kept any trace of emotion out of his voice, which wasn't hard to do, since he'd practiced that technique most of his life. "I had to wear heavy, orthopedic shoes until I was fourteen years old. Believe me, they were not the coolest shoes in town." He could still remember the kids calling him Big Foot, making him feel like the monster by the same name.

Faith put her hands on his shoulders, sending a reassuring warmth through his body. "I'm sorry. That must have been difficult."

"I was the class klutz. I couldn't run in the shoes. I used to trip over everything. We had those desks where the seats would pull up. Once I was jumping over one of the desks and I got my foot stuck in the seat. It took the janitor an hour to free me." He could still remember the embarrassment, the shame. How he'd longed to be like everyone else, strong, agile, normal. He closed his eyes, struggling against the memories that threatened to swamp him with feelings he no longer wanted to feel.

He felt Faith touch his face, and he opened his eyes to see her concern, her understanding.

"It's tough being an outsider," she said. "But as one of my foster moms used to say, 'That which does not kill us makes us stronger.' I used to think I had to be the strongest person on the planet."

"Maybe you are."

"Maybe *you* are."

Alex shook his head. "I didn't get through my childhood all that gracefully. I complained, argued, whined about being picked last for every team. I used to beg my dad to let me wear tennis shoes to school, but he always said no. He never understood how hard it was to be different. Did I mention I was pretty good at self-pity?"

She simply smiled at him.

"Well, it's true. Anyway, I began to covet shoes. I'd cut out pictures in magazines and put them up on my walls. I told myself that as soon as I could stop wearing the orthopedic shoes, I would get the best pair of athletic shoes known to man, and they would change my life. I'd be able to run fast or at least outrun the bullies. I'd be able to play baseball. I'd be able to shoot baskets, and not just free throws, but layups and jump shots. I would be the most popular kid in school. I had big dreams."

He glanced over at her with a rueful smile. "Too big. I did finally get into a pair of tennis shoes, but the other kids were so much further along than me. They could already do all the things I'd dreamed about. I was still the worst athlete in my class. It took forever for me to catch up. I used to practice free throws in my driveway every night until the moon came up. I figured if I could do that one thing—just that one thing—it would help. Eventually I made the basketball team, and dreamed of hitting the free throw at the buzzer to win the game."

"Did it happen?"

"No. I never even got up to the line. The coach didn't have confidence in me."

"Stupid man."

"Thanks." He put his hand on her leg and squeezed it. "When I got out of school, I went to work for Nike. I figured at least I could get a discount on the shoes.

Eventually I wanted more. I wanted to be in control, to call the shots, to design the shoes. So after several years of learning everything I could about the business, I took a risk and opened Top Flight. The rest is history.'' He didn't feel like mentioning the early years of poverty and bad business decisions. She didn't have to know he wasn't the overnight success he appeared to be.

''You should be proud of yourself. You had a dream and you accomplished it. I'm impressed.''

''Why doesn't it feel like enough?'' he murmured, wondering why he'd said the words aloud when he saw the answer in her face.

''You know why.''

''Family.''

''Family,'' she confirmed. ''Sometimes I have a really great day at the bakery, and I want to run home and share my success with someone, only there's no one there. I'm sure you must feel the same way at times.''

''Yeah, but I get over it.''

Faith smiled at him and leaned forward, nestling her face in the crook of his neck. He rested his head on top of hers, content to hold her. Or at least he told himself he should be content, especially with his grandfather and Jessie sleeping just down the hall.

They sat quietly for so long Alex thought Faith might have fallen asleep, until she suddenly lifted her head and said, ''You wore socks the other night.''

''Did I?'' he asked warily. ''I wear socks just about every night.''

''When we made love, you didn't take your socks off.''

Her green eyes had gone from gentle to determined, and he had a feeling he was in big trouble. ''As I recall, we were in a hurry.''

''You have a thing about your feet, don't you?''

''No. Don't be silly.'' He tried to laugh off her comment, but she didn't buy it.

"You do."

Faith slid off the couch and onto the floor before he could stop her. She knelt in front of him and slowly began to untie the laces on his tennis shoes.

"Don't," he said, putting a hand on her shoulder to stop her. "This is ridiculous."

"You have to trust me, Alex."

"I do trust you."

"Enough to show me your feet?"

"I'm not a monster. I don't have six toes."

"Then what are you afraid of?"

"I just don't think my feet are that attractive. Don't tell me you have a foot fetish?" He tried to make a joke of it. "Because there are other parts of my body that would certainly appreciate your attention."

"Let's start with your feet." She slipped one shoe off and went to work on the other one.

Alex stiffened. It was true, he didn't make a habit of showing off his feet, not that he really made a point of hiding them. Most women didn't care about his feet. Most women didn't want to know that much about him, he realized suddenly. Just as he picked women he could keep at a distance, those women usually kept him at a distance. But not Faith, no, she wanted to own him heart, body, and soul.

"Faith, stop. It's late and you should go home."

"You saw all of me, Alex. I think it's only fair I see all of you." She paused. "If you'll let me. If you'll trust me."

"Oh, hell, go ahead, take off my sock." He stuck out one foot and wished she'd hurry up so he could get this over with. But Faith pulled off the sock with excruciating slowness as if she were performing a strip tease, and when the sock disappeared onto the floor and she pulled his foot into her lap, he felt a rush of desire that had no place in a moment such as this. She was trying to prove a point, not turn him on; unfortunately her fingers playing with his toes reminded him of her fingers on another part of his body, which immediately hardened into a painful knot of desire.

He wanted to tell her to stop. He wanted to tell her to keep touching him. In the end he didn't say anything, he just watched in fascination as she bent her head and touched the tip of his big toe with her mouth. Her pink tongue came out and trailed a circle of erotic wetness around his toe that almost sent him off the couch.

"My God, Faith. Your mouth . . ." Alex drew in a ragged breath. "Come here." He pulled her into his arms and kissed her, giving her everything she wanted, because hadn't she just given him the most generous gift of all, loving a part of him that had never been loved by anyone, not even himself?

When he finally lifted his head, he could barely breathe without inhaling her scent. He could barely look at her mouth without wanting to kiss her. She'd gotten under his skin, into every pore, every nerve ending, until she'd become a part of him. How had he let it happen? How could he ever let her go?

"I want you, Alex, every part of you," she said.

"You picked a hell of a time to show me."

She smiled somewhat sadly. "It's always the wrong time, the wrong place, the wrong people. I never get it right."

"We could go to your house," he said impulsively. "It would only take a few minutes. Let's go."

"We can't. Tomorrow is Easter."

"A reason to celebrate."

"You should be here with Jessie and Julian. It's a family day. I better go."

"Let's just sit for a while," he said, unwilling to let her go just yet.

"Well, all right." She snuggled into his arms and closed her eyes. "But just for a few more minutes." Had she said that before? Oh, well, she was too comfortable to move. She'd leave in a while.

* * *

"Wake up, Faith. Wake up."

Faith jolted awake at the sound of Jessie's voice. It took her a moment to rub the sleep out of her eyes, to realize that she was not at home in bed, but still on Alex's couch, still wrapped in his arms. And Jessie—Jessie was staring at both of them with an excited look in her eyes.

Faith scrambled out of Alex's arms as he yawned and stretched. She tried to straighten her clothing, to calm down her flyaway hair, so she wouldn't look like she'd spent the night making love to Alex. Although sleeping with him was bad enough. It was hardly the appropriate message she wanted to send Jessie, but Jessie didn't seem to care about them at all.

She held out the basket in her hands. "Look, Faith. An Easter basket. I found this at the end of my bed."

"Imagine that," Faith said, enjoying the look of pure childish pleasure on Jessie's face. "You know, when the Easter Bunny comes, he usually hides candy around the house, too. Sometimes he even takes the eggs and spreads them around, just to be naughty."

Jessie dove under the couch, her gaze catching on a chocolate kiss. "I found one. And there's another one." She raced around the living room in delight, squealing at each new find.

"I think you made our girl very happy," Alex muttered, exchanging a poignant look with Faith.

Faith just wished she could make him happy, too. But it would take more than a few Easter eggs and chocolate candies to make Alex believe in anything, especially love.

"What's going on out here?" Julian asked, as he walked into the living room in his bathrobe. "Did I hear word of an Easter Bunny?"

"He came, Julian, he came!" Jessie danced over to him and showed him one of the eggs they had colored. "Look, he hid my egg. Can you believe it?"

"Actually, I'm having a lot of trouble believing it," Julian said with a pointed look at Alex. Then his gaze moved over to Faith, and he nodded. "Ah, now I understand. Good morning, my dear."

"Good morning," Faith replied, feeling awkward and embarrassed. She should not have spent the night in Alex's apartment. What on earth would Julian think?

Actually, Julian didn't look particularly distressed. He just murmured something about getting dressed and disappeared from the room.

"Relax, Faith," Alex said quietly. "We didn't do anything wrong."

"Maybe I did. I stayed all night." She darted a quick look to see if Jessie was listening, but she was oblivious to anything but her hunt. "You don't like to wake up with a woman, remember?"

"I remember. It wasn't so bad." But he jumped to his feet rather quickly, making a mockery of his words. "I'll make coffee. Jess—don't eat all that candy before breakfast, okay?"

"Okay." Jess popped a chocolate egg into her mouth.

Faith tried to smile. She would not let Alex's insecurities ruin the morning. "It's Easter, Alex, a good day to gorge on chocolate."

"Will you stay for breakfast?"

She wanted to stay for breakfast and lunch and dinner and anything else she could get, but slowly she remembered her commitments. Easter was important to the Porters, and she'd said she was coming. She couldn't disappoint them. "I—I can't."

Alex's voice turned even cooler. "That's right. You have somewhere to go."

"I promised."

He shrugged his shoulders. "It's no big deal."

She felt the wall go up between them. Last night she'd gotten through to him. But now the stranger was back. Damn him. Damn the Porters. And damned if she wasn't caught in the middle. "I could come back," she offered impulsively, taking a chance that he wouldn't reject her idea outright. "For dinner."

Alex hesitated, then shook his head. "I'm not good at holidays. You're better off staying with your friends."

She got to her feet. "Don't do this, Alex. Don't shut me out."

"You're the one who's leaving."

"But I want to come back."

"Then come back."

"Okay, I will." She reached for her purse on the end table. "I'll see you later."

"If you change your mind and want to stay . . ."

"I won't change my mind."

"Fine."

"Fine."

Faith turned to Jessie. "I have to go. Happy Easter."

Jessie came over and gave Faith an awkward hug. "Thanks for being the Easter Bunny."

Faith smiled. "I had help."

"Alex?" Jessie's eyes widened.

"Yes."

"Wow."

"Wow," Faith echoed as she watched Jessie run to Alex.

Alex opened his arms and Jessie fit right into them as if she'd always belonged there. Alex looked at Faith over Jessie's head, his expression a mix of longing and pain. She didn't know how Alex could bear to let Jessie go. Real father or not, he loved Jessie. He just didn't believe in forever. Faith wished she could prove him wrong.

Chapter 22

Faith drove home, changed her clothes, then got back into the car to drive to the Porters' house. She'd prepared a special bunny cake as well as a tray of mixed pastries and a lemon torte. Since her first Easter celebration at the Porters' three years earlier, Faith had come to love their traditions, the family unity that spilled out of every corner of their home during the holidays.

She would have felt better if she could have come as she'd come the year before, as a friend of the family, not as a possible wife for Ben. As she stepped out of her car and shut the door, she prayed that Ben had finally told his parents the truth.

"Faith." Kim waved from the porch, then ran down the walkway to help her with the desserts. "I saw the cutest bridesmaid's dress. It's a pearl pink, and although I don't normally like pink, this was gorgeous. And best of all, it wasn't that expensive. I know I'm getting ahead of myself. You haven't officially asked me, and if you'd rather have a friend, that's okay, too. But I still think you should look at the dress. Maybe tomorrow we could go at lunchtime. It's not far from the bakery."

Faith was saved from replying as Nancy met her at the door with a kiss on the cheek. "I'm so glad you're here, Faith, and so sorry I let you down this week, but I finally kicked that horrible cold."

"I'm glad."

Nancy took the other tray from Faith's hands. "Ben will be here any second. He just called, and I asked him to pick up a carton of ice cream from the store. It turns out Chuck had a midnight snack."

Faith smiled. She loved the give and take of this family, the way they scolded each other with love shining out of their eyes.

"Would you mind giving me a hand in the kitchen?" Nancy asked. "I made a pesto dip to go with French bread, and I'd love to have you take some into the backyard. Chuck's brother and his wife are already out there with the kids."

"Sure."

The doorbell rang again and Nancy yelled, "Come in."

Chuck's sister and husband and their oldest daughter with her three young kids came into the house, exchanging hellos and hugs with Nancy, Faith, and Kim. Then the bell rang again.

Faith slipped into the kitchen with a laugh. If she was going to serve appetizers, she'd better get started before the next crew arrived.

Ben arrived fifteen minutes later. He greeted his mother with a kiss, and Faith with a pleading smile to stay quiet. She nodded her head, knowing this was not the time or the place to tell the Porters they were not getting married. Instead, she allowed herself to be cornered by Ben's grandmother, who wanted to tell her all about Ben as a little boy. Their conversation lasted throughout the lavish buffet and well into dessert.

"That's enough, Grannie," Ben said an hour later, as his grandmother was preparing to bring out the family scrapbooks. "The Easter egg hunt is about to begin."

"Thanks," Faith said, as she followed Ben into the backyard where his parents had set up an Easter egg hunt. "I love your grandmother, but she was getting ready to name our children."

"Sorry."

Faith sat down in a lawn chair, pleased to feel the sun on her face. It relieved some of the tension racing through her body. The Easter egg hunt was another Porter family tradition, and one Faith had watched with much pleasure for the past couple of years. She'd often fantasized about a time when she and Gary would have a toddler to throw into the fray, but sadly, that hadn't happened.

"How are you, Faith?" Esther Porter asked. She was one of Ben's aunts, a lovely woman who'd stitched a beautiful sampler for Faith at the time of her first engagement to Gary.

"I'm fine," Faith replied. "How about you?"

"Arthritis is making my fingers ache, but Nancy tells me it may be time to start my stitchery again. You'll have to tell me your color scheme, dear."

"I haven't decided yet."

"Well, I've always been partial to blues. So restful and soothing, the way a home should be."

"I'll keep that in mind."

Ben pulled up a chair next to her as Esther wandered away with one of her grandchildren. Dressed in casual beige slacks and an ivory-colored, long-sleeve shirt, he looked fresh and well rested, not at all the way she felt, she thought resentfully. Ben didn't look like he had a care in the world. But then, he was awfully good at pretending.

"Still mad at me?" he asked.

"Yes."

"Well, thanks for being a sport." Ben leaned forward, lacing his hands together as they both watched the children scamper for treasure. "I didn't want to ruin Easter. That's one reason why I haven't said anything."

"I hate lying to your parents."

"I know you do."

Faith breathed in the scent of spring flowers and tried to relax. It was a beautiful day, not too warm, not too cool. The birds were singing, the children laughing. It was a perfect day for Easter, for rebirth, for renewal. And time to move on. Way past time, she realized.

"I wish it would have been me," Ben said heavily, interrupting her thoughts. "The one who died."

Faith turned to him in shock. "Don't ever say that."

"My parents would have been happier if Gary had lived."

"No. They love you, Ben. I know you think they loved Gary more, but it's not true. Your father used to argue with Gary all the time."

"Are you kidding?" Ben looked at her with amazement and disbelief. "Gary and my father agreed on everything."

"They didn't. For example, Chuck didn't want Gary to invest in the bakery, but Gary did it anyway—for me. Chuck didn't speak to him for three days."

Ben looked at her in astonishment. "I never knew that."

"You didn't know a lot of things. Gary respected your parents, but he made his own decisions and he lived his own life. You should do the same."

"Gary wasn't—abnormal."

"Oh, Ben." Faith sighed with heartfelt compassion. "I can't imagine what it must be like to be you. I'll be honest. But your sexuality is only one part of your personality."

"A big part. Too big for my parents to accept."

"I hope you're wrong. Because they need you, and you need them, but not this way, not with so many lies."

"I'm terrified of losing my parents, Faith. I can't be all alone. I'm not as strong as you."

"Sometimes you have no choice but to be strong."

"But I do have a choice."

She looked into his warm, worried brown eyes. "Do you, Ben? I think you've been fighting this for a long time." She paused. "Do you care about that man—the one you were with?"

"I don't know."

"Lying to yourself now?"

"Okay. I like him—very much."

"Are you going to give him up for your parents?"

Ben let out a breath. "How can I have both? It's hopeless."

"What's hopeless, dear?" Nancy asked, coming up behind them, her round face reflecting a happy weariness. "Good heavens. The two of you look positively depressed. What's happened?"

"I didn't get any candy," Ben said, standing up to kiss his mother on the cheek.

"Oh, you. As if you don't know there's an Easter basket with your name on it in the living room."

"Mother, I'm a little old for Easter baskets."

"You're my baby boy, you're never too old to spoil." She gave Ben a hug, then smiled at Faith. "I have one for you, too."

"You shouldn't have."

"You're part of the family, Faith."

"Aunt Nancy, can I have some lemonade?" one of the children asked.

"I'll get it for you, Robert," Faith said quickly. She couldn't stand to look into Nancy's generous, loving eyes for one second longer.

The kitchen was filled with relatives, but Faith found some lemonade and poured Robert a glass. Rather than return to the Easter egg hunt, she made her way into the living room and up the stairs. Eventually she found herself outside of Gary's bedroom door. She hadn't made a conscious decision to come to his room, but now that she was here, she knew she had to go inside.

Faith hadn't been in Gary's room since the day of the funeral. She'd always stayed away, too afraid of the painful memories. But somehow, today, she needed to see his room, his things.

Taking a deep breath, she pushed open the door and saw—a boy's room. There was a double-sized bed with a cherry frame and matching desk and dresser. Gary's stereo stood on a table in one corner along with his collection of records. Everything was exactly the way he'd left it at eighteen years old when he'd gone to college. Even then Nancy had kept his room ready for him to come home. Here it was, still the same, decades later.

Faith went in and sat on the bed. She picked up a raggedy old tiger and held it in her arms. "Lucky," she whispered, tracing the tiger's worn-out nose. She remembered Gary telling her that Lucky had been his "lovey," the animal he'd slept with every night of his life until he turned eight and his father had decided he was too old to need a 'lovey'.

Gary said he'd stuffed Lucky into a drawer, but sometimes late at night he'd get up and take it out. Then in the morning he'd put him back. What was it about the Porters that made their boys want to hide their true selves from their parents? She knew Nancy and Chuck loved their children.

Maybe that was just the way families were. What did she know?

She hugged the tiger to her chest, thinking of all the toys she'd tried to hang on to. She'd had a doll once, Emma Lou, she'd call her. But Emma Lou had been left at the house for the next foster kid. And she'd had a bear once. She'd just called him "Bear," afraid to give him a name for fear he'd disappear as well. He had.

Just like Alex, she thought. She'd loved and lost, over and over again. But unlike Alex, she still kept hoping for that miracle, that once in a lifetime that would last forever.

Tears gathered in the corners of her eyes. She hadn't cried since the funeral, but today she couldn't stop the emotion from spilling out. She cried for everyone and everything she had lost. And she cried for the Porters, because she knew that she would soon be leaving. After they learned the wedding was off, nothing would be the same. They'd be done with her. And her last link to Gary would be broken.

She squeezed her eyes shut and saw Gary's image. She felt his smile, warm and tender, wash over her like a soft rain. And then he was gone.

Faith didn't realize Nancy had come into the room until the door shut. Hastily she wiped her eyes and set the tiger down on the bed.

Nancy looked at her with concern. "Are you all right?"

"Fine."

"You don't have to pretend with me." Nancy sat on the edge of the bed. "I've cried in here many times, wishing I could have just a few more minutes with Gary, one last chance to tell him how much I love him."

"He knew. He always knew."

"I hope so. He loved you, too. He told me so many times. In fact, I was a little jealous at first, hearing the way he said your name with so much longing that I knew he'd found his true love."

Faith had to swallow hard to keep the tears from coming back. "Why are the good things in life so short?"

"I don't know. But there are more good things waiting just around the corner for you—with Ben."

Faith stared at Nancy, feeling the truth rushing to her lips. She bit down hard, tasting blood.

"It will be a different love with Ben, I suspect, but just as good. Just as sweet."

Faith couldn't stand it. She tried not to say the words, but they poured out of her like a tidal wave intent on destruction. "I'm not going to marry Ben."

"What?" Nancy's mouth dropped open. Her eyes looked shocked as if she'd just seen a horrible accident.

Now that she'd said it, Faith had to explain. There was no point in hiding, no point in wishing she hadn't told the truth on Easter Sunday. It was done. "I'm not going to marry Ben."

"I—I don't understand. Of course you're going to marry Ben. He loves you. You love him. It's all so perfect."

"I can't marry Ben," Faith said gently. "I love him very much as a friend, but not as a husband. I'm sorry."

"Sorry? You're breaking my son's heart, and all you can say is you're sorry?"

"I *am* sorry." Faith didn't know what else to say.

"Sorry for what, Faith? For leading him on? For lying to him?" Nancy's compassion turned to ugly, bitter anger. "You built up his dreams and now you're throwing them back in his face. How could you do such a thing to him?"

"That's not the way—"

"Ben was there for you when Gary died. He held you in his arms while you cried. He took you food when you wouldn't eat. He washed your car. He did your laundry. He helped out in the bakery until you could face working again."

Faith knew all that. Ben had been a great friend, supportive, loving, kind. But she knew now what she hadn't known then or even a few days ago, that Ben had never had that kind of love for her. She couldn't tell Nancy that. She couldn't let those words cross her lips. It was not her secret to tell, and she owed Ben that much.

"We opened our hearts to you," Nancy continued. "We welcomed you into our home. We treated you like a daughter."

"And I appreciate—"

"My God!" Nancy clapped a hand over her mouth. "You made love to Ben just the other night. You slept in his bed." She jumped to her feet.

"I didn't—"

"How could you do this to him? Gary would be so ashamed of you."

Faith felt like she'd been slugged in the gut, and she didn't have a chance to catch her breath before Nancy landed another blow.

"You don't deserve our love, our family. I want you to go." Nancy walked to the door and opened it. "Now."

"Nancy, please let me explain." But what could she

say that would change anything? She would never be able to convince Nancy that she hadn't deliberately broken Ben's heart.

"Get out of my house, Faith. You betrayed me. You betrayed all of us. I don't ever want to see you again."

Faith slid off the bed and walked to the door. She looked into the eyes of a woman who had been like a mother to her. But Nancy's true allegiance had always been to her boys. Even now she was like a mother bear protecting her cubs. She would have eaten Faith alive if she could.

"I didn't mean to hurt you," Faith said one last time.

Nancy didn't speak, her face taut with anger and disappointment. Faith walked down the stairs and out the front door. Once on the sidewalk, she took a last look at the house, and suddenly realized how many times she'd stood on the sidewalk, taking one last look at a family that no longer wanted her.

"Good-bye, Porters," she whispered. "It's been fun."

Chapter 23

Faith wasn't coming back. It was almost seven.

Alex glanced at the dining room table he and Jessie had set so carefully with a knife, a spoon, and two forks on a linen napkin. They had put out the crystal wineglasses and lit candles, which were now dripping wax on the silver candleholders. The flowers in the center of the table drooped from loneliness. The china glistened in the candlelight, mocking him with the beauty, the promise, of a family dinner.

Why had he done all this? He should have known better than to believe in a family holiday. How many had he spent alone, eating his dinner in front of the television set, watching the Christmas specials, the happy families with their happy relatives, while his father had celebrated elsewhere? Too many to count.

Faith was with her ideal family—the Porters—and her ideal man—Ben. Maybe she'd changed her mind, decided to marry the guy after all, buy in to the family she'd always wanted, the white picket fence, the dog, and the 2.5 children.

Well, good for her and good for him. He didn't need Faith messing up his orderly life. It was about time he got back to his priorities, to Top Flight. His company made him happy. He didn't need anything or anyone else.

He returned to the kitchen and opened the oven door.

The roast was drying out slowly but surely, looking as exciting as his future—a future without Faith.

"Is dinner ready yet?" Jessie peered into the oven as if seeking an answer from its dark depths. When none came, she looked up at him, her eyes as hopeful but as wary as his. He wanted to reassure her, to tell her it would all be perfect, this family holiday, this family dinner. But the words wouldn't come.

"It's ready," he said shortly. He picked up an oven mitt and took the pan out of the oven and set it on top of the stove. "Would you call Grandfather?"

Jessie hesitated. "What about Faith?"

"She's not here, Jess."

"She said she'd come back. We should wait for her."

"How long do you think we should wait?"

Jessie stared at him for a long moment, her gaze drifting from the roast to the clock. He wondered how many times she'd watched a clock, waiting, hoping. The answer came as the light in her eyes grew dull, as her mouth drooped into a disappointed pout. But she didn't cry. She didn't whine. She just said simply, "I guess we might as well eat."

"Might as well," he agreed.

Jessie walked over to the kitchen door and called for Julian. Then she returned to his side, watching as he took the meat out of the pan and set it on a platter.

Julian poked his head into the kitchen. "Something smells good in here. And the table—fabulous. Did you do that, Jessie?"

Jessie shrugged. "It was no big deal." She picked up the casserole dish of beans that Alex had placed on the counter and headed for the dining room.

Julian watched her go with troubled eyes. "Is she all right?"

"She'll live."

"Are you sure you don't want to wait a few more minutes? Miss Faith—"

"I'm sure." Alex cut him off with a shake of his head.

"Something must have come up."

"She's where she wants to be, Grandfather. You know what that feels like, don't you? You picked up and moved on often enough. Damn." He slammed his hand down on the counter, hearing the bitterness in his voice and wishing it away. He should be past caring about old transgressions by now. He was a grown man. He'd moved on. "I'm sorry. Forget I said that."

"You don't have to apologize for speaking the truth. I probably deserve worse."

"You have your own life, Grandfather, and I have mine. Just because we share some blood doesn't mean we have to share anything else."

Julian gave a sad shake of his head. "I made many mistakes, Alex. You'll never know how sorry I am about the ones that hurt you."

Alex picked up a knife and sliced the meat into several long wedges and placed them on a plate. Jessie returned to pick up the platter of beef, leaving Alex to bring the mashed potatoes and the rolls. Julian followed more slowly, settling himself into a chair at one end of the dining room table.

As Alex sat down at the other end, he took a deep breath, feeling as if he would need all of his strength to get through this meal without losing it completely. Faith's empty chair reminded him of another broken promise. He'd been a fool to believe in her.

He tightened his lips and reached for the bottle of Chardonnay on the table. In doing so, he caught a glimpse of Jessie's worried face, and guilt kicked him in the stomach. He was thinking only of himself, and he should have been thinking about Jessie.

Although by this time next week Eddie Saunders would be back in town, and Jessie—He couldn't finish the thought even in his own mind. For Jessie had crept into his heart. In a few days she'd lost the waifish look in her eyes, the defiant slant of her mouth, the rebellious attitude, and instead had become an entertaining companion.

They'd spent the day at the Marina Greens, tossing a Frisbee, wading into the bay, and sharing crab cakes at an outdoor café. They'd laughed—a lot. He couldn't remember a day he'd enjoyed so much.

"This looks wonderful," Julian said as he surveyed the table. "I didn't know you had it in you, Alex."

"You don't know anything about me, Grandfather.

"I'm trying."

"Too little, too late."

"I hope not," Julian said evenly, carefully choosing his words, his own words for a change. "I do care about you, Alex. I know I haven't always shown it. I'm sorry for that. I'm sorry for a lot of things. I'm sure you'll do a better job with Jessie." He smiled at Jessie reassuringly. "You're lucky to have Alex."

"I know," she said. "That's why Melanie wanted to come back to California. She wanted to find Alex before . . ." Jessie's voice suddenly drifted away. "Could someone pass the potatoes?"

"Before what?" Alex asked. "I thought Melanie got sick rather suddenly."

"She did."

"But you weren't in California when she got sick?"

"No, we were in Nashville."

Alex saw the guilty look in Jessie's eyes and put two and two together. "Melanie came back to California to find me?"

Jessie hesitated, then nodded. "Yes."

"Why wasn't she looking for Eddie Saunders?"

"I don't know. She never said. She wanted to find you before—before she—she died." Jessie stumbled over the words, her eyes glittering with wetness. "But she ran out of time. So she asked the lawyer to look for you. She made him promise to find you. She said you were the best thing that ever happened to her and she wanted you to be the best thing that ever happened to me." Jessie stared down at her plate. "I guess if she'd have asked you herself, you would have had a chance to say no."

And he would have said no, too. Only then he would have missed one of the best weeks of his life. Alex felt suddenly ashamed of his behavior. This family dinner wasn't for him or even for Faith; it was for Jessie, and it was about time he made it right.

"Why don't we eat?" he suggested.

Neither Jessie nor Julian moved a muscle. "I'm sorry for acting like a jerk," Alex added. "It's Easter, and we should have a nice family dinner."

"Did that hurt?" Julian asked with a gleam in his eye. "Mentioning family and dinner in the same breath?"

"Not as much as it used to. Pass me the meat. I'm starving."

Jessie cleared her throat. "We should say grace, Alex."

"What?"

"You know. A prayer."

"I don't know any grace."

"I do." Jessie held out her hand to Alex. "We have to hold hands."

Alex sighed, but knew he might as well play this family dinner out to the last detail. He took one of Jessie's hands and waited as Julian took the other.

Jessie bowed her head. "Dear God. Thank you for this wonderful meal. And thank you for all the Easter candy. By the way, I'd really like to have a CD player, if there's any way you could convince Alex to get me one."

"Amen," Alex said.

"And thank you for giving me Alex, even if he doesn't want to be my dad forever. And thank you for Faith, because she's really nice, and she makes the best cookies."

"Amen," Alex said, hoping to end it, but Jessie wouldn't let go of his hand.

"And thank you for giving me a great-grandfather, who says more shit than I do."

Alex shot her a dark look. "Is that it?"

"Amen," she said.

He released her hand. "So where did you learn about grace?"

"Melanie screwed a preacher once."

Julian choked on his water.

Alex frowned at her. "Jessie!"

"What? I could have said she fu—"

"Don't." He held up his hand. "Don't say anything more. Let's just eat."

Before he could take a bite, the doorbell rang, and all three of them froze. Alex knew who it was, but now that she was here, he was almost afraid to answer it. Because then he couldn't be angry at her, and it was much safer to dislike Faith than to like her.

"Aren't you going to get it?" Julian demanded.

"I'm getting it." Alex stood up. He took his time walking to the door. He didn't know what to say, how to react, how to protect himself . . .

When he opened the door, his anger fled at the sight of Faith's sweet, ravaged face. Her cheeks were pale, her lipstick smudged, her eyes swollen and red. She'd obviously been crying. He couldn't imagine who could have done this to her, and a wave of fury made his fists clench.

"My God, Faith, what happened to you? Did you get mugged? Did someone hurt you?"

"I didn't get mugged, at least not by a stranger." She paused, shaking her head as if she just realized she'd knocked on the wrong door. "I'm sorry. This was a mistake. I shouldn't have come."

"Wait."

"I feel so . . . I don't even know how I feel."

Alex grabbed her hand and pulled her into the apartment, shutting the door behind her. He ran his hands up and down her arms, expecting to find broken bones or scars or bruises, but the hurt was obviously on the inside.

He didn't know what to say, so he did the only thing he could do. He pulled her into his arms and kissed her tenderly. He'd never felt protective about anyone, never gotten close enough to feel that way, but he felt it now.

Faith pulled back, her eyes still sad but less teary. "Thanks. I needed a hug."

"Any time."

He kept his hands on her waist, reluctant to let her go. "What happened?"

"It's a long story. The bottom line is, they kicked me out."

"Who kicked you out?"

"The Porters." Her mouth trembled as she struggled with her emotions once again. "I deserved it," she said with a sniff.

"Why? What did you do? Break one of their precious Easter eggs?"

She tried to smile but didn't quite make it. "No, I broke their son's heart."

"Ben?"

"Yes. No. I don't know."

"You're not making any sense."

"They just think I broke Ben's heart, but I didn't."

"I'm not so sure about that. I imagine he was pretty upset about losing you."

Faith shook her head. "He wasn't upset because he loved me. He was upset because his plan didn't work. Ben is gay."

Alex looked shocked. "No way!"

"Yes. He's gay."

"And he asked you to marry him? Why?"

"To keep up the facade. His parents were pressuring him to marry, to have children. Since Gary died, Chuck and Nancy have pinned all their hopes on Ben. They want him to carry on the family name. Tradition is very important to them. And I think the idea of Ben marrying me worked the best, because I'm their link to Gary. Ben wants to please his parents. In fact, he has this almost obsessive need for their approval, and I guess in some crazy moment he decided he could forget about being gay and marry me.''

''That's an interesting decision.''

''The only problem is, Ben didn't tell his parents he's gay, nor did he tell them I'd refused to marry him. So today, when Nancy was going on and on about me being a part of the family, I lost it, and I told her I wasn't marrying Ben. She said I was—I was ungrateful and she never wants to see me again.'' Faith drew in a deep breath. ''I probably deserved it.''

''Why? For not going along with their plans? You can't replace their son, no matter how hard you try.''

''I know. I guess I wanted to please them, too. They're the first family who really wanted me—but not anymore. Not anymore.''

Alex studied her tense face, sensing she needed a distraction and fast. She was wired, close to the edge, and he could not let her fall. ''Do you want to talk about this now?''

''No.'' She smiled weakly. ''I'm not sure I ever want to talk about it.''

''Then come and have dinner with us. I just served the roast beef, and, well, if I say so myself, it's a fine Easter dinner I've made.''

''Easter dinner, huh?''

''You'll have to see it to believe it.''

''I wasn't going to come. I'm not sure I can do this anymore.''

''Do what?''

''Get involved with families that aren't my own. How many times do I have to get hit with a brick before I start realizing that my head hurts?''

He cupped her face with his hands and gazed deep into her eyes, seeing all the doubts, the fears, the lonely nights of the past and the future. It was almost like looking into a mirror. ''Don't, Faith. Don't turn into a cynic like me.''

''Why not? Maybe you're right. Maybe it's better not to hope, then you're never disappointed.''

"Somehow I just can't see you wallowing in the dark side of life." He tilted his head to one side. "Tell me this—are you hoping my roast beef tastes like ambrosia?"

She looked startled. "I hadn't thought about it."

"Good, then you won't be disappointed." He planted a quick kiss on her lips. "Come on, have some food. Have some wine. We may not be the Porters, but the Carrigans can definitely do dinner. Too bad you missed grace, though. It was a doozie."

"You said grace?"

"Jessie did." Alex took her hand and pulled her toward the dining room.

"I'll have to get a recap."

"Better ask for the G-rated version."

"I'll remember that."

Faith got a recap of not only grace but everything else the Carrigans had done that day. It wasn't a typical holiday, but it had obviously worked for them. Jessie looked happier than Faith had ever seen her.

"Well, how did we do?" Alex asked as Faith brought in the last few dishes from the table.

"Not bad. You're getting the hang of this family stuff, Alex." Faith leaned against the counter, watching him scrape and rinse. "You know, there is something very sexy about a man doing dishes."

He sent her a skeptical look. "That's a good line, sweetheart."

"It's true. All that male strength channeled into soaping off grease spots. It's downright erotic. I think you should do the dishes all the time."

"And what do I get if I do?"

"Mmmm, what do you want?"

His wicked grin said it all, and Faith felt her cheeks grow warm. "Never mind, I shouldn't have asked."

"I want you naked."

"Well, that's direct." She reached for the sponge on the counter, looking for a distraction.

Alex put his hand over hers, standing so close to her, his breath tickled her cheek. "I want you on top of me, beside me, beneath me, with nothing—and I mean nothing—between us."

She drew in a breath. "All that just for doing the dishes? You ask a lot."

"Honey, I've only just begun."

She ducked under his arm and away from his lips. "We're supposed to be cleaning the kitchen."

"You make me forget all my good intentions."

"I'm not so sure your intentions are good."

Alex started to say something, but the phone rang, so he wiped his hands on a towel and answered it.

"Hello? Yes, Mrs. Conrad. Thanks for calling me back. You spoke to Suzannah?"

Faith tensed, wondering what would come next. Had Suzannah agreed to see Julian?

"I see. Hold on a minute. Let me get a pen."

Faith handed Alex the pen and pad sitting on the kitchen counter. Just then Julian walked into the kitchen, his expression anxious. Apparently he'd heard the phone ring.

Alex jotted down an address. "Thank you." He paused. "I understand. I'll tell my grandfather. Goodbye."

"Tell me what?" Julian asked, his face tense.

Faith put a hand on Julian's shoulder to steady him, but he didn't even notice her. All of his attention was focused on Alex and the piece of paper he held in his hand.

"Suzannah doesn't want to speak to you on the phone," Alex said.

"Why not?"

"She wants you to come to Arizona." Alex held up the paper in his hand. "I have her address in Flagstaff."

Julian's mouth dropped open. He let out a gasp and

swayed slightly. Faith grabbed his arm at the same time Alex rushed over. Together they pushed him gently onto a kitchen chair.

"Easy, Grandfather. Take a breath. There you go." Alex held on to his grandfather's shoulders with both hands, keeping him steady. "Better?"

"Here's some water," Faith said, handing Alex a glass of water.

Alex raised it to his grandfather's lips and Julian took a grateful sip.

"Better," Julian said.

Alex set the glass down on the table, but stayed kneeling in front of his grandfather. "Should I call the doctor?"

"No, I'm all right. I just can't believe you found Suzannah."

"This isn't good for you. I think we should drop it right here," Alex said.

"No, I can't. Suzannah is expecting me, and I will go to her."

Alex looked to Faith with desperation in his eyes. "You see what this is doing to him. Tell him he can't go to Arizona. He'll listen to you."

Faith wanted to do as he asked. In truth, she was alarmed by Julian's pallor, by the trembling of his limbs, but she could also see the light of hope burning in his blue eyes. He wouldn't listen to her. He could only listen to his heart. And Suzannah was calling him.

"I can't. I'm sorry. I don't think any of us can stop him. I'm not sure we should try."

"Faith, for God's sake—"

"Alex, it's all right." Julian held up a hand. "I'm not having a heart attack, and I don't need you or Miss Faith to tell me what to do. I know what to do. And I will do it. I've come this far. I'll see it to the end."

"What about your health?"

"My heart will last. I'm meant to do this, Alex." Julian shook his head, his eyes bemused with memories.

"I'm going to see Suzannah again. I can't believe it."

"You could be disappointed," Alex said.

"I won't be. I just want the chance to tell her I'm sorry for what I did. That's all. And, of course, I'd like to put the pot back so that you and Miss Faith—"

"Let's just worry about you for now."

"Very well. We must go tomorrow, Alex. There is no time to waste. Please, say you will go with me."

Alex hesitated, then slowly nodded. "All right. I'll go with you." He turned to Faith. "I'll have my secretary book us on a flight to Arizona in the morning."

Faith started at the purposeful look in his eyes, and it took a moment for his words to sink in. "Not us. You. You and Julian and Jessie."

"And you."

She put a hand to her necklace and gave it a nervous twist. "No, I couldn't."

"You have to. You helped my grandfather get this far. You're not going to let him down now."

"You don't need me."

"Oh, but we do."

"I have a business."

"So do I. You can find someone to cover for you, just as I can. We'd both be lying to say otherwise."

Faith saw Julian watching her with a hopeful expression on his face. She should say no. She was already far too involved with the Carrigans. Hadn't she learned anything with the Porters? Once this search was over, once Suzannah was found, the Carrigans would have no more need of her. And she'd be left alone, again. Maybe she should take a page out of Alex's book and make a break now.

"Could I speak to Faith alone?" Alex asked, obviously sensing her indecision.

"Of course." Julian got to his feet with more energy, more vigor, than Faith had ever seen. The discovery of Suzannah's whereabouts had taken years off his age.

When they were alone, Faith turned to Alex. "I can't go."

"Why not?"

"Because this isn't my problem."

"You made it your problem when you became friends with my grandfather. I told you not to get involved, remember? But you wouldn't listen."

"I helped him find Suzannah. I never said I'd help him put the pottery back. Besides, this is a good chance for the three of you to bond together."

"We need you, Faith. You're the bridge between us."

She ran a hand through her hair in frustration. "I'm tired of being a bridge, of being someone's link to someone else. What about me, Alex? Is my only purpose in life to serve as a conduit for other people's dreams?"

"Of course not." He looked taken aback by her words. "That's not what I meant."

"You're using me, just like Ben used me."

"That's not true."

"Then why do you want me to come with you if not to soothe your grandfather when he gets upset and keep Jessie out of trouble? Isn't that what you envision me doing? Isn't that my role?"

Alex didn't say anything for a long moment. "I care about you, Faith. Maybe I want you to come along for me."

"Why?"

Alex didn't answer.

"You can't say it, can you?"

"Say what?"

"Three little words. I'll give you a hint. One of them is *love*."

"Do you want me to say I love you?"

"Only if it's true."

Alex sighed. "Dammit, Faith. I've got my hands full right now. Can't we talk about this when we come back?"

"When we come back, I won't be of any use to you.

My job will be done. Either the curse will be broken or it won't. Your grandfather will either stay with Suzannah or find some other place to live. And Jessie—well, we both know what you have planned for her. So tell me, Alex, how are you going to need me when we come back? You won't need a bridge, because everyone will be gone."

"Except me."

"A man who's afraid to love."

"You're beginning to sound like a woman who's afraid to love."

"I learned from the master."

Alex shook his head in bewilderment, as if he wasn't sure what to make of her new attitude. It wasn't surprising really. She felt as confused about things as he did.

"Okay, look at it this way. If you come with me to Arizona, we'll both be taking the same risk. Maybe at the end, I'll want you and you won't want me. Maybe you'll break my heart."

Faith considered his words. "I suppose that's possible. If you have a heart to break."

"Oh, it's there, all right. And if anyone has a shot at ripping it in two, it's you."

She supposed that was as near a declaration of love as she was going to get. "All right. I'll go with you to Arizona."

Relief filled his eyes. "Thank you."

"But not just to make things easier for you, Alex. I have to admit—I want to find out what happens."

"To Suzannah and Julian?"

"And to the people in my dream. I think they're all connected. Maybe we were meant to go to the desert all along. What's that your grandfather always says?"

" 'The winds will curse your life until you return to where it began.' "

"I guess we'll find out if that's true."

"I guess we will."

Chapter 24

By late Monday afternoon, Faith was on her way back to where it began. With Alex at her side and Julian and Jessie sitting across the aisle, the plane took off for Arizona and the long-awaited reunion with Suzannah.

Faith let out a breath as the plane lifted off the runway, banked to the west, and headed south.

"All right?" Alex asked, covering her hand.

She smiled, realizing her fingers were wrapped tightly around the ends of the armrests. "I'm fine. I don't fly much."

"Really? I thought your head was always in the clouds."

"Very funny." She settled back in her seat. "How about you? Do you like to fly?"

"I love it. I like that rush when the plane lifts off. Almost as good as . . ." He smiled wickedly. "Well, you know."

Since his words conjured up a memory she preferred not to dwell on, Faith ignored him by pulling out the magazine from the seat pocket in front of her. Inside was a map showing the route from San Francisco to Phoenix, Arizona. In two short hours they would be in the desert.

Faith passed the next few minutes by glancing through the magazine, but there was little to hold her attention, so she slipped it back in the seat pocket and laced her hands together in her lap.

Alex had the tray table down and was going over a file he'd pulled out of his briefcase. All she could see were columns of numbers. Alex seemed satisfied, a pleased smile curving his lips as he studied his reports. She liked watching him work.

When Alex was focused on something, he gave it his all, 150 percent. She remembered when those intense blue eyes had been focused on her. Lord, how she remembered. Her stomach made its familiar gut-clenching twist, and she tried to focus on something besides Alex. But that was part of the problem. He simply overpowered everything around him. He was sharper, clearer, brighter, louder—a man who commanded attention—and a man who had no idea just how many people looked up to him.

Faith had a feeling Alex saw everything in his life through a pair of out-of-focus glasses that screamed *failure* and *rejection*. On the outside he was confident and secure, a successful businessman, but on the inside, he was still that kid who got his oversized foot stuck in the desk.

Alex caught her smile. "What's so funny?"

"Just imagining you with your foot stuck in a desk."

"I shouldn't have told you that story. I have a feeling you don't forget anything."

"Then we're even, because neither do you. Tell me something. Do you ever see your mother or your father?"

"Rarely."

"Are they mad at you as well, or is it one-sided?"

Alex closed the file in front of him and slipped it back into his carry-on. "No one is angry with anyone. You have to care about someone to get mad."

"You're still angry."

"I'm not."

"You are."

"And you're a stubborn woman."

"A survival skill learned early."

"Okay, I don't respect my mother for walking out on me. I guess you could say I'm still mad at her. My father—we never had much in common. He didn't hang around long enough for us to find things in common. He's a photographer and travels all over the world. I don't even know where he is right now. And he doesn't know where I am. That's the kind of family I grew up in, Faith. It wasn't the Cleavers."

"That's too bad."

He shrugged. "Speaking of families—did you talk to the Porters this morning?"

Faith tensed, wishing she'd never brought up the subject of family. "No."

"Why not?"

"Nancy is no longer working at the bakery. When she threw me out of her house, she also quit."

"What about Ben?"

"He never worked there."

Alex shot her a pointed look.

"I haven't spoken to Ben."

"Ben must have talked to his mother. He must know that she kicked you out of the house. I'm surprised he wasn't waiting for you when you got home last night."

"He wasn't."

"And he didn't call to apologize for putting you in an awkward position?"

"No."

"I thought the guy was your friend."

Faith squirmed in her seat, irritated with Alex for echoing her own thoughts. "He was my friend. Is, I mean."

"I think you were right the first time. Ben let his mother eat you alive, and he didn't do anything to stop her."

"Ben wasn't even there."

"He knew. Don't tell me he didn't know."

"Fine, I won't tell you." She sighed and crossed her arms in front of her chest. "Ben is a dear, sweet—coward. He couldn't stop his mother from throwing me out because that would have meant telling her the truth or at least some other lie that would have reflected badly on him.''

''So he sacrificed you.''

''I guess.''

''Come on, Faith. You should be mad at this guy. You should be calling him every name in the book.''

Alex's eyes blazed with an anger that seemed completely irrational. If Faith hadn't known better, she would have thought he was feeling protective toward her, furious with Ben because Ben had hurt her. But that would have meant Alex cared. A tiny, dangerous seed of hope took root.

''Why does it matter to you?'' she asked.

''Because—it's not right.''

''I thought maybe you were angry with Ben because he hurt me.''

''Well, I am.''

''That would mean you care about me.''

Alex frowned, his eyebrows curving down in a wary line. ''You're putting words in my mouth.''

''Someone has to.''

Alex rolled his eyes. ''Why do I bother trying to talk to you?''

''Because you're a marshmallow, Alex. All tough and crusty on the outside, but inside you're as mushy as they come.''

''You know, you could switch seats with Jessie.''

''And risk letting you fall in love even more with your daughter? I wouldn't dream of it.''

Alex tapped his fingers restlessly against the tray table. He glanced out the window, then back at her. ''I left a message for Eddie Saunders this morning. I told him to call me as soon as he got back to town. I also asked Melanie's attorney to follow up with him for me.''

''Why didn't you tell Mr. Saunders that you had his daughter?'' Faith lowered her voice. Jessie had on headphones and was sitting on the other side of Julian, but she didn't want to risk being overheard.

"I didn't think it was a good idea to tell him that over the phone." Alex tipped his head toward Jessie. "You know, she should be in school today. And here I am trekking out to the desert with my crazy grandfather to chase down a curse. What kind of a father am I?"

"One who cares very much about his grandfather, despite his best efforts not to do so."

"I've cared before, Faith."

"I know, and look where it got you." She let out another sigh. "Look where it got me. I guess you have the last laugh after all."

Alex looked into her eyes, his own gaze a troubled blue. "I'm not laughing. I can't stand the thought of anyone hurting you. I know you haven't had it easy over the years."

"I survived. One of the social workers told me I was just like a weed. I could grow anywhere. I didn't need much, just a little sunlight, a little water, and a little space."

"Kids need a hell of a lot more than that," Alex said fiercely. "And you're not a weed. You're a rose, a beautiful, prickly, sweet rose."

Faith felt her tiny seed of hope grow bigger. "Thank you. That's one of the nicest things anyone has ever said about me."

"Someday you'll meet a guy with a great family, and you'll fit right in."

She frowned. "I think that might be the meanest thing anyone has ever said to me."

"Why? I just wanted—"

"To remind me that I have no place in your long-term plans. I know."

"Faith, I don't have long-term plans. That's the first problem."

"And the second problem is you're too hardheaded to

see that you and I could be absolutely perfect for each other."

He looked stunned by her directness. "I know we're good in some areas, but—"

"I'm not talking about sex. I'm talking about love."

"I don't know much about love."

"Neither do I. Maybe we could figure it out together. At least we'd both know we were starting from ground zero. We could make our mistakes together."

He shook his head, not willing to give an inch. "I have a habit of disappointing people. It runs in the family. Ask my grandfather. The Carrigans have bad genes. I'm not husband material. I'm not a family man."

"Since I don't even know whether my genes are bad or good, then I suppose I'm not good wife material either."

"You are. Anyone just has to look at you to see that you would be . . ." His voice turned husky, as tender as his eyes. "You would be an incredible wife."

His words stole her breath away, and she wished for the impossible. "Someday, Alex, I'm going to remind you of that."

The flight attendant interrupted their conversation with drinks and peanuts, and by the time she'd finished serving, they were flying over the desert. The pilot came on the speaker to direct their attention to the Grand Canyon below.

Faith had never been to Arizona, never seen the Grand Canyon or the desert, and she wasn't prepared for the incredible sight. The land was vast, the earth a glorious orange-red, contrasting with the deep blue sky. Occasionally white, puffy clouds blew through the landscape, but they disappeared before long as if they were not allowed to shade the ground from the hot sun above.

"It looks so big," Faith murmured. "There's so much land to cover. Even if Suzannah has the pot . . ."

Alex sent her a skeptical look. "Do you really think she kept a piece of broken pottery for fifty years? And if she did, why didn't she try to find Julian?''

''Maybe she did try.''

''He hasn't been in hiding.''

''True, but he was married. And so was she. Maybe she felt it would be disloyal. As for keeping the pottery all these years—yes, I think she kept it.''

''There's my Faith. You're back. I knew the optimist in you had not completely vanished.''

She made a face at him. ''I can't help looking at the bright side. It's what gets me up in the morning. You should try it sometime. Anyway, I think Suzannah kept the pottery because she knew it was important. Julian said that when Suzannah touched it she became afraid. She heard voices in her head. Just like me.''

''Tell me about the dreams.''

Faith hesitated, not sure she wanted to reveal the dreams to Alex, to his skepticism and his doubts. Still, perhaps he needed to know. ''They take place in a deep canyon. There are caves, dwellings in the rocks; some can only be reached by climbing up the face of the canyon. There's a woman in the dreams, me, I guess. I don't know. There's an older woman, my grandmother, I think, or the woman's grandmother.'' She laughed nervously. ''This isn't making any sense.''

''You see yourself in the dreams?''

''Not me exactly. I feel like I'm someone else, someone who lived a long time ago. There are two men, one that I'm supposed to marry, and one that I love. The old woman is angry with me, because I'm supposed to marry the one guy, but I'm resisting.'' Faith thought back to the dreams, trying to remember the details. ''The pot is there, too. I think I made it for the man I love. Whenever the other man sees it, he becomes angry.''

''Faith, I hate to be pragmatic—''

''But you're going to anyway.''

''I think your dream is reflecting your life, your ambivalence towards marrying Ben, your relationship with Mrs. Porter, the whole bit.''

"And the warrior, the man I love, that would be—you?"

His eyes darkened as he turned his gaze toward the window. "You don't love me, Faith."

"How do you know?"

"Because you shouldn't."

"That doesn't mean I don't."

"We barely know each other."

"Sometimes I feel like I've known you for hundreds of years." She paused. "But I digress. In the last dream, the moon was full and the wedding ceremony was beginning. My face was painted, and they were taking me toward the circle of fire where people were dancing and chanting, and the drums were beating. Then I saw him—the warrior. He stood in the shadows, and he put his hand out to me."

"What happened?"

"I ran to him. Then he disappeared. I couldn't find him. The walls started closing in on me, and I felt like I was being buried alive. Then I woke up."

"Wow. When you dream, you really dream."

"The warrior looks exactly like you."

Alex leaned back in his seat. "It's just a dream. It doesn't mean anything."

"Maybe not. But somehow . . ."

"What?"

She looked him straight in the eye. "I think something terrible happened to the woman when she made her choice, something evil, something to do with that pot. I feel it deep down in my soul, Alex. And somewhere out there in the desert is the rest of the story."

They landed in Phoenix a few minutes later. After disembarking from the plane, they made their way to the rental car desk where they picked up a four-wheel drive. The trip from Phoenix to Flagstaff took several hours, but the time passed rapidly for Faith. She had expected miles of flat, brown, dusty land, but the scenery changed a hundred times during their trip, from the blistering heat of the lowlands to the red bluffs of Sedona, and the mountains covered with ponderosa pine near Flagstaff.

Having spent her entire life in various California suburbs, Faith had not been prepared for the vastness of this state, the endless horizon of land, the rivers and streams that wove through mazes of canyons, the incredible buttes that came out of nowhere to touch the sky.

Along the way, she glanced through the guidebook Alex had bought at the airport gift shop. In the front was a map of the entire state. She saw notations for all the natural wonders, from the infamous Grand Canyon to the Painted Desert, the Petrified Forest, and the Badlands. She learned that the Navajo reservation covered almost the entire upper third of the state, stretching into the Four Corners area where Arizona, New Mexico, Colorado, and Utah meet. Within the Navajo reservation was the Hopi reservation, and the two tribes were still arguing over boundaries.

The book also went on to describe the various sites of prehistoric peoples such as the Anasazi. Discussion of archaeological sites was followed by pictures of pottery and baskets. Some of the pots looked similar to the half Julian owned, but nothing exact. That didn't surprise Faith. She had a feeling that particular pot was one of a kind.

Julian remained quiet during most of the trip, occasionally commenting on the scenery, but otherwise he seemed to have little to say until they neared their destination. Then he became jittery, nervous, talking a mile a minute about that summer trip fifty years earlier.

Julian told them that he and Suzannah had met in Flagstaff and spent a month taking day trips to various other parts of the state, sometimes staying overnight in rundown motels or campgrounds. He told them Suzannah had worn her mother's ring, pretending they were married, so no one would ask questions about who they were and what they were doing. Not that many people did.

Arizona had been even less crowded fifty years earlier, and most people minded their own business.

Faith let him talk. Through his stories she began to piece together a picture of Suzannah. She imagined a young, impetuous redhead with fire in her eyes and love in her heart, flouting the conventions, running off with the boy of her dreams, dancing in the moonlight in a meadow filled with wildflowers. Their story was pure romance, almost a fairy tale. She wondered if it would have a happy ending—after all these years.

Julian ran out of steam when they turned off the highway. In fact, as they stopped at a light, he began pulling at the collar of his shirt as if it were too tight, as if he couldn't breathe.

"Alex, stop the car," Faith said, suddenly terrified by Julian's color, his trembling limbs.

"What?" Alex glanced at his grandfather and immediately pulled into the next lane, finally turning in to a gas station. "Grandfather? Are you all right?"

"Water. I need some water for my pills." Julian reached into his pocket and took out a bottle of pills.

Faith handed him the water bottle she'd brought with her on the trip. He took a long sip and let out a breath of relief.

"All right now?" Alex asked, his voice tense.

"Yes."

"Are you sure? Take a deep breath. Is there any pain?"

"No. My chest felt tight for a minute there, but it's fine now."

"Do you get these attacks often?"

"Sometimes—when I feel stress."

"That's it. We're going to find our hotel and get you some rest. I knew this trip would be too much for you."

"It's not too much, and I want to go straight to Suzannah's house. *Now,* Alex."

Alex glared at his grandfather. Julian glared back. Standoff. They needed a bridge, so Faith leaned forward.

"Why don't we compromise? We'll find our hotel, get some dinner, and decide what to do next."

"Fine," Alex said.

"Fine." Julian replied, crossing his arms in front of his chest.

Faith sat back and smiled at Jessie. "Boys," she muttered.

"I heard that," Alex said as he started the engine.

He drove through town until they found the hotel his secretary had booked for them. Alex and Julian were to share a room, with Faith and Jessie doing the same. They agreed to meet in thirty minutes for dinner in the coffee shop.

"This is nice," Jessie said, as she walked into the hotel room. "Ooh, two double beds." She flopped down on onc, bouncing in appreciation. "Cool. I never stayed anywhere as nice as this. I'm going to check out the bathroom. Can I take a shower?"

"Sure, honey, whatever you want."

Faith stretched out on the bed, relieved to have a few moments peace. She felt tired and cramped after the plane trip and the long car ride. Too much movement, she decided, closing her eyes.

The silence soothed her, and she drifted off almost immediately.

He was there in the moonlight, waiting for her with the pot in his hands. He opened his arms. She ran into them. He kissed her long and hard, pledging his love, his life, his soul. It was over too fast. But they could not linger here in the open canyon floor. The others were coming.

Her betrothed would not allow her to be with anyone else. That she had chosen another—a man who had come from another place, who had always walked alone, who called no other a friend—would shame her betrothed. He would be an outcast for the rest of his life unless he sought revenge. He would have to kill them to save his pride. They had to get away.

The warrior pointed to the rock formation in the distance where the butterflies danced. He told her his grandfather had spoken of another land, a world they had never seen. Beyond those rocks, he said, they would find their freedom.

He took her hand and she gave him her heart . . .

Faith groaned as the drums got louder and louder. She sat up in bewilderment, finally realizing the pounding was coming from the hotel room door. Jessie was singing in the shower and obviously hadn't heard a thing. Faith got to her feet and walked over to the door, wondering how long she'd slept.

She pulled the door open and Alex fell into the room, his hair wild and restless, his eyes frantic.

"What's wrong?" she asked.

"Grandfather. He's gone."

Chapter 25

"Gone? What do you mean? Is he downstairs?"

"No, he's not downstairs," Alex yelled. "He's gone. While I was in the shower he disappeared. He's not in the gift shop or the coffee shop or the bar. When I came back to my room, I found this." He held out a piece of paper.

Faith took it from his hand and read aloud. " 'Gone to meet Suzannah. I can't wait another second. Love, Julian.' " She handed it back to him. "At least we know he's all right."

"Do we? An hour ago he looked like he was having a heart attack because of stress. What kind of stress do you think he'll be under when he sees Suzannah for the first time in fifty years?"

"A lot. I'll get my purse."

Jessie came out of the bathroom, wearing a clean T-shirt and a pair of shorts, her hair wrapped in a towel. She stopped when she saw Alex. "Is it dinnertime already?"

"Julian has disappeared," Faith said gently. "Apparently he couldn't wait to find Suzannah."

Jessie's eyes widened. "Oh."

Faith turned to Alex. "Did he take the car?"

"No, I've got the keys right here."

"Then he must have found a cab. We'll just have to

go to Suzannah's house and make sure he's all right."

"I don't like this, Faith. Why couldn't he wait?"

"Your grandfather has a mind of his own."

"He's selfish and arrogant and does whatever the hell he wants, no matter who gets hurt in the process."

Faith read through the anger in his eyes. "And you're worried about him."

"I guess I've gotten used to having him around. Come on, let's go."

"I'm ready. Jess?"

Jess ran a brush through her wet hair and slipped on her sandals. "I'm ready, too."

With the help of a local city map and the concierge, they found Suzannah's house without too much trouble. It was in a neighborhood on the outskirts of town facing the San Francisco Peaks, where snow could still be seen on the very tops of the mountains.

Suzannah's house was a one-story white stucco building with red tiles. The lawn was well kept with colorful flowers planted in baskets along the walkway. The porch light cast shadows along the edges of the yard. There were a few lights on inside the house, but everything was quiet.

Alex rang the bell and they waited for long, tense seconds. "Where is she?" he muttered.

Faith started to answer, then heard movement from inside the house. Her stomach tightened and she couldn't help the nervous flutters of excitement that ran up and down her spine. She was going to meet Suzannah. Finally. Faith could only imagine what Julian must have felt when he'd stood on this doorstep waiting for his long-lost love to open the door.

Faith held her breath as the door slowly opened and a woman stepped into the light. She was a slender reed, barely five feet tall, her hair a dark, rich shade of copper, her eyes a light hazel or green. They seemed to change as she stepped into the light.

"Yes?" She looked at Faith, then at Alex. Her jaw dropped open as she stared into his blue eyes—so like his grandfather's. "Oh, dear." She put a hand to her mouth. "You're—you must be—who are you?"

"Alex Carrigan. Julian Carrigan's grandson. And you are?"

"Suzannah." She closed her eyes for a moment, then opened them again. "You have the same eyes as your grandfather."

"So I've been told. This is Faith Christopher, a friend of mine, and my—and Jessie."

Suzannah said hello to Faith and Jessie, still looking uncertain, unsure of what to do next. That was when it occurred to Faith that something was wrong. Suzannah did not look like a woman who had just been reunited with her long-lost love.

Alex seemed to come to the same conclusion, his eyes narrowing as he tried to peer past Suzannah into the house. "I'd like to speak to my grandfather."

"Your grandfather?"

"Yes," Alex said impatiently. "Can we come in?"

"Your grandfather is not here."

"He has to be. He said he was going to meet you. He left at least a half hour ago. He has to be here."

"I'm sorry, but I haven't seen him, not in more than fifty years."

"Faith?" Alex turned to her with his heart in his eyes. She'd never seen him look so worried.

She put a hand on his arm. "He's okay. We must have misread the message."

"All he had was this address."

"Is Julian all right?" Jessie asked, as she bit down on her bottom lip.

"Yes," Faith said fiercely. "We didn't come this far to lose him now." She turned to Suzannah. "May we come in for a few moments, so we can think about what to do next?"

"Yes, of course." She stepped back so they could enter the house.

Suzannah's living room was a kaleidoscope of colors, reds, greens, oranges, and blues. There were handmade rugs warming the hardwood floors, Native American crafts, baskets and dolls adorning every corner of every table. There were paintings on the wall that were purely Southwest, spectacular views of the Grand Canyon and the Painted Desert, Monument Valley and the Sunset Crater.

Faith couldn't help wondering if Suzannah had always surrounded herself with such things or if her return to Arizona had revived an old passion.

"Would you like something to drink?" Suzannah asked, as she led them toward the back of the house where the combined kitchen/family room led onto a small deck. The windows and French doors had been left open to offset the balmy night, and a light breeze blew through the house.

"I'd like something to drink," Jessie said. "Do you have any soda?"

"I have orange juice or cranberry juice. I also have several different teas."

"Orange juice is fine."

"Tea," Faith replied to Suzannah's silent inquiry.

"Nothing for me," Alex said, taking a seat at the kitchen table. "I can't believe my grandfather isn't here. He's been looking for you for years, and now that we've found you, he's missing."

Suzannah handed Jessie a glass of orange juice, then filled the teakettle with water. In the light of the kitchen, Suzannah's face showed signs of age. There were fine lines running across her forehead, around her eyes and the corners of her mouth. She wore a light dusting of makeup, but it did little to shield the freckles or weather spots dotting her skin. Despite her years, she moved with an athletic grace that made every movement seem effortless. Faith could see why Julian had fallen in love with her. She must have been strikingly beautiful in her day

Suzannah walked over to the table and sat down as she waited for the teakettle to get hot. "I didn't know your grandfather was looking for me until two nights ago, when my sister-in-law called me. I felt this momentary panic when I heard his name. I knew that I couldn't speak to him on the phone, not after so long." She paused. "I really didn't expect him to come here. Maybe a part of me wondered if he would, but I really didn't expect it."

"It would have been easier if you had just called him back," Alex said.

"I was afraid. It's been so long. I didn't know what I would say." Her gaze feasted on Alex's face. "You look so like him, at least the man I knew. I can hardly believe I'm sitting here talking to Julian's grandson. Sometimes it seems like only a moment ago that Julian and I were dancing in the meadow next to the old gray sedan he'd bought for a hundred dollars. Other times it seems like centuries ago."

The teakettle let out a cry and Suzannah stood up abruptly. She busied herself fixing two mugs of tea, then brought them over to the table for Faith and herself.

"Thank you," Faith said as Suzannah settled back into a chair.

They sat quietly for a few moments until Jessie finally spoke. "Aren't you going to ask her about the pot?"

Suzannah stiffened, sitting straight up in her chair as if she'd been called to task. "The pot? Julian told you about the pot?"

"Thousands of times," Alex replied. "He's hoping you still have the other half."

"Why? What does it matter now?"

"He has the crazy idea that this pot can be put back together and returned to its resting place. My grandfather believes that he was cursed when he took that pot and the only way to break the curse is to return the pot."

Suzannah bolted out of her chair. "Cursed? I don't know anything about a curse."

''It's probably not even true,'' Alex said.

''I knew he shouldn't have taken it. But I didn't know about a curse. What is it?''

''Apparently neither my grandfather nor anyone in his family will ever find true love as long as he has the pot.''

Suzannah stared at Alex, her light eyes shadowing with fear or guilt, Faith couldn't tell which. ''Your grandfather—Julian—he's never been in love?''

''He's imagined himself to be a few times, but it never worked out. He blames the pot. I'm not so sure that isn't just an excuse for his lack of commitment.''

Suzannah stared out the window at the darkness. She didn't move for several seconds, completely lost in thought. ''I always wondered,'' she murmured.

Alex rose to his feet. ''We need to find my grandfather, Mrs. Conrad. I'm sure he'll be willing to answer all your questions, but right now I need you to answer one of mine.''

''No, I want you to go,'' Suzannah said, her voice turning shrill. ''This was a mistake, a horrible mistake.''

''Now, wait just a minute,'' Alex said angrily. ''It's your fault my grandfather has come all this way, and—''

''And,'' Faith said, interrupting Alex with a sharp voice, ''we want you to know how important you are to Julian.'' Faith knew that she had to smooth the way between Alex and Suzannah. Alex was worried and impatient, but that wouldn't get Suzannah to help them. She was ready to put them on the next plane back to San Francisco.

''I don't mean anything to Julian,'' Suzannah said, her eyes anguished as she turned to Faith. ''It was a summer romance, a month of foolishness that ended in disaster. I have no wish to remember it or relive it.''

''I can understand that, but Julian doesn't feel the same way. He speaks very fondly of you. He read me some of your letters and—''

''He kept my letters? All these years, he kept my letters?" Suzannah sank back into her chair, her eyes filling with moisture. "Why did he do that?"

"Because he loved you."

Suzannah drew in a long breath and slowly let it out. "I loved him, too. But our love was not meant to be. I married someone else, you know. I lived with him for fifty-four years. He died two years ago last fall."

"That's when you came back to Arizona," Faith said.

"Yes. I'd been happy here, at least in the beginning. It was the only place I'd truly felt free to be myself, to live without restraints, without guilt or shame. I guess I hoped I'd find that happiness again."

"In all those years, you never thought to look up my grandfather?" Alex asked.

Suzannah shook her head. "No. I was a married woman. I assumed Julian had gone on to marry someone else. Which he obviously did, since you're his grandson."

"Several someones," Alex commented dryly. "But I'll let him tell you his life story. Right now I just want to find him. His heart isn't so good anymore."

She paled. "I'm sorry to hear that."

"Will you help us find him?" Alex asked. "Please?"

His gentle tone brought Suzannah around. "All right. If I can."

"I think you might be the only one who can," Faith said. "Alex, do you want to try the hotel? Maybe he went back there."

Alex did as she suggested, but there was no answer in his room. A follow-up call to the front desk and the coffee shop added no further information. Julian had disappeared.

"You could try calling the cab company," Jessie said. "Melanie always paid the cab driver extra so he wouldn't say where he took us. Maybe Julian didn't know to do that."

Alex stared at Jessie in amazement. "The things you

know. Thanks, I'll see if I can find out which cab company picked him up."

While Alex was doing that, Jessie wandered into the backyard to look at the stars, leaving Suzannah and Faith alone at the table.

Suzannah stared at Faith thoughtfully. "It's funny. We have similar features, don't we?"

"Yes. That's why Julian picked me."

"Picked you? I don't understand."

"He came into my bakery one day and told me this wild story about a prehistoric piece of pottery and a long-lost love. He asked for my help. I just thought he was a lonely old man. But then I saw the pot, and I touched it, and I felt an electrical current run through my body from the past to the present."

Suzannah drew in a sharp breath, her eyes glittering in the evening light. Faith put a hand on her arm. "You heard them, too, didn't you?"

"Yes. I've never been so frightened in my life."

"I think the woman who owned that pot looked like me—and like you. Maybe that's why she speaks to us and not to the others."

"I wondered, but the dreams were so long ago. They haunted me for days until I married Harry, and then they disappeared. I never touched the pot again. I never wanted to feel the way I felt that night."

"That's why you ran away."

"It was a sin, what Julian did, made worse by my actions. I'm the one who broke the pot. I deserved to be punished."

"So you went home and married a man you didn't love." Faith sat up straight, suddenly seeing all the parallels in their stories. "And she stopped speaking to you because you would no longer understand. That's it. You made a different choice, and you could no longer hear her. It all makes sense now."

"Not to me." Suzannah looked even more confused. "What choice did I make?"

"You married a man for duty and not for love."

"You don't know that."

"Don't I?" Faith sent her a steady look, seeing the truth in her eyes. "And the woman who owned the pot chose love over duty. Please tell me you kept the pot, Suzannah."

"I—I need to speak to Julian before I say anything else."

"Then you'll have to help us find him," Alex interrupted, returning to the room. "If he didn't come here to meet you, he must have gone somewhere else. The question is, where?"

Julian stared at the enormous warehouse in front of him. It was nine o'clock and the warehouse was closing. The last shoppers had left the building with their shopping carts filled with toilet paper and dish soap and boxes of cookies and trays of muffins. He'd watched as one family loaded up the back of their Suburban with several boxes of foods and goods.

The world had changed so much in fifty years, and the land had changed too. There was now an enormous parking lot and a cement monster where there once had been dirt and trees and wildflowers and a sky filled with stars, filled with magic.

Julian sat down on a bench outside the front door. He knew this was the spot they had come to all those years ago. He was sure of it. Because one thing hadn't changed: the cross on the nearby hillside, marking the grave of some unknown person.

He remembered many nights when he and Suzannah had come to this very spot. It had been deserted then, nothing but trees and shrubs and walking trails. They'd parked the car on the dirt and turned on the radio. They'd laughed over crackers and cheese, and when the night had grown old and the moon had grown full, they'd danced under the stars.

Tears blurred his vision. It was just as well. He no

longer wanted to see the parking lot, the building behind him, the proof of progress. Another generation had taken over their spot. It was too late to recapture his dreams or his love. Alex had been right all along. He was chasing windmills, seeing a world that didn't exist.

His heart filled with sadness as the coolness of the evening chilled his bones. He had left it too long. He had had his chance, his time in the sun, and it was gone.

He couldn't go to Suzannah's house. He couldn't walk up to her door and simply ring the bell—not after all these years. He had no courage left, no strength to go on. The curse had won. He would die alone.

"Do you have any idea where we're going?" Alex asked Suzannah as she squinted to see a road sign. They'd gotten into his car thirty minutes earlier and so far appeared to be driving in circles.

"So much has changed," Suzannah said. "I'm not even sure if Julian would remember where we used to go, much less be able to find it. I've lived here for two years, and I still don't know my way around. Turn here—I think."

Alex groaned but did as she requested. He couldn't believe he was now looking for his grandfather when he'd spent the past week looking for Suzannah. Why, oh, why had he come on this wild-goose chase?

"Don't give up now," Faith said from the backseat. "We'll find him."

"Then I'm going to kill him," he said darkly. "And I swear if he jumps out of the shadows and yells 'gotcha' . . . well, you won't want to be around." Actually, right now Alex longed for his grandfather to do exactly that. Something was wrong. He could feel it in his bones. Maybe Julian had set out for Suzannah's house and collapsed on the way. He could be lying in a hospital bed right now, or worse yet—he could be alone and needing help.

Alex took several calming breaths. He'd never had a big imagination, but it was working overtime tonight. He checked his rearview mirror for cars and saw Faith staring out the back window, looking as alarmed as he felt. For all her belief in the goodness of life, she didn't look too optimistic, and another knot formed in his gut. Even Jessie looked grim, not to mention tired.

What the hell was he doing—driving aimlessly around Flagstaff, Arizona, without a clue as to where he was going?

"That's it," Suzannah said suddenly.

He slammed on the brakes, throwing them all forward in the car. "What?"

"Turn down that street." She pointed off to the right. "It was over there. I remember, because there's a cross on the hillside, and we used to look at it and wonder who was buried there."

"Sounds like a fun place to go."

"This spot was empty then. We used to drive out here in Julian's old car. It rattled and rolled all the way. When we got here, we'd turn on the radio and we'd dance. I loved to dance. We were supposed to come here that night—that last night. In the morning we were planning to drive into New Mexico, to leave Arizona. But that didn't happen." Her voice grew wistful. "I never danced with anyone as good as Julian. Poor Harry couldn't carry a rhythm to save his life. But Julian, he literally swept me off my feet. He was a wonderful man, kind, caring, considerate, always willing to listen. I'd never met anyone like him."

Alex couldn't believe what he was hearing. His grandfather had always been selfish, arrogant, interested in getting what was his, making his point, and not listening to others. Had time colored Suzannah's memories as well as Julian's or had they truly had such a romantic love affair?

He had to admit the longing in her voice had taken him by surprise. He'd believed all along that Julian's memories were one-sided, but Suzannah seemed as lost without Julian as he was without her.

"That's the spot," Suzannah said. "Pull into the parking lot."

"It's a shopping warehouse," Alex said in surprise.

"I told you things have changed."

"Grandfather wouldn't have come here."

"Maybe not. I don't know where else to go." She shot him a desperate look that matched his own feelings exactly.

Alex drove farther into the parking lot. It was dark and empty; the warehouse was closed. "This is ridiculous. We'll just go back to the hotel and wait. He has to return sometime." Alex pulled into a parking spot so he could turn around and go back the way he'd come in.

"Wait," Faith said abruptly. "I think we should take a closer look."

"What's the point? He's not here."

"There's someone by the front door. I think it's a man. He's sitting on the bench." Faith had the door open before he could turn off the engine. Jessie jumped out as well, leaving only Suzannah and him in the car.

"Shall we go check it out?" he asked her.

"I'm not sure I can do this."

"You can."

"Do you think he'll remember me?"

"I don't think he's ever forgotten you. Why don't we find out if it's him?"

Chapter 26

"Julian?" *Faith called. Her heart sped up as she* saw the man slumped on the bench. His head hung so low it touched his chest. He didn't appear to be moving. Oh, God! What if he'd had a heart attack? Could they have come all this way only to be stopped now? As she got closer, she turned to Jessie. "Honey, maybe you should wait here."

Jessie looked stricken. "Is he dead?"

"I hope not."

Faith went over to the bench, praying all the way. "Julian, are you all right?" She touched his shoulder with her hand, and he opened his eyes, his clear blue, weary old eyes.

"Miss Faith?"

"Oh, thank heavens. We've been looking all over for you."

"I shouldn't have come here. It's too late."

"It's not too late."

"She was a dream, my Suzannah. But she's gone, and I can't get her back. Everything has changed. I just want to go home."

"Julian, she's here."

He looked at her without comprehending. "What?"

"Suzannah is here. We found her." She smiled at him with encouragement. "She told us about this spot."

"No," he whispered, shaking his head in disbelief.

"Yes. Don't you think it's time you said hello?"

Faith took a step back, and Suzannah walked into the light. Julian stood up and the air crackled between them. Faith held her breath wondering what would happen next. What would they say, what would they do?

"Suzannah." Julian drew himself up to his full height, no longer slumping with age and fatigue but standing proud and tall. He looked like a new man.

"Julian," she acknowledged, tossing her head back ever so slightly. She held herself as stiff and straight as a poker.

Another moment of silence followed, so excruciatingly painful Faith wanted to jump into the breach, to yell at them to start talking, to make up for lost time, to say something, anything.

But all they could do was stare at one another, looking, searching, wondering . . .

"I can't believe it's you," Julian said finally. "My God! You look as beautiful as the last time I saw you."

Suzannah trembled ever so slightly, obviously touched by his words. "I'm an old woman now, Julian. Not at all the young girl you remember."

He looked into her eyes. "I never thought I'd see you again."

"And I never thought to see you. But here you are." She tipped her head toward their surroundings. "In our spot . . ." Her voice broke and she took in a deep breath and let it out. "So many years have passed. I see all the signs of age—in both of us. And yet you look so very much the same. How can that be?"

"You look the same to me, too." Julian slowly extended his hand. "And I believe, if memory serves me right, that you owe me a dance."

A lone tear dripped down her cheek. "Julian. It's too late for us."

"Just a dance, one dance."

"Here?"

"Yes, here. In our meadow of wildflowers."

Suzannah took his hand. She went into his arms as if it had been five minutes since they'd seen each other. And slowly they began to dance.

"Go get the car, Alex," Faith whispered. "Pull it over there and turn on the music."

Alex sent her a skeptical look but did as she requested. He pulled up a second later and opened the windows so that a song of romance filled the night, transforming the warehouse parking lot into a starlit meadow for one last time.

Alex got out of the car and slipped his arms around Faith's waist, pulling her back against his chest as Julian and Suzannah danced in the middle of the parking lot.

"It's incredible," Faith murmured. "I think true love really does last."

"There were people in between, Faith. My grandfather married five other women."

"But they weren't Suzannah."

Alex's arms tightened around her body, holding her close. She wished Alex could believe as she did. But she feared he saw only the warehouse parking lot and not the magic of the night. Then his lips trailed down her cheek and she wondered . . .

An hour later they sat around Suzannah's kitchen table once again. She and Julian seemed to be in a daze, unable to speak coherent sentences or form rational thoughts. They'd spoken only haltingly in the car on the way home, disjointed phrases that meant little to Faith but obviously something to them.

Upon arriving at Suzannah's house, Jessie had disappeared into another room to find a television set. Faith didn't blame her for wanting some space. It had been a very long day. But there were questions that still needed to be asked and answers that needed to be given.

"Can I get anyone anything?" Suzannah asked.

Alex and Faith murmured no, while Julian continued

to stare at Suzannah as if he were afraid she would vanish before his very eyes. Finally Julian spoke.

"We must talk about what happened, Suzannah." He put his hand over hers. "Please tell me why you ran away that night."

Suzannah took a moment to gather her thoughts. "I was frightened. The wind grew fierce after you left. It blew through the trailer like a hurricane. I couldn't breathe. I was choking on the dust. So I grabbed my bag and the pot and ran outside. I thought of going to you, but the wind knocked me over. At that point, all I wanted to do was get away from the voices in my head. I took your car and drove to the bus station. There was a bus leaving for Los Angeles, and I got on it. I hoped you would find your car."

"I did, eventually."

Suzannah stared down at their entwined hands. "I was a coward to run away as I did, but I felt so terrible. And in the beginning I was angry with you. I knew stealing the pot was wrong, but breaking it was even worse. Everything my aunt had told me was true. I was wicked. I was a sinner. It all made sense to me. When I returned home, my aunt was ill. She begged me to marry Harry Conrad. He was a good man, she told me. He was studying to be a minister, and perhaps with him I would be able to find God."

She paused for a long moment. "I thought maybe it was the right thing to do after all that had gone wrong in Arizona. It wasn't fair to Harry, of course. But at eighteen, I didn't realize that, or else I just didn't care. Years later, I did care, and I tried to love him back, to be a good wife. We didn't have a bad life together. I lacked for little, except children, but that wasn't meant to be."

"Perhaps because of what we did, the curse I brought down on our heads. I was never sure if it had hurt you. I'm sorry." Julian touched her hair with a tenderness that caught at Faith's heart. "I wish you had waited for me that night, or called me when you got home. I would have come for you. I would have tried to help you."

She smiled at him. "It's so easy to say that now. But we were young. It was a different world then. And we had our lives ahead of us. You were heading for Broadway as I recall. Did you make it there?"

"I spent most of my life there."

"I'm glad."

"But you never became a dancer?"

"I became a minister's wife, and I was pretty good at it, most of the time."

"Did Harry ever ask you about . . ."

"No, and I never told him. Maybe that was wrong. But I couldn't share you with anyone." She offered him a sad, twisted smile as she struggled not to cry. "But now I guess it doesn't matter anymore."

"Okay, let's cut to thc chase," Alex said abruptly.

"Alex, you're not being very sensitive," Faith said with a frown. "They're just getting to know each other again."

"I'm tired, Faith. And I have a feeling tomorrow is going to be another long day, because if I know anything about my grandfather, I know this. He has a plan, and you and I figure prominently in it. That is, if Suzannah still has her half of the pot."

"I have it," Suzannah said slowly. "Let me get it."

She left the room, and Julian turned to Alex in a panic. "I didn't bring my half. Someone must go and get it from the hotel."

"Relax, Grandfather, I brought it. It's in the car. I'll get it."

Faith smiled at Julian once they were alone. "You did it. You found her."

"No, you found her."

"Well, it doesn't matter who did what. How do you feel?"

"Like I'm eighteen years old again. She's still as beautiful as I remember."

"Yes, she is. And you're still a handsome man."

''Hardly that. But at least she didn't turn away in horror. When I took her in my arms, it was as if all the years had slipped away. In my heart I'm still that young man and she's still that young woman.''

''Maybe what's in your heart is all that matters.''

Julian and Faith stood up as Alex and Suzannah returned to the room. Alex handed Julian his half of the pot while Suzannah set a box on the table. She slowly removed the lid, then pulled away layers of tissue paper. Finally she reached the bottom.

''I'm afraid,'' she said. ''I haven't touched it since I packed it away almost fifty years ago.''

Julian touched her hand. ''It will be all right. I think we should do this together, put it back the way it was.''

She nodded slowly. ''Okay, here goes.''

As she picked up the pot, the breeze blew through an open window, stirring the curtains and sending shivers through everyone in the room. Faith slid closer to Alex, wanting his strength, his protection—from what, she was not completely sure.

Slowly, deliberately, Julian and Suzannah moved their hands together until the two pieces of the pot were almost touching.

''Do it,'' Faith whispered. ''Do it.''

And the pot became one.

Faith's heart stopped as the overwhelming smell of smoke filled her senses. Faith saw Suzannah put a hand to her mouth and knew the other woman could smell it, too. She wondered if she could hear the voices, the screams, the terrible mournful wailing. She looked into Suzannah's eyes and saw the same recognition. There was a woman in pain, and her grief had reached across thousands of years.

''What's happening?'' Alex demanded.

Faith could barely speak, but finally she got the words out. ''She's crying, Alex, so hard I can feel her tears dripping down my cheeks, onto my hands.'' Faith held out her hands, wondering how they could look so normal when they felt so strange. "We will take the pot back tomorrow. Because if we don't—she'll never see him again."

"Who?"

"The warrior." Suzannah and Faith said the two words at the same exact time, drawing gasps of shock from both Julian and Alex.

"Yes," Suzannah said to Faith's unspoken question. "I saw him, too. He looked like Julian."

"He looks like Alex to me."

"You're both nuts," Alex said, his eyes worried. "It's just a pot."

"It's more than that." Faith wished she could make him understand. "It's a symbol of their love. It's what holds them together. Oh, I can't explain it. You just have to believe." She looked into Alex's eyes. "Can you do that, Alex? Because I need you with me."

"I can try. You say we need to put this back, but where? Where is this canyon? This cave? And how in hell are we going to find it?"

Faith turned to Julian. "Do you remember where it was?"

"Of course. I remember everything. It was called Coal Mine Canyon, at least it was called that back then. It's on the Navajo reservation, not far from Tuba City. There's a windmill that you can see from the road. From that spot you hike into the canyon. It's an amazing place. The wind rolls through the canyons like a runaway freight train. You will have to be careful. It is a desolate place, not a tourist spot. I hope you can find it."

"You will need a guide," Suzannah said. "I know someone, a young Navajo. I think he will help us. I will call him tonight, and tomorrow perhaps . . ."

"We will go," Alex said. He turned to Faith. "That is, if you're sure you want to do this."

She wasn't sure about anything. She just knew she had to get to the end of the story or she would never have peace. "I'll do it."

"Then we'll leave in the morning."

* * *

Jimmy Mitchell, a strong, young Navajo about twenty years old, arrived at Suzannah's house just after 10:00 A.M. After discussing the canyon landmarks with Julian, Jimmy felt confident he could take them to the same spot. He said that part of the land had remained virtually untouched as it was a dry, desolate place with little water. The only people who went into the canyon were intrepid hikers intent on exploring the backcountry away from the more popular tourist sites.

Jimmy had stocked his Jeep with backpacks and provisions in case they needed to spend the night. Despite Jimmy's confidence, Faith felt uncertain about the trip. She'd slept little the night before, tossing and turning, her dreams haunted by images of canyons and rocks and shadows, but the dreams had never become clearer than a distant haze, their meanings remaining elusively out of reach.

While Jimmy checked their water supplies one last time, Faith slipped into the Jeep. She wore jeans and a long-sleeve plaid shirt over a tank top. She'd borrowed a pair of hiking boots from Suzannah as well as a baseball cap to protect her face from the sun. Alex was dressed in similar attire but had bypassed the hiking boots, content to wear a pair of Top Flight tennis shoes.

Alex got into the backseat. "Ready to go?"

She sent him a wry smile. "As ready as I'll ever be."

"Having second thoughts?"

"Oh, yeah."

"I thought you had faith."

"Occasionally I recognize that there is a place in life for logical, rational thinking."

"Which would send you heading back to San Francisco on the first plane."

"Right, so I'm trying not to think at all. I just want to get this over with."

"Me, too."

Alex leaned forward and kissed her slowly, slipping

his tongue into her mouth, tracing the line of her teeth, the softness of her lips. When he lifted his head, she couldn't remember her own name, much less what she'd been worried about.

"I've missed you," he said. "When this is over, you and I will have to get reacquainted."

"Let's not wait fifty years, okay?"

He smiled, but it didn't quite reach his eyes, and she had no idea what he was thinking. Before she could ask him, Jimmy got into the Jeep and started the engine.

Jimmy drove with a lead foot that had them out of town in no time. He talked as fast as he drove, switching subjects every few minutes. Fortunately, his chatter kept Faith's mind off the trip ahead of them. She didn't want to think too much about the canyons, because she was afraid of what she would see there, what she would feel. Would the dreams return? Would they take over her life? Would she somehow lose herself in the desert?

The questions rattled around in her head as they drove north, finally reaching Tuba City a few hours later. They turned east then, heading toward an area the Navajos call Ha Ho No Geh or "too many washes." They traveled another twenty minutes, then turned off onto a dirt road.

The Jeep bounced with every turn of the tires, and Jimmy grew silent as the wind blew up, covering them with thick layers of desert dust. There were no trees in this area, nothing moist or lush, just an intense feeling of desolation.

"I don't understand," Jimmy mused. "This wind—it's stronger than I remember."

And the winds will curse your life until you return to where it began . . . Faith turned in her seat, exchanging a solemn look with Alex. She knew exactly what he was thinking—that the wind would not help their journey.

"Suzannah told me about the pot your grandfather stole," Jimmy said, mentioning out loud for the first time their real reason in going into the backcountry. "She said it was broken, but now it's fixed."

"That's right," Alex said.

The wind blew Jimmy's baseball hat into the backseat. Alex grabbed it before it blew out of the Jeep entirely.

"I don't like this at all." Jimmy pressed his foot down on the gas. "You know, my grandmother said any person who touches a holy object may forever lose favor with the spirits. I don't want to see it—the pot, I mean. Just keep it to yourselves, okay?"

"Sure," Alex said. "Remember, we're trying to put it back, not steal it. The spirits should be happy with us, don't you think?"

Jimmy started to reply, then began to cough and choke as the dust swirled into a small tornado heading directly for them. Faith put her hands over her eyes, trying to protect them from the flying dirt and pebbles. She felt terrified. They were going too fast. The wind was too strong.

"Stop," she cried.

Suddenly the Jeep went out of control, spinning them into the dry, prickly brush in a dizzying ride of terror.

Faith screamed, wondering if they would ever come to a stop. Then her head hit the ground, and there was nothing but darkness.

Chapter 27

"*Faith! Faith!" Alex tried desperately to get upright,* hearing nothing from the two passengers in the front seat. The Jeep had landed on its side, Faith's side, and Jimmy's body was sprawled over hers.

The wind had quieted down, almost as quickly as it had arisen, blowing gently now, as if to soothe them rather than to punish them.

"Faith, say something," he begged, finally freeing himself from his seat belt. He couldn't lose her, not now, not when it was all so new, when the future looked so bright, so full of hope. God! He hadn't realized until just this second how much she'd come to mean to him. He wanted to hear her voice once more, oozing with optimism and idealistic dreams. He wanted to see the ever-present smile glistening on her lips and shining out of her eyes. He wanted to hold her and touch her . . . "You have to be all right," he whispered. "You have to be."

Alex leaned over the front seat and patted Jimmy on the shoulder.

Jimmy stirred, uttering a pained moan. He squinted his eyes against the midday sun. "What happened?"

"I don't know. Are you hurt? We need to get you off of Faith." Alex tried to speak calmly, tried to give Jimmy the consideration he deserved when all the while he wanted to rip the other man out of the Jeep so he could get to Faith.

Jimmy muttered something about his leg, and when he held up his hand it was covered in blood.

"Do you think you can move?" Alex asked.

"Yeah. I think so." Jimmy bit down on his bottom lip as Alex helped him get out of the Jeep. When he was lying on the ground, Alex could see a long, ugly gash in his leg.

"We've got to stop that bleeding."

"It's okay. Get Faith," Jimmy said, his black eyes worried. "I couldn't hear her—I couldn't hear her breathing."

Alex's heart stood still. He wouldn't believe that she was dead. She had to be alive. She had to be all right.

Trying not to jiggle the Jeep from its precarious position, Alex climbed into the front seat. Faith was lying on the ground, against the door. There was a cut on the side of her head and blood dripping down her cheek. He used his fingers to wipe it away from her eyes, then he felt for the pulse in her neck, hoping against hope . . .

It was there, slow, quiet, but definitely present, and he heard a gentle whoosh of breath leave her lips.

"Faith." He stroked her cheek with a gentle hand, bracing himself against the seat so his body wouldn't bump into hers. He didn't know how badly she was hurt, if she'd broken anything. "Faith, honey. You have to wake up."

He was calling her name, and she could feel his fingers touch her face. When she opened her eyes, he was there, watching her. It was still dark, but nearing dawn. They would have to leave now. It would be their last chance to get away.

She couldn't move. Her cheeks felt hot, but her body felt chilled. She shivered as a light wind blew through their hiding place. Her stomach heaved in silent agony. She was sick. Her limbs felt weak. It was a chore just to keep her eyes open. Yet if they didn't leave now, they would be found, and they would be killed.

She struggled to lift her hand to the warrior's face, and she whispered to him to go.

He shook his head and settled down next to her. He pulled her into his arms and pressed her head against his chest.

She knew it was wrong, madness. He had to leave. She pushed against him, telling him to go with every particle of her being. She did not want him to die.

He shook his head again, his eyes resolute. Then he picked up the pot they had filled with water, their last few drops, and he held it to her parched lips. She drank just enough to cool her throat, then handed it to him, and he finished it off. There would be no more water. There would be no more time. But they would be together . . . forever. It seemed so easy to let life go, to journey to the other world, to . . .

Something sharp pinched her cheek, a voice hammered in her head. She didn't want to wake up. It would be easier to die now than to let the others find them.

"Faith, dammit. You wake up right now!"

Faith grimaced, feeling the dream slide away, as Alex's irritated voice sank into her subconscious.

"You are not going to leave me alone here in the wilderness, not to mention with a crazy grandfather and a trash-talking daughter and . . . well, you just can't leave. So wake up—or else," he threatened hopelessly.

"Or else what?" she murmured, slowing opening her eyes. She saw his worried face lit up by the now brilliant sun. She remembered the swirling wind, the dust, the accident. She was lying on her back and her head hurt. In fact, it was throbbing.

She saw blood on Alex's fingers. "Are you all right?"

"I'm fine. It's you I'm worried about."

"Jimmy?"

"He hurt his leg. Now, what about you? Where is the pain?"

"My head."

"Anywhere else? Can you move your fingers?"

Faith was almost afraid to try, the vivid memory of languid weakness still fresh in her mind. But her fingers moved and so did her toes. She wiggled her legs and arms as well. Nothing hurt. Nothing tingled.

"I think I'm okay."

"Are you sure? I don't want to move you if anything could be wrong."

"Can you help me out?"

He nodded, and with much care and patience Alex got Faith out of the Jeep. She sat down on the ground next to Jimmy, her own worries forgotten as she saw his leg. He'd taken off his T-shirt and tied it around his wound to act as a tourniquet, but he was pale and his eyes were glittering with pain.

"We need to get you to a doctor," she said.

"Cell phone," Jimmy muttered. "It's in the car. See if it still works."

Alex immediately returned to the Jeep, and Faith prayed he would find the phone intact.

"Got it," he yelled. "It's working."

Jimmy gave him a number to call, faster than 911, he told Alex. Alex dialed the number and handed the phone to Jimmy. Someone must have answered, because Jimmy told the person he needed an ambulance or a ride as soon as possible. He hung up the phone and told them someone would be there within thirty minutes.

"I hope that will be soon enough," Alex muttered.

Jimmy gave him a weak smile. "The bleeding has stopped. I'll be okay. I've been hurt worse."

Faith doubted that was true but silently applauded Jimmy's brave attitude. "Let's see if we can make you more comfortable," she said, finding some of their things strewn about the dirt road. She pulled out a folded blanket and placed it under Jimmy's head. Then Alex brought over a canteen filled with water, and Faith helped him take a drink.

"Thanks. My mouth was filled with dirt," Jimmy said. "How's your head?"

"It's just a bump."

"You were unconscious," Alex said. "For at least three or four minutes. I hope you don't have a concussion."

Faith didn't think so. She could see clearly, and she didn't feel faint or dizzy, just disturbed. "I dreamed about them again," she told Alex. "When I hit my head, they came into my mind. They're in a cave, and the woman is sick. She can't move. But if they don't leave, they will be found, taken back, or killed on the spot." Faith paused, realizing she had the undivided attention of both men. "The woman begs the man to leave, to escape, but he won't go. Instead he lies down next to her, and they take the last drops of water from their pot."

"What happens then?" Alex asked.

"I don't know. Someone was pinching my cheek."

"You seemed to be fading away, Faith. Your pulse got so faint."

"I felt like I was her, Alex—dying." Faith met Alex's eyes and knew that he was starting to believe.

"That's it. We're going back, and we're leaving this pot right here. It's close enough, if it's even still intact."

In some ways, Faith wanted to agree, because she was afraid of what would happen to her when they took the pot back. Would she simply fade away into this other woman's soul, or would she be herself again, without this strange connection to another life?

While she was thinking, Alex searched for the pot. He found the box still intact, and he opened it carefully, checking to see if anything was broken.

"It's okay," he said with surprise. "Still in one piece."

"You must take it back," Jimmy said. "You cannot leave it here."

"But you're hurt," Faith began.

"And we can't find the way without you," Alex finished.

Jimmy stared at them, his eyes so dark, so compelling, that he reminded Faith of a younger warrior. He no longer appeared to be the modern Native American kid who wanted to go to college and forget the old ways. He seemed transformed, as taken aback by what had happened as Faith was.

"The wind came out of nowhere—fury," Jimmy said. "I was not meant to go with you. The spirits have spoken. You must go alone. I will tell you the way. And somehow you will find the cave you seek and return the pot to its resting place."

"Oh, hell, this is crazy!" Alex threw up his hands. "How are we going to find some cave out there in this wilderness? We don't know these canyons. Think about it, Faith. There are snakes out here, quicksand, tarantulas. Do you really want to go on?"

"We don't have a choice. We have to do this."

"You should go now," Jimmy said. "So you can find the cave before dark. There is food and water in the packs, blankets and sleeping bags. Take the cell phone, just in case. Now, listen carefully, and I will tell you the way."

Alex didn't move.

Faith didn't move.

They simply stared at each other.

"I want to finish this," Faith said. "I want to end it today if we can."

"What about your head?"

"It's fine." Faith turned to Jimmy. "How much further will we have to go?"

"Three or four hours walking from the windmill up ahead," he said, pointing to a structure in the distance. "Follow a compass heading fifty-five degrees from the windmill down an old coal-mining cut. You'll come to a narrow chute of loose sand that leads to a trail below. You should pass by a very strange looking rock formation they call 'the ghost.' From there you'll have to figure out which of the side canyons you want—there are many to choose from. The wind can be very strong. Be careful."

"We'll wait until help comes for you," Alex said.

Jimmy shook his head. "No. Absolutely not. It will be too late then."

"We can't just leave you like this," Faith said.

"You must go now. I will be fine. Please. I feel this is very important. Go." He pressed the phone into Faith's hand.

She gave it back to him. "You need this, Jimmy, just in case they can't find you."

Jimmy considered her words. "All right. I will send a friend back for you tomorrow. He will be here at ten in the morning. He will wait until four. If you have not come back by then, he will call for help. There is room for the pot in that backpack," Jimmy said, pointing to the larger pack.

Alex did as Jimmy suggested and finally they were ready to go.

"Thank you, Jimmy," Faith said, shaking his hand. "I hope you'll be all right."

"I wish the same for you."

Faith took a deep breath as she looked up the trail. Alex put his hand on her shoulder, following her gaze. "Scared?"

"Terrified. And you?"

"I'd rather be getting a root canal."

"We can do this," she said, as much to garner her courage as his. "After all, you're wearing your Top Flight tennis shoes. You said you could do anything in those shoes."

Alex glanced down at his feet, then sent her a slow, confident smile. "You're right. I'd forgotten. Come on, let's go find ourselves a canyon."

Faith shook her head in disgust as Alex charged ahead. "Well, at least you believe in something," she called out after him. "Even if it's only your shoes."

* * *

They found the windmill and checked their compass heading, then took the winding path down to the canyon floor. They found themselves walking under 150-foot rimrocks, shaded from pink to gray with streaks of black coal at the top. They passed two springs that were completely dry, and as the day wore on they stopped several times to take refreshing sips of water.

The wind that had blown their Jeep onto its side seemed oddly quiet now. They saw no one during their journey. Faith couldn't imagine why anyone would have chosen to live in a place like this, so dry, so desolate, so frightening. As the afternoon shadows fell across the canyons, some of the rock formations took on monstrous appearances, and Faith began to feel distinctly uneasy.

They were all alone and yet she felt as if someone were watching them.

Alex stopped a few minutes later to wipe some sweat from his face. He looked back at her, his face a picture of grim determination. "Have you ever seen such a place?"

"No."

She glanced over her shoulder, trying to make mental notes of the way they'd come. She'd hate to get lost in this maze of canyons and rocks. She had a feeling it would be days before anyone would find them.

"Shall we keep going?" he asked.

"We've come this far."

"We won't get out of here before dark, Faith. We'll have to spend the night, unless we turn back now."

"Let's keep going. I feel like we're getting close." In the past few minutes, the canyon walls had begun to look familiar. She could almost remember running through them once before.

Alex continued to lead the way, and Faith slowly followed. Fifteen minutes later she looked up to the sky to see how far the sun had gone down and saw the rocks, the butterflies. They had run toward those rocks. They had believed that love, freedom, happiness, lay just beyond. "Alex, stop!"

Alex came to an abrupt halt. "What's wrong?"

She pointed toward the sky. "Look."

"Is that it?"

"I think so." She saw a path off to the side. "That way. Let's go that way."

As they followed the path, the sandstone earth began to crumble, leaving Faith to wonder if they could actually make it to the top. And what if they got there and there was no cave?

She paused and shaded her eyes, hoping to catch a glimpse of some type of crevice, but the rocks went in and out of her view, hiding the landscape above until she was almost on top of it. That was probably why they'd gone there, hoping to stay hidden, away from the angry eyes of those searching below.

As they climbed, the wind began to blow stronger. Faith had to stop to pull her hair away from her eyes. Alex shot her an occasional worried look, but they were both too tired, too tense, to speak. The cliff path grew steeper, but they were getting closer to the butterflies, and Faith felt an impatience to reach the top.

Just then her foot slipped and she began to fall. She cried out for Alex and tried desperately to grab on to something, but the loose dirt slipped through her fingers.

"Hang on, Faith." Alex reached for her, slipping and sliding himself as they rolled partway down the side of the cliff. Finally he caught her hand and held on, steadying her until the rush of pebbles and rocks stopped.

Faith felt absolutely terrified as she saw the sharp, pointed rocks below. If Alex let go, if her hand slipped . . .

"Look at me," Alex commanded. "Look at me, dammit."

Faith struggled to turn her gaze. Finally she looked into his stark blue eyes and saw determination, courage, strength, so much strength she felt reassured. He would not let her go. He would not let her fall.

"Don't think about what's down there. I'm going to pull you up, okay?"

She gave him a small nod, too terrified to move. Alex slowly set his feet on more solid ground and began to pull. She kept her gaze on him, trying to think calmly, to believe. He strained against the weight of his backpack combined with her weight and her backpack. She'd never seen a man so determined to succeed. This was the man who had built a shoe empire. This was the man who had battled his own insecurities to rise to the top. And this was the man of her dreams—the warrior. She had the sense they had played this scene before.

In fact, she knew what was about to happen. As Alex pulled her back to the path, to safety, she fell backward against the side of the cliff and her hand came down on a—

"No!" she screamed. "Get it away."

"What?" Alex yelled.

She shifted ever so slightly and looked to the right where she had almost put down her hand. It was there—the snake.

"Don't move, Faith. There's a rattlesnake right next to you."

"I know," she whispered. "Do something, Alex. Please, do something!"

Chapter 28

Alex picked up a heavy rock the size of a brick and weighed it in his hand. "The snake is about a foot away from you, Faith," he said calmly, as if he were talking about a book or some other inanimate object. "I'm going to nail it with this rock. And then we're going to run like hell up the path."

"Do you think you can hit it?"

"It's just like a free throw," he muttered. "I can do this. I know I can."

Faith stared at his face and prayed that he was right.

Alex lifted the rock, took aim, and heaved it at the snake. Faith jumped to her feet and ran. Alex followed her down the path, and they didn't stop running until they were twenty yards away.

Faith stopped, breathless, adrenaline surging through her body from the near fall and the near snakebite.

Alex stopped, too, his own chest heaving with ragged, triumphant breaths. "We did it!"

"You did it." Faith slipped out of her backpack and flung her arms around Alex's neck. "You saved my life."

"I wouldn't go that far. I'm not even sure I hit the damn thing."

"You did. Oh, Alex." She stared into his eyes and felt

so much love for this man that it completely overwhelmed her.

Their mouths met in a hungry, passionate kiss that knew no boundaries, no barriers. The fear of the past few minutes had heightened every emotion. His mouth gave her exquisite pleasure, and she took everything he had to give.

Alex lifted his head and looked into her eyes. "Damn, Faith. What have you done to me?"

"The same thing you've done to me."

"I want to make love to you—right here, right now."

Her heart caught at his words. "There's a cave not far from here. It's just around the next bend." She stopped, seeing the question in his eyes. "I know because—"

"Because you've been there before."

"Yes." She paused, taking a deep breath. "The last time the warrior had to carry me because I'd been bitten by a snake, and the poison was sweeping through my body."

Alex's mouth tightened grimly. His eyes darkened. "You knew there was a snake. You said . . ." He shook his head. "I don't understand. This can't be happening."

"It is happening. I don't know why or how, but it's real to me. I know now why I felt sick in my dreams. I'd been bitten by a snake. I think I was dying." She turned toward the trail, suddenly impatient to see the cave.

Alex followed closely behind her, steadying her when she stumbled. Finally they saw an opening before them, almost completely covered by brush.

"It's there," Faith said in bemusement, stunned they'd actually found it. "Right there."

"Are you sure?"

She nodded, setting down her backpack in the small clearing in front of the cave.

"There's a flashlight in my pack," Alex said. "Let me get it out so we can see what's inside."

Alex retrieved the flashlight and they crawled in

through the mouth of the cave. Once inside, he focused the light on the walls.

It was a small cave, barely six feet by eight feet. There wasn't enough headroom for a man to stand. Faith followed the light with wary eyes, not sure what they would find in the cave. If two people had died here, their skeletons might still remain. But she didn't see anything but dust and dirt and some carvings on a distant wall.

She'd seen them before. She'd watched as the warrior had carved out the symbols, knowing that one day they would be read by the people following them, and they would know that they had died for love.

"Faith? Is this the place?"

"Yes. This is it."

"I'll get the pot. Hold the flashlight."

Faith did as Alex asked, crawling deeper into the cave while he went to retrieve the pot. She closed her eyes for a moment, letting the images come into her head.

The warrior soothed her with his kiss and his touch. He promised her an eternity in his arms. And that was where she would soon be. She could feel the poison killing her slowly, inch by inch, the pain so excruciating she wanted to die now. Only that would mean leaving him so much earlier.

She still wanted him to go, to escape. He could be free just over the cliff. They had seen the butterflies dancing on the rocks. They had heard the stories of another land, one green with grass, wet with water, filled with harvest.

She looked into his eyes, imploring him to go. She did not want him to die.

He would not leave her, he told her. And he would not let them take joy in killing him. He held the stalk of a plant in front of her eyes and placed it against his lips.

Her heart stopped. The plant would kill him as surely as the snake had taken her life. She used every last ounce of her strength to stop him. And finally when he was looking at her, she tipped her head to their pot, the sym-

bol of their love, which would surely be smashed to bits when they were found.

He understood and placed a gentle kiss on her lips. He set down the stalk and picked up the pot. He walked over to the farthest, darkest corner of the cave. Digging through the loose rocks, he placed the pot in the corner where it could not be seen. Then he went outside and brought in more rocks, more shrubs. He covered up the entrance to their cave, shutting out the last bit of light, the last bit of air. When he was done, he came back to her and took her in his arms. She thought he ate the plant then, but she didn't want to watch.

She knew the end was near, but with his heart beating steadily beneath her cheek, she felt strong and brave, as if she were the warrior. The sun filled her heart and lifted her to the sky. The pain faded away, and she danced toward the butterflies, feeling gloriously free. He followed her minutes later and together they found a new world.

Faith felt the tears dripping down her cheeks, the heart beating beneath her cheek, and when she opened her eyes she was wrapped in Alex's arms.

"Over there," she said with a small sob. "He put it over there."

Alex's eyes met hers. "They died here."

"Yes. They were running away from the man she was supposed to marry. When she couldn't go on, they knew they would be found and murdered. So the warrior boarded up the cave as best he could. He hid the pot over there." She pointed to the most distant part of the cave. "Then he ate a poisonous plant, deliberately killing himself, because he couldn't bear to live without her."

Faith was almost afraid of what she would see in Alex's eyes, mockery, amusement, sarcasm—all of those would have been in character, but instead she saw kindness, compassion.

"Let's put the pot back," he said.

Faith nodded and helped him place the pot carefully

behind some rocks, hoping it would stay untouched for centuries to come.

"Be happy," she whispered, then followed Alex out of the cave. The air was refreshing, and she took long, deep breaths, relieved to be out of the cave, away from the haunting memories of a tragic past.

While she was trying to calm her shattered nerves, Alex began to pile rocks and brush in front of the entrance to the cave. At first he could find little to work with, then the wind began to blow, harder and harder until rocks crumbled and the earth began to shake. Alex gave up his efforts, grabbed their packs, and shouted at her to run.

She went up instead of down, toward the butterflies dancing, toward freedom. It wasn't far, she realized with stunning clarity. Another fifty yards and they would have reached the top. They would have seen . . .

She stopped abruptly. She'd expected a lush green valley, fertile land, water, rivers, colors, but the land ahead of her was a maze of canyon peaks, gargoyle rocks, sharp spires painted red and brown. It was a shockingly brutal vista. She'd heard of the Badlands, but she'd never seen any land so desolate, so frightening, so sad. "Would you look at that? They had nowhere to go," she murmured. "They thought this was the way out, but it wasn't."

"Maybe it's better that they didn't know," Alex said. He dropped their packs on the ground and put his arms around her waist, pulling her against his chest. They didn't speak for several minutes, caught up in the sight before them.

"I've never seen anything like this," Alex said. "It's almost ghostly."

"They would have been horribly disappointed to see this, believing their freedom lay just on the other side of these rocks. They don't look like butterflies anymore. They just look like rocks."

"Sh-h," he whispered.

"Their love was such a tragedy." She turned in his

arms. "What are we supposed to learn from this?"

"I don't know, Faith. Does there have to be a lesson?"

"She followed her heart, and look where it took her."

"They're together now, wherever they are. And they're no longer bound by these canyon walls. They're free, Faith. That's what you have to focus on."

"I know, but I wanted a happy ending."

"And you got one. They're resting in peace now. Besides . . ." He swung his hand across the vista in front of them. "There is a certain beauty here, a mystical, ghostly beauty."

Faith looked at him in surprise. She'd never expected to hear such a romantic statement from such a cynic. And as the sun streaked over the horizon, painting the rocks in various startling pastel shades of color, she saw the beauty he spoke of and she shivered.

They stood there quietly, watching the last lingering traces of the sun.

"It will be dark soon," she said.

"Yes. Afraid?"

"Not with you here by my side. You've already saved my life twice."

"Let's not go for three."

"Let's not," she said.

"You know, I think we should celebrate our victory. We found the canyon. We put the pot back. We broke the curse. Hell, we're standing on top of the whole damn world. It's unbelievable."

Faith grinned at him. "You're finally happy."

"Deliriously happy."

"So how are we going to celebrate? I don't see any fancy restaurants, any bottles of champagne or plates of caviar."

"Mmmm, that could be a problem. Hold on a second." Alex dug through his backpack and pulled out two bottles of water and a box of crackers. "Champagne and appetizers."

"Not bad. I didn't think you had this much imagination.'' She took a swig of water, the cool liquid easing the parched feeling of her throat. She felt better now. The wind had died down. The sun had set and she was standing on this incredible windswept peak with the man of her dreams.

She turned to Alex and caught him watching her in a way that made her toes curl and her stomach tumble. She didn't just see the desire in his eyes, she felt it in every nerve ending, every breath.

''Well, we're finally alone,'' he said. ''Just you and me and the universe. What do you think we should do now?''

She answered him the only way she knew how. She ran toward him and he met her halfway. Their mouths met in a hot, passionate kiss. Their hands wrestled with buttons and zippers. Stripping down to nothing, they tumbled to the ground, eager, impatient, the need to be one overwhelming their sense of propriety.

When Alex parted her legs with his, when he slipped into her body, Faith welcomed him, feeling like she'd just recaptured a part of herself that had been missing for a very long time. She clung to him, matching him move for move, stroke for stroke, until she couldn't think straight. She could only feel him inside of her, on top of her, surrounding her with love and warmth, burning the ice away from her heart and the loneliness from her past.

Later they lay together in sleeping bags, staring up at a starlit sky.

''Incredible,'' Faith murmured.

''I didn't think I was that good.''

She poked him in the ribs. ''I was talking about the sky. Have you ever seen so many stars?''

''Never.''

She turned over on her side so she could study his face, his handsome, strong, courageous face. She'd seen so many sides to Alex. He was so much more complex than she'd ever imagined, vulnerable yet confident, insecure but arrogant, kind and compassionate but still a cynic, generous with his money and his help but not with his heart.

"Alex?" she murmured.

He turned his head. "What?"

"I want to tell you something. It doesn't require a reply or a comment or anything. It's just something I want to say." She paused and took a deep breath. "I love you. That's it. I just wanted you to know how I felt."

She waited hopelessly. She'd told him not to reply and yet . . .

He put his hand on the back of her neck and pulled her face toward his. He kissed her long and hard, his lips and tongue demanding access to her mouth. It wasn't exactly the answer she'd wanted, but she took it.

He rolled on top of her, nuzzling her collarbone, trailing kisses down to the valley of her breasts, sucking each nipple into a tiny hard point that drew fire down to her thighs. He worked his way down her body, loving her, cherishing her as if every part of her was incredibly precious.

Faith's need grew stronger with each touch of his lips on her body until she was crying out for him to join her. She needed to feel him again, within her body, her heart, and her soul.

"Now, Alex, please."

He came to her with love, unspoken, but as true as the earth and the sun and the moon and the stars. She'd never known such longing or such satisfaction. And when it was done, she slept dreamlessly. For there was no need for dreams.

The next morning the sun came up bright and startling. A new day. A new forever.

Faith gave a lazy stretch. She had aches in all the right places, but she couldn't help smiling. They'd done what they'd set out to do, reunited the spirits and broken the curse. She frowned, realizing something wasn't quite right. She was alone in the sleeping bag.

She sat up, holding the bag to her bare breasts. Alex was already dressed and sitting with his back to her several yards away. He was sipping some bottled water and staring out at the view.

The sight of him so far away, so distant, smashed her happiness into tiny little bits. He probably would have left her in the night if they hadn't been so far from civilization, she told herself grimly. After all, the man could not stay with a woman until morning, not after he'd made love to her at any rate. The only day they'd awoken together was the night they'd slept in each other's arms in Alex's living room. Apparently he'd felt more comfortable with a night spent in less intimate occupation.

She dug around in the sleeping bag for her clothes and put them on. Alex didn't even move. She didn't know if he couldn't hear her or if he was ignoring her.

It didn't matter, because she was suddenly angry. Damn him for drawing away from her again. She thought she'd broken down the barriers, but this morning they were back in place, and she was tired of chipping away at an inpenetrable wall. He was probably scared now because she'd told him she loved him.

Faith stumbled to her feet, and Alex finally turned around. He smiled at her, then realized something was wrong, his smile evaporating like the morning mist under the hot sun.

"What?" he asked warily. "Don't tell me you're not a morning person."

"Are you ready to go?"

"We have time."

"Not as far as I'm concerned." She rolled up her sleeping bag and stuffed it into her pack.

Alex came over to her, watching, waiting. "Do you want to tell me what's wrong?"

"Nothing."

"Oh, right. Like I believe that."

She sat back on her heels and looked up at him. "You couldn't stay with me all night. After everything we've been through, everything we've shared, you're still afraid to wake up with me."

"Faith, I'm right here."

"Because you wouldn't leave me alone on this cliff, but you got dressed and put that old wall up around your heart just as soon as you could."

"I woke up early. I couldn't go back to sleep, so I thought I'd get up. That's it. I wasn't trying to get away from you."

"Sure, whatever you say." She stood up and put the backpack over her shoulders.

"Don't you want something to eat, to drink?"

"I'm not hungry. I just want to go home."

Alex stared at her, his own lips drawing into a taut line. "Fine, you want to go home, we'll go home."

"Fine."

They didn't speak on their way back down the path. They paused for a moment at the place where they'd gone into the cave, then continued on without a word. Faith didn't feel like talking. She just wanted to go home and lick her wounds in private. She'd given Alex her heart and he'd thrown it right back at her. When would she ever learn?

They returned to the Jeep several hours later, hot, tired, and angry. Faith's bad mood had apparently rubbed off on Alex, who seemed no more inclined to speak to her than she was to speak to him. Fortunately, Jimmy's friend was waiting for them, and unlike Jimmy, he seemed content to drive them back to Flagstaff in silence.

They arrived at Suzannah's house by late afternoon to find Julian, Suzannah, and Jessie waiting eagerly for their report. Faith just wanted to lie down, but she knew that wouldn't be fair to Julian or to Suzannah. She could see the strain in their eyes, the tension written in the lines around their mouths.

"We put the pot back," she said simply. "It's done."

Suzannah let out a long sigh of relief. Julian's eyes glittered with unshed tears.

"You broke the curse," Julian said. "Thank God." He walked over to Alex and gave him a hug. "I'm proud of you, Alex. You're a good man and now you can be happy."

Alex didn't look happy. He looked annoyed. "Well, at least you can get on with your life now, Grandfather. And without any more curses to blame your bad luck on."

"I don't intend to have any more bad luck."

"Did you see any ghosts or skeletons?" Jessie asked, her eyes wide and eager.

"Not a one," Faith replied. "But I know what happened now between the lovers. I'll tell you all the whole story as soon as I have a chance to catch my breath. Right now I'd love a hot shower and maybe a nap."

"Of course," Suzannah said. "You and Alex must be tired. You can rest here if you like."

"But first . . ." Julian began, looking from Alex to Faith. "There's something you should know."

Faith tensed. "Please don't tell me there's more to this curse."

"Suzannah and I are going to be married. Now that the curse is broken, I can finally be with the love of my life."

Alex's mouth dropped open. "Isn't this a little sudden? You've only been together two days."

"I don't want to waste any more time, Alex. When you get to be my age, you'll understand that time is precious and spending that time with someone you love is the ultimate happiness." Julian smiled at Suzannah as he took her hand in his. "Tomorrow we plan to fly to Las Vegas to be married. We'd like you and Faith and Jessie to come and stand up with us."

"Wow," Faith muttered. She didn't know what to say, although she had to admit that Julian and Suzannah looked incredibly happy. "Are you sure?"

"It's so fast," Alex said. "You should get to know each other again, at least give yourselves a week, two weeks, maybe a month."

"We know each other," Suzannah said confidently. "We've had a lifetime to think about what we had together."

" 'Two souls with but a single thought. Two hearts that beat as one,' " Julian quoted. "That is the way we feel about each other."

Alex sighed. "Right. You always have the last line, don't you?"

"Not quite the last," Faith said. "Congratulations, Julian, Suzannah. I hope you'll be very happy. And I think you're right—you were meant to be together, just as the other two were meant to be together."

"And you and Alex?" Julian said hopefully.

Faith turned to see Alex slipping out of the room. "Two out of three isn't bad."

"I'm sorry. The boy doesn't know what he has."

"He knows. He just doesn't want it. He doesn't want me."

Chapter 29

*They arrived in San Francisco late Wednesday af-*ternoon after a quick stop in Vegas to watch Julian and Suzannah get married. After a brief honeymoon, Julian and Suzannah planned to return to Arizona to live.

It was cold and gray in San Francisco, a far cry from the hot desert sun. And there were no awe-inspiring peaks, just buildings, traffic, and reality.

The cab pulled up in front of Alex's building a little after four o'clock. Alex had suggested Faith drop off her bags at his apartment, then go down the street and check on her bakery. Later he'd drive her home.

She wasn't particularly looking forward to later. They hadn't spoken any private words to each other since they'd left the canyon, but she knew the words were coming, and she had a feeling they would not be "I love you" but more along the lines of "It's been fun."

Faith was trying to mentally prepare herself for that moment, but wasn't having much luck. Every time she told herself that Alex could not commit to anyone, that he couldn't love a woman forever, she'd remember their night under the stars. She'd felt his love then. Why hadn't it lasted until the morning?

She let out another sigh, drawing Alex's attention as he helped her out of the cab.

"Tired?" he asked.

"Yes." She smiled shortly and turned to Jessie. "Do you need help with your bag, honey?"

"I'm okay. Do I have to go to school tomorrow, Alex?"

"It's about time, don't you think?" He ruffled her hair and urged her toward the building. "Let's get this stuff upstairs."

The doorman held open the door for them with a smile. "Good morning, Mr. Carrigan. How was your trip?"

"Successful," Alex replied.

"A gentleman came by for you several times yesterday and again this morning. He said he'd prefer to talk to you here rather than over the phone or at his house. Said it was a private matter. Let's see, his name was . . ." The doorman pondered for a moment. "Edward Saunders, I believe. I told him I didn't know when you'd be back. He seemed quite anxious to see you, though."

Faith put an arm around Jessie's shoulders as she let out a small, panicked cry. The doorman looked startled as Jessie began to sob.

"Is something wrong?" he asked.

"We're fine. Thank you, George."

"Come on, Jess, let's go upstairs." Alex tried to take her hand, but Jessie pulled it away, her eyes flaming with anger and betrayal.

"Why should I go upstairs when you're just going to send me away? I'll just wait down here for my—my—my real father." Jessie barreled her head into Faith's stomach, lacing her arms around Faith's back, and she sobbed as if her heart were breaking in two.

Faith looked at Alex and saw the uncertainty, the fear, the hopelessness. She knew he was going to let Jessie go, just as he wanted to let her go.

"Fight, dammit," she said, shocking him with her words.

"If he's her real father . . ."

"Then what? You let her go to a man she doesn't know?"

"She didn't know me two weeks ago."

"But she knows you now, and you know her. You love her, even if you can't say the words out loud. I've seen it in your eyes, and I've heard it in your voice, and if you tell me that's not the truth, then you're only lying to yourself. I feel sorry for you, really, really sorry. Because you could have the most incredible family, if you'd only open up your heart."

Alex's fists clenched at his side in silent rage. "Don't you dare feel sorry for me. You don't know what I'm thinking, what I'm feeling."

"Don't I?" She dared him to argue. She wanted him to fight her, Eddie, whoever. At least then he'd be letting out emotion instead of keeping it inside where it could only hurt him.

The door opened, and Alex and Faith turned in accord. A slim man with golden blond hair and an impossibly dark winter tan strode through the door. He stopped when he saw Alex and Faith. He paled when he saw Jessie, when he heard her crying.

"Alex Carrigan?" he asked.

"Yes. You must be Eddie Saunders."

Eddie stopped a few feet away. "I got your message. I came home early."

"Let's go upstairs," Alex suggested.

Jessie cried harder, and the doorman slipped out to the sidewalk, leaving them alone in the lobby.

"Look, if you're going to try and tell me that she's my kid, you can stop right now. Melanie told me I wasn't the father." Eddie shot Jessie a quick look. "Sorry, kid, but that's the truth."

Faith's arms tightened around Jessie. "Come on, honey, let's go upstairs."

"No. I'm never going upstairs again," Jessie said defiantly. "Not with him." She shot Alex a hateful, devastated look.

Alex felt like he'd been stabbed with a long, sharp knife. "Jessie, please."

"Go on. Tell him you're not my real father," she dared Alex. "You've been saying it all along."

"He is your real father," Eddie said. "Melanie told me so."

"Melanie told me you were the father," Alex said. "You were there in the hospital with her."

"Right. Because Melanie wanted a free trip to Hollywood. Oh, I took her there, all right, believing I was the dad, until nine months later when Melanie told me the truth. She said you wouldn't take her to Hollywood. You were more interested in college than her dreams of being an actress."

Alex couldn't breathe. He heard the words, but they didn't make sense. He vaguely remembered Melanie talking on and on about being an actress. But he'd assumed she'd put that dream aside, because they were having a baby, because she was seventeen and he was eighteen and it was all they could do to make enough money for food and a crummy studio apartment, not to mention having to raise a child.

"I figured she went back to you," Eddie continued. "She kept telling me what a great guy you were, how much you loved the baby. One day I said, I bet you wish he was the real father. That's when she said you were, and she left. I never saw her again."

"She didn't come back to me." At least Alex didn't think she had. He'd moved by then. He couldn't stand living in their apartment, remembering all the happy times when he'd imagined having a family, being a father. An unexpected pain ripped through him. He didn't want to feel anything, but it was too much. There were too many emotions to contain, and they began to spill over one after the other, until he thought he was drowning.

And all the while Jessie cried and Faith looked at him as if he were the coldest man on the face of the earth. Didn't she know how much he cared about Jessie? About her? Why did she need him to spell it out for her? Why couldn't she just see the truth in his eyes?

"I'm not the father," Eddie pushed on. "And I don't want kids. If you press this, I'll ask for DNA testing, whatever it takes to prove she's not my child."

Alex felt an overwhelming anger. The truth suddenly became crystal-clear. And he knew exactly what he had to do.

"We won't need DNA testing," Alex said. "You're right. Jessie is not your kid. She's mine. She always has been, and she always will be."

Jessie stopped crying. She looked at Alex with tear-streaked cheeks, a wondrous hope blooming in her eyes. "I—I am?"

"You are. You most definitely are my daughter."

"Are you sure? This isn't just a joke?"

"Absolutely, positively sure." He took a deep breath. "I love you, Jessie. I guess it's about time I told you that."

Tears dripped down her cheeks as she bit down on her lip. "You mean it?"

"I mean it, Jess. I want you forever. If that's okay with you."

Jessie ran into his arms and he held her tightly against him. His daughter, his child, his family. He would never let her go. Never. He raised his head and saw Faith slip out of the building. He wanted to call after her. He had so much left to say. But this moment belonged to Jessie.

"I love you, too," Jessie said shyly. "I'll try to be a good kid."

"Just be yourself, Jess. That's all I want you to be. Come on, let's go home."

Faith's Fancies was warm and cozy, smelling like cinnamon and sugar, smelling like home. Faith took a deep breath as she stood inside the front door. This was where she belonged, here with her pastries and her rolls and her friends.

Pam came out of the kitchen, let out a welcome yell, and ran around the counter to give her a hug.

"You're back," she said with a grin. "I've been worried about you, the way you took off to Arizona at the drop of a hat with that gorgeous man and his wacky family. How did it go?"

"It was fine. We did what we needed to do."

Pam's sharp eyes slid over every inch of Faith's face. "Oh, dear."

Faith tucked a strand of hair behind her ear. "I don't look that bad, do I?"

"You do. I want to hear everything."

"You will, but not today. I need some time."

Pam nodded understandingly. "Ben has been haunting the place the past two days. I told him I didn't know when you'd be back. He seemed pretty upset. I guess his mother told him she kicked you out of the family. Although I'm still not sure why."

"I wasn't willing to marry her son. I don't think Nancy ever really cared about me—or at least she only cared in the sense that I was connected to Gary and then to Ben. A bridge," she said sadly, remembering that Alex had called her that, too. "But no more bridges for me. I'm done with all that."

"Tired of having people drive over you all the time, huh?"

"Yes. How are things going here?"

"Business is good. A little slow today, but not bad. Leslie is turning into quite a good pastry chef, not as good as you, of course, but you don't have to worry about giving her more work."

"That's great."

"Why don't you go home, Faith, get some rest."

"That sounds like a fine idea. Can you call me a cab? I'm too tired to take the bus, and my car is at home."

"How did you get here?"

"It was easier to go to Alex's place. He was going to drive me home, but I think I'll just take a cab."

"Things didn't work out with him the way you wanted?"

"No. But I'll survive. I always do."

Faith walked outside and sat on the brick planter in front of her store. She hoped the cab would come quickly. She didn't want Alex or Jessie to come down the street and try to talk to her or invite her back to the apartment. She needed some time alone. She needed some time to cry, because there were so many emotions whirling around inside that she could do nothing but let them out.

The tears held until she walked through the front door of her apartment. Then she sank down on the couch, pulled the warm afghan up over her shoulders, and cried herself to sleep.

She woke up hours later to a dark apartment and a ringing doorbell. A spark of hope ignited within her. Maybe Alex had come to her.

She ran to the door and threw it open, her arms wide, her smile spreading across her face, and saw—Ben. Her smile faded, and her arms fell to her sides. She didn't know how she felt about Ben anymore.

"Hello, Faith. I guess that greeting wasn't for me. Can I come in anyway?"

"Sure." She stepped back and let him in.

"You look like hell."

"Thanks." She sat down on the couch and didn't bother to fix her hair or even straighten the wrinkles out of her clothes. She didn't have the energy left to pretend.

Ben sat on the far side of the couch and laced his fingers together. He stared down at the floor for the longest time, then over at her. "I'm sorry about what happened on Easter. My mother gave me her version. I know she hurt you, and I know it was my fault. I did try to explain to her that I was okay with our breakup."

"Well, that's something, I guess. And it wasn't your fault, Ben. It was mine."

He let out a short, bitter laugh. "Hardly. After all, I had the great idea that we should get married."

"Well, that was your fault, but the rest . . . I let myself get too close. I pretended I was a part of your family, but I wasn't, not really."

"You were a part of the family. I messed things up big time." He shook his head in disgust. "I wanted to call you last Sunday night. I even picked up the phone a few times, but I didn't know what to say, so I just hung up. I came by the bakery Monday afternoon, but Pam told me you'd gone to Arizona with that guy." He paused. "You like him, don't you?"

"Yeah."

"I'm glad you found someone."

"He doesn't want me either."

"Are you sure?"

"I'm sure."

Silence fell between them once again. "His loss," Ben said finally.

"You're right."

Ben looked at her in surprise. "I am?"

"Out there in the desert, there was so much space, so much aloneness—it made a mockery of how lonely I'd felt living amongst all these people. I'm going to fill my space with people I love. And it doesn't matter to me if they love me back or if they share a common family name or a bloodline. I'm going to start making my own traditions and stop trying to live in everyone else's family. And if it's just me for a while, then it will be just me. That's okay, too. I hung on to you, Ben, the same way your parents hung on to me. We were all afraid to let go. But I'm glad we did let go. I loved your brother, and I love your family still. I even love you. So there."

She smiled, wanting him to understand. "I thought I had to be someone else. Maybe that doesn't make sense, but all this time I didn't think I could be Faith Christopher, because it was just a made-up name. But you know what? I am Faith Christopher, and that will just have to be good enough."

"It is good enough. I hope you'll still be my friend,

because last night I took Tony to my parents' house for dinner. They told me I could bring a date," he said with a mischievous smile that couldn't wholly cover the sadness. "I told them everything. My mother became hysterical. My father stormed out of the room. And Kim cried, but she gave me a hug and said she'd still be my sister. I guess that's something."

Faith slid down the couch and put her hand over his. "I'm sorry they didn't react the way you wanted."

"They reacted better than I expected. I should have done it a long time ago. You were right. I couldn't spend the rest of my life living a lie. I don't know if my parents will ever come around, but at least if they do, I'll know they love me for who I am and not just who they want me to be."

"You can't change people," Faith said, feeling more sadness settle into her heart. "I've learned that the hard way, more than once."

Faith spent the rest of the evening watching television, catching up on the newspapers and her bills, and letting the answering machine pick up her calls. She couldn't help jumping every time the phone rang, but it was never Alex. She thought he might have called or dropped off her bags at least, but he'd stayed away.

It was for the best, she told herself over and over again. She had to start getting over him sometimes; it might as well be now.

But her heart wouldn't quit hoping, and when the doorbell rang just before ten, she jumped to her feet. She forced herself to walk slowly, to take her time. He was probably going to drop off her bags and give her the big breakup speech, the one he'd probably given dozens of times. After all, Julian was married now and Jessie was settled as Alex's daughter. They had no more need for a bridge.

As she opened the door, Faith wished Alex hadn't worn a navy blue polo shirt and blue jeans for this breakup, because he looked handsome and sexy and overwhelmingly appealing.

Alex picked up the bag next to his feet and set it inside the door. "You left your suitcase at my building."

"I thought you and Jessie needed some time alone."

"Really? I thought you just couldn't wait to get away."

"That wasn't the reason."

"Wasn't it?" He walked into her apartment and shut the door. "Then why don't you tell me why you left?"

"I told you." She looked away, uncomfortable with the fire in his eyes. "I thought you and Jessie needed to spend time together, and I wanted to check on the bakery."

"Then why didn't you come back? Why didn't you let me drive you home? Why did you run away like a coward?" he challenged.

"A coward?" A wave of fury raced through her, and she looked him straight in the eye. "I'm not the one who can't spend the night with a lover. You're the coward, not me. You're so afraid of getting hurt, you're barely alive."

"Oh, I'm alive, all right." He grabbed her by the arms. "And I'm damned confused. You tell me you love me one night, and the next morning you won't speak to me. Why? Because I happened to get up and dressed before you?"

"You just couldn't stand to wake up with me in your arms, to have to say something back to me," she said, not feeling as certain of herself as she had before. She had expected him to brush her off, not to be angry with her. "That's why you got up, isn't it?"

"Actually, my ass was freezing. We were naked in that sleeping bag as you recall, and you were hogging the covers."

Faith licked her lips, bewildered by his blunt words, sudden smile. "What are you saying?"

"I'm saying that two nights ago, on a windswept cliff,

I thought I'd found the love of my life and that she'd found me. Only, before I could tell her, she got mad and walked away.'' He paused. ''It took me a while to figure out that she was only doing what I've been doing most of my life.''

''Which is what?'' she asked breathlessly, still reeling from his words of love.

''I always left before someone could leave me. The way I figure it—you just couldn't take one more departure, so you bailed out.''

''You're right. I couldn't take one more person saying, 'She's a pretty girl, but we can't keep her.' ''

''You are a pretty girl.'' Alex cupped her face with his strong hands. ''But I do want to keep you—for the rest of my life. I want to tell you something, and you don't need to reply or even answer. I love you, Faith.''

Her stomach took one last inevitable tumble as his words sent a thrill down her spine and joy through her body. ''Oh, Alex, I love you, too.''

He sealed her words with a kiss, a warm, melting, everlasting kiss. ''Promise me you'll tell me again—in the morning.''

She smiled into his eyes. ''Are you going to be here in the morning?''

''Yes. I arranged for my housekeeper to stay with Jessie tonight.''

''Maybe you should go home, Alex. Jessie needs you, too.''

''Jessie told me I couldn't come back without you. I want you to be my wife, Faith, my lover, my partner, my best friend.''

''Yes, yes, yes, yes.''

''And Julian's granddaughter?''

''Yes,'' she said with a laugh.

''And Jessie's mother?''

Faith felt the tears well up in her eyes. She'd waited a long time for this moment. ''Are you sure?''

''I've never been more sure of anything in my life.''

His expression turned serious. "I don't need a bridge, Faith. I need a wife."

"And I need a husband."

"We'll be Mr. and Mrs. Carrigan," he said with a smile.

"Yes, and we'll dye Easter eggs and buy big Christmas trees and make up lots of traditions."

"And we'll fill our mantel with pictures of our family, our children."

"Children?"

He pressed his lips against her mouth. "Yes, and I think we should start right now. But this time we're going to go slow, because we have all night."

"And all morning."

"And the rest of our lives," he promised. "In fact, maybe we should make a pot together."

"Shut up and kiss me."

And he did exactly that.

The Avon Romance Superleaders, where all your dreams can—and do—come true.

What would it be like . . . to be swept off your feet by a handsome stranger . . . Or to be a princess for a day? What if your world was turned upside down by an English lord? Or if your one true love came back to you?

It's like a wonderful, romantic dream . . . Enter a glittering ballroom in Regency London, wearing a gossamer gown and dancing with the most scandalous rake of the ton *. . . Find yourself an independent woman of the Wild West, pulled into the arms of a jean-clad cowboy who lives by his own set of rules . . . Have your every need fulfilled by a handsome millionaire . . .*

At Avon, each month we bring to you love stories written by some of romance's best dreamspinners—Kathleen Eagle, Christina Dodd, Barbara Freethy, and Lorraine Heath. Following are sneak peeks of their latest Superleaders . . .

"Kathleen Eagle is a national treasure."
Susan Elizabeth Phillips

Available now from Avon Books
Kathleen Eagle's latest romantic bestseller
The Last True Cowboy

Everyone knows a cowboy is as good as his word, but what if the words are "I love you?"

When Julia Weslin returns to the High Horse ranch, she knows she has finally found a place to call home. And there she meets K. C. Houston, a long, lean cowboy . . . a man who's never stayed in one place for very long. K. C. promises to help Julia revive the cash-strapped ranch, and Julia knows he'll keep that promise. But even though they find strength—and passion—in each other's arms, Julia also knows that K. C. has never promised he'd stay forever.

"Readers who liked *The Horse Whisperer* will love this romance from Eagle."
Publishers Weekly

THE LAST TRUE COWBOY
by Kathleen Eagle

Julia turned her face to K. C.'s neck, and he could feel the warmth of her breath when he whispered, "Where are you staying tonight?"

"Haven't thought that far ahead."

"Where are you going from here?"

"South, maybe west." He slid his hand slowly from the small of her back up to the center, pressing her close so that he could feel the rise and fall of her chest against his. "But that's beyond tonight. Way beyond where I am right now."

She tipped her head back and looked up at him. Her face was dewy, and her eyes glistened. "What are you thinking about now?"

He smiled. "Don't have to think when I'm dancin'. Comes natural."

"Maybe you'd like what I'm thinking."

"Maybe you'd like what you're feeling if you'd just . . ." He taught her with his hips. She laughed, and her hips improved on his move. "There, that's it. Just dance with me."

"It's easier than I thought." She gave her head a sassy toss. "Past tense. I'm not thinking anymore."

"Attagirl."

Suddenly, she studied him hard, then smiled. "I think you *would* be easy to love."

"You do, huh?" He smiled, too, but he was wondering what he'd said to bring her to that conclusion.

She slipped her arm around his neck and gave him a peck on the cheek. "And that you can do without. Good night, sweet cowboy."

He felt a little stung by her abrupt departure, by the motherly kiss that was about as welcome as a pat on the head, but when he saw how unsteadily

she made her way toward the door, he followed her. He caught up with her just as she was stepping off the boardwalk. She turned the corner, and he wheeled around her, shoving his hands as far as they would go into the front pockets of his jeans as he matched her pace.

"Nobody's ever loved me and left me quite so fast before."

She laughed and linked her arm with his as though they'd been friends forever, and they strolled together. He figured she was headed for the little parking lot behind the bar, which was where he'd left his pickup. He decided that if she was heading home, he'd be doing the driving.

"You haven't told me your name."

"I assumed we had a tacit agreement to keep our names a mystery, since you're just passing through." She tipped her head back. "It's a pretty night, isn't it? Peaceful and still. No wind to blow you anywhere."

"It'll pick up tomorrow. Always does."

"And then you just go? South or west or wherever the road takes you?" She glanced askance, measuring him up for something. "Maybe I should hitch a ride. Would you take me with you?"

"Sure." He nodded toward the parking lot. "South or west? You choose."

"Right now? Choosing would take some thinking."

"True. We don't want that."

"So just take me with you." She tightened her grip on his arm. "Anywhere. This is a one-time-only offer, cowboy. I'll go with you anywhere."

"How about if I take you home?"

If you loved this excerpt from Kathleen Eagle's *The Last True Cowboy*, then you'll also love her newest hardcover, coming in August 1999 from Avon Books. Don't miss it!

Have you ever longed to be a princess for a day? To wear beautiful clothes, live in a palace, and have a handsome prince as your intended? Evangeline Scoffield gets to live that fantasy when a sensuous, virile man tells her that he is Danior and she is his runaway princess . . . his fiancée since childhood who he is bringing back to their homeland to marry. And as you read Christina Dodd's Runaway Princess, *you must decide if Evangeline is truly his bride . . . or the English orphan she claims she is . . .*

THE RUNAWAY PRINCESS
by Christina Dodd

"G*et your hands off of me."* *She spoke with a fair* imitation of calm.

"No, princess." He sounded very sure of himself, and as his grip tightened, her delicate glove escaped from his other hand.

Evangeline followed its descent with wide eyes. It landed on the toe of his black boot, an incongruous decoration on that serviceable leather. Then, slowly,

her gaze traveled up his long legs, clad in black trousers. Up his torso, with its black jacket over a snowy white shirt. To his face.

No kindness softened the carved features. No flaw gave humanity to his godlike looks. He appeared to be an element of nature: inhuman, dangerous, harsh. Perhaps even . . . mad?

She had to do this.

Grabbing his wrist, she twisted. His fingers involuntarily opened, and she continued twisting until she stood next to him, his arm tucked, pale side up, beneath hers.

"I'd like to know where you've been to learn all that. If you hadn't hesitated . . ."

If she hadn't hesitated, she'd be free.

But she didn't say so. This man was, after all, mad. And she was a paltry orphan.

She remained still and the stranger relaxed slightly, looking her over as if he were a banker who'd been forced to foreclose on a hovel and found his new possession quite unprepossessing.

Fine. So she wasn't a beauty. The London dressmaker had clucked in disapproval at her coltish arms and legs, and the London hairdresser had refused to cut her long brown hair, citing distressing lack of curl. Her odd-colored eyes were faintly slanted, a heritage that would always be a mystery, and her chin tended to jut aggressively.

Only her skin had passed her personal test of nobility. So she might not be an enchantress, but she also wasn't this stranger's property, so he had no call to sneer like that. "Who are you?" she asked, this time in English.

His mouth, firm, full-lipped, and surrounded by a

faint black beard, twisted in disgust. "You're playing a game." He spoke English, too, only slightly accented.

"No . . ." Well, yes. The game of staying alive.

"You'll come back with me, whether you like it or not."

"Back?" *Where*?

He *towered* over her, and she had little experience with towering men. Actually, she had little experience with men at all. None had bothered to visit her eccentric guardian Leona, who viewed men as primitive, given to sweeping a woman away for the excitement of her mind and the pleasure of her body.

She started to inch toward the door, but without glancing at her he said, "If you move, I will have to give in to my baser instincts."

He didn't say what those instincts were; he didn't have to. Her imagination galloped on like a runaway horse.

She replied, "I think there's been a mistake. I am not who you think I am. That is, if who I surmise you think I am is really . . ."

He looked at her, and her voice trailed off.

"You dare deny you are Princess Ethelinda?"

If the truth weren't so pathetic, she could almost laugh. "I'm not any of the things Henri or the guests say I am. I'm only Miss Evangeline Scoffield of East Little Teignmouth, Cornwall."

Her declaration made no dent in his imperious stance, and he dismissed her claim without consideration. "What nonsense."

"There must be some superficial resemblance between us, and I'm flattered you think I'm a princess,

but actually I'm a"—her laughter dried up—"nobody."

It was quite clear he didn't believe her.

Alex Carrigan, named one of the "Ten Most Eligible Bachelors," can command the best table at a restaurant, has the best-looking model-of-the-moment on his arm . . . and always flies first class. But things are missing from his life, important things like a real home and a family. And when he meets Faith he soon discovers that the best things in life don't always come with a price tag . . .

In The Sweetest Thing, *Rita Award-winning author Barbara Freethy shows us that finding your one perfect love might take a lifetime, but that sometimes it's worth the wait . . .*

THE SWEETEST THING
by Barbara Freethy

"Well?"

Faith played with the medal that hung around her neck. She could see the amusement in his eyes, and it irritated the heck out of her. She felt like a blushing schoolgirl, and she was nothing of the kind.

"Maybe I should come back later."

"Maybe you shouldn't have come at all. In fact,

why did you come?" Alex's stance was purely aggressive. "Did you come to help my grandfather search out his lost love? Because I don't get it. Why would you take the time to bother? You're a busy woman. You have your own business. Your own life. Why do this? Unless . . ."

"Unless, what?"

"You're looking for an inheritance. If so, I hate to break it to you, but the old man hasn't got much more than that broken pot and a million stories to sell."

"How dare you! I have no interest in your grandfather's money."

"Then maybe it's me you're after. *San Francisco Magazine* called me one of the ten most eligible bachelors in the Bay Area."

"Bully for you. I didn't see the article, and if I had, I'd probably question their taste."

"Ooh, that hurts." Alex put a hand to his heart.

"I hope it does."

Faith tried to walk past him, but he caught her by the arm.

"Wait."

"Why? So you can insult me again?"

Alex let out a breath and shook his head. "You were in my dreams last night. I didn't like it."

His words startled her. When she looked into his eyes, she no longer saw dislike but fear. The emotion humbled him, made him far less arrogant, far more likeable.

"I can't stop thinking about you," he muttered. "What is it about you? You're not my type. Not at all."

"And you're not mine. That's why I haven't been

thinking about you at all . . ." Her voice drifted away as she realized that wasn't true.

Grayson Rhodes is a maverick, the son of an English duke who refuses to live by society's rules. He leaves the stuffy drawing rooms of London behind to seek his fortune in a rough, rugged land called Texas. There, he discovers a place where a man is as good as his word, where you earn your fortune—not inherit it. And there he meets Abbie Westland . . . a woman whose fragile heart he dares not break.

In A Rogue In Texas *by Rita Award-winning author Lorraine Heath, you'll meet a powerful, passionate man who rediscovers the promise of love . . .*

A ROGUE IN TEXAS
by Lorraine Heath

A*bigail stared at the man who had just made himself* at home on her back porch. "It's scandalous for you to be out here while I'm bathing. You're . . . you're . . ." She couldn't think of a word bad enough to describe him or his behavior. In the moonlight, she saw him flash a grin.

"Disreputable?"

"You're no *gentleman*!"

"I never claimed to be. I've always thought of myself as a rogue."

She thrust out her hand. "Give me the towel."

"Finish your bath and I'll dry you off."

"No!" She rued the tremble in her voice.

"What are you afraid of?" he asked quietly. "I won't ravish you. At least, not without your permission."

Beneath the water, she clenched her hands. She was naked and vulnerable, and she could feel his gaze latched on to her, watching her, studying her.

"I never would have thought to take a bath outside, but it must be rather relaxing to have the hot water caressing your skin while the stars look down."

He had the gall to laugh loudly, joyfully. "I'm not stopping you from washing. You're only a shadow in the night, Abbie."

Lord, she hated the way her name rolled off his tongue, soft and lyrical like a song she'd sing to put the babies to sleep.

She felt along the bottom of the tub until she found the soap she'd dropped when his hand had accidentally caressed her breast. The memory caused the heat of embarrassment to scald her cheeks. Her fingers closing around the soap, she brought it up, rubbing it back and forth across her breast, but she seemed unable to wash away the feel of his palm cradling her flesh . . .

If you liked these sneak peeks
at the Avon Romance Superleaders,
then don't miss the latest
Avon Superleader by Lisa Kleypas,

SOMEONE TO WATCH OVER ME,

her breathlessly awaited
new romantic bestseller . . .

What if you awakened in a stranger's bed, with no memory of your past? Your rescuer tells you he's Grant Morgan, that he was once your lover, and that you are Vivien Rose Duvall, a woman whose life has shocked Regency society to its core. Deep in your soul, you know he has you mistaken for someone else, but you have no proof... and he soon becomes your only hope to find out the truth.

In Someone to Watch Over Me, *Lisa Kleypas creates an unforgettable hero who is determined to rescue the one woman who has ever bewitched him...*

SOMEONE TO WATCH OVER ME

by Lisa Kleypas

Grant gathered Vivien in the mass of bedclothes and carefully pulled her into his arms. She gasped at the relief of it. He was so infinitely strong, holding her hard against him. Resting her head on his shoulder, she crushed her cheek against the linen of his shirt. Her vision was filled with details of him; the smooth, tanned skin, the silky-rough locks of dark brown hair...

"Who are you?" she whispered.

"Don't you remember?"

"No, I..." Thoughts and images eluded her efforts to capture them. She couldn't remember anything. There was blankness in every direction, a great confounding void.

He eased her head back, his warm fingers cupping around the back of her neck. A slight smile tipped the corners of his mouth. "I'm Grant Morgan."

"What h-happened to me?" She struggled to think. "I-I was in the water . . ."

"How did you end up in the river, Vivien?"

"Vivien?" she repeated in desperate confusion. "Why did you call me that?"

"Don't you know your own name?" he asked quietly.

She shuddered with frightened sobs. "No . . . I don't know, I don't *know*. Help me," she whispered.

Long fingers slid gently over the side of her face. "It's all right. Don't be afraid."

And incredibly, she took comfort in his voice, his touch, his presence. His hands moved over her body, soothing her shaking limbs. Hazily, she wondered if this was what it was like when heavenly spirits ministered to the suffering. Yes . . . an angel's touch must be like this.

AN IRRESISTIBLE REBATE
WHEN YOU READ THIS ROMANCE

LORRAINE HEATH'S
A ROGUE IN TEXAS

"Lorraine Heath writes the most powerfully moving Love stories in romance today."
—Jill Barnett

When you open a book by Lorraine Heath you'll experience the amazing joy and the tender heartache of falling in love. Come discover what so many readers already know, and Avon will pay you to do it. Simply purchase a copy of A ROGUE IN TEXAS (available in bookstores in April). Then mail in your proof-of-purchase (cash register receipt) along with the coupon below by December 31, 1999, and we'll send you a check for $2.00.

Void where prohibited by law.

- -

Mail to:
Avon Books, Dept. BP, P.O. Box 767, Dresden, TN 38225

Name__________________________________

Address________________________________

City___________________________________

State/Zip_______________________________

RTX 1298